THE MAUNALOA CURSE

A Novel of Romantic Suspense

Irma Walker

THE BOBBS-MERRILL COMPANY, INC.

Indianapolis/New York

ALSO BY IRMA WALKER

The Lucifer Wine
The Murdoch Legacy
Someone's Stolen Nellie Grey
The Man in the Driver's Seat

Copyright © 1978 by Irma Walker

All rights reserved, including the right of reproduction
in whole or in part in any form
Published by The Bobbs-Merrill Company, Inc.
Indianapolis   New York

Designed by Rita Muncie
Manufactured in the United States of America

First printing

Library of Congress Cataloging in Publication Data

Walker, Irma.
  The Maunaloa curse.

  I. Title.
PZ4.W1783Mau [PS3573.A4253327] 813'.5'4   78-55657
ISBN 0-672-52450-3

Walker

To my father,
Earl M. Roden

I

KING OF SWORDS

It had been that rarity for San Francisco—a hot, muggy summer day. Tempers had flared at the small free clinic where Lani worked, and patients who were usually cooperative had kept the staff in an uproar all day. As usual, she was late getting off work, so it was well past seven when she finally covered her typewriter. Although overtime pay was unheard of at the chronically underfunded clinic, she didn't really mind working late. After all, there was nothing waiting for her in her stuffy little apartment in the Avenues except a cool shower and another salad-and-sandwich meal in front of the TV set.

After the muni bus left her off at her corner, she strolled without hurry along the street, moving in and out of the patches of shade under the plane trees. It was a quiet neighborhood, a little rundown but still respectable, and sometimes she liked to pretend that she had always lived there, had grown up in one of the aging Victorians that lined both sides of the street. When she came opposite the house where she'd been living for the past year, a large Queen Anne that had been converted to apartments, she saw her landlady on the front steps, bending over to pick up a newspaper.

Although she sighed inwardly—Mrs. Costello was a compulsive nonstop talker—she waved and started across the street.

And then it happened.

The car came out of nowhere, a juggernaut of steel and glass, bearing down upon her. Although the driver must have seen her there in the middle of the empty street, the car didn't swerve. Instead, it seemed to pick up speed; and it was only instinct, the reflexes of her healthy young body, that saved her.

In one fluid movement she flung herself toward a car parked at the curb, rolled over its hood and fell to the sidewalk on the other side, jarring the breath out of her lungs.

As she lay there, stunned and disbelieving, a woman screamed. There was the screech of tires cutting a corner too sharply, and then the sound of running feet. Her landlady's shocked face swam above her; it seemed part of the madness of the moment that Mrs. Costello should be babbling numbers, the same ones over and over.

Later, in her landlady's cluttered living room, this part of the nightmare, at least, began to make sense. By then a policeman had been summoned, and Mrs. Costello, her brown eyes snapping with excitement, held the center of the floor.

Lani listened, fighting a hysterical desire to laugh, as her landlady described the car in detail, including its license plate number, its mismatched hubcaps, and the dent in its left rear fender. Mrs. Costello wasn't as sure about the driver, but she thought it had been a man, probably a young one. The policeman, middle-aged and polite, took down her statement. Lani sensed his skepticism as Mrs. Costello insisted that the driver had deliberately tried to run her tenant down.

He studied Lani with thoughtful eyes. "Have you received any threats, Miss Brock? Stepped on anyone's toes at work, maybe?"

"No, I get along fine with everybody at the clinic."

"How about boyfriends? Any trouble along those lines?"

"I haven't had much time lately for boyfriends, I'm afraid."

"And no wonder," Mrs. Costello said. "Working all hours at that clinic—"

"And you can't think of anyone who might have a grudge against you, Miss Brock?" the policeman cut in.

Lani started to shake her head, but Mrs. Costello wasn't finished yet. "Tell the officer about that man, the one who came here asking all those questions about you," she urged.

"He was making a credit check on me," Lani said. "I gave you as a reference when I applied for a charge account at the Emporium, you know."

Mrs. Costello sniffed. "So why would a department store care what hours you work and if you have a steady boyfriend? When I asked him for his credentials, he showed me a private investigator's permit and said he was checking you out for an insurance policy. I sent him packing, but maybe I should have called the police."

Lani was silent. It was true that she'd applied for a charge account, part of her decision to put down roots here in San Francisco, but it did seem strange that the department store would use a private investigator to check out her references. And why had he lied about an insurance policy?

The policeman snapped shut his notebook. "Well, we'll run a make on the car. It's probably some weirdo who gets his kicks out of scaring pretty—from scaring young women." He paused, and this time his smile seemed less professional. "Just in case, I'd be careful, Miss Brock. No use taking chances until we catch up with this joker. And you'd better have a doctor check you over. That's an ugly-looking scrape on your elbow."

While Mrs. Costello showed the police officer out, Lani took inventory of herself. Her dress was a mess, and she'd probably be covered with bruises tomorrow; but aside from her skinned elbow, her wild plunge over the hood of the parked car had done little damage.

Impulsively she reached for her purse, which Mrs. Costello had rescued from the gutter, and took out a small scythe-shaped shark's tooth. Before Kawena, the old Hawaiian woman who'd been her nurse, had given it to Lani, she'd threaded a tiny silver chain through a hole in the top so it could be worn around the neck. Now, thirteen years later, the chain was tarnished and the tooth had taken on the patina of old ivory.

With long familiarity, Lani's fingertips traced the outlined head of Lono, the Hawaiian harvest god, carved with exquisite care into one side of the tooth. At one time she would have credited her escape today to the *mana* of the shark's tooth, but it had been a long time since she'd believed in magic charms, Hawaiian or otherwise.

And yet—after all these years, she still had the tooth. Had she really kept it, as she'd always told herself, because it had been Kawena's last gift to her before her banishment from Maunaloa Island? Lani had been only eight when her father sent her away, but she could still remember Kawena's anguished face, the pity in her eyes. Was this the only reason she'd kept the shark's tooth? Or did some of the old superstitions still cling, despite her efforts to free herself from the past?

Suddenly angry with herself, she put the shark's tooth away again. Mrs. Costello trotted back into the room, looking like a worried Pekingese with her too-short nose, her prominent eyes. Although Lani was sure her landlady's concern was genuine, she also knew that Mrs. Costello was enjoying the excitement. Her landlady was a short, plump woman with a penchant for gossip; for years she'd been the housekeeper for a wealthy Hillsborough family, and she still read the society pages religiously, following the social activities of "her" family.

For all her insatiable curiosity, she was comfortable to be around, and Lani was well aware how lucky she was to have found a decent place to live for the kind of rent she could afford. Living here made it possible to stay on at the clinic, doing work she loved, instead of being forced to look for a better-paying job. So when Mrs. Costello asked her how she was feeling now, she forced a smile and said she was fine, just fine, thank you.

"Well, I don't believe you," Mrs. Costello said crossly. "You look ready to cave in. What you need is a glass of warm brandy. Now you settle down on the sofa and relax while I heat up some Korbel's. And don't you worry. They'll pick that man up fast now that they have a description of the car."

She bustled off, and Lani tried to follow her advice. Already the whole episode seemed like a nightmare. Here in this comfortable room with its wall-to-wall furniture, the framed family photographs lined up along the fireplace mantel, it was hard to believe that she'd just had a close brush with death. Her skin chilled as she remembered the hot breath of the car, the smell of burning rubber, the shriek of tires. Although she didn't believe for one minute that it had been a deliberate attempt to kill her, it was sobering to realize that there was someone in the world who was so hideously callous that he could almost run down a stranger and then not stop to see whether she was hurt.

She realized she was shaking again, and rather than give in to her nerves, she reached out quickly and picked up a newspaper that was lying open on the sofa beside her.

It was the current issue of *Society West*, a West Coast publication Mrs. Costello subscribed to so she could keep up with the family who had employed her for so many years. Her attention caught by the word *Honolulu*, Lani glanced down at a photograph spread across two columns under the headline HONOLULU SOCIETY AFFAIR PLANNED.

There were two women in the photograph, one young and the other past middle age; they were standing in front of an elaborate floral arrangement of torch ginger and bird-of-paradise, smiling into the camera.

Lani's eyes settled idly on the older woman—and the blood drained from her head, leaving her shaken and weak. It was the second shock she'd sustained within an hour. The first had shaken her up physically, but this second shock was far more destructive, because it brought back to her, all too painfully, the things in her past she'd been trying to forget.

She had been so sure, had prided herself on the belief that she'd finally conquered her fear—and her hatred—of Berta St. John. After all, it had been ten years since she'd run away from her aunt's house in Boston. In two weeks she

5

would be twenty-one; she was no longer a twelve-year-old child at the mercy of a woman who hated her. So why was the old panic crowding up in her throat? She took a deep breath, then another, and immediately felt better—and also a little ashamed of her easy panic. After all, she wasn't even sure the woman in the photograph *was* Aunt Berta. Why would her aunt's picture appear in a publication that catered to West Coast society, three thousand miles from Boston? There must be dozens of women in the world with Aunt Berta's dissecting eyes, her cool, well-bred smile. . . .

She focused her eyes on the photograph and read the caption under the picture. Then, in disbelief, she read it again.

"One of Honolulu's most important social events of the year, the annual fund-raising ball for the Prince Kuhio Hospital Benefit Fund, will be co-hosted this year for the first time by Iolani Stevenson and her aunt, Berta St. John, a former resident of Boston who now resides on Maunaloa Island with her niece."

Lani's eyes moved back to the photograph, but this time it was the second woman who held her attention. Even in the grainy newspaper reproduction, it was obvious that the girl was young; with her brilliant smile, her smoothly planed cheekbones and cap of blond hair, she was also very beautiful.

Lani stared at the picture for a long time. Slowly she shook her head from side to side.

"But that's a lie!" In her agitation she spoke out loud. "How can it be true when *I'm* Iolani Stevenson?"

6

II

Lani had just turned twelve and had been living in Boston with her aunt for almost four years when she found the orchid lying on the sidewalk.

She had taken the long way home from school, and because she was late, she was hurrying as fast as her legs would carry her. Even so, when she saw the flower, a splash of purple on the grimy sidewalk in front of a florists' supply store, she skidded to a quick stop.

Cautiously she looked up and down the busy street, then pretended an interest in the dusty plastic flower samples in the window of the florists' wholesaler. The oblique rays of the afternoon sun threw back her reflection from the tinted glass—the reflection of a small, too-thin girl with tawny skin and thick, pale hair skinned back so severely from her forehead that it gave her eyebrows a perpetual slant.

When she was sure no one was watching her, she bent swiftly and scooped up the flower. The orchid, a tiny vanda, felt cold, satin-smooth in her hand as she thrust it deep into her jacket pocket and hurried on.

Her heart thumped painfully as she ducked into a narrow alleyway. She turned a corner and was almost upon a gang of youngsters playing touch football in the middle of the street before she saw them. By then one of the boys had spotted her, and it was too late for retreat.

"Hey, there's Crazy Lani!" he shouted, and in a moment

they were surrounding her, blocking her path. A fat girl with lank blond hair started up a chant, the one they'd been tormenting Lani with lately, and the others joined in, their voices shrill and penetrating.

"Crazy Lani, full of hate . . . killed her ma when she was eight . . ."

The words fell on Lani's ears like tiny drops of acid. The chanting was new; until recently, although they'd always teased her about her name and her whispery voice, they hadn't been sure why she was so different from them. Now they had a focus for their teasing, and as the chanting went on, she squeezed her eyelids together to shut out the hot excitement in their faces.

"Who's the kid?"

It was a boy's voice, but it held an edge of authority—or maybe it was arrogance. Lani opened her eyes; she recognized the newcomer, and her mouth went dry. He was a new boy in school; his name was Kore, but no one had ever laughed at his queer name the way they did at hers. He was several years older than the other boys in his class, but no one teased him about that, either. As he came toward her, Lani remembered the whispers she'd heard about the knife he carried—some said it was strapped to his leg, others that he kept it in his back pocket—so she wasn't surprised when the others drew back, leaving her standing alone.

"What's she done?" he wanted to know.

They were only too glad to tell him, to curry his favor by repeating the tales they'd heard from their mothers, who'd heard them from one of Aunt Berta's bridge cronies. The boy listened silently; he studied Lani with opaque black eyes, taking in her too-large jacket, her too-serviceable shoes, the rolled white ankle socks that no other girl in school would have been caught dead in.

"Well, how about it, Iolani?" he asked finally. "Did you really shoot your old lady like they say?"

From the corner of her eye she caught movement, and she knew the others were crowding closer, that her brief respite was over.

"Hey, you kids—you get away from that girl, you hear?

She's got enough trouble without you pestering her. Now you scat or I'm going to call the police."

It was old Mr. Purdue, who lived next door to her aunt. Although he seldom spoke to Lani, he'd given her a ten-dollar bill once when she'd helped him find his lost dog. Lani edged forward cautiously, but no one tried to stop her as she threaded her way through them and fled down the street.

She slowed to a walk when she came in sight of her aunt's home, a large yellow brick house that stood alone, surrounded by a high iron fence.

Moving quietly, she went up the broad front steps and let herself into the entrance hall that always smelled of disinfectant and lemon oil. Through the half-open doors of the front parlor, women's voices filtered out into the hall. From long experience, Lani identified them, matching names to the voices.

When Lani heard her own name, she stopped to listen, one foot resting on the bottom step of the staircase, ready for instant flight at the first sign that the bridge game was breaking up.

"—nobody can accuse me of not doing my Christian duty by Lani," her aunt's well-modulated voice was saying. "Of course, if I'd had any idea her father would leave her here so long, I might have had second thoughts."

There was a murmur of commiseration, then Miss Quincy's simpering, "I'm sure you'll get your reward in heaven, Berta."

"I certainly hope so." Aunt Berta's voice was sour. "It was so different with my sister, you know. She was twelve years younger than I, but I never had a minute's trouble with her until she met John Stevenson. Sometimes I find it hard to believe that Lani is Carol's daughter. Of course they do say blood will tell, and there've been some very strange stories about that Stevenson family."

There was a short silence. Mrs. Arnold broke it first. "Surely you don't believe that nonsense about a curse—a good Christian like you!"

"Not really. But it does seem odd that nothing ever happens to *them*. It's always their wives or husbands who end up getting murdered, while the Stevensons live to a ripe old age and die in bed."

"Are you saying your sister's death *wasn't* an accident? Surely you don't believe the girl is capable of—of violence, do you?" Miss Quincy's voice quivered with excitement. "Of course, you did tell us that the girl was in shock afterward, that she completely lost her voice for months after it happened—"

"All I'm saying is that it was a sad day when my sister met John Stevenson. If she hadn't married that half-breed, maybe she'd be alive today."

"A half-breed?" Miss Quincy said sharply. "Are you talking about his Hawaiian mother? I thought the Island people were proud of their Hawaiian blood, especially if they could trace it back to royalty."

"Royalty! A raggle-tailed bunch of royalty *that* was. Those people were still making human sacrifices to their heathen gods when the first white man got there. Carol never would have married him if she'd known what he was."

"And yet he's been pretty generous with you, hasn't he?" There was a touch of malice in Mrs. Arnold's voice. "You did tell us once that he paid you well for taking care of Lani."

"I hope you aren't suggesting I'm doing it for *money*, Madge Arnold! John Stevenson is getting a bargain. It would cost him a small fortune to keep that child in a sanatorium."

For a while, except for the slap of cards, there was silence. This time it was Mrs. Arnold who took up the conversational reins.

"What's this I hear about the kids at school making up a nasty little poem about Lani? My cousin's daughter is a teacher there, you know, and she said she felt sorry for the girl, the way those kids torment her about—you know, what happened to her mother."

"Well, I wouldn't let it bother me, Claire." Berta St. John's voice was silky. "If they *have* been teasing her, it must be for some other reason. After all, I've only confided the details of my sister's death to you three, and I know none of you would discuss my private business behind my back."

There was a small, strained silence, then a rush of protestations. When the conversation drifted back to the bridge game, Lani climbed the stairs and went to her room.

Before she took off her jacket, she fished the orchid from her pocket and laid it on the bed. It glowed like the outer rim of a Maunaloa rainbow against the white spread. She stroked it gently with her fingertip and briefly allowed herself to pretend that the past four years had been a bad dream, that she was back on Maunaloa Island with her father, that he still loved her, wanted her. . . .

A sob forced its way through her tight throat. She turned away and began taking off her school clothes and hanging them up in the closet. She had stripped down to her panties when her eyes fell on the orchid again. The room with its somber dark furniture faded, and she was back on the lanai of Kawena's little cottage, dancing in the morning sun, while Kawena, her voice pitched to a falsetto, sang a song about a bird in flight, the song that always seemed to have been written especially for Lani because her name— Iolani—meant soaring hawk.

> . . . *I luna la, i luna; na manu oke lewa.*
> *I lalo la, i lalo; na pua oka honua. . . .*

Above, above, birds of the heaven./Below, below, flowers of the earth. . . .

Involuntarily, as if they had a will of their own, her fingers began to arch in the gesture that meant a soaring bird, then a flower. Her hips swayed, slowly at first, then faster, in the lovely movements that Kawena had taught her. . . .

There was no warning. She'd been so lost in the past that she'd forgotten to be careful, and she hadn't heard the door open. The first hint of disaster was the odor of her aunt's lilac cologne, and by that time it was already too late.

She started to turn, and the slap caught her on the ear. The second slap drove her lips against her teeth, and its force sent her crashing against the bed.

Too stunned yet for pain, she crouched there, looking up into her aunt's pitiless face. With blinding clarity she saw herself through her aunt's eyes—her naked body, just beginning to show the first buds of womanhood, swaying back and forth in the lascivious movements of a heathen dance.

In her shame she tried to cover her nakedness with her hands. Her aunt hit her again, driving her the rest of the way to the floor. There was no way to escape; she retreated deep inside herself to a place where her aunt couldn't reach her. With part of her mind she knew her aunt had snatched up a belt and was raining blows on her naked back and arms, and in her fear she called out her father's name.

Berta St. John's mouth twisted into a thin line. "Daddy!" she mimicked. "*He* won't help you. He can't stand the sight of you. Your fine, rich father's got other things to do these days, he and that new wife of his—"

She broke off, and an odd expression crossed her face. Stonily, because pride was the only weapon she had, Lani stared up at her. Her aunt averted her eyes first. She turned away, dropping the belt on the bed. Over her shoulder she told Lani to clean herself up and get to bed.

When she was gone, Lani hoisted herself to her feet. There was a queer wet feeling inside the ear her aunt had slapped; the welts on her back and arms burned like fire; and her lips were already swollen to half again their normal size, but she had one small satisfaction: she hadn't whimpered in front of Aunt Berta, even though she knew it would have gone better for her if she had.

In the bathroom down the hall, she stood under a lukewarm shower for a long time, then patted herself dry with a towel. She found a bottle of antiseptic in the medicine cabinet and dabbed it on the abrasions she could reach before she put on her pajamas. She heard the clatter of dishes from the kitchen as she was returning to her room. To shut out the sound—and the odor of frying ham—she crawled into bed and pulled the covers over her head.

Although the antiseptic had helped to ease the sting on her back and arms, her mouth throbbed with pain and her brain seemed to be on fire. An image of her aunt's face, distorted with rage, swam into her mind. Although Aunt Berta often struck her, she'd never whipped her with a belt before, and she'd always been careful to strike her where the bruises wouldn't show.

For as long as Lani could remember, she had known that her mother's sister disliked her and her father. Her father, who was so wise, must have known it too. So why had he sent her away with Aunt Berta? Why hadn't he ever come to check up on her? Was it really because he couldn't stand the sight of her, as Aunt Berta said?

For a moment her memory played a trick on her, and she was back on Maunaloa Island, crouching among the giant leaves of an a'pe plant, listening to her parents quarreling inside the Folly. Her mother's voice, unnaturally shrill, sounded in her ears again.

"—before I'll give you a divorce, I'll stand up in court and swear that Lani isn't really your child—"

Lani shuddered and retreated from the too-painful memory. She told herself she had finished waiting for her father. Now that he had a new wife, he would never come for her. And she couldn't stay here either, not after today. From now on her aunt—and the neighborhood kids—would make her life unbearable; so it was time to leave. Surely there must be a place where she would be welcome, where her aunt couldn't find her.

She waited until the TV set in her aunt's bedroom had been off for almost an hour before she slid out of bed and switched on a lamp. When she took off her pajamas, she saw that they were stained with blood; she shuddered, dropped them on the floor and pushed them under the bed with her foot.

She pulled on jeans, a wool sweater, her hooded jacket. In her jacket pocket she stuffed her toothbrush and comb, a quarter she'd once found in the gutter near school, the ten-dollar bill Mr. Purdue had given her for finding his dog, and the shark's tooth that had been Kawena's last gift to her.

Everything else, including the orchid, she left behind.

The house was quiet as she crept down the stairs and out the front door. The wind pushing against her face was cold, tainted with the odor of marsh gas from the creek bottoms several blocks away. As she paused to pull up the hood of her jacket, it came to her where she could hide—at least until she could think of something better.

But before she went on, she turned for one last look at the house where she'd been so miserable for the past four years. All that time—she'd waited all those years for a sign from her father. Even when it hadn't come, she had made excuses for him. Well, she would never make that mistake again. From this moment on, no matter what else happened, she would never again accept anything—not food or clothing or shelter—from her father. Either she would survive on her own, without his help, or she'd die trying. Because whatever waited for her out there, it couldn't be worse than what had happened to her in her aunt's house—or on Maunaloa Island four years ago.

She turned her back on the house and plunged down the street, headed for the old abandoned viaduct that crossed the creek bottoms several blocks away.

For decades, the viaduct had provided fast access from the suburbs to downtown Boston; now, replaced by a newer overpass, it had been allowed to deteriorate as it waited for the steel balls of the wrecking crews. Near the center of the viaduct, where it crossed a small creek, the cement covering on one of its giant supports had crumbled along a fault, and a large chunk had fallen away. It lay against the creek bank now, partially blocking off the opening of a drainage pipe.

Lani spent the night crouching just inside the pipe's opening, too terrified of rats and other horrors to crawl further back into the pipe where it would have been warmer. Although it was dry inside the pipe, cold radiated from the metal casing, chilling her to the bone. An evil odor made her empty stomach roll, and she was sure something was watching her from the black hole behind her. When a rustling started up in the dry leaves near her feet, she jerked her legs back with a scream. A low humming vibrated through the metal pipe, setting her teeth on edge. She told herself it was only the wind blowing in from the marshlands at the other end of the pipe, but she couldn't make herself believe it.

When the first grey light of dawn showed through the opening, she finally slept. She awoke, hours later, with cramped muscles and a burning thirst. Incautiously she stretched her shoulder muscles. Pain shot through her body, and she wondered how her hands and feet could be so cold when her arms and back felt as if they were on fire.

The day passed slowly, miserably. Several times she heard voices, and each time she ducked back inside the pipe and huddled there, afraid. Toward noon a small white dog came along and stared at her with bright, curious eyes. When she didn't move, it went away.

At dusk she ventured far enough away from her refuge to stretch her legs and drink greedily from the creek. Unwilling to spend another night in the evil-smelling drainpipe, she gathered a few armloads of dried weeds and piled them in a sheltered spot nearby. The earthy odor of the weeds was a welcome change as she sat with her back against the fallen block of cement, staring up at the sky.

After a while she dug into her pocket for the carved shark's tooth. Although she no longer believed that its *mana* worked for her, she put it around her neck. She fell asleep, her chin on her chest, so she didn't know that she'd been found until the crunch of footsteps awakened her. Before she could jump up, a figure was standing over her.

He spoke first. "You're the kid who killed her ma, ain't you?"

Lani's skin chilled as she recognized the new boy she'd met the day before, the one named Kore. He looked very tall, more like a man than a boy as he loomed above her, his shoulders silhouetted against the moon, and she suddenly remembered the rumors she'd heard about his touchy temper, his dangerous fighting habits, the knife he carried. When he squatted down a few feet away, watching her, she stared back warily, ready to run if he came any closer.

"The cops think some gang snatched you," he said.

"Snatched me? You mean—kidnapped me?" she said, startled into speech. "Why would anyone do that?"

"For money, dummy."

"But—but that's crazy."

"Well, that's what I heard on the radio. I guess they found blood on your sheets and on your—y'know, pajamas; so they figure someone got in your room and grabbed you."

She started to say again that it was crazy, and then she remembered the bloodstains on the pajamas she'd kicked under the bed and was silent.

"So how come you ran away?"

"I—I didn't run away," she said. "I've been camping out."

She expected a snort of disbelief, but instead he said, "I ran away once."

"How long was it before they found you?"

"They didn't look for me. I went back on my own in a couple of days."

"What did they do to you—your parents, I mean?"

"My pa gave me a licking, but my mom cried and hugged me, and then she gave me a whack on the head for worrying her." He picked up a stick and began gouging out holes in the soft ground at his feet. "What happened to your mouth? It's all puffed up," he said.

Involuntarily her hand went up to cover her mouth. "I fell down," she said quickly.

"Your aunt zapped you, didn't she? How come you let an old dame like that push you around?" Lani didn't answer, and he looked impatient. "What's the matter with you? Can't you talk, runt?"

"Why don't you go away?" she said, goaded into boldness.

"Who's going to make me—you?" His voice was challenging, and again uneasiness stirred inside Lani. She studied the bulge in the front of his sweater. Was that where he kept the knife? Had he really pulled it out and threatened to cut off Danny O'Reilly's ears? Of course everybody at school knew what a liar Danny was, but still—

"Maybe you'd better go back home," Kore said. "There's a bunch of hoboes camped out in the freight yard on the other side of the hill, and they get their water from the creek here. You know what they'd do to you if they caught you, don't you?"

Lani resisted a strong desire to look into the shadows behind her. "I—I can't go back to my aunt's house," she whispered.

"Why not? Now that she's had a good scare, maybe she'll lay off you."

Silently Lani unbuttoned her jacket, took it off and pushed up her sweater sleeves. The angry welts on her arms looked black in the grey moonlight.

Kore studied them with clinical interest. "What did she use on you?" he asked.

"A belt."

"She do that often?"

"Not with a belt. Usually she slaps me or locks me in her closet, and once she whipped me with a fly swatter. I was dusting her desk and knocked her journal off onto the floor."

"What's a journal?"

"It's a—well, sort of a diary. She thought I was trying to break the lock so I could read it, I guess."

"What did you do this time?"

"She caught me dancing the hula in my room."

"Dancing? What's wrong with that?"

Lani thought a moment. "She says it's wicked," she said finally.

"That's dumb. My mom used to be in a hooch show when she was younger. That's where she met my old man—he was a talker for a ten-in-one." He caught her blank look and added, "You know—freaks. What kind of name is Iolani, anyway?"

"It's Hawaiian," she said reluctantly.

"You're Hawaiian? So how come you've got that blond hair?"

"I'm only part Hawaiian," she said.

She braced herself for a derisive remark, but he fooled her. "Yeah, it's kind of that way with me. My ma's a Rom but my pa's *gadje*."

His words could have been spoken in Greek for all they

meant to Lani. "What's a Rom?" she asked.

"A Gypsy—don't you know nothing?"

Lani felt a small thrill of alarm; her aunt's deepest antipathy was reserved for the people she called "the dirty, thieving Gypsies."

"And your father is a—a non-Gypsy?" she said.

"That's what I said, didn't I?" Kore played with his stick, his expression brooding. "When we're working a show, the other Roms won't have nothing to do with us because of pa, and the *gadje* hate us because ma's a Rom. It's a drag, being half one thing and half something else—y'know what I mean?"

Lani didn't—not exactly—but she nodded anyway.

"You want some candy?" he asked abruptly.

Lani's empty stomach gurgled. "Yes, please," she said.

He produced a Hershey bar from his pocket. "You got any money?" he asked, his voice businesslike.

Lani got out the quarter she'd found and handed it to him. His face expressionless, he put it into his pocket before he gave her the candy bar. He watched her silently as she unwrapped it and began cramming it into her mouth.

"I can get you more food, but it'll cost you," he said when she was finished. "What else you got in your pockets?"

Lani hesitated, thinking of the ten-dollar bill. If she gave it to him, how could she be sure he'd bring her any food? "That's all the money I have," she said.

"What's that thing hanging around your neck?"

She had forgotten she was wearing the shark's tooth. She put her hand up quickly to hide it. "It's my lucky piece," she said.

"You don't believe in that junk, do you?" His voice was scornful. "How much luck have you had lately, anyway?"

Lani shivered. He had a point; why hadn't the *mana* of the shark's tooth worked for her? Maybe Aunt Berta was right. Maybe she was too wicked to deserve help.

Her stomach growled again, reminding her how long it had been since she'd had a real meal. Since the boy wanted the shark's tooth, why not trade it for food? After all, she already knew its magic didn't work for her, didn't she? She slipped the chain over her head and held the shark's tooth in her hand. It gleamed in the moonlight with a pearlescent whiteness, and unexpectedly she felt a fierce possessiveness toward it.

"I—I can't give it away." She dropped it into her pocket. "Kawena gave it to me—"

"Who the hell's Kawena?"

"She was my friend before I came to Boston. It wouldn't be right to give away her present."

"Well, you're going to get awful hungry, runt." Kore's voice was disgruntled. "How come you didn't rip off some food from your aunt when you ran away?"

"Because—because my father pays for the food at my aunt's house."

She didn't expect him to understand, but again he surprised her. "Yeah, my ma's like that about her old man. After I was born he wanted to make up with her, but she wouldn't have nothing to do with him. What it is, I'm the only grandson he's got, and besides, my ma's the best fortune-teller in the *familia*. They want her to take a *duikkerin* booth in the carnival they work, but she knows they'll treat my old man like dirt, so she's signing up with another show."

He paused to give Lani a long, considering look. "Don't you have no folks except your aunt?"

"There's my father."

"Does he travel around a lot?"

"No, he lives on Maunaloa."

"What's Maunaloa—a boat?"

"It's an island. It belongs to my father."

"Your pa owns a whole island?" Kore sounded skeptical. "How many people live there?"

"About—well, about fifteen, counting the kids. The Kealoha family works for my father, but they live in their own cottages."

"And all those people have to take orders from your old man?"

"I—I guess so."

"How come you don't live with him?"

"He's married again. He doesn't want me around."

"He must be rich. I'll bet he'd pay a lot to get you back."

The pulse in Lani's throat jumped. "I'll give you some money if you promise not to tell anyone you saw me," she said quickly.

Again his features seemed to sharpen. "How much?"

"Ten dollars." She took the ten-dollar bill from her pocket and showed it to him.

"You had that all along? Why didn't you give it to me for food?"

"I wanted to save it for something more important."

"There ain't nothing more important than food." Kore's voice was flat. He reached forward lazily and plucked the bill from her hand. She was sure he would walk away then, taking her money with him, but he didn't move. He stared at her so long that she grew uneasy again.

"You'd better come with me," he said abruptly.

"Are—are you going to turn me over to the police?"

"That'll be the day. I don't like cops and they don't like me. I'm going to take you to a better place to hide."

When she didn't move, he grabbed her by the arm and hauled her to her feet. His hand felt heavy on her arm, and it smelled of woodsmoke, of garlic. With a quick jerk she freed herself and scuttled backward, out of his reach.

The boy shrugged, the shrug she was beginning to realize could mean many things—irritation, disbelief, indifference. "Okay, it's your funeral. That's what I get for trying to help a *gadje*."

"You really want to help me?" she asked, her voice small.

"I said so, didn't I? I figured you could crash out in this old shack next to our house until things cool down, but if you want to stay here it makes no difference to me."

It was the indifference in his voice that decided her. Silently she put on her jacket and followed him up the creek bank.

There were few people in the streets they passed through;

the ones they did meet eyed Kore nervously and drew aside to let him pass. Lani's legs were beginning to ache by the time they finally stopped in front of a small cottage. Like her aunt's house on St. John's Court, it was isolated from its neighbors by an iron fence, but there the resemblance ended. Lani's breathing quickened as she stared up at the sign painted on the front of the building.

MADAME PEARSA, READER AND ADVISOR.
LOVE OR CAREER OR HEALTH—IT'S ALL IN YOUR HAND.
LET MADAME PEARSA ADVISE YOU.

"Who's Madame Pearsa?" she whispered.

"That's my ma. She reads hands and tarot cards. This is her *ofisa*—y'know, where she works. Right now, we're living here, too."

Uneasily Lani stared up at the windows of the house. "Can she really see the future?"

"Sure. She was born with a veil over her forehead." But his voice was too glib, and she gave him a suspicious look. He grinned back at her. "Most of it's a scam, but sometimes she really does have the gift—"

He broke off as a car turned into the street. Roughly he pulled Lani into the shadows behind a tree. When the car had passed, he ducked through a small opening between two overgrown shrubs. She followed him closely, trying to move as soundlessly as he did.

When they got to a door he stopped, opened it and shoved her through. The odor of decay enveloped her, and she stood very still, not daring to move for fear of what she might touch. Kore brushed past her; a moment later a match flared, then the flame of a kerosene lamp. She saw that she was standing in a shack, obviously a lean-to of the house. It was piled high with stacks of banded newspapers and remnants of boards and planks.

Kore pointed out a canvas cot. "You can sack out there. But if my old man catches you, I don't know nothing about you, see? If you say different, you'll be sorry as hell." His black eyes held hers until she nodded. "I'll bring you some food in the morning—"

He broke off, listening. She saw his face change even before the door slammed open and a man's voice demanded, "What the hell's going on here?"

The man standing in the doorway was tall, gaunt; except for his coloring—fair where Kore was dark—he was an older, rougher version of Kore. His eyes raked Lani, and her legs began to shake.

"Ain't you got no better sense'n to bring your girls around here?" he growled, glaring at Kore.

"She ain't my girl. I don't make out with little kids," Kore answered, his face sullen.

"So what's she doing here?"

Kore shrugged. "I was cutting across the yard when I heard something moving inside the shed. I found her crashed out on the cot. She told me her aunt beat her up and kicked her. Maybe it's the truth—someone's sure been working her over."

The man stared at Lani. "Say, ain't you that kid the cops are—"

"Show my pa what your aunt did to you, Lani," Kore interrupted.

Wordlessly Lani pushed up her sleeves and showed the man the welts on her arms. He whistled softly, his eyes speculative. "So that's how it was, huh? Now I wonder why her aunt is so all-fired anxious to get her back?"

"She says she hasn't eaten for a couple days, Pa. Maybe we'd better feed her before—y'know, we ask her any questions."

The man nodded; he seemed to have forgotten his anger as he led the way outside, around a corner of the house and through another door.

The room they entered, a kitchen, was poorly lighted. Its only furnishings were several folding chairs and a table, a hot plate sitting on a packing crate, and a portable icebox.

Kore's father pushed aside a strip of red cloth that served as a door, and Lani eased past him into another room. Like the kitchen, this room was small. Other than two folding chairs, the only piece of furniture in the room was a round table covered with a red velvet cloth. A woman was sitting at the table shuffling a deck of cards. Lani stared at her, fascinated by the gold loops in her ears, the scrap of bright cloth tied tightly over her forehead. Somehow it was easy to believe that this woman with her swarthy skin, her black glossy hair, had some kind of magical powers.

The woman looked up; Lani met her black eyes, and her breath caught sharply. "You've brought one of your little school friends home with you, Kore?" she said, her voice as warm and rich as hot chocolate.

"Her name's Iolani. I found her hiding in the lean-to." Kore's eyes warned Lani not to contradict him. As if he'd lost interest, he said around a yawn, "Show my ma what your aunt did to you, Iolani."

Lani took off her jacket. She turned away from the woman and pulled up her sweater and T-shirt to expose her back. The T-shirt had stuck to several of the abrasions, and she whimpered as the cloth pulled free, taking the scabs with it.

There was a hissing sound behind her. Panic held her immobile as the woman swooped down upon her. Then her hands, surprisingly gentle, were stroking Lani's hair back from her eyes. "You're safe here with us," the woman crooned. "Pearsa won't let nobody hurt you."

"Don't you go getting no crazy ideas, woman," the man said sharply. "We ain't adding kidnapping to our troubles."

"Who said anything about kidnapping, Clay? We're joining the Tatum Brothers show in Philadelphia in a couple days, ain't we? Who's going to pay any attention if we turn up with two kids instead of one?"

"It won't work. There's other Roms in the Tatum show. That family of yours is sure to find out, and you know they've been waiting for years to get me in trouble with the cops."

"She could pass for Yula. I've still got all of Yula's papers."

"What about that blond hair? She'd stick out like a sore thumb."

"No, she wouldn't. Yula had blond hair at first—and

anyway, no one in the *familia* saw her after she was first born."

"Well, it don't make no sense to me, taking on another mouth to feed," Clay grumbled.

Kore, who had been listening silently, spoke up. "She could sell flowers. I'm getting too big for it, anyway. I can teach her all she needs to know. Later on, she could help ma with the *boojo* or learn to tell cards if she's got the knack for it." He helped himself from a plate of sticky-looking candy on the table. "She says she can dance that Hawaiian hula stuff. Maybe she could go into a fat show when she gets a shape."

Clay's eyes flickered over Lani. Her heart beat faster as she realized he was weakening. "She's a good-looking kid," he said grudgingly. "Maybe it'd work out if— No, dammit, it's too risky. There wasn't no talk on the radio about the aunt mistreating the girl."

Lani spoke for the first time. "Aunt Berta took me in only because it was her Christian duty. She was always saying she hoped I'd die young so she could lay down her burden."

The woman said something in a staccato language. She brushed a strand of stray hair away from Lani's forehead. "How'd you like to live with us, Iolani? We'd call you Yula, just like our little girl who had the blood disease and died. Would you like to be Pearsa's little girl?"

Lani looked into the woman's eyes; under heavy, untrimmed eyebrows, they were shrewd—and very warm. She smelled of some musky perfume that reminded Lani of a sandalwood fan her father had once brought her from Hong Kong.

"Yes, thank you," she said in her politest voice.

That night she slept on a quilt spread out on the kitchen floor, and two days later she left Boston with Kore and his family. That had been ten years ago, and in all that time she'd had no news of her aunt or her father until she picked up her landlady's newspaper and saw her aunt's face smiling up at her from the front page.

III

From somewhere in the room, Lani was aware of her landlady's voice, but she was so immersed in the past that it took an inordinate amount of effort for her to concentrate on Mrs. Costello's words.

"—as white as a duck, Yula! There—I *knew* you were taking that accident too calmly. Now you just let go and have yourself a good bawl, while I dab some medicine on your elbow . . ."

Mrs. Costello went on talking, and Lani was relieved that, as usual, she didn't wait for an answer. She let her landlady treat her scraped elbow and put a glass of warm brandy in her hand. When she took a sip it felt like fire in her mouth, but its warmth spread through her body, driving back some of the coldness. When her eyes strayed back to the newspaper lying open beside her on the sofa, Mrs. Costello craned her neck to see what had caught her interest.

"Did you see that article about the Cinderella Girl?" she asked. "I guess Honolulu society will turn out in droves, trying to get a look at her."

"Cinderella Girl?"

"Why, yes. Surely you've read about her. It was in *Newsweek*, I'm sure. There was such a fuss when that girl was kidnapped ten years ago, you know— No, that would be before your time, wouldn't it? Well, she was snatched right out of her aunt's house in Boston in the middle of the night. Everybody thought she was dead. There was blood all over the place, I guess. Come to find out, it was her kidnappers who were dead."

"Her kidnappers? I don't understand—"

"It was in a big pileup on one of those turnpikes in the East. The Stevenson girl was only—oh, ten or eleven then. She was in shock at first, and later the doctors found out she'd lost her memory. Well, one of the families that got wiped out in the pileup had a girl around that age, so naturally they assumed— There was no one left to identify her, see, especially since the girl couldn't help them. So she was raised in a foster home, never knew the difference until a few months ago when she started going to a psychiatrist and her memory came back—"

"No one connected the girl in the wreck with the missing girl?"

"Lord, no—it was several states apart. I guess there were bodies all over the place, most of them so badly—" She stopped, gave Lani a contrite look. "There—I've got you upset again. Now you relax, and I'll go see if I can dig out that *Newsweek* article about the Stevenson girl. Do you good to have something to keep your mind off—y'know, what happened."

She bustled away, leaving Lani feeling a little numb. She tried to relate the things Mrs. Costello had told her with the things she knew to be true, but it was like trying to put together a jigsaw puzzle in the dark.

The girl was an impostor, of course; but was it possible that she'd made an honest mistake? Maybe the girl had been listening to a radio newscast about a missing girl her own age just before the terrible accident that had killed her family and destroyed her memory. And years later, when she'd gone to a psychiatrist, maybe the newscast she'd heard had surfaced, creating a whole false past for her. . . .

Lani picked up the copy of *Society West* and studied the girl's picture. She discovered that she felt indifference, even pity for the impostor. This girl with her self-possessed smile had taken nothing that Lani valued. She was welcome to the burden of that old tragedy, to Aunt Berta, to a father who disliked her; to a share of the Stevenson estate, if it ever came to that. Lani felt no desire to expose her to rain on her parade.

"There—I knew I had it somewhere." Mrs. Costello presented the newsmagazine with an air of triumph just as the phone rang in the hall. She made an exasperated sound and trotted away, leaving Lani alone with the magazine.

It didn't take her long to find the article. It was two columns long, and as she read the heading above it, several words leaped out at her from the printed page.

—*heiress to the estate of the late John K. Stevenson, wealthy Oahu businessman and rancher—*

The *late* John K. Stevenson . . .

She closed her eyes against the rush of grief. As if he were standing in front of her, she could see her father, black hair tumbling over his forehead, eyes that were as blue as hers were green; hear his exuberant laugh . . . it seemed incredibly sad that he who had always seemed so much more alive than other people should be dead.

She blinked rapidly and clenched her teeth until the tears dried in her eyes. She returned to the article then and read it to the end. When she had finished, she closed the magazine and tried to sort out the things she'd read. Her father was dead—and so was his second wife, both killed three years ago in a motorboat accident in Kaneohe Bay. But they had left behind a souvenir of their brief marriage.

"I have a sister," Lani said aloud, like someone trying to memorize a difficult lesson. "She's eleven years old and her name is Maile."

Something unexpected happened to her, to the cold lump she'd carried inside her for so long. She felt a sudden warmth, a longing to see this young half-sister, to find out what she was like. Had she inherited their father's charm—and his quick temper that could flare up like a Kona storm and sweep away everything in front of it? Or was Maile like her mother, the stepmother Lani had never seen?

And what had they told Maile about her older sister, Iolani? That she had killed her own mother long ago? Or had they hidden the whole tragic episode from her? What did Maile think of the girl who had suddenly turned up, claiming to be her sister? And who was taking care of Maile, now that her parents were dead? Did she live on Maunaloa Island, or had she been sent off to school on the mainland or maybe in Honolulu? Did she have relatives on her mother's side of the family to watch out for her interests, to protect her, or was she all alone in the world except for the impostor—and Aunt Berta?

Lani shivered in the hot, humid room. Surely her father would never have entrusted another child to Aunt Berta. And yet—hadn't the *Society West* article referred to her as Berta St. John of Maunaloa Island?

Her hands shook as she picked up the society publication. She read the caption under her aunt's picture again and found that her memory hadn't been faulty. Aunt Berta lived on Maunaloa Island now, and if Maile also lived there— *Oh, God, I can't let that happen*, she thought. *I can't let Aunt Berta terrorize another child. . . .*

Mrs. Costello's homey living room seemed suddenly unreal. She was back in the old house in Boston, locked in the smothering darkness of her aunt's linen closet. It had been the dark, not the missed meals or her aunt's abuse, that she'd hated so much. The dark inside the closet always seemed to be peopled with leering faces; she'd kept her eyes shut, no matter how long she was confined, afraid of what she might see if she opened them.

The trembling in her hands started up again. She put the paper down and tried to use reason to stay the storm building up inside her. Her father had been a careful man. Would he have entrusted a second child to the woman who had proved to be such a poor guardian for his first? And how could she possibly find out for sure, one way or the other, without going there to see for herself?

She shook her head violently, repudiating the idea. She could never go back to Maunaloa. She had turned her back on that part of her life ten years ago—for good. The *Newsweek* article had called Iolani Stevenson an heiress. Well, she didn't begrudge the girl anything she could get from her father's estate. But Maile—could she turn her back on her sister so easily? What if the impostor were *not* some confused person who had identified herself with a missing girl? What if she were an opportunist, maybe even a criminal? How safe would a child be, left in her care?

She heard footsteps outside in the hall; by the time her landlady came into the living room, she had herself under control and was able to smile convincingly, just as though she were the same person Mrs. Costello had left a few minutes ago.

"That was Officer Gowan on the phone, Yula," Mrs. Costello announced. "They found the car parked a couple of blocks from here—it was reported stolen earlier. They think now it was some youngster out joyriding in a stolen car."

"That would explain why he didn't stop," Lani said. Although she hadn't really shared Mrs. Costello's suspicions, she was more relieved than she cared to admit.

"Well . . . maybe. Or maybe he was smart enough to steal a car that couldn't be traced back to him."

"Him? You're sure now that it was a man?"

Mrs. Costello chewed her lip, thinking. "Well, I couldn't swear to it, of course. The driver was kind of slumped down behind the wheel. It could have been a woman or a kid, I guess." She fixed Lani with a hard stare. "Either way, you be extra careful, Yula."

Lani nodded meekly. She cast around for a way to change the subject, but before she could speak, Mrs. Costello gave an exclamation and began searching through the capacious pockets of her smock.

"In all the excitement, I almost forgot your letter." She found an envelope and held it out to Lani. "I'm afraid it's another one of those letters you sent out, trying to find your brother."

Lani recognized her own handwriting on the envelope with a pang of disappointment. After the first of the letters she'd sent had come back, she had been forced to satisfy her landlady's curiosity by explaining she'd lost touch with her brother and was trying to find him. But she'd never told Mrs. Costello that Kore wasn't really her brother or even her foster brother in a legal sense.

"That's the fifth one that's come back, isn't it?" Mrs. Costello said. "Well, you keep trying, dear, and one of these days—is that the last of those letters you sent out?"

"No, there were seven, but the trouble is—" Lani broke off. How could she explain to Mrs. Costello that she wasn't sure if Kore wanted to be found? She'd had no word from him since the night of Pearsa's funeral when he'd slammed out of the trailer—and out of her life. At the time she'd been too numb with grief to realize how badly she'd handled his marriage proposal. Later it had come to her that she'd hurt Kore's pride, that prickly Rom pride that was as much a part of him as his black eyes, his lithe body, his fear of showing weakness.

Her mistake had been that she hadn't made it clear to Kore why she was refusing him. It wasn't, as he must have believed, because the idea of marrying a Rom was repugnant to her. No, she had turned him down only because of the promise she'd made Pearsa just before her death, and if Kore hadn't stormed off, she would have told him so, made him see that saddling himself with a wife he didn't love would be the worst mistake of his life.

Unbidden, an insidious question slipped past her defenses. *And if you hadn't made that promise to Pearsa, what would your answer have been that night?* Even now, four years later, she still wasn't sure what she would have done. After all, she had been in love with Kore for such a long time. She had dreamed of being his wife, living with him, bearing his children—would she have turned him down, even though she had known in her heart that he was proposing only because he felt responsible for her?

Pearsa, who knew them both so well, must have guessed what would happen once she was gone, and to prevent Kore from making a tragic mistake, she had made Lani promise she would never marry him. At the time, alone in that coldly impersonal hospital room with Pearsa, knowing Pearsa was dying, she would have promised anything, done anything to make Pearsa's last moments easier. It was only later that she'd realized how hard the promise would be to keep.

And so she had removed herself from temptation. For the second time in her life she had run away. Had Kore gone back to the trailer looking for her? If so, what had he thought when he found she was gone? This was something she probably would never know. When she found Kore—*if* she found him—she would tell him the whole story; and then, four years late, she would give him Pearsa's *sumadjii*, the breastpiece of gold eagles and gold Mexican pesos that rightly belonged to him.

Although Pearsa, before she sank into the coma from which she had never awakened, had made Lani promise that she would sell the coins in the *sumadjii* and use the money to finance her education so she could break away from carnival life, Lani had known that this was one promise she couldn't keep. Traditionally, a Rom woman's *sumadjii* went to her daughter, or, if she had no daughter, to the wife of her son. Pearsa, there at the last, had forgotten that her real daughter was dead—but Lani hadn't. When she left, she had taken the *sumadjii* with her, afraid to leave it in the trailer for fear Kore wouldn't return, but she had kept it locked up in a metal box ever since. Even when she had been working at two jobs to pay her tuition to secretarial college, she had never been tempted to sell any of the coins.

"I see this one came back from the Showman's League in Tampa," Mrs. Costello said, breaking into Lani's thoughts. "Do you think he's working in some carnival or circus?"

"It's possible—I tried the Seamen's Unions, too. He shipped out once as a merchant marine." Lani didn't add that at the time Kore had been dodging a paternity suit which had been brought by one of the carnival girls who flocked around him like bees around spilled honey.

"How on earth did you lose track of him so completely?"

"We had a—a misunderstanding right after Pearsa—our mother—died," Lani said.

Mrs. Costello made a tut-tutting sound. "Your father's dead, too, isn't he?"

Lani hesitated. During the years that Pearsa had nurtured her, loved her, she had become Lani's mother in a way her own restless, impatient mother had never been; but that remote, silent man Pearsa was married to—no, she had never thought of Clay Brock as her father. But it was impossible to explain all this, so she said, "My father was killed in an accident several years before my mother died."

"No wonder you want to find your brother," Mrs. Costello said. "It isn't easy, being all alone in the world."

But I'm not alone, Lani thought. *I have an eleven-year-old sister I've never seen. What's more, I'll get no peace until I know that she's getting good care, that no one is mistreating her. . . .*

As easily as that, Lani made up her mind. Mrs. Costello caught the tightening of her lips and gave her a curious look.

"In the excitement," Lani said carefully, "I almost forgot my own news. A seaman came into the clinic today, and we got to talking . . . it's just possible that my brother is working out of Honolulu on a freighter. I have a week's vacation coming, you know, and I've decided to take it now and go over to the Islands to see if I can locate him."

IV

It was night when Lani returned to the Islands.

From her window seat on the big 747, she looked down at the lights of Honolulu, at the white breakers, luminous in the moonlight, that defined the beaches, and she gave herself a lecture about keeping her cool during the next few days, about remaining aloof from old memories, old pain.

She took the airport bus to Waikiki Beach, where she had made reservations in a small hotel on Prince Kuhio Street. Although the charity ball, where she hoped to get a look at her aunt and the girl who'd usurped her identity, was to be held that evening, she decided, after a restless night, to rent a car and do some sightseeing, mainly because she was determined to keep so busy that she wouldn't have time for worry—or second thoughts.

For breakfast she bought a sackful of *malasados* at a bakery on Kapiolani Street and shared the hot, crispy doughnuts with a small brown Filipino boy on a bench near the Ala Wai Canal. She watched a free hula show in the International Market Place, then bought Mrs. Costello a lauhala purse at a store in the Ala Moana Shopping Center. At lunchtime she ate a bowl of *saimin* at a small open-fronted diner on Beretania Street, then drove slowly through the pineapple and sugar cane fields to the windward side of the island.

· It was late afternoon when she parked the rental car at the Nuuanu Pali lookout. A busload of tourists were swarming over the rocks, snapping pictures, buying plump apple bananas from the rear of a truck, and listening to the practiced spiel of their tour guide, a jovial and very large Hawaiian man.

She leaned against the waist-high wall that outlined the top of the cliff. A thousand feet below, the Kaneohe basin spread out to the ocean, a patchwork quilt of greens and browns and tans. Although she knew the lookout faced away from Maunaloa Island, she fancied she could make out a familiar saddle-shaped outline in the haze on the horizon, and a wave of homesickness, as unexpected as it was intense, washed over her.

She turned away from the wall so abruptly that she almost bumped into the driver of the tour bus, who was sitting on the wall having a cigarette. He grinned at her cheerfully when she apologized.

"No big t'ing." He looked her over with frank interest. "You a local girl, miss?"

Lani hesitated, then said cautiously, "I was born in the Islands, but my family moved to the mainland when I was pretty small."

He nodded. "Soon as I see you, I t'ink, that *wahine* not all *haole*."

"You could tell, just by looking, that I'm part Hawaiian?" Lani said.

"Sure." He thumped his chest with the flat of his hand. "Same with me. I got one part kanaka, one part *haole*."

He grinned at her, showing an expanse of large, square teeth. Lani smiled back and said, "I was trying to locate Maunaloa Island. It's out there in Kaneohe Bay, isn't it?"

"Sure, but you no can see from *pali*." He hesitated, shaking his head. "That island, it's got one bad reputation. My cousin Kamaki, he's got this boat for hire out and sometimes he take supplies out there, but he never stay *pau poele*—you know, after dark." He stared at Lani curiously. "Where you hear about Maunaloa?"

"I read about it in a—a magazine article about the girl who was missing so long and was finally found."

"Yeah, that was somet'ing, all right. Make plenty big splash in the papers."

"There's another Stevenson daughter, isn't there? A much younger girl?"

"Sure—that po' little girl. Alla time got bad luck. One time, she eat akia berry, get plenty sick; then she fall down, break her leg—"

The tour guide called an impatient "Hele on!" from the bus, and the man shrugged good-naturedly and ambled off, leaving Lani feeling disappointed that there hadn't been time to pump the bus driver for more information about her sister.

On the trip back to Waikiki, she thought over what she'd learned, and her uneasiness deepened—the same uneasiness that had brought her to Honolulu. What had the man meant when he'd talked about Maile's "bad luck"? He'd mentioned akia berries, but surely there were no poisonous plants on Maunaloa, unless it was a specimen plant in the greenhouses or in Kawena's garden, where she grew the herbs and succulents for her tonics.

Lani spent an hour wandering through the stores on Kalakaua Avenue, shopping for a dress to wear to the charity ball. She finally found one she could afford, a long sheath with understated lines in a not-too-gaudy Hawaiian print, and carried it back to her hotel room.

Since it was still early, she stretched out on the bed for a nap, only to discover that her mind was too active for sleep. Growing within her was the feeling that she had embarked on a wild goose chase. After all, what could she possibly learn just by looking at her aunt? Aunt Berta had always been an expert at hiding her true nature behind a façade of gentility. Even Pearsa's training, drilled into Lani during those years when her foster mother had been hopeful of making a *boojo* woman out of her, wouldn't be much help in seeing behind those china-blue eyes, that bland face. Of course Aunt Berta and the fake Iolani Stevenson would be the center of attention at the ball. It was always possible that if she kept her ears open, she might pick up some more of the same kind of gossip she'd heard from the bus driver at the *pali*. . . .

When it was dark outside, she dressed carefully in the new sheath she'd bought. The print, in muted shades of green, was becoming, and she was satisfied that she wouldn't look out of place at the charity ball. For a long time she stared at her reflection in the bathroom mirror, wondering if her aunt could possibly recognize the colorless, too-thin girl of ten years before in this woman of almost twenty-one. Her skin was still tawny, but her hair had darkened several shades, and she was no longer colorless or too thin.

She turned away from the mirror and went to get her purse. Since the hotel where the charity ball was being held was a couple of miles away, she decided to take her car and was lucky enough to find a parking place a few blocks from the hotel.

After she left the car, she walked through the voluptuously warm night, the scent of flowering plants, of the sea—that elusive odor that was uniquely Hawaiian—enveloping her, and she felt a stab of regret that there was no one to share it with her. Although there were other people on the sidewalk, she felt invisible, a ghost among the chattering couples she met, and she was glad when, a few minutes later, she reached the hotel.

The hotel was old, dating from the last days of the Monarchy. It was built around a huge courtyard which featured a giant banyan tree that was even older than the hotel. Tree ferns cast shadows on the coral walls of the courtyard, and the music, from one of the island's cosmopolitan bands, was discreet and unobtrusive. Tables and chairs, already full, had been set out on graduated tiers that rose from a dance floor in the center. To Lani's relief she saw every kind of dress, from casual muumuus to gowns that might have been just unpacked from a Paris couturier's box. Although she felt conspicuous without an escort, she realized it was so crowded it was unlikely that anyone was paying any attention to her. Even so, she found it nerve-wracking to stand quietly in the shadow of a huge potted palm, pretending a poise she didn't feel.

She was prepared for a long wait, if not for complete disappointment; so it was unnerving when, less than half an hour after she entered the courtyard, her aunt, looking regal and haughty in floating voile, came sweeping in, accompanied by a tall, dark-haired man. As far as Lani could tell from the glimpse she got before the older woman swept past, her aunt looked much the same as she had ten years earlier. Time, it seemed, had dealt more kindly with Aunt Berta than it had with her own beloved Pearsa.

She waited until her breathing was back to normal before she turned to look behind her. Her aunt was standing so close that it took all her control not to gasp out loud. Another couple had joined Aunt Berta and her escort, and Lani's heartbeat picked up speed again as she recognized the girl from the newspaper photograph.

Superficially, the girl resembled Lani, but only in the most general way. Her hair, although blond, was silvery, a shining cap that hugged her small head. Her eyes were light, probably green, although it was hard to tell in the yellowish torch light, and she was inches taller than Lani, with a model's lean hips and small, high breasts. The price of her gown, a shimmering silver that matched her hair, would probably have paid Lani's salary at the clinic for a year. Without her perfect posture and grooming, the gown would have seemed too daring; on her, it looked as if it had been created just to complement her sleek figure and the unusual color of her hair.

It was a long time before Lani turned her attention to the two men. The dark-haired man was the taller of the two and, Lani realized now, extraordinarily good-looking, with strong, regular features and thick dark hair. The second man was leaner, his body wiry, tightly knit. In the flickering light of the luau torches, his hair looked russet. When he smiled at something the blond girl said, Lani wondered why, a moment earlier, she had been thinking he was rather ordinary looking.

The man turned his head; for a moment he looked directly into Lani's eyes. When she realized that she'd been staring openly, she whirled and melted into the crowd behind her. There was a queer weakness in her legs; seeing her aunt had been even more traumatic than she'd expected it would be. She looked around for a place where she could be alone for a few minutes. She saw a discreet sign—THIS WAY TO THE LOUNGES—above a door and headed toward it thankfully.

The women's lounge, at one end of a T-shaped hall, was dimly lighted and blessedly empty. It was furnished with high-backed wicker chairs and sofas and a row of dressing tables with lights encircling their mirrors. Lani found a chair that faced away from the door and sank into it gratefully. Although she didn't smoke, she found herself wishing she had a cigarette, if only to give her tension an outlet. As soon as she was back to normal, she promised herself, she'd return to her hotel. She had accomplished her mission—for all the good it had done her.

The door behind her opened with a sigh of displaced air. Not yet ready to face anyone, she slid down in the wicker chair, thankful for its high-winged back. With part of her mind she realized that two women had entered and were seating themselves at the dressing tables, but their voices didn't register immediately—not until she recognized her aunt's flat Bostonian accent.

"Really, Vivian, the idea is to be discreet, to be seen a few times under controlled situations, to satisfy their curiosity, but certainly not to make a spectacle of yourself."

"Just because I decided to wear my new Givenchy, I have to listen to another of your lectures?" The voice was thin, breathy—and sulky.

"You know this business has to be staged carefully. We can't prevent the curiosity, but we can control it, keep it strictly a local matter. The less you exhibit yourself, the better. If you could manage to look a little—"

"A little dowdy, like the missionary-family bitches in this town?"

"—a little less flamboyant, it would help. That gown—well, it *is* more suitable to New York, don't you think? Why didn't you wear the print, as we decided?"

"*You* decided, you mean. I hate those tacky Hawaiian prints. In fact, this whole damned Hawaiian scene bores me."

"Well, that's too bad. You knew this affair tonight was for a local charity. We chose it—remember?—because it was not likely to attract any mainland publicity. We can't allow your picture to be splashed all over the mainland newspapers. Until we're sure about the girl, we can't take the risk that she might read about you, realize her father is dead, and come forward at the last minute to complicate things."

"There's no chance of that, is there?" The girl's voice was alarmed. "You told me she was dead—"

"What I said was we have good reason to *assume* she's dead."

During the years Pearsa had trained Lani to read the small physical signs that reveal hidden emotions—the twitch of an eyelid, a tensed muscle, the contraction of the pupil—she had also taught her to listen to voices, and Lani knew that her aunt was lying now—or at least that she was being evasive.

"I don't see how she could still be alive, but even if she should turn up, she'll be taken care of."

"What do you mean by that? There won't be any rough stuff, will there? I don't want to get involved in—"

"You're already involved." Aunt Berta bit off the words. "It's too late for second thoughts, Vivian. You know what he'd do to you if you tried to double-cross him, don't you? He's completely ruthless, as you very well know. And anyway"—her voice took on a conciliatory tone—"Lani's father spent a fortune trying to trace her, and there was nothing, not the slightest evidence that she was still alive. Personally, I've always been convinced she was murdered, her body buried somewhere, probably by some tramp. And even if she should turn up at this late date, it would just be her word against mine—and against the physical evidence. Why do you think we went to so much trouble, having you write those fake letters to John Stevenson and planting your fingerprints on her old brush? That was insurance, just in case it was ever needed—"

There was a swishing sound at the door, and a bevy of chattering women invaded the lounge. A few minutes later, when Lani peeked cautiously over the top of her chair, her aunt and the girl she'd called Vivian were gone.

It was several minutes before Lani could bring herself to follow them. Still in a state of shock, she found it hard to make sense out of what she'd overheard. She had assumed the impostor was an innocent victim of circumstance, or, at worst, an opportunist. Now, realizing the girl had been working hand-in-hand with her aunt, Lani wondered at her own blindness. Without Aunt Berta's help, an impostor would have been exposed, no matter how well prepared or how plausible her story. For one thing, Berta St. John was the only person who had known Lani intimately as a child, who could identify her— No, that wasn't quite true, Lani thought suddenly. Because there was also Kawena—and Kawena's family.

She stopped in the middle of the hall, oblivious to a pair of passing women. How had the girl, this Vivian, fooled Kawena? Had Aunt Berta found a way to banish Kawena and the Kealoha family from Maunaloa before Vivian came forward? Was it possible she had that kind of power? Had she been appointed Maile's legal guardian? And whom had Aunt Berta meant when she'd told Vivian that "he" would never let her back out of the scheme? Was there a third conspirator involved, the man her aunt had called ruthless?

Still deep in thought, she started on down the hall. She opened the door to the courtyard, then stopped dead. Berta St. John and Vivian were standing almost directly in her path, talking with the two men she'd seen them with earlier. Her aunt's eyes rested on her briefly, then moved on. Nothing changed on that genteel face; no recognition or alarm flickered in her blue eyes. But the shock of seeing her aunt again so unexpectedly was too much for Lani. She turned on her heel and fled back through the still-closing door.

She was halfway down the hall when she heard the door open behind her and the sound of footsteps. Although common sense told her that it was very unlikely her aunt would be returning to the lounge so soon, she found it impossible to look around. The thought of being trapped in the lounge alarmed her, and when she saw a red light and an EMERGENCY EXIT sign above a door, she hurried toward it. Without breaking her stride, she flung it open and plunged out into the night.

The self-closing mechanism of the door swooshed softly as it closed behind her. It was so dark that it was a few seconds before her eyes adjusted enough to the change of light so that she could see she was standing in an alley. As far as she could tell in the near-total darkness, she was alone. She stared up uneasily at the dark walls of the old hotel. No light showed in any of the windows that over-looked the alley, and she wondered if they had been painted over, if the rooms behind them were used as storage.

Although there was a lamppost at the far end of the alley, its moon-shaped globe had been engulfed by the branches of a banyan tree, and the light it shed was so feeble that it barely penetrated the darkness at the mouth of the alley. As Lani stared into the darkness around her, a feeling of disorientation swept over her. Even the beat of distant music, filtering out into the alley from the courtyard, had a disembodied sound, as if it came from another dimension.

Lani made a sudden discovery about herself: she would rather risk a face-to-face encounter with her aunt than walk down that dark alley alone. Although she was ashamed that she'd let her old fear of the dark rout her, she turned and felt for the doorknob—only to discover there was none. Too late she realized that since it was an emergency door, it could only be opened from the inside.

There was nothing else to do but start down the alley. She forced her reluctant legs forward, trying not to notice how far away the street light was. As she was passing a row of trash cans, there was a flash of light behind her, so brief that she couldn't be sure she hadn't imagined it. She stopped and held her breath, listening. There was a faint click, then a scuffling sound that could have been a cat—or someone running lightly on tiptoe.

She turned her head stiffly to look back, but as far as she could tell, nothing was moving behind her, and the small sound had already stopped. Although she told herself she was dreaming up horrors where none existed, she moved faster now. A minute later she stopped again to listen, and this time there could be no doubt. The sounds were closer, and they were unmistakably footsteps, light and sure, moving toward her.

She began to run. Her sandals slapped against the cement paving, setting up echoes along the dark walls of the hotel. She tried to scream, but as so often happened, her voice had deserted her when she most needed it. Ahead, a darker rectangle among the shadows, she saw the outline of a door. She headed for it, her breath sobbing in her throat. When her outstretched hand touched wood, she began a frantic search for the doorknob, but again there was none, and she knew it was another fire exit door that only opened outward.

Abandoning all caution, she pounded on the door, and when no one came to open it, she began to run again, knowing that she wasn't going to make it to the street—and safety—in time.

Even so, the first blow took her by surprise. It struck her on the back of her head and sent her reeling into a row of garbage cans. Even before she struck the ground, she was twisting her body, rolling frantically, trying to find a hiding place among the cans. The second blow came down out of the darkness, and this time it landed below her ear. Pain shot through the back of her head, paralyzing her. Although she was only half-conscious, she was aware of something gritty under her cheek, and she sensed, rather than saw, someone bending over her, blotting out the little light there was.

Starkly, as if a voice had said them out loud, words came to her. *I'm going to die in this filthy alley and I'll never see Maunaloa again....*

It seemed like an eternity that she lay there, unable to move, waiting for the next blow to fall. At the end of the alley, fifty or more feet away, there was the shuffling of feet on cement, a rush of bantering male voices, a hoarse laugh. With every nerve in her body working overtime, Lani sensed that her attacker was listening as intently as she was, waiting for the group of men to move on.

Mercifully, they seemed in no hurry to leave. They were arguing good-naturedly about whose car to use and where to go next. Lani prayed as she'd never done before in her life, willing them to linger there under the street light—at least until she recovered enough strength to call out for help.

She was never to know exactly what saved her. Maybe one of the men glanced toward the alley, or maybe her attacker simply got tired of waiting. She heard footsteps, the same quick, light footsteps that had followed her earlier, this time moving away from her, and a few moments later she was alone in the alley again.

In her relief she moaned deep in her throat, and the sound galvanized her to action. She rolled to her side, got her knees under her and strained to a standing position. At the end of the alley the group of men had moved on, and the only sound now was the thumping of her own heart.

It was instinct that sent her stumbling back toward the hotel. With its faded gentility, its understated luxury, it seemed the epitome of safety, and it was only later that she realized that she should have headed for the well-traveled street as fast as she could go, even if it meant following her attacker.

She was almost to the exit door when she remembered that it only opened outward. Simultaneously she realized that at some point during the attack she'd dropped her purse. She staggered to a stop, uncertain what to do next. Her head seemed full of bubbles, and it ached abominably, making it hard for her to think, much less make a decision. The thought of pounding on the door for someone to open it, of drawing attention to herself, made her cringe, and yet she wasn't sure she could make it back to her car without help. And her purse—how could she find her purse in the dark? It held her driver's license, the ID cards that were so difficult to replace, her money . . .

Ahead of her, glowing in the dark like a stationary lightning bug, she saw a small pinpoint of light. Frantically she turned to run. Her outstretched hand struck a trash can lid, and the metallic sound echoed through the alley.

"Who's there? Is someone out there?"

There was nothing furtive about the voice; it was authoritative, strong—and male. With relief she realized that the pinpoint of light was a cigarette, that someone had stepped outside to have a private smoke. She tried to speak, but her coordination was still poor, and she could only lean against the trash can, trying not to fall.

A small beam of light came out of the darkness, moved over the wall behind her, then down to her face.

"What the devil—what's wrong with you, miss?"

Lani closed her eyes against the light. It would be all right now. Whoever this man was, surely he would help her.

"Are you ill? Can't you speak?"

She opened her eyes. "I fell," she whispered. "I knocked

myself out." It wasn't until she heard her own voice telling the lie that she knew she wasn't going to report the attempted mugging to the police.

The man came closer, still holding the tiny flashlight beam on her face. "What did you say? I can't hear you."

With an effort she raised her voice. "I was walking down the alley, going to my car, and I stumbled over something. I took a bad fall—" She took her hands away from the trash can to show him her skinned palms; the gesture threw her off balance and she began to topple forward. There was an exclamation, and then hands had plucked her out of the air.

She sagged against the man. His jacket smelled of tobacco, of after-shave lotion and something else that was indefinably male, and she was suddenly aware of the strength of the arms holding her, of the warmth of his hands through the thin material of her dress.

A floating feeling, as if she were having an out-of-the-body experience, held her motionless. She told herself it was shock, but she knew it was something else, too. For one of the rare times in her life, she felt a desire to cling to a man—and she still hadn't seen his face.

Then he was setting her back on her feet, steadying her. "Can you walk?" he asked, and his voice was so matter-of-fact, she knew that whatever significance the moment had held for her, he obviously hadn't shared it.

"I'm fine. It was just a dizzy spell," she answered, and because she was ashamed of her momentary weakness, her voice came out distant and cool.

"Do you need medical help?"

"I don't think so—no, I'm sure I don't. It was just the shock. It happened so quickly. But I did drop my purse. If you'd help me find it—"

"No problem. If you can walk, I'll take you to your car after we locate your purse—or call you a taxi. How far do you have to go?"

"I left my car about three blocks from here," she said, thankful for his impersonal offer of help.

"That's a pretty long hike in your condition. Look, my

car's in the hotel parking lot. Suppose I drive you to your car or take you on home. You can send someone back for your car or pick it up tomorrow."

"Oh, I couldn't—"

"I'm perfectly respectable." His voice sounded amused. It occurred to her that it was a very attractive voice, deep and vibrant, and she felt a sudden desire to see if his face matched it.

"Won't someone be wondering what happened to you?"

"Not for a while. There's quite a crush inside. I'll explain to my friends later. The important thing now is to get you off your feet before you cave in again."

This was so self-evident that Lani made no more protests. Since, as he told her now, he'd be going back in through the hotel lobby, he secured the exit door, which he'd unlocked when he came out for his cigarette. While she leaned against the wall, he looked for her purse, finding it after a short search. He handed it to her and took her arm. Trying not to lean too heavily on the man, she forced herself to move forward and soon discovered that the brief rest had restored most of the strength in her legs. Except for the throbbing in the back of her head and the sting in the palms of her hands, she seemed to be back to normal.

When they moved into the circle of light at the end of the alley, she looked up at her rescuer—and recognized him immediately. He was the dark-haired man who had escorted Aunt Berta into the courtyard; later, he had been one of the group standing outside the entrance to the lounges, talking to her aunt and the impostor.

Her arm must have tensed, because he gave her a curious look. She turned her face away, fighting the desire to run. He stopped her directly under the street light, took a card out of his wallet and handed it to her. She made a pretense of reading it, but other than his name— Wade MacMasters—the words on the card made no impression on her.

"What's your name?" he asked abruptly.

"Yula—" The word was so faint that she cleared her throat and tried again. "Yula Brock."

The man frowned at her. "Did you hurt your throat when you fell?"

"I have trouble talking when—when I'm tired."

"Or when you've had a scare." He studied her disheveled hair, her skinned hands. "What really happened? Was it a mugger?"

"It was a fall," she said sharply.

She was sure he would question her further, but instead he said, "Yula—that's an unusual name. Romany, isn't it?"

At her start and quick stare, he added, "I was stationed with a Rom while I was doing my stint in 'Nam. I remember he told me once that his grandmother's name was Yula. His mother made the mistake of letting his birth be recorded, and the draft board in New Jersey nailed him—or maybe someone in a rival family blew the whistle on him, the way he suspected. At any rate, he was pretty much like a fish out of water, being cut off from his people, and he opened up a little to me—not that we ever became really good friends."

"No, he might act friendly if he could use you in some way, but he'd never trust a *gadje* enough to become real friends with you," she said absently. It had just occurred to her that since this man knew Aunt Berta, he might also know something of the relationship between her aunt and her young half-sister. Maybe she should take advantage of this opportunity that had been thrust upon her so unexpectedly to pump him. The question was—how to begin? She glanced up at Wade MacMasters and found him studying her, his eyes too intent for politeness. His next words were like a dash of cold water.

"Is that why you told me you'd had a fall? So I wouldn't call the police? Are you a Rom?"

She could have bitten off her own careless tongue, but she rallied quickly. "I told you I had a fall because that's what happened. And no, I'm not a Rom. I know a little about them because I once had a friend who—who was raised by a Gypsy family. As for my name, my mother got it from a novel she was reading just before I was born."

"I see. Well, that explains why you don't look like a Gypsy. Your coloring is all wrong, for one thing, and most of them, including the women, have rather strong features, don't they?"

Lani thought of Pearsa, of her roughhewn face, and her eyes that could pierce the soul of a *gadje* she was setting up for a con one minute and be as warm as a kiss the next. Unexpectedly her throat closed up, and she was glad when a passing couple diverted Wade MacMasters's attention. The woman's gaze lingered on Wade, moved to Lani. When her eyes narrowed, Lani realized for the first time that her struggle in the alley had left her dress wrinkled, with one sleeve almost torn off.

Wade MacMasters had noticed the woman's stare, too. "Is your dress ruined?" he asked.

"I'm afraid so, and I just bought it yesterday."

"Just be thankful you weren't badly hurt. You can always replace a dress."

The casualness in his voice annoyed her. "Not this dress," she said a little stiffly. "I spent more than I can afford on it. I wanted something nice for the charity ball tonight."

"And yet you were leaving early, weren't you?"

"I—I thought there would be a stage show," she improvised. "When I realized it was a dance, that it was mostly couples, I decided to go back to my hotel—"

"Your hotel? Then you don't live here in Honolulu?"

"I'm a tourist. I had some idea I might like to live here, but I understand jobs are very hard to find if you're an outsider."

"That's true. The patronage system is very strong here in the Islands. What kind of job were you looking for?"

"I've been working as a sort of Girl Friday in the office of a medical clinic in San Francisco for the past year. It's understaffed, so we all have to pitch in where we're needed. I've done a little bit of everything, including helping the physical therapists—" She broke off, realizing that she was talking too much because she was nervous.

Wade MacMasters regarded her thoughtfully. "Look, I could use a cup of coffee, and I have a hunch you could, too. There's a little place just down the street where you can still get a decent cup."

Lani nodded, secretly pleased at the prospect of prolonging the evening. Surely, she told herself, she could find a way, over coffee, to bring her aunt into the conversation.

The coffee house was small, intimate; although it was tucked away behind a new, modern hotel, it still retained the charm of an earlier era. The walls were covered with lauhala matting; the tables were Philippine mahogany and rattan, scarred by long usage; and the lighting was so discreet that she didn't feel conspicuous in her torn dress.

In the establishment's tiny restroom, she washed her face and hands, renewed her makeup and tidied her hair, pinned the rip under her sleeve together as best she could. When she rejoined Wade MacMasters, she was sure his eyes registered surprise as he rose to let her slip into the booth.

As they waited for their coffee, he talked about the changes that had come to the Islands since his boyhood on a ranch on the big island of Hawaii. He spoke with assurance, with the confidence of a man who has no doubts that his own opinions are worth listening to, and Lani found herself relaxing a little, although she was too much aware of him as a man to relax completely.

The coffee arrived, and as she sipped the hot, fragrant brew, she realized how much she needed it.

"When do you plan to return to the mainland, Miss Brock?" the man asked abruptly.

"At the end of the week. My vacation will be over then." An idea of how to bring her aunt into the conversation came to her, and she added, "Won't your friends be wondering what happened to you, Mr. MacMasters? Didn't I see you with an older woman and a blond girl?"

"That was Berta St. John and her niece, Iolani Stevenson." Although she thought she was prepared, her aunt's name made her flinch, and the man's eyes sharpened. "I see you recognize Iolani's name. There's been a lot of tripe written about her since she returned to her family."

"Is she—are you related to Miss Stevenson?" she asked, because it seemed a natural question.

To her surprise he nodded. "In a way. My sister was John Stevenson's second wife. Iolani's half-sister Maile is my niece. Since I'm Maile's guardian and also manage the Stevenson estate, I live with the Stevenson girls and their aunt on Maunaloa Island."

Lani set her coffee cup down very carefully. "Maunaloa Island?"

"It's a privately owned island off Kaneohe Bay, not the sort of place a tourist would have heard about." He was silent for a moment. She kept her eyes fixed on her cup, aware that he was watching her.

"If you're serious about making a change in your employment, I may be able to help you," he went on. "Would you mind answering a few questions about yourself?"

She shook her head a little warily. Why should this man, a complete stranger, offer to help her find a job? He certainly didn't act like the average male on the make. In fact, he was almost too businesslike as he began asking her questions.

"How much did you help with physical therapy treatments at that clinic in San Francisco?" he asked.

"Quite a bit," she told him, her puzzlement growing. "We were so shorthanded that I often helped with the youngsters who needed special exercises and—"

"You worked with children?"

"Most of the time. The doctors said I had a knack for getting them to cooperate."

"Do you come from a large family?"

"No, I was an only child, but—well, I enjoy kids."

"They mind you? Do what you tell them to do?"

Lani shook her head, amused. "Not always. Some of the treatments are very—well, the doctors and nurses call them uncomfortable, but actually they can be very painful. Mostly it's a matter of gaining their trust by being honest, by using diversions when necessary—"

"Diversions, Miss Brock?"

"Telling them stories, getting them to talk about their friends and pets, teaching them simple songs and dances that can double as therapy exercises."

"What about bribery—you know, with candy and such?"

She shook her head. "Bribery doesn't work very well, even though most of the youngsters we treat at the clinic come from underprivileged homes. It's better to use other methods. It's surprising how much pain they will put up with, trying to please someone they—they trust."

He was silent for a moment, his eyes probing hers. "Do you have any relatives or close friends here in the Islands?" he asked.

Belatedly, caution stirred inside Lani. "Look, Mr. Mac-Masters, I don't mind answering questions about my job qualifications, but what does my personal life have to do with it?"

"Bear with me a minute," he answered crisply. "There's a good reason for my question. Do you have any relatives or friends in the Islands?"

"No, but—"

"Then it's possible I have a job for you."

From her first glimpse of the man in the hotel courtyard, she had known he was unusually attractive, with his strong, masculine features, his grey eyes that contrasted so sharply with his dark hair and tanned skin. Now, when he smiled at her, she realized something else: Wade MacMasters had a very potent personal charm.

"I'm offering you a job as my secretary," he said. Lani started to speak, but he held up his hand. "Wait. There are some things you should know about the job before you make up your mind. Although I maintain a full office staff here in Honolulu at our offices in the Stevenson Building on King Street, I usually take work home with me weekends and at night. There's also my personal correspondence, and records concerning the management of Maunaloa Island to be maintained. Most importantly right now, I need someone to help out with my young niece, Maile. Transportation back and forth to Oahu is limited, although we have a cabin cruiser, and the company leases a helicopter, which is usually available. But you can see why I can't use anyone who'd always be running off to Honolulu to meet her friends. I went that route before, and it just didn't work out."

He paused, as if expecting a comment, but this time Lani was silent. "There are benefits, too, of course," he went on. "The pay is above average, even for the Islands, and you'll have ample time off when I'm on business trips. When I *am* home, I work irregular hours, sometimes at night, always on the weekend for at least a few hours a day. So this is not a job for someone with a large social life—"

He went on talking about her duties, and although she was careful to look receptive, her mind was in a whirl. It was such incredibly good luck . . . or was it pure luck? Could it be something more sinister, or— No, how was that possible? It had to be a coincidence, and the opportunity she'd been hoping for. A chance to see for herself what the relationship was between her half-sister and Aunt Berta.

"You said something about needing help with your niece," she said when there was a lull in the conversation. "Isn't there a domestic staff on the island?"

"There's an excellent staff, but I need someone who can supervise the physical therapy my niece's doctor recommends for her. She broke her leg a few months ago, and we haven't had much luck getting her to do her exercises."

"How did the accident happen?" Lani asked.

"It was just one of those crazy things. The bolts that secure the balcony railing outside her room had worked loose. She was leaning over it, talking to her aunt below in the garden, and the weight of her body finished the job of loosening the bolts. Luckily, she landed in a shrub, which broke her fall, or it could have been worse. As it was, she spent several months in a cast. The leg is out of the cast now, but it has atrophied enough that she needs therapeutic exercises. Unfortunately, Maile hasn't been cooperating. After what happened to her sister, her father overprotected her, and—well, I'm afraid she's rather a difficult child."

He looked so harassed that she felt a pang of sympathy— or maybe it was envy for the sister her father had cared enough about to overprotect. Wade MacMasters glanced down at his watch.

"Do you think you'd like to take a stab at the job, Miss Brock?" he asked.

Lani forced herself to smile coolly. "Yes, thank you. It might be interesting, living on an island."

Wade MacMasters nodded; from his lack of surprise, it was obvious he'd expected her to accept. "I'll need references, of course, and there'll be an application form to fill out." He took a business card from his wallet and handed it to her. "Call my office tomorrow and we'll get things started. I won't be going back to the island for a couple of days. That should give you ample time to wind up your own affairs."

He paused, his eyes moving over her. "That's a painful-looking place on your arm. Maybe you'd better have a doctor check you over."

"Oh, that's an old scrape. I got it a couple of days ago when a car almost ran me down."

"Two accidents in three days? Does this sort of thing happen to you often? You don't suffer from dizzy spells, do you, Miss Brock?"

Lani felt the heat rise to her face. "I'm in perfect health," she said.

Unexpectedly, Wade MacMasters laughed. "And you also don't like total strangers prying into your business and asking you personal questions, do you?" he said. "Well, I'm not fond of nosy people, either. I think we'll get along just fine, Miss Brock."

He looked around for their waitress and beckoned for the check. "I'd better get back, but first I'll see you to your car. Or would you rather I called you a cab?"

"Oh, I'm fine now," she told him.

Wade MacMasters was silent as they walked the two blocks to the side street where she'd parked the rental car. Even after he'd unlocked the car door for her and watched her slide behind the wheel, he only nodded and stepped back. Following his lead, she gave him a polite smile and drove off, but when she glanced in the rear-view mirror, she saw that he was still standing at the curb, staring after her. The expression on his face was so strange that some of her original doubts returned. Did he already regret hiring her? He didn't seem like an impulsive man; why had he hired her, a strange woman he'd rescued from an alley?

The phone inside her hotel room was ringing when she unlocked her door a few minutes later. She hurried across the room, pausing only long enough to shut the door behind her. Had Wade already had second thoughts about hiring her? Was he calling to tell her he'd changed his mind?

She snatched up the phone, and a voice so faint it could have come from another world spoke in her ear.

"What? I can't hear you—"

"Lani? Is that you, Lani?"

"Kore—" She sat down on the edge of the bed, her knees suddenly weak. "Is it really you, Kore? How did you find me? Are you here in Honolulu?"

"I'm in Seattle. Your letter caught up with me late this afternoon—it was forwarded by the Seamen's Union. When I called the number you gave me in San Francisco, your landlady told me you were in Honolulu. She gave me the name of your hotel—"

"Oh, Kore, I'm so glad to hear from you! I thought you were—"

"Dead? No way. Listen, I'm sorry as hell I went off half cocked like that. It was a real shock to my ego, having you turn me down. I always thought—hell, I'd been waiting for you to grow up for eight years. Why do you think I was always punching out other guys for trying to come on with you?"

"I—I didn't have any idea you felt like that, Kore," Lani said carefully.

"Well, you always were a dumb little *gadje*." But there was a hint of laughter in Kore's voice now. "And we'll talk about this later. What happened to you after I split? When I cooled off and went back, you were gone, and nobody knew what had happened to you. I almost went out of my mind."

"I went to St. Louis, got a job and finished high school at night. Later I went to business college, and—oh, there's so much to tell you, but this is long distance."

"I'm flush. You'll be glad to learn I'm a reformed character and a respectable businessman. Some of that Pollyanna stuff of yours must have finally rubbed off." Again there was laughter in his voice. "But you're right. History can wait. I'll be in San Francisco in a couple of days."

"But I won't be back by then," Lani wailed. "I just took a job here. I start working on Maunaloa Island in a couple of days."

There was a brief silence. "Maunaloa? Isn't that the island you used to talk about all the time, the one your old man owns? I thought you were turned off him for good. Did you change your mind?"

"I haven't changed my mind. But I found out recently that I have a half-sister, and I have to find out if—if she's being cared for properly."

"You lost me there. And what did you mean when you said you'd taken a job on Maunaloa? Why would you have to do that?"

"I was hired as Yula Brock. They have no idea who I am. I'm going to work for the man who manages my father's business affairs now."

"How did that come about? Where did you meet this— what's his name, anyway?"

"His name is Wade MacMasters, and I met him by accident. Someone tried to mug me in an alley tonight, and he came along— Oh, it's much too long to go into now. He has no idea who I am, and if I find out my sister is getting good care, there's no reason why anyone should ever know. I don't look anything like I did when I ran away."

"No, that you don't. You looked like a half-starved puppy someone had left out in the rain the night I stumbled over you."

"The night you conned me out of every penny I had, you mean," she retorted.

"Sure. You were a *gadje*. Any Rom worth his salt would have done the same."

"And would any Rom have taken me home to his mother?" she asked. "Would any Rom have been a big brother to me all those years?"

"I'm not your big brother, Lani. Maybe Pearsa got confused about that sometimes, but I never did. I made up my mind to marry you when you were twelve—"

"We'd better talk about that when we see each other," Lani said hurriedly. She had a lot of things to explain to Kore, but this wasn't the time, not over the phone. "This shouldn't take more than a few days. When I'm satisfied that my sister is being treated well, I'll quit my job and come back to San Francisco."

"I'll be waiting for you." He hesitated a moment before he asked, "How do you expect to fool your father? Won't he recognize you? And what about your old nurse—hell, I never could remember her name."

"Kawena. I'll just have to keep away from her, I guess. As for my father, he's been dead three years, Kore. And I've already seen my aunt. She looked right at me, and I'm sure she didn't recognize me."

"Your aunt? Is that the one who—"

"Yes, Aunt Berta. She's living at Maunaloa with my half-sister now. I have to be sure she hasn't been mistreating Maile—"

"Maile?"

"My sister. She's only eleven, the same age I was when I was living with Aunt Berta."

Kore was silent for a moment. "Well, I don't like the smell of this, Lani. I think you should hop on a plane and go back to California. If you want, I can go to Honolulu, do a little snooping around or even hire a detective."

"No, I want to do it myself."

"So what happens if you find out your aunt's been up to her old tricks? Are you going to try to get guardianship of the girl? And why all the secrecy, anyway? Why didn't you speak up and tell this MacMasters guy who you really are?"

"It might not be that easy. It's too complicated to explain over the phone, but I have good reason to believe it would be very difficult to prove who I am. And that part isn't important. I don't want anything from my father's estate. But I can't turn my back on my sister, either."

"Okay, but be careful. It might be dangerous if your aunt should recognize you."

"I promise I'll be careful." A laugh bubbled up in her throat. "I'll use the training Pearsa gave me. Surely I can fool a bunch of *gadje*."

"You were a lousy Rom. Who ever heard of a Rom who wouldn't steal? And how many times did you scare off one of Pearsa's *bozurs* just when she was ready for the payoff?"

Lani sighed. "You're right. I always felt sorry for them, and I guess they could sense it. But I did okay selling flowers, and in the fat show later on. You have to admit I can dance, Kore."

"Yeah, but that meant I was always punching out some rube for coming on too strong with you," he grumbled. "And don't change the subject. Are you sure I can't talk you out of this crazy scheme?"

There was a coaxing tone in his voice now, and it brought a reluctant smile to Lani's face. Except for that one time, she'd never been able to refuse Kore anything—as he well knew. During her years with his family, she had done his chores for him, lied for him to save him from his father's thrashings, lent him the money she earned dancing when he was short. In return he had let her tag along behind him, had listened silently while she talked about Maunaloa, about her homesickness for Kawena, about all the things she couldn't say to Pearsa for fear of hurting her foster mother.

Pearsa had given her love and emotional security, but it had been Kore she had poured her heart out to. It had been a harsh life, living as they had in a succession of grubby trailers on the outskirts of small Southern towns, exposed to all the raw edges of life. But Kore had protected her from the worst of it. From the beginning he had made it clear that a terrible retribution awaited the first man who stepped out of line with his sister, and she'd been as safe as if she'd been shut up in a convent—at least from the carnival men.

"Yes, I guess you *could* make me change my mind," she said ruefully. "And that's why I'm not going to give you a chance to try."

"Okay, okay, but don't take any chances, Lani. What's this about a mugging? And your landlady mentioned something about a car trying to run you down—"

"That was an accident," she broke in. "And it was my own fault I almost got mugged tonight. I took a shortcut through an alley, and—well, it was a stupid thing to do. I promise it won't happen again."

But after she hung up, she felt chilled, despite her joy at finding Kore. Because he was right about one thing—there *was* something odd about being the victim of two near-fatal incidents within the space of two days.

Was it possible they weren't coincidences, after all? Her landlady had insisted that the driver of the car had tried to run her down. And whoever had assaulted her in that alley had certainly intended to do more than just snatch her purse. If they were deliberate attempts to scare her or even kill her, that meant that someone knew who she was, someone with a reason for wanting her out of the way.

Her aunt had told the blond girl that if Lani turned up, she would be "taken care of." What exactly had she meant? Murder? Surely even Aunt Berta wouldn't go that far, especially since they—her aunt, Vivian, the mysterious man Aunt Berta had described as ruthless—had everything on their side.

Even if I wanted to claim the estate, Lani thought bleakly as she began getting ready for bed, *who would take the unsupported word of a Gypsy against a pillar of Boston society like Aunt Berta?*

VI

It was still early morning, two days later, when Lani got out of the cab that had brought her to downtown Honolulu from her hotel in Waikiki. She stood at the curb with her suitcase, waiting for Wade MacMasters, aware that she was a little early. Although the clouds that hovered over the Koolau range behind the city hadn't yet lost their morning tinge of rose, already the trade winds pushing against her face were awash with car exhaust, the odors of hot metal and burning rubber.

She looked at the tall buildings surrounding her, taking in the hustle and bustle of the busy street; and the strains of an old song slipped into her mind—". . . *a perfume of a million flowers, clinging to the heart of Old Hawaii . . .*"—and she felt a sharp prick of nostalgia for what had been, what had disappeared.

She put up her hand to stifle a yawn. She had slept poorly the night before, and she felt sluggish and dull. For the first time in months she had dreamed about her aunt, and the tatters of the nightmare still clung to her. All night, whenever she'd dozed off, her aunt had pursued her in her dreams, while in the background the neighborhood children had chanted the hateful words that had haunted her long after she'd run away from Boston.

She pushed the memory away and looked up at the name—THE STEVENSON BUILDING—above the entrance of the building behind her. Although she knew that her father had been comfortably off, she was surprised by the size of the building that housed the Stevenson interests. With the cost of land and construction in the Islands, it must have been enormously expensive to build. Had the family fortune increased during the past ten years, or was her memory wrong? A child had little interest in such things; and yet, wouldn't she have known if her father had been really rich? She made a note to find out the answer, then put it out of her mind as a car zoomed out of the garage under the building and stopped at the curb beside her.

The car was a small foreign one, as understated and expensive as the building it had erupted from. To her relief she saw that Wade MacMasters was alone. Although she knew she'd have to face her aunt eventually, at least she'd been given a reprieve.

Wade got out to load her suitcase and makeup case into the back of the car. In the morning light he looked different—or maybe it was the sports coat and open-necked shirt he was wearing that made him seem more approachable. She met his eyes. In the full daylight, the contrast between his grey eyes and his dark hair was so startling that she had to resist an impulse to blink.

He took her arm to help her into the low-slung car, and she was nonplussed by her response as his hand cupped her elbow. "Cool Lani," Kore had called her once; what would he think now if he knew how her pulse leaped at the touch of a man she'd met only twice?

At first, as Wade steered the small car through the downtown traffic, their conversation was mainly one-sided as he explained that the Stevensons' cabin cruiser, the *Kauhelani*, was docked near Kahaluu, a few miles north of Kaneohe. Once, when they stopped for a traffic light, she felt his eyes on her, and she had a sudden feeling of disquiet. Was he having second thoughts about taking an outsider to live on Maunaloa Island?

"Your references checked out okay," he said, breaking a short silence. "I talked to Dr. Fredericks on the phone, and he told me you were one of the most competent and versatile members of his staff. He was pretty unhappy that you were staying in the Islands."

"Dr. Fredericks is a wonderful man to work with," she said warmly. "He's been a good friend to me."

"Just friends? Somehow I got the impression it was something more than that."

His unjustified assumption stung, and she retorted, "Dr. Fredericks is seventy years old. He's old enough to be my grandfather—and that's exactly how he treated me and *all* the members of his staff."

She was sorry as soon as the words cleared her mouth, but Wade's face relaxed into a smile. "Sorry. That was stupid of me, wasn't it?"

Since it would have been imprudent to agree, she was glad when he pointed out a Buddhist temple they were passing. For the rest of the forty-minute drive the conversation was pleasant but impersonal.

The tension she'd been fighting for the past two days began to build again as they pulled into a fenced-off parking lot at the base of a long wharf at Kahaluu. Wade let her off with her luggage. While he went to park the car, she studied the cabin cruiser rocking gently in the swells at the end of the wharf.

The boat was new, or at least it wasn't the ungainly one she remembered. She smiled to herself as she read the name painted on its side. *Kauhelani* meant floating island, but the sleek, modern lines of the boat bore no resemblance to any island she'd ever seen.

A stocky brown-skinned man was loading supplies into the boat. He was a tall man with a thick neck that rose from wide, thick shoulders. His lips were full, and his rugged features could have served as the model for the faces she'd seen carved into tree-fern trunks. He paused to wipe the sweat from his broad forehead, and her pulses jumped as she recognized David Kealoha, Kawena's grandson.

She felt a rolling wave of panic as he padded down the wharf toward her. Although he was nine years older, they had been good friends as children. Would he recognize her now as easily as she had recognized him?

Then Wade, who had joined her, was introducing David Kealoha, and she realized there was nothing except curiosity in David's ingenuous eyes.

"Aloha, Yula," he said, his broad white teeth flashing in a smile.

He returned to his task, and Wade motioned for Lani to board the boat. Still a little numb from her first encounter with one of the people she'd known as a child, Lani picked up her makeup case and moved toward the gangplank. She was glad when Wade stopped to talk to David, since it gave her time to get herself under control. She glanced through the open door of the boat's cabin, and when she saw a shadowy figure sitting inside, she skirted the cabin and went to stand in the prow, out of sight of the wharf.

She leaned against the metal railing, wondering why, all of a sudden, she was filled with doubts about the course she had decided upon. Was it because of her nightmares the night before? Or had Kore infected her with his concern over her safety?

Unexpectedly she felt a yearning to see Kore, to talk with him face-to-face. For so long he had been her bulwark, her protector. Talking with him on the phone had made her realize just how alone she had been since Pearsa's death. How would it be, having him back in her life? Would she have to be on guard against the old attraction he'd always had for her? Surely, after all this time, that was all over. So why did she have this strong urge to get off the boat and go back to San Francisco to wait for him?

The deck beneath Lani swayed, and she saw that while she had been lost in thought, the *Kauhelani* had left the wharf and was heading out into Kaneohe Bay. The water was rough, spiked with white crests, and the wind stung her lips and whipped her hair out from under her scarf. To the left, the coast curved in a giant arch, like a finger pointing directly at Maunaloa Island, which lay separated from Oahu by some twenty miles of open ocean.

"Are you trying to get a look at Maunaloa?" The voice was male; it held a subtle amusement. "It's well outside the bay; you can't see it from here."

She turned and looked into the eyes of the russet-haired man who'd been so attentive to her aunt and Vivian in the hotel courtyard two nights earlier. At close range he looked a little older than he had in the flickering light of the luau torches. She was thinking that he must be Wade's age, in his early thirties, when she found herself smiling at him, not really sure why—unless it was because his own smile was so infectious.

"How large is the island?" she asked.

"About twelve square miles, some of them straight up and down." He braced his lean body against the swell of the waves as he surveyed her with frank interest. He was rangy rather than solidly built like Wade MacMasters, and there were tiny golden freckles on his forearms and across his forehead. Although he had a redhead's fair skin, he was deeply tanned, as if he spent a lot of time in the sun.

"I'm Jason Richards, and of course you're Yula Brock, Wade's latest typist."

"Latest typist? Have there been many?"

"A whole covey. The island's too isolated for most outsiders, but maybe in your case we can all make a special effort to persuade you to stay for a while."

There was a glint in his eyes as if he were laughing at some private joke, and Lani stiffened, instantly on guard. "How long have you lived on Maunaloa?" she asked.

"Lord, I don't *live* there. As beautiful as it is, it would drive me up a wall, being isolated anywhere for more than a few weeks. I'm a people-watcher. Why should I settle for a few when I can be entertained by a few million? I live in New York when I'm not off on an assignment."

"Are you a writer?"

"A journalist-photographer. Right now I'm doing a book on the history of the Islands. I always try to get extra mileage from my research, so I've also taken on several magazine assignments, including a spread for *National*

Geographic and another on the ethnic makeup of Oahu for *Society*, the sociology magazine."

"Are you including Maunaloa Island in your book?"

"Of course. I'm probably the only writer in the country who has access to Maunaloa. Wade isn't too happy about the prospect of publicity. I had to promise not to exploit the Maunaloa curse angle, of course. Too bad—it would add dimension and a touch of the macabre to the *National Geographic* piece."

"The island has a curse? What kind of curse?"

"Well, things—some very unpleasant things—have happened to outsiders on Maunaloa." At her involuntary flinch, his wide, mobile mouth stretched into a smile. "Oh, you'll be safe. It's the men and women intrepid enough to marry a Stevenson who seem to come a cropper."

A chill settled inside Lani; for a moment she saw her mother's face, grey and waxen in death, the blood on her throat as scarlet as the lehua lei that Lani had made for her that morning. . . .

"Surely that's just superstition," she said.

"Well, Wade will tell you that the violent deaths of so many Stevenson brides and grooms are pure coincidence." He slanted his eyes at her; they were very unusual eyes, she noted, the same amber color as the stones the Hawaiians call Pele's Tears, and like the stones they were translucent, with tiny specks of brown. "Now, I have a theory that the island was cursed a long time before the first Stevenson enraged the local *kahuna*—that's a sort of witch doctor—by building a gazebo on the site of one of the sacred *heiaus*."

"Heiaus?"

"An altar—a temple."

"And you have a theory about the island?"

"I do indeed. It's my theory that there are evil places in this world, as well as people who are inherently ill-fated. In the California gold country, there's a house that stays cold even on the hottest summer day. A whole succession of suicides have taken place there and at least four murders, yet it looks like a perfectly ordinary house. Certain bridges and high buildings, no different from others in the same locale, seem to draw the morbidly inclined. It's quite possible that people with a penchant for violence are drawn to Maunaloa Island—and to the Stevensons."

Lani spoke around a cold lump in her throat. "What exactly is the curse?"

"Well, the old *kahuna* must have figured it would be more effective to wipe out the spouses, presumably beloved, than to have the curse fall directly upon the Stevensons themselves, so he put the curse on anyone who married into the family." He shook his head, his eyes glinting. "The local Hawaiians still believe in the curse. It's too bad my cousin doesn't."

"Your cousin?"

"Wade. We're first cousins."

"Then Maile must be your niece, too."

"She calls me Uncle Jason, but actually we're cousins once removed."

Lani digested this information for a moment. "Why would you care if your cousin believes in the curse?" she asked finally.

"Because it might keep him from getting too cozy with Iolani Stevenson." The amusement was back in his voice. "Wade is much too pragmatic to believe in curses. Or maybe he doesn't dare believe, since—"

"I'm sure Miss Brock isn't interested in my failings, Jason," Wade's cool voice said behind them.

Jason turned to look at his cousin, his smile unabashed. "Oh, you're wrong about that. I can't remember when I've had a more receptive audience."

"Well, you'll have to postpone the rest of it. I have some business to discuss with Miss Brock."

"Which is my cue to cut out, I suppose. Okay, I'll go say my alohas to Kawena and give you a few minutes of privacy."

He winked at Lani and ambled off. She felt dizzy, off-balance, as she watched his tall, lean body swing easily along the narrow deck beside the superstructure and disappear inside the cabin. Kawena, here on the boat? Had that shadowy figure she'd seen sitting inside the cabin been Kawena? Surely Kawena hadn't recognized her or she would have called out.

She jumped nervously when Wade spoke. "I hope Jason hasn't been filling your head with a lot of wild tales about the Maunaloa curse," he said. "Every old family has its share of tragedy. The Stevensons are no exception."

"It isn't really any of my business," she said, a little formally. She wondered why it had been so easy to talk with Jason, even though she suspected he'd been laughing at her half the time, and so difficult to talk naturally with Wade MacMasters. Was it because she was so aware of his physical presence, his maleness? If so, she had better take herself in hand. It wouldn't do to forget, not even for a moment, her real purpose for coming to Maunaloa. "And I wasn't pumping Mr. Richards about your private affairs," she went on. "I'm not a gossip, Mr. MacMasters."

Unexpectedly, Wade's eyes lost their chill. "No—no, I'm sure you aren't that, Yula," he said. He leaned against the railing, smiling at her. "Since Jason has brought up the curse, maybe I should give you a brief rundown—and then warn you not to discuss the curse with my young niece. Maile's far too interested in the supernatural as it is."

"I'll be careful," she promised, and earned another of the smiles she found so attractive.

Lani didn't have to pretend her interest as Wade told her how Aaron Stevenson, an Australian sea captain, had been shipwrecked on the shoals off Maunaloa Island in 1851. He had gone inland to find wood to repair his ship and instead had discovered a treasure grove of sandalwood. Part of what Wade was saying she already knew, but this was the first time she'd heard that her ancestor had sold his ship's ballast of iron to the metal-hungry Hawaiians for the money to buy Maunaloa Island from the royal estate.

"Captain Stevenson banished most of the natives from Maunaloa, but he was shrewd enough to placate the local *kahuna* by allowing him and his family to stay on the island.

Then, after he'd married the daughter of one of the missionary families, he let her coax him into ripping up the stones of the island's chief *heiau* so she could build a Folly on the site—"

Lani flinched again, and he paused to give her a questioning look.

"A Folly?" she managed.

"That's a name the Victorians sometimes used for their retreats. It's still known as Abigail's Folly—which, as it turned out, is a damned appropriate name."

"Couldn't they have built it somewhere else?"

"Of course, but Captain Stevenson was a very obstinate man. To demonstrate his contempt for the *kahuna*'s threats, he had his sailors carry the *heiau* stones up the bluff behind the site with the intention of tossing them into a natural sinkhole at the top. They were almost to the top when a sudden storm came up, and three of the men lost their footing and were killed. The other sailors abandoned the stones on a ledge halfway up the cliff. You can still see them there, although the ledge is overgrown with vegetation now."

And the curse won't be lifted until the sacred stones again rest beside Lono's Spring, Lani thought, remembering how she'd always shivered with a delicious fear when Kawena had reached this part of the old legend.

"I wonder why Captain Stevenson didn't give in after three men had died and have the stones returned," she mused aloud.

"As I said, he was a very stubborn man—and also a strict Calvinist. He believed that the best way to fight superstition was to defy it." Wade hesitated briefly before he went on. "All the Stevensons are stubborn, as you'll find out when you meet my niece. I'm counting on you to see that she continues her therapeutic exercises."

"I'll do my best, but I'm not a child psychologist."

"Your former employer told me you have a knack for establishing a rapport with youngsters." His eyes, which she already had discovered could be so remote, were warm now, and she felt a pang of disappointment when Jason strolled up and hooked his elbows over the railing.

Lani couldn't help comparing the two men as they talked together. Despite his casual clothes, Wade had the mark of success about him, while Jason—just how much of that indolent air of his was a pose? If he could get assignments from top magazines, he must work hard at his profession. What was he really like behind that lazy smile?

David Kealoha called Wade from the helm house, and he went off, leaving her alone with Jason again. Beside her at the railing, Jason was silent. His expression sober, he was staring straight ahead. Automatically she followed the direction of his stare, and her breath left her in a long sigh.

Ahead, little more than a speck on the horizon, lay a small island. In the late-morning light the island seemed to float above a silvery haze, and she knew that saddle-shaped outline so well, knew that in the heat of a summer day its twin mountain ranges could look as grey and insubstantial as smoke; that later on, silhouetted against the setting sun, their razor-sharp edges could take on a metallic glow, as if dusted with powdered copper.

I'm home, she thought. *For better or worse, I'm finally coming home to Maunaloa. . . .*

She clutched the damp railing with numb, bloodless fingers. Too many memories had been thrust upon her in too short a time, and her nerves seemed overloaded, out of control. Since it would have been impossible for her to carry on a normal conversation, she was grateful that Jason, standing beside her at the railing, was still silent.

Not daring to look at him, she stared at the island ahead, at the sheer cliffs with their sharp ridges, softened only by a thin green veil of vegetation and a crown of scrub ohia trees. The color of the water changed from deep, dancing blue to aquamarine as the boat edged closer to shore. Although they were approaching the island from the southwest, she knew that the cliffs extended around most of the north side of the island, exposing their rocky shanks to the prevailing winds and the full assault of the storm tides.

Although the island seemed as timeless as the sea that

surrounded it, she was aware that there must have been changes in the thirteen years she'd been away. Would this make it easier for her, or more difficult? And if she was so affected just by looking at the island, how could she possibly get through the next few hours and not give herself away?

Beside her, Jason turned his head to smile at her, and the sun fell directly across his face. He had a clown's smile, wide and humorous and crescent-shaped. His eyes were very clear, and she had a sudden feeling that if she stared into their amber depths long enough she would see the real Jason Richards hidden inside. Would she find a friend, someone she could trust? Or someone who posed a threat to her?

"It's easy to see why the local real estate developers would sell their souls for a chance to buy Maunaloa Island, isn't it?" he said. "It has all the advantages of being completely isolated, and yet it's only a few minutes by helicopter from Honolulu airport and an hour's boat ride from Kaneohe. More importantly, it has its own artesian wells, and fresh water is very rare for an island this small."

"Surely the Stevensons aren't interested in selling," Lani said. "The island's been in their family for generations, hasn't it?"

"They can't sell, not for several years. The estate's tied up until Maile comes of age. After that—who knows? The latest offer, from a hotel chain, was in the millions, I understand."

Lani felt chilled. *Millions*, he had said—and yet it was out of her aunt's reach until Maile came of age. But what if her aunt and her co-conspirators weren't content to wait for those millions? And what if they wanted it all, not just half? If Maile had died when she'd eaten those akia berries, or if she'd been killed when she'd fallen from the balcony, would the whole estate have gone to Vivian? To a girl who had no reason to feel sentimental about an island—or about a child who wasn't really her sister?

"Are you cold?" Jason asked, and she realized she was shivering.

"No—no, I'm fine," she said. "It's the excitement of going

to a new place, starting a new job. This is all so different from what I've been used to."

"And what exactly have you been used to, Yula? Where do you come from? Why did you come to Hawaii?"

"I came here on vacation—from San Francisco. When Mr. MacMasters offered me a job, I decided it might be fun, something different, to live on an island, so I accepted."

"Well, it certainly will be different," he said. "Whether or not it will be fun, time will tell."

Lani frowned at him. Was there a warning in his voice? "Is Mr. MacMasters difficult to work for?"

"Not in the way you probably mean. But he could be very hazardous for a susceptible girl. Are you a susceptible girl, Yula?"

Lani felt a prick of anger. "Not in the least," she said coolly.

"Good. Then there's no danger that you'll get hurt, is there?" He gave her a lazy smile. "On the other hand, while Wade might not be available, keep in mind that I have no attachments."

"Not available? Do you mean he's married?"

"Not any longer, he isn't. But he's been very badly burned. His wife put him through hell before she took their youngster and ran off with a tennis bum."

"He has a child?"

"He *had* a son," Jason corrected, his face suddenly sober. "The courts gave Wade custody, so Gloria waited until he went on a business trip and then took off with the boy. Both of them were killed when the car she was driving went off the highway near Koko Head. Gloria always did drive like a maniac."

Lani had a sudden image of a speeding car, a small boy, the screeching of brakes. . . . She shuddered, and the man gave her a thoughtful look. "So that's why Wade is so wary of women these days," he added.

"He seemed very interested in Miss Stevenson at the charity ball," Lani said without thinking.

"So you *were* there! I was sure it was you. You were standing in front of a palm, looking very cool and collected—and as if you had butterflies in your stomach."

His description was just a shade too accurate. "Imagine your noticing me," she murmured.

"Purely professional. I was thinking I'd like to photograph you."

Lani was sure this was another of his jokes—or maybe part of his line with women. She decided not to play his little game and was silent.

"There—you don't believe me." Jason's voice was rueful. "It's one of my crosses that no one ever believes a word I say. The truth is, I'm much too lazy to lie."

"Then maybe you should change the way you say things," she retorted, amused in spite of herself. "Aren't you ever serious?"

"Often, but I try not to overdo it. Most of the world's troubles are caused by sober, well-meaning, self-righteous people. As it happens, I am very serious about wanting to photograph you. I need a warm body to liven up the scenery shots I'll be taking the next few weeks."

"Surely a professional model would be more appropriate. Or maybe Miss Stevenson—she looks like a model."

"Yes, she does. But she's also camera shy, a trait that rather surprises me. When she wasn't looking, I took a few candid shots anyway. Unfortunately, they have a plastic quality that—well, it happens sometimes. It isn't true, you see, that the camera never lies."

"Well, I probably wouldn't be very photogenic either," she said.

Jason surveyed her, his eyes probing. "You're wrong about that. That tawny skin and those green eyes of yours are extraordinary; and with that kind of bone structure, you're going to be a very beautiful old lady someday. It's my guess you'll come across on film as a warm, earthy woman."

His too-thorough scrutiny, the personal turn of the conversation, made her uncomfortable. To change the subject, she asked the first question that came into her mind. "What did you mean when you said Mr. MacMasters didn't dare believe in the curse?"

"Because the last Stevenson spouse to meet an early

death was Wade's own sister. I think that's one reason why he gets a little paranoid when anyone mentions the curse. After all, he was all in favor of that marriage."

"Was it because he wanted to become manager of the Stevenson business interests?"

"Oh, Wade was already in charge when John married his sister. He was doing a damned good job, too. Thanks mainly to his efforts, Iolani and Maile are two of the wealthiest females in the Islands. Iolani would probably be smart to marry the guy and keep him in the family."

Lani tried to read the expression in his eyes. "And yet— you wouldn't really like to see that happen?" she asked.

"Maybe I have my own plans for the young heiress," he said.

Although he was smiling again, she felt oddly disconcerted. Was he joking? Or did he really have a yen for the impostor? She gave herself a mental shake. Why should she care if either of them was in love with Vivian? She had returned to Maunaloa for one purpose only. It would be stupid to allow herself to be drawn into the personal life of anyone she met during her stay here.

"Miss Stevenson is very attractive," she said aloud.

"Indeed she is. Who would have thought she'd turn out the way she did? She was such a funny little thing as a kid, all eyes and legs."

"You knew Miss Stevenson when she was a child? But I didn't—" She stopped just in time.

"You didn't think I was that old? Oh, I was just a kid myself, only eighteen, but I was in and out of the Stevenson house a lot that last year. I had an enormous crush on Carol Stevenson. I guess it amused her to have a lap dog in attendance."

Lani stared at him fixedly. There had been so many young men around her mother . . . didn't she remember a tall, thin one with rusty hair who had called her "Princess" and who had spent hours playing Monopoly with her in the hau arbor? She probed her memory, but the name of the red-haired young man was gone. Had it been Jason?

"Carol was bored with the Islands," Jason was going on.

"John was gone a lot on business. I guess their marriage was a stormy one. I suspect that's why Carol always had a houseful of people staying here."

A stormy marriage? Lani tried to reconcile his words with what she remembered. Had she been living in her own private world, too young to sense the trouble between her parents? And how much of her feeling of security during those years had been due to Kawena and her family, who had enveloped her with their own special warmth, treated her as one of their own?

Unexpectedly a deep yearning for Kawena swept over her. She wanted desperately to dash into the cabin and throw herself down beside her old nurse, to have her worries, her fears rocked away again in Kawena's thin, wiry arms. . . .

"The woman Wade is talking with is Kawena Kealoha," Jason said, and Lani realized she had turned and was staring into the dark cabin.

"Kealoha." Her voice sounded thin and breathy. "Is she related to David Kealoha?"

"His grandmother. She's the matriarch of the family and as much a fixture on the island as Maunaloa House—but not for long, if Iolani's aunt has her way. She'd like to turn the whole Kealoha family off the island."

"Why does she dislike them?" Lani asked, although she already knew the answer.

"Because Berta St. John is a dyed-in-the-wool bigot," he said. "She's also up in arms because Kawena has been on a Hawaiian Power kick lately. Right now the movement is trying to get the Navy to stop using Kahoolawe Island for a bombing range, but their next target could be Maunaloa. It would be a natural choice, since there's plenty of documented proof that the island was sacred to the old Hawaiians."

"Do you think there's a chance the Kealohas could be forced to leave Maunaloa?" Lani asked.

"I wouldn't underestimate Kawena if I were Berta St. John. She might discover she has a shark by the tail."

"What does that mean?"

"It means Kawena is a very shrewd old woman. She's also a prime mover of the Kaahumanu Society, and those old Hawaiian ladies have a big clout in the Islands. Any attempt to oust the Kealohas would cause the Stevensons a lot of ill will. And it isn't as if the Kealohas aren't useful to the Stevensons."

He gestured toward David Kealoha in the wheel house. "David does most of the gardening at Maunaloa House, maintains the power plant, brings in supplies—he's something of a master-of-all-trades. His mother, Moana, is the housekeeper, and his wife, Lehua, helps with the cooking and the housework. The others have drifted away; Kawena's twin grandsons live in Honolulu. One is a doctor and the other a lawyer who's already involved in Island politics."

It was all Lani could do not to laugh. She thought about the twins, dark-haired, stocky boys ten years her senior who had teased her, tolerated her, let her tag along after them. Which one had become the lawyer and which the doctor? It had been their mother, Moana, who had taught her to play the ukulele, patiently positioning her clumsy fingers for the chords. Would Moana turn out to be a danger to her now? David hadn't recognized her, but then women were so much more perceptive about people than men were.

"Kawena was John Stevenson's nurse, then Iolani's," Jason went on. "If she hadn't lost her eyesight, she would have been Maile's nurse, too, I suspect." He stopped, his eyes sharpening. "Are you okay? You look pale—"

"I'm just—just excited, I think." She swallowed hard, forced a smile. "You were talking about Kawena. I didn't realize she was blind."

"It's one of those progressive things. Being Kawena, she hasn't allowed it to slow her down."

"If she was Miss Stevenson's nurse, she must have been very happy when the girl was found."

"I'm sure she was. Unfortunately, Iolani doesn't remember Kawena or much else about her childhood. Her psychiatrist says her memory may never come back fully."

Lani felt a reluctant admiration for the impostor. Any

slip, any blunder Vivian might make could be explained away to loss of memory. It was all so Machiavellian—too subtle, in fact, for her aunt. Had Vivian come up with this cleverly worked out plan, or was it the man they both seemed to fear? And just who was their accomplice? Was it possible it could be Jason—or Wade MacMasters?

She had almost forgotten the man at her side, and she recoiled instinctively when Jason touched her arm. His amber-colored eyes regarded her curiously as she stammered something about woolgathering.

"We're almost there," he said, pointing.

Lani turned, and her breath caught sharply. While they had been talking, the boat had rounded the southernmost tip of the island, and they were edging into the small cove where Maunaloa Island's one wharf was located.

It was just as she remembered it. The wharf, weatherbeaten and sturdy, still jutted out into the cove, large enough for several boats to dock there simultaneously. To its left, like a great unset emerald, the lagoon lay, surrounded by a heavy growth of coconut palms. And behind, brooding over it all, were the bluffs, a crumbling, cindery bulwark that protected the inhabited side of the island from the constant trade winds.

Lani braced herself against the railing, looking for signs of change. She had learned to swim in the green waters of the lagoon, had lazed for hours, playing with her dolls, on a raft that Amoka, David Kealoha's father, had built for her. The raft was gone now, but tall, slender coconut palms still defied gravity to lean far out across the lagoon, their fringed tops dipping toward the water, and a new generation of ferns crowded up against the coral wall that protected the sides of the lagoon from erosion.

There was a scraping sound as the boat nudged the wharf, and Jason left her to help Wade and David with the lines. Unable to resist the opportunity to see what the years had done to her old nurse, Lani watched as David, his big hand cupped protectively around his grandmother's elbow, led her down the gangplank.

Some things, she discovered, hadn't changed. How many times had she seen Kawena dressed as she was now in a long black fitted muumuu, a lei of orange feathers around her neck and a small-crowned hat riding her coiled hair? And yet—had Kawena always been this small and fragile-looking? The last time she'd seen her, her hair had been black as a mynah bird's wing; now it was streaked with white. And if Kawena, who had once seemed so regal and tall, had diminished to this tiny, birdlike woman, would Maunaloa Island seem cramped and small to her adult eyes?

On the wharf Kawena paused. As if she sensed Lani watching her, she lifted her face toward the spot where Lani was standing. For a long moment Lani felt the impact of those blind eyes. It wasn't until Kawena moved on that she realized she had been holding her breath.

Lani waited until Kawena, walking arm in arm with Wade, was gone before she joined Jason, who was waiting for her on the wharf. As they walked along the seawall toward the house, Jason pointed out the bathhouse, a long, low rustic building that blended well with its setting. Lani was glad that he didn't seem to expect an answer as he rambled on, obviously enjoying the role of guide.

Soon after they left the lagoon area, the seawall curved outward to skirt a large grove of trees. The trees were old, a spectacular mixture that her grandfather, who had been an amateur botanist, had brought in from all over the world. At any other time she would have welcomed the chance to see how the trees, all old friends, had survived the years. But today her nerves were too raw and hurting, so she stared straight ahead at the brown tile roofs of Maunaloa House as they came into view, looming above the giant umbrella-shaped monkeypod trees that surrounded the old house. Then Jason drew her attention to a heron, fighting the wind currents overhead, and incautiously she turned her head to watch it. She followed its flight as it dropped below the tops of the bluffs—and the blood rushed from her head.

Thirteen years earlier, the Folly had been hidden from view by a grove of rainbow shower trees; now all that remained of the trees that flanked its left side was a giant heap of rubble. A raw slash in the bluffs behind the pile of rock and earth showed what must have happened.

For a long moment she had one starkly clear look at the red pagoda-shaped roof of Abigail's Folly, and then all the horror of the day when her mother had died was back, multiplied by the black despair of the years between. She felt her knees buckle, felt herself falling—and then felt nothing at all.

Jason must have caught her, because the next thing she was aware of was his voice calling her name, and the pressure of arms under her knees and behind her shoulders.

She opened her eyes and fixed them on his face, using the concern she saw there as an anchor to pull her back to reality. He held her easily, obviously without strain; and despite her giddiness—and embarrassment—she realized that his lean body was surprisingly strong.

"What happened, Yula?" he asked.

"I—I forgot to eat breakfast this morning," she said, saying the first thing that came into her mind.

"Well, that's easily mended. We'll get Moana to fix you something when we get to the house." His face made one of its lightning transformations from plain to near-handsome as he grinned down at her. "There I was, playing the Good Samaritan, trying to divert your attention from what I thought was *mal de mer* with my sparkling travelogue, when all the time it wasn't seasickness at all but just plain hunger. I should have offered you a candy bar instead."

Lani smiled back at him. "Your history lesson was diverting—and very interesting," she said.

"Well, I appreciate those kind words—"

"And *I'd* appreciate it if you'd play your little games with someone else, Jason," Wade's cold voice said behind them. Over Jason's shoulder, Lani caught the distaste in Wade's grey eyes, and she felt heat flooding her face. "As for you, Miss Brock, entertaining my cousin is not part of your duties."

Jason let her slip to her feet, but he kept a protective arm around her shoulders. Under his tan his face was flushed too, but there was anger, not embarrassment, in his eyes as he turned to face his cousin.

"Yula passed out," he said shortly. "I caught her as she fell."

"I see. Well, she seems to make a habit of passing out when there's a man around to catch her," Wade said.

The unfairness of his remark infuriated Lani, but before the angry words that rose to her lips could escape, Jason's arm tightened warningly around her shoulders. "You'll have to take my word that she passed out cold, Wade. If I hadn't caught her, she'd be lying at the bottom of the sea-wall right now."

Wade stared at his cousin for a long moment, his lips set in a hard, tight line. Lani had discovered earlier that his eyes could be warm and solicitous, but there was no warmth in them now as he nodded stiffly, turned on his heel and stalked away, and she knew that he still had reservations about the incident, that even before she had started her new job she had already managed to alienate her employer.

VII

As they resumed their walk along the seawall, it was obvious that Jason was taking no chances. He kept his hand resting lightly on her arm and was careful to stay on the beach side, where the seawall rose six or more feet above the sand. Listening to his lively conversation, Lani made a discovery about herself: for a person who had just fainted dead away from shock, she was feeling surprisingly normal.

She glanced up at the tall man at her side. How much of her quick recovery stemmed from the feeling that she had just made a new friend? Although she knew it was foolish, maybe even dangerous, to trust anyone she met on Maunaloa, especially a man who might be her aunt's accomplice, she couldn't forget that Jason had sensed her distress on the boat and had been thoughtful enough to try to divert her from what he'd thought was an attack of seasickness. Nor could she forget how he had defended her when Wade MacMasters assumed the worst about her.

So she let her guard drop a little and found she was enjoying herself as he started another anecdote about her grandfather. She wondered what he would say if she told him she was well aware of her grandfather's eccentricities, that the trees he was pointing out were old friends. Better than he, she knew that when the jacarandas were in full bloom, their apple blossom–like flowers seemed to turn the air around them blue; that when the pods of the false wiliwili opened, the ground beneath the trees would be covered with a carpet of tiny red seeds.

She was wondering if Maile ever gathered the seeds to make necklaces for her dolls when Jason's hand tightened on her arm, and she realized they had reached the stone steps that led from the seawall to the wide concourse in front of Maunaloa House.

The concourse was another of her grandfather's conceits, since it was purely ornamental. The coconut trees that lined it on both sides were very old, and because they were protected from the winds by the bulk of the old house, each stood tall and proud and very straight. A circle of shining metal encircled the thick base of each tree, protection against the crabs that came up from the beach to feed upon the tender immature coconuts.

Since a falling coconut, when mature, can crack the skull of a grown man, it had been one of the duties of the Kealoha men to remove the pods before the coconuts inside had a chance to become a hazard. On the days the trees were trimmed Lani had followed the men from tree to tree, pouncing upon the biggest of the brown pods to use as boats in the lagoon, gorging herself on the custard-like flesh of the immature coconuts that the men obligingly slashed open for her with their bolo knives.

The Hawaiians on the island had been patient with her. Amoka, David's father, who called her his calabash daughter, had taught her the thirty words that describe the coconut in all its phases of ripeness. Even now, she remembered them better than she did her multiplication tables.

They started up the center of the concourse, walking slowly, and as Lani stared at the house where she had been born, something deep inside her winced for a moment, almost as if a cold finger had moved along the base of her neck.

It was a large two-storied structure, and because it had been built by Aaron Stevenson for his New England wife, it was an odd blend of New England formality and practical plantation-house comfort. Like many Island homes of its era, its walls were coral block more than two feet thick; its windows were jalousied, and wide verandas protected the rooms inside from the tropical sun. Two wings jutted out, one on each side of the main house, adding an air of informality to the original square house. The older, called the *makai* wing because it faced the ocean, had been added during the '70s, while the *mauka* wing, which faced the bluffs, was comparatively new, having been added by her great-grandfather at the turn of the century.

Although they were hidden from the concourse, Lani knew that sprawling gardens lay behind the house. Placed at random among the grove of monkeypod trees beyond the gardens were small auxiliary buildings—guest cottages, a laundry-and-pump house, the building that contained the power plant, oil storage tanks, and the greenhouses that had been her grandfather's pride and joy.

"The old house is quite a museum piece," Jason said, breaking his silence. He took out a pipe, tamped tobacco into it, lit it behind a cupped hand. "And maybe that's what it will be someday—a maritime museum, with Maunaloa Island a state park."

Lani gave him a startled look. "Is that your own idea?"

"Not exactly. There's been some talk about it. Before John Stevenson was killed, he once told me he was thinking about changing his will so the island and house would be turned over to the state eventually. But he obviously didn't have time to set it up before he died."

He paused to watch a pair of quarreling mynah birds as they ruffled their glossy neck feathers and stalked in circles around each other. "You'll probably be assigned to one of the guest cottages," he went on, his eyes on the birds. "I have the one in the middle. I hope my typewriter doesn't bother you. Sometimes I'm still pecking away until late into the night. If you ever get lonely, I'm always available."

Lani was aware of a feeling of disappointment. So far, Jason had been the model of the perfect gentleman; was she going to have *that* kind of trouble from him?

81

Jason gave her a sidelong look, and she knew that again he had read her thoughts. From the glint in his amber eyes he was highly amused by her reaction.

As they started up the broad steps of the front veranda, Wade came out of the house and stood waiting for them. His voice cool, he told Lani, "The housekeeper will show you to your room. I've asked her to put you near my niece. I also talked to Maile, and she knows you'll be supervising her physical therapy from now on. I told her I expect her cooperation, or I'd take away a few of her privileges."

"Oh, I wish you hadn't done that!" Lani said impulsively. His thick eyebrows came together in a frown, and she added, "It might be better if Maile didn't think of therapy in terms of punishment."

Wade gave her an impatient look. "There's already been too much indulgence of that child's whims. John pampered her, and my sister—well, she was so young when Maile was born that she treated her more like a doll than a child. Maile's been badly spoiled. Even her aunt, who is a very strong-minded woman, can't seem to control her—"

A dark-haired woman dressed in a gaily flowered muumuu came out onto the veranda, interrupting him. Lani's heart gave a convulsive leap as she recognized Moana, Kawena's daughter. She was taller than her mother, but she had Kawena's perfect carriage, and her thick lustrous hair was still black, although Lani knew she must be in her late forties. Although she wasn't pretty, she had the self-possession that is usually associated with beauty as she smiled at Jason and eyed Lani with frank curiosity.

Wade made introductions, then glanced down at his watch and went back into the house. Lani, seized with a sudden reluctance to be left alone with Moana, hoped Jason would stay and act as a buffer, but he excused himself, saying something about having a date with a hot typewriter. He drew Moana aside and spoke to her briefly before ambling off, his hands in his pockets, whistling an off-key version of a Hawaiian chant.

"Bettah come along with me, Yula," Moana said. Although she spoke with the easy informality of the Islands, her voice lacked David's warmth. She led the way into the house; Lani followed silently, mentally braced for a fresh assault of memories. The entrance hall, as spacious as a full-sized room, looked just as it had the day she'd left. The same chinoiserie desk, made by New England cabinetmakers and shipped around the Horn to Hong Kong to be decorated with scenes of Old China, still stood in its place of honor at the base of the graceful staircase. The big double doors that led to the living room were closed, but through another door to her left Lani caught a glimpse of the graceful Sheraton dining room furniture that had been part of the first Abigail's dowry.

A familiar odor, a combination of pine disinfectant and lemon oil, made her nostrils flare. It was the same odor she associated with her aunt's house in Boston, and she knew that Aunt Berta had already put her own indelible mark on the house. Had she been given carte blanche to run the house as she chose? And if so, did Moana resent this intrusion into the domestic arrangements of Maunaloa House?

Lani resisted the temptation to question Moana about her aunt as she followed in the Hawaiian woman's wake, up the long curve of the stairs, down a dark hall. When they passed the room that had been her mother's, she averted her eyes, glad that its door was closed. What had her father done with her mother's personal possessions—the antique perfume bottles, the silk screens and cloisonné vases and the ivory-and-jade collection? Did someone else—Aunt Berta or Vivian, perhaps—have the room now? And did the odor of crushed jasmine, her mother's signature perfume, still linger in the closets where she'd stored her clothes, in the bed where she'd slept?

They turned a corner and passed into the *mauka* wing. Halfway down the long corridor that ran through the center of the structure, Moana stopped in front of a closed door.

"Here we are. Mr. Wade tell me to put you close to Maile. A couple days ago she took it in her head to move out of the *makai* wing and into room Iolani used to have. This is third time that child's moved in the past couple of months."

She hesitated, and Lani waited, sensing that the

Hawaiian woman had something else she wanted to say. "About Maile—I expect she'll give you plenty trouble about those exercises the doctor ordered."

"Is she hard to handle, Moana?"

"*Auwe!* That girl is *huikau*—all mix up. Used to be, we got along fine. Now she's got her nose in the air, won't talk to me, won't listen when I try to talk to her."

"Isn't there anyone she does listen to? What about her sister, or her aunt?"

Moana sniffed. "Iolani's got too much other stuff on her mind. As for her aunt—if you ask me, Maile already listens too much to *her*. That woman is numbah one troublemaker. Alla time poke her long nose where it don't belong. She tells Lehua and me how to cook and clean house, tells David how to run boat. Someday I'm going to tell that woman what she can do with her schedules and her *haole* food."

Lani, remembering her own woes with her aunt's rigid schedules, gave her a heartfelt smile. Unexpectedly Moana's face softened, and she leaned forward to touch Lani's arm.

"Mr. Jason say you no eat yo' breakfast," she said, slipping into the rich patois of the Islands. "Well, no *pilikia*—you catch little nap, and bymby I bring you plenty *kaukau*."

Before Lani could tell her she didn't expect to be waited on, a bell rang three times at the end of the hall. "That means Mr. Wade wants to talk to me," Moana said, her voice formal again. She hurried away, leaving Lani to congratulate herself that she had passed one more hurdle. She would be willing to swear that Moana hadn't recognized her. And why should she, she thought as she pushed open the door, when there was already one Iolani Stevenson in residence at Maunaloa House?

Although the room she was standing in was large, as were all the rooms at Maunaloa House, its heavy dark furniture seemed to overwhelm it. Since the rooms in this wing had been furnished when the wing had been added, the furniture was late Victorian—marble-topped commodes, unwieldy upholstered chairs, ornate tables with bulbous legs, and beds with tall, cathedral headboards.

The room had no closet, but there was a darkly varnished armoire in one corner which she knew would provide more than ample space for her spartan wardrobe. Another door opened into a tiny bathroom; it had been installed during her grandfather's time, and its fixtures were outmoded, a little rusty. The thought of a warm bath was tempting. She got her terrycloth robe from the suitcase David had already left on a luggage rack at the foot of the bed and took it into the bathroom with her.

A few minutes later, up to her chin in hot water in the high old-fashioned tub, she let her thoughts drift to the two men who had come into her life so recently. What was the reason for the tension she had sensed between the two cousins? Was it rivalry over Vivian? A simple difference of personality? Or could it be something rooted in their childhood?

When the water had cooled, she rubbed herself dry, slipped into her robe and went to get her makeup kit. She had forgotten her slippers, and her bare feet made no sound as she pushed open the bathroom door. She was already in the bedroom before she realized she had a visitor.

The girl standing by the bed, completely absorbed in the contents of Lani's open suitcase, was small for her age; with her delicate features, her oval-shaped face, she looked as fragile as an old-fashioned china doll. The only traces of her Hawaiian ancestry were the almond shape of her eyes and the glossy black hair that flowed smoothly down her back to her waist. She was wearing a long Thai-silk shift, slit to her knees, and there were velvet thongs on her narrow feet. Lani realized that subconsciously she had been expecting a waif, but this girl was as well-tended as a hothouse flower.

Lani took another step into the room, and the girl looked up. For a moment the surprise on her face was comical— until her finely shaped eyebrows came together in a scowl.

"You must be Maile," Lani said, her voice a little husky. "I'm Yula—"

"You're not supposed to be here," the girl interrupted rudely. "Aunt Berta doesn't allow the servants to sleep in the big house. Just wait until she finds out Moana gave you this room. She'll send you packing, just like she did the other nurses."

Lani knew she was being tested; she mustered up a smile. "I'm your uncle's secretary, not a nurse," she said lightly. "As it happens, I worked at a clinic in San Francisco, and sometimes I helped the physical therapists with the children there."

"Uncle Wade said you were going to supervise my exercises," Maile said, obviously unappeased. "He told me *he* would do them with me, but he's always too busy. And anyway I hate those old exercises"—her voice rose shrilly— "and I'm not going to do them anymore!"

Lani was silent. She got her brush from her suitcase, sat down at the dressing table, and began brushing her hair with long, even strokes.

"Didn't you hear me?" Maile demanded. "When Aunt Berta gets back from her shopping trip, I'm going to tell her I don't want you in the *mauka* wing."

Lani turned to regard Maile with thoughtful eyes. After a moment Maile looked away, her mouth sulky. She stared down at the bits of jewelry that Lani had dropped on the bed earlier when she'd undressed for her bath.

"What's that?" she asked, pointing to a small gold locket.

Lani went to the bed, picked up the locket and opened it to show Maile the tiny picture of Kore inside. "It's a locket—for carrying around the picture of someone you care about."

"Is he your lover?" Maile said, staring greedily at the trinket.

"He's my brother."

Maile studied her, her head to one side. Lani braced herself for another insult, but instead Maile gave a doleful sigh. "If *I* had a locket like this, I'd put my father's picture in it. He's dead, you know."

It was such an obvious hint and bid for sympathy that

Lani almost laughed. Even so, she was tempted to give the locket to Maile. It was an inexpensive trinket; its only value to her was the picture it held. She had bought it with the first money she'd earned dancing in a midway show at a time when it had seemed important to keep Kore's picture close to her heart. It was only because of habit, she reminded herself now, that she still wore the locket occasionally, just as it was habit that made her cling to Kawena's gift, the carved shark's tooth.

She started to ask Maile if she'd like to have the locket, then thought better of it, deciding it would be a mistake to start off their relationship with a gesture that might seem a bribe. So she smiled at Maile and began unpacking her suitcase, shaking out her clothes and putting them away in the armoire and in the drawers of a marble-topped commode.

Maile perched on the edge of the bed, watching her. From the disdain on her face, it was obvious what she thought of Lani's wardrobe.

"Vivian won't want you here either," Maile said.

"Vivian?"

"That's my sister. Her name's really Iolani, but while she was lost, her name was Vivian." Her lips curved in a small, secret smile. "She doesn't like it when I call her Vivian—that's why I do it sometimes."

"Why would your sister care if I'm here or not?"

"She doesn't like other girls, especially pretty ones, around Uncle Wade and Uncle Jason."

"What about you? Does she mind having you around?" Lani asked, careful to make the question sound casual.

"She doesn't pay any attention to me. Even though I'm pretty, I don't count because I'm not grown up yet."

"You're modest, too," Lani said, smiling at her.

"What does that mean?" Maile demanded.

"It means that—well, it isn't considered very good manners to compliment yourself, even if it's true."

Maile shrugged. "Everybody is always saying you should tell the truth, and then they get mad when you do."

Lani laughed, genuinely amused. "You're right, Maile. It's all very confusing, isn't it? When is something a social lie and when is it just plain lying? I still can't figure out how it works sometimes."

For a long moment Maile studied her. Something flickered deep in her hazel eyes, but if it was a smile, it never reached her lips.

"I didn't mean that I think I'm as pretty as Iolani," she said. "I don't have anything up here yet"—she touched her chest—"and my legs don't match now, but when I'm grown up, Iolani will be old, like Aunt Berta." The prospect seemed to please her. "I'm going to have a lot of boyfriends someday, and I'll make them buy me presents or I won't let them make out with me. I'm only going out with rich men, too. Poor ones can't afford to buy you jewelry and take you to expensive places to eat."

Lani concentrated on keeping her face expressionless. "It might be more fun to get a job and buy your own nice things," she commented.

"Why should I work?" Maile said, looking surprised. "I'm going to be very rich when I turn twenty-one. Then I'll make everybody who's been mean to me sorry. Aunt Berta says that when you have a lot of money, people have to crawl to you."

"Your aunt must have been teasing you. Or maybe you misunderstood her."

"Oh, she didn't say it to *me*. She was talking to Iolani in the garden, and I was hiding behind—" Maile stopped; her eyes got very still.

Lani pretended not to notice. "Well, I don't think it would be much fun, having people crawl around you," she said thoughtfully. "Can't you just see poor Moana, trying to cook your meals on her knees? And David—he'd probably run the *Kauhelani* into a reef."

Unexpectedly, Maile giggled. As if the sound surprised her, her eyes widened and she put both hands over her mouth. Again Lani pretended not to notice. She set a pair of shoes inside the armoire and shut the door. When she turned around, she found that Maile had moved to the bed and was staring at the small metal box that held her private papers and Pearsa's gold coins.

She expected a question about the box, but Maile said, "My mother was very pretty. There's a painting of her in one of the bedrooms in the *makai* wing. I don't look at all like her. And I don't look much like my father, either. I guess I'm a throwback—that's what Aunt Berta says."

Lani held her breath, let it out slowly. "You'll probably look more like your mother as you grow older."

"Aunt Berta says I'm never going to grow up—not unless I mend my wicked ways."

The words were matter-of-fact; the expression in Maile's eyes was not. Lani's mouth went dry as an old memory surfaced: Aunt Berta, in one of her cold rages, standing over her, telling her that she was such a wicked little girl that she was never going to live long enough to grow up.

Maile's eyes sharpened, and Lani realized she was trembling, that her palms were wet. "Well, you look very healthy to me," she said briskly. "And your legs will be the same size again when the muscles strengthen. There were a lot of youngsters at the clinic who had the same problem after they'd been in a cast for a long time. They all returned to normal eventually." She didn't add the obvious, that they had all cooperated with the therapists.

"Did you like those kids? I suppose they never gave you any trouble," Maile said scornfully.

"I liked most of them—and some of the ones I liked best gave me the most trouble," Lani said honestly.

"Well, *I'm* going to give you a lot of trouble," Maile announced.

Lani knew this was another test; silently she began braiding her hair, arranging it in a coil high on her head.

"You're as pretty as Iolani, I guess." Maile's voice was grudging. "Are you a slut, too?"

Lani waited several moments before she turned to look at Maile. "Do you know what that word means?"

"Something bad, or Iolani wouldn't have been so mad

when Aunt Berta called her that." Maile rubbed the tip of her nose reflectively. "What *does* it mean, anyway?"

"I'm sure it's in the dictionary," Lani said. "And you're right about its not being a nice word."

"Does it have something to do with sex?"

"In a way."

"Oh well, I think sex is silly," Maile said, obviously losing interest.

"Are you very close to your Aunt Berta?" Lani asked, trying for a casual tone. "You seem to quote her a lot."

A mask seemed to drop over Maile's eyes. She slid off the bed, smoothing her shift over her hips in a curiously adult gesture. "And you're pretty nosy, aren't you?" she said.

"Not really. I do want to know all about you, Maile, since we'll be together a lot in the next few weeks. I hope we can be friends. If not, I'll settle for your cooperation."

"Well, I don't want to be your friend. I'm not going to cooperate, either."

She was gone, leaving the door open behind her. Feeling thoroughly disgruntled with herself, Lani went to close it. Why hadn't she handled Maile differently, treated her as if she were a new patient at the clinic? Why had she let the conversation become personal? The truth was, she had made the mistake of expecting a replica of herself at that age, only to discover that Maile was an entirely different kind of child. It was evident she hadn't been abused, that she didn't fear her aunt—and maybe, Lani thought suddenly, this was Maile's real danger. That Aunt Berta had already passed along her materialistic standards to Maile was obvious. Had she also passed along her bigotry, her snobbishness?

Her thoughts were so unpalatable that she was glad when a light tapping on the door interrupted them. She went to open it to Moana and the welcome tray of sandwiches and salad she was carrying. It wasn't until later, when Lani was turning down the white counterpane on the bed to take a nap, that she discovered the tiny gold locket that held Kore's picture was missing.

VIII

Lani didn't take her nap, after all.

She curled up in one of the upholstered chairs in front of the windows, stared out into the ferny leaves of a monkeypod tree, and tried to decide what to do about the missing locket.

Although the locket held little sentimental value, Kore's picture was a different matter. It was all very well to tell herself that she had no need to carry his picture around in a locket now that he had come back into her life, but she had treasured that faded snapshot too long to take its theft calmly.

Of even more immediacy was the problem of how to deal with Maile. Surely something more than simple avarice lay behind the theft. Was this Maile's way of challenging her authority, another test to see how far she could go? And if nothing was done to get the locket back, wouldn't Maile consider this an admission of weakness? If she ever hoped to gain Maile's confidence, she must first win her respect, and that meant she couldn't turn to Wade, not even for advice.

Seemingly out of nowhere, an idea came to her. It was such a simple solution that in her relief she laughed aloud. For the present she would say nothing, pretend she hadn't yet discovered her loss, but at the proper time she would handle the theft in her own way.

Having made a decision, Lani put the whole business out of her mind and rested her head against the scratchy velour of the old chair. The sun, moving downward in the western sky, fell obliquely across her lap, adding to her drowsiness. There was the odor of some half-remembered flower, as elusive as a dream, in the wind that ruffled the Swiss organdy curtains at the windows.

Pikake, she thought, remembering the pikake vines that grew so profusely on the bluffs behind Maunaloa House. She closed her eyes, and her thoughts drifted to the two men she'd just met, then to Kore, who had been so miraculously restored to her. Three men—two of them strangers and one from her past. How odd that just before Pearsa's final stroke, she had talked about three men who would shape the pattern of her life. . . .

That day, Pearsa had been sitting at the tiny breakfast bar in the cramped trailer that had been their home for the past year. She had been laying out her worn tarot cards in the form of a cross, muttering to herself in Romany.

Lani, who was sitting cross-legged on the cot that filled the tiny alcove where she slept, was mending a pair of rehearsal leotards. She had been too absorbed in her own thoughts to pay much attention to her foster mother at first. Lately there had been a change in her relationship with Kore that puzzled—and excited—her. She sometimes felt as if time had stood still and she had remained a little girl. Kore, as protective as any Rom father, had kept the men of the carnival away from her, and while there was no one in particular she was really interested in, she had been restive since her seventeenth birthday, resentful of his constant vigilance.

They had quarreled the night before when he'd caught her talking to the carnival's young advance man. At the climax of the quarrel, she'd shouted that she wasn't his sister and she didn't have to take his orders. He had cut off her tirade by grabbing her by the shoulders and kissing her. There had been nothing brotherly about the kiss, and when he finally released her, she could only stare at him, her hand pressed against her throbbing mouth.

Even after he turned on his heel and stalked away, her mind was in such a turmoil that she hadn't been able to sleep last night. She had been in love with Kore since the day he had taken her home to his mother; was it possible that he finally felt the same way about her? Then why did he still treat her like a child? Why hadn't he said something before, done something about it?

She was thinking about this and only half-listening to Pearsa, who had decided to read Lani's cards that day, something she rarely did for the members of her own family.

Although Lani no longer believed in tarot cards or crystal balls or any other of the trappings of fortune-telling, she had shuffled the thick deck of cards and tried to concentrate on a question. Inevitably, with her mind so full of Kore, she had asked about love, about marriage, and then had retreated into her own thoughts.

"—the Six of Pentacles, the Devil, the King of Cups—" Despite her preoccupation, Pearsa's voice, queerly pitched and slurred, penetrated her reverie, and she looked up. Pearsa's eyes were glazed; she was swaying back and forth.

"Three men will shape your destiny, my daughter," she said in a voice Lani had never heard her use before. "One is as steady as a rock, but he can never be anything more to you than a friend, no matter how you wish it otherwise. The second man—the face of the second man is pleasing, but it is greed that drives him, that perverts him. Beware of the devil who hides behind a pleasing face, because he carries the worm of death with him wherever he goes. And the third man—ah, this one is the King of Cups, and he is your own true love. You will walk many dangerous paths before you find him, and you must be wise and brave; above all, you must be brave. Death will touch you several times before you find your own true love. Be careful it is not your own death, my daughter. . . ."

"But how can I tell the three men apart, Pearsa?" Lani asked, fascinated in spite of herself.

"All will please you; and each one, in his own way, will love you in return. You will need all your wits, all your courage; but if you listen to your own heart, you will make the right choice—"

Her voice faltered; a sigh escaped her throat, and a moment later the glazed look left her eyes. But she seemed dazed, disoriented, and Lani asked her no more questions. Later that afternoon, Pearsa had been struck down by a stroke; three days later she was dead.

And now, Lani thought, *three men have come into my life, all at the same time*. Were they the three Pearsa had told her about? Was it really true that the devil lurked inside one of them? Which of the three could never be anything more than a friend? Had Pearsa meant Kore? In her own oblique way, had she been warning Lani that what he felt for her was affection, not love? Was that why, just before Pearsa had lapsed into her final sleep, she had made Lani promise not to marry him?

Lani sighed, remembering with shame how she had been tempted to break her promise to Pearsa when Kore had come to her after the funeral and asked her to marry him. She had run away from temptation that time, without even a note of explanation. This time, when she saw Kore again, she would be honest with him. When he found out about her promise, surely he would see that she had done the right thing. . . .

Her thoughts blurred, and perhaps she dozed after all, for when the bell outside in the hall aroused her, she discovered that the sun had already dropped behind the bluffs, that the room was much darker.

She rose, stretched and yawned, and went to examine her wardrobe. She had left San Francisco in such a hurry that there hadn't been time to buy anything new for the trip, and last year's summer clothes looked limp and dull, hanging in the dim recesses of the big mahogany armoire.

She finally settled for a turquoise blouse with a ruffled collar and a long dark green skirt, and she took special pains with her makeup. Although she was aware that she looked younger with her hair down, she let it hang loose about her shoulders, and when she examined herself in the oval mirror above the dressing table, she knew she looked her best, that the turquoise blouse was becoming to her green eyes and her dark gold hair.

Even so, she couldn't help thinking of Vivian, so sleek and self-assured and ravishingly beautiful. It was ironic, she reflected ruefully, that the girl who had appropriated her identity should look so much the aristocratic heiress, whereas she, the real Iolani Stevenson, had a—what was it Jason had called it?—an earthy look.

She made a face at her reflection in the mirror and turned away. What was the opinion of a stranger to her, anyway? It shouldn't matter—it *didn't* matter, any more than the look of distaste on Wade MacMasters's face when he'd found her in Jason's arms had mattered. Both men were strangers, and strangers they would undoubtedly remain, since she didn't intend to be here long enough for anyone to become important to her, especially a man.

The bell gave a second warning, and she went downstairs feeling composed and in control of herself, and determined to remain that way.

When she came through the French doors, Wade and Jason were waiting for her, standing side by side at the edge of the lanai. Wade's greeting was cordial, but it was Jason who asked how she felt and who told her that she looked ravishing in turquoise.

Dinner was a buffet, the food set out in chafing dishes on a long rattan table on the lanai. To Lani's secret amusement, the food was the everyday dishes of the Islands, and she suspected that Moana was taking advantage of Berta St. John's absence to serve the foods she herself preferred.

Like so many things in the Islands, the menu was a mixture, foods borrowed from various Island cultures and adapted by the practical Hawaiians for their own use. There was teriyaki steak—thin strips of broiled rib eye, marinated in shoyu and gingerroot, then threaded onto slivers of bamboo and broiled; butterfish, wrapped in ti leaves and steamed until succulent and flaky; fried rice, rich with green onions, crumbled bacon and bits of seafood, each grain of rice coated with a last-minute application of beaten egg; a salad of tender taro leaves and watercress; fried green bananas and Samoan coconut bread; a compote of fresh Island fruits—papaya, mango, watermelon and pineapple.

Lani filled her plate and carried it to a round rattan table, which was already set up with crystal and silver and a centerpiece of torch ginger. Maile, looking more than ever like a collector's doll in a yellow holoku, the Hawaiian version of the formal gown, was already settled there. Her response to Lani's greeting was a demure smile—a little too demure, Lani decided, remembering her missing locket.

Of the two men, Jason showed Maile the most attention, telling her she looked like a buttercup in her yellow holoku, and then explaining patiently what a buttercup was. It was obvious that Maile was flattered; she hung on Jason's every word, ignoring Wade and Lani. Lani resisted Jason's attempts to draw her into their conversation, sensing that it would be a mistake to compete with Maile for the attention of either man.

On the trip from Kaneohe, Lani had felt a thinly veiled ill will between the two men, but their conversation seemed cordial enough now. Only once, when Jason, who had been teasing Maile about her sweet tooth, told her that she'd better be careful or the Night Marchers might be tempted to steal a little girl who only ate sweets, did the antagonism between the two men surface again.

"Your Uncle Jason is teasing you, Maile," Wade said sharply. "He knows very well that the Night Marchers are a legend and don't really exist."

Lani wasn't surprised that Maile looked unconvinced. She too had grown up believing in the Night Marchers, that legion of dead chiefs and their warrior attendants whom the Hawaiians believe walk the dark nights.

"But they *are* real, Uncle Wade," Maile said earnestly. "Kawena saw them lots of times, right here on Maunaloa, before she went blind—and so did Amoka, Keaka and Peter's grandfather." She shivered suddenly and hugged her chest with her thin arms. "Sometimes, when I'm playing in the Folly, I can hear them, the drums and the nose flutes and the *ukekes*—"

"I've already explained all that to you, Maile," Wade said impatiently. "You know the sinkhole is up there on the hill behind the Folly—what you hear is sea water filling up the underground passages under the sinkhole at high tide. The water compresses the air in the lava vents, and it acts like a drum—or like a giant whistle sometimes. As for Kawena—she is a superstitious old woman with far too big an imagination."

"But Keaha said—"

"Keaha was teasing you—just like your Uncle Jason has been teasing you. And I think it's time to change the subject." He directed a hard stare at Jason, who looked amused.

The two men began discussing a mutual friend, and Maile returned to her food, her lips set in a rebellious line. Although she pushed the food on her plate around with her fork, Lani noticed that very little of it reached her mouth. A few minutes later, when Moana brought in a plate of coconut cake cut into squares and set it unceremoniously in the middle of the table, Maile eyed it greedily. She glanced at the two men, absorbed in their conversation, then at Lani, who pretended to be busy with her own food. Deftly Maile slipped three squares of the cake onto her napkin, tied the ends together to form a pouch, and dropped it into her lap. A few moments later it disappeared into the depths of a lauhala carryall sitting on the floor by her feet.

Troubled, Lani absentmindedly buttered a bit of coconut bread. There seemed no logical reason for Maile to steal the cake. If she wanted it, she had only to take it. It was obvious that neither of the men was paying any attention to what she ate or didn't eat. Was this some game Maile was playing, or did it have some connection with the stolen locket? When she'd discovered her locket was missing, the word *kleptomaniac* had crossed Lani's mind briefly, but she'd dismissed the possibility as unlikely. Now she was forced to ask herself whether it was possible that Maile was addicted to stealing for its own sake. If so, why hadn't someone done something about it, or were the adults at Maunaloa too absorbed in their own lives to notice?

Surreptitiously Lani studied the two cousins. Although Jason was very attractive, with his dark red hair, amber eyes and wide, humorous mouth, it was Wade she found herself watching, trying to decide what there was about him that made her so aware of him as a man. Was it his striking good looks, his well-muscled body, the quiet authority in his voice? Or was it the vitality that was so apparent, even when he was talking quietly, as he was now?

She realized she was staring. She looked away and met Jason's glance. He was looking very casual in a gaily patterned aloha shirt worn outside his trousers, Hawaiian style. "You haven't said half a dozen words all evening," he said. "Are you always this quiet, Yula?"

"I never waste time talking when I can eat food like this," she said, thinking of the overaged stews, greasy hamburgers and shriveled hot dogs that had been her fare so often during the years with the Tatum Brothers show.

"Well, you are a novelty—a woman who puts good food ahead of idle chitchat. I think I approve of your choice of secretaries, Wade."

"I'm relieved to hear that." Wade's voice was dry. "See that you don't let your approval interfere with Miss Brock's duties."

"It's a promise. Of course"—Jason paused to snare a shrimp from a plate of *pupus*—"I *am* hoping to persuade Yula to let me photograph her while I'm here."

Lani saw Wade's face stiffen. To forestall another flare-up between the two men, she asked quickly, "What is this vegetable, Jason? It tastes a little like squash, but—"

"It's breadfruit, a staple in the diet of the old Hawaiians. In fact, they brought breadfruit tree saplings with them in their outriggers when they made their treks here from Tahiti." Although his voice was casual, Jason's eyes told her that he knew exactly why she had asked the question. "Ordinarily, it's too bland a food for my taste, but Moana can turn just about anything into gourmet eating."

"Aunt Berta doesn't like the local food," Maile announced. "She says it's too full of starch. That's why the kanakas are so fat and lazy—they eat too much poi."

"That's enough, Maile." Wade's voice was sharp. "We

made a bargain, remember? You weren't going to call the Hawaiians kanakas anymore—"

"Keaha and Peter call me *pupule*—and it isn't nice to call someone crazy. And Moana hates me. Today she pinched me when she was helping me with those exercises. She was mad because I told her I'm going to make all the kanakas leave Maunaloa when I 'herit my money."

"Moana doesn't hate you, although sometimes she has good reason to. And from now on, Miss Brock will be in charge of your physical therapy. See that you don't give her any trouble or you'll answer to me."

"Just wait until Aunt Berta gets back and finds out about *her*," Maile said sullenly. "You know she doesn't let the servants sleep in the house."

Wade tossed his napkin down beside his plate. "Okay, that does it. Off to bed with you. Since you've only been playing with your food, you obviously aren't hungry."

A dark red flush spread over Maile's face. She groped sideways for her lauhala bag and stood up. Her mouth began to quiver; when she began to cry, Lani stood too and took a step toward her. Maile must have caught the movement, because she flew around the corner of the table and flung herself into Lani's arms. Although Lani's concern was tempered by the suspicion that she was being manipulated, she couldn't help feeling flattered when Maile insisted between sobs that Lani go upstairs with her. Without waiting for Wade's permission, she put her arm around Maile's shaking shoulders and led her from the lanai and up the stairs.

She had been prepared for a certain amount of pain when she saw her old room again, but a quick glance around told her there'd be no old memories here to haunt her. The posy-strewn wallpaper she remembered was gone; the walls were painted an oyster-white now, and the comfortable old maple and cherrywood furniture had been replaced by modern pieces of bleached mahogany.

Maile, who had stopped crying as soon as they left the lanai, stood with downcast eyes as Lani unzipped the yellow holoku, found a pair of pajamas in a huge triple dresser, helped her into them, then brushed and braided Maile's long silky hair for the night.

While Maile brushed her teeth in the bathroom, Lani turned down the bed covers. Like the room's furniture and wall decorations, the boldly modern bedspread seemed much too adult, and Lani remembered that Moana had told her that Maile had changed her room several times lately.

Maile, looking very pleased with herself, came back into the room and climbed into bed. Under the thin material of her pajamas, her shoulder blades showed plainly, and she looked very small and frail in the middle of the full-sized bed.

"Do you have anyone your own age to play with?" Lani asked impulsively. "How old are David Kealoha's two boys?"

"Peter's twelve and Keaka's eleven, but I don't like them anymore. They always have secrets, and they say I'm *pupule* and call me a coast *haole*, when they know I've never been to the mainland. They're hateful and mean, and anyway I don't want any kanaka friends. Kanakas are lazy and stupid, and they don't take enough baths, either."

A sharp retort rose to Lani's lips, but she suppressed it and said mildly, "Moana looks very well scrubbed to me, and so does David. And didn't Jason tell me that two of Moana's sons were professional men? That doesn't sound so stupid. As for being lazy, this house is spotless. Since the Kealohas do the work—or am I wrong? Do your sister and aunt help with household chores at Maunaloa House?"

Maile looked scornful. "Of course not. That's what the kanakas get paid for. Since Uncle Wade put Aunt Berta in charge, they have to take orders from her, and she makes sure they earn their pay." She drew her lips together, and for a moment she looked so much like Berta St. John that Lani's breath caught. "When I 'herit *my* half of the island, I won't let any of them, especially those nasty boys, live on Maunaloa."

Again, it was all Lani could do to hold back an angry reproof. To give herself time, she wandered over to the windows. Of necessity, the sills were high enough to keep out the torrential kona rains, but the full-length windows opened inward, French-door style, to allow easy access to the balcony outside. Through an iron railing, the glossy leaves of a mango tree were silhouetted against the glow of a concealed floodlight in the garden below. When Lani had left Maunaloa, the mango tree had been little more than a sapling. She had helped Amoka, David's father, plant the tree a few weeks before the heart attack that had left Moana a widow. He had told her that when the tree bore fruit, she could reach right out her window and help herself.

Unexpectedly her eyes stung; she fought against a fresh wave of nostalgia, knowing that she couldn't trust her memories, since so many of them were false.

"What are you looking at?" Maile asked curiously. "You keep staring out that window, and you haven't said anything for the longest time."

"I was thinking how lucky you are to live on such a beautiful island," Lani said.

"Well, I don't think I'm so lucky. I wish Maunaloa would sink into the ocean."

"Why do you say that? Islands are very special places."

"I hate islands! You can't go anywhere when you live on an island. If I lived on the mainland I would run away and join a circus."

Lani felt a small shock. She swung around to stare at Maile.

"Why are you staring at me like that?" Maile demanded.

"Because—because I once knew a little girl who ran away from home," she said.

"What happened to her?"

"A family of Gypsies took her in. She lived with them until—for a long time."

"Gypsies? *Real* Gypsies?"

"Real ones—only they call themselves Roms, not Gypsies."

Maile studied her, her hazel eyes suspicious. "Is that true? Did it really happen, or did you just make it up?"

"It's true. It really did happen."

"Did they live in a caravan?"

"Sort of. They were carnival people, so they lived in trailers most of the time—"

"Then she really did join a circus!" In her excitement Maile sat up in bed. "Did you work in a circus too, Yula? Is that how you met your friend? What else did she tell you about the Gypsies—the Roms?"

Belatedly Lani realized that she had already said too much. "We did work together, but not in a circus," she said. "It must be your bedtime, Maile. Why don't I tuck you in and turn off the lights so you can get some sleep?"

"I'm not a baby. I don't need anyone to tuck me in." The corners of Maile's mouth turned downward in a pout. "And I don't care about that silly girl—or the Gypsies. Everybody knows they steal from people and—and they've got loose morals, too."

Although Lani knew that Maile was quoting her aunt again, some of her anger spilled over into words this time. "As it happens, the Roms have a very strict moral code," she said sharply. "But they have been treated so badly by *gadje*—by outsiders—that they consider anyone not a Rom their enemy. That's why they have no compunction about cheating outsiders whenever they get the chance. This doesn't make it right, of course, but it does explain why they have such strict rules for their behavior toward other Roms and can still cheat the *gadje* with their *boojos*."

"What's a *boojo?*" Maile asked eagerly, brushing aside Lani's neat little moral.

"A *boojo* is a—a confidence game, a trick," Lani said. "The Rom women who tell fortunes are very shrewd about people. If the customer seems prosperous and especially superstitious, the *boojo* woman tells her—it's almost always a woman—that her money is unclean. She offers to purify the money, but first it has to be drawn out of the bank. Once the Rom woman gets her hands on the money, there's any number of ways to switch it for worthless paper, or sometimes for smaller bills."

Maile was silent a moment, her eyes reflective. "I wish I were a *boojo* woman," she said then. "I'd like to play tricks on people and make them sorry for being mean to me."

"Well, the little girl I was telling you about didn't feel that way," Lani said firmly. "Even though the Roms were good to her, she knew it was wrong to steal from vulnerable old women. It's true that the Roms have been exploited, but so have the Hawaiians, and yet they don't make their living extorting money fron the helpless and the superstitious."

Maile fixed Lani with an unblinking stare. It was impossible to guess what she was thinking. "Tell me more about the little girl," she said finally. "What was her name? Did she grow up and marry a Gypsy boy?"

"I'll tell you more about her tomorrow," Lani said. "Right now, I'd better get back downstairs. I rushed out of there without even saying good-night to your uncles."

"Oh, they're not downstairs. I heard Uncle Jason whistling in the garden while I was in the bathroom, and Uncle Wade is working in his office. You can see his office lights on across the garden."

She didn't try to hide her satisfaction, and Lani knew her earlier suspicions had been right. Maile's outburst had been a deliberate—and successful—attempt to get her away from the two men. Where had an eleven-year-old child learned to be so devious? And why had Maile developed such a taste for eavesdropping? Had Aunt Berta been her teacher, or someone else in this house? Suddenly Lani was remembering another little girl who had lingered on the stairs of her aunt's house to listen to the gossip around a bridge table. She had risked her aunt's fury because she had been so hungry for any scrap of news about her father. Was there something Maile was trying to find out? Or was it simple boredom? Well, whatever the reason, Maile was a very lonely child—and for all her outward aplomb, a very vulnerable one.

She stared down into her sister's too-wise eyes, and pity stirred inside her. Before she had time to reconsider, she bent and kissed Maile gently on the cheek.

"Happy dreams, Maile," she said, as she reached out to switch off the lamp beside the bed.

Maile's gasp stopped her. "Don't do that!" she said shrilly. "I have to—to read a verse in my Bible before I go to sleep."

Lani hesitated, arrested by the expression on Maile's face, before she nodded and turned away. At the door she glanced back. Maile was lying on her back, her thin arms folded across her chest; although she was staring directly at Lani, she didn't respond to Lani's smile.

Lani was halfway down the hall when she heard a soft click behind her, and knew that Maile had locked her bedroom door.

Later, when she was lying in bed in the warm darkness of her own room, the night wind stirring the curtains at the windows, she thought back over the day, trying to bring order from her impressions. Above all else, one clear image stood out in her mind. As she had reached out to turn off the lamp beside her sister's bed, she had caught a look of stark terror in Maile's eyes.

There was no longer any use trying to convince herself that Maile was a normal child. A normal eleven-year-old didn't lock her door at night or sleep in a lighted bedroom. Wade had warned her that Maile was "difficult," that she had an abnormal interest in the supernatural. Why hadn't he also told her that Maile was terrified of the dark?

Well, this was one area where she could help her sister. Before she left Maunaloa Island and went back to San Francisco to pick up the threads of her own life, she meant to find out why Maile, who had been coddled and protected all her life, still felt she had to lock herself in her bedroom at night. And if her plans to throw Maile and the Kealohas together worked out, Maile would have a chance to find out just how wrong her aunt was about the Hawaiians, too.

IX

During the next two days, Lani got reacquainted with the island. It was a bittersweet experience.

Every room she entered in the old house, every path she walked on, seemed to hold the ghosts of her father and mother. Although she explored the beach, the gardens, the grove of specimen trees, and the greenhouses that had been her grandfather's special joy, there were other places she was careful to avoid. It was easy to stay away from the circle of cottages where the Kealohas lived and the cemetery just beyond where her parents—and her father's second wife—lay buried, but it was more difficult to ignore Abigail's Folly.

Twice Jason invited her for a swim in the lagoon, and each time, although she found herself enjoying his company more and more, she made an excuse, knowing she was not yet ready for a second encounter with the Folly. The structure, a replica of a Chinese temple, was one of the landmarks of the island, and Jason was sure to point it out. The next time she looked at the place where her mother had died, she meant to be alone, not in the company of a man who had a disconcerting habit of plucking her thoughts—and her emotional responses—out of the air.

Wade's manner toward her, although courteous and patient, remained reserved. Only occasionally, as if his guard slipped a bit, did he show flashes of his initial warmth. Her job, mostly routine office duties, was interesting, mainly because it gave her a chance to find out more about Wade MacMasters and the business he administered for the Stevenson estate.

The first day, when he set her to work culling outdated business letters from a business correspondence file, she was struck by the diversity and scope of the estate her father had left. She already knew about Halelaulea, the Stevensons' ranch on the big island of Hawaii, which had been in the family for generations, but she had no recollection at all that her father had owned controlling interest in several large Island businesses, as well as huge blocks of real estate in downtown Hilo and Honolulu. So much money at stake, she thought uneasily; no wonder her aunt, always so covetous and greedy, had been willing to risk everything to get control of it.

Even with the constant assault on her emotions and the stress of learning a new job, Lani would have been content if her first physical therapy session with Maile had gone more smoothly. Because she had been successful in handling recalcitrant children at the clinic, she had been sure she could win Maile over; but she soon discovered she had been overconfident.

During their first hour together, Maile ran the gamut from sulks to a full-blown tantrum, and when Lani finally coaxed her into trying one of the easier exercises, she did it listlessly for a few times and then flatly refused to do any more that day. Lani tried incorporating a simple hula dance into the physical therapy routine, but Maile refused to cooperate, telling her scornfully that she wasn't allowed to do those "nasty heathen dances," an obvious quote from Berta St. John.

The second afternoon, when Maile failed to turn up on the lanai for her exercise session, Lani was obliged to go looking for her. She searched the house, the gardens, the guest cottages, the greenhouses and even the bathhouse, although she was careful to keep her eyes averted from the pagoda-shaped roof of the Folly. An hour later she was standing on the seawall in front of Maunaloa House, ready to admit defeat, when she remembered she hadn't searched the hau arbor.

The hau arbor sat on the narrow promontory of land that formed the easternmost boundary of the cove; like the Folly, it had been built at the whim of the first Abigail, Captain Aaron's ill-fated bride. With its fluted columns, its arches and marble benches, it must once have been a fair reproduction of a Roman grape arbor; during the decades, the six hau trees which had been planted between its arches had taken over, and now their vinelike branches and heavy foliage covered the entire structure and formed a thick, impenetrable roof overhead.

It had been one of Lani's favorite hideaways when she was a child; its cool, shadowy depths were a perfect place for reading, for playing with her dolls, or just for dreaming away a hot summer's afternoon. One of its attractions had been its isolation, so she wasn't surprised, when she moved quietly across the sand toward it, to hear a low murmuring coming from inside.

As she rounded the corner of the arbor, skirting one of the clusters of succulents that grew wild in the sandy soil of the promontory, she reached up and plucked a hau blossom from a dangling branch. She tucked the hibiscuslike flower behind her ear, remembering that she'd never been able to explain to her mother why she would waste time making leis from the fragile blossoms which lasted for only a few hours. How could she explain to her mother, who was always so practical about material things, that there was something magical about the way the hau petals changed from a morning yellow to apricot at noon to a deep red just before, at nightfall, they finally closed and withered to nothingness?

She stepped through the arched entrance of the arbor, ducking low to avoid a trailing hau branch. Maile was sitting cross-legged on a marble bench; her eyes were closed, and she was rocking gently back and forth, crooning a wordless song to the doll cradled in her arms. There was something so defenseless about her oblivious face that Lani immediately felt like an intruder.

Before she could back away, Maile's eyes flew open. For a long moment she stared at Lani, and then, like a mask dropping into place, the tenderness on her face was replaced with wariness.

Lani looked around the sun-dappled enclosure. "What a lovely place," she said, determinedly cheerful. "Would you prefer to do your exercises here, Maile? It seems cooler than the lanai."

"This is *my* place," Maile said loudly. "No one comes here except me. I don't want you here."

"Well, I can understand that. I had a place like this when I was your age, and I hated sharing it, especially with people I hardly knew. So why don't we go back to the house and do your exercises on the lanai? Then we can have some pineapple juice and cookies—"

"I hate pineapple juice, and I'm not supposed to eat sweets between meals. And I'm not going to do those exercises because they don't do any good. My legs are still different sizes—see?"

She thrust her legs out in front of her. She was wearing shorts under a loose-fitting top, and her thin legs, so fleshless and mismatched, made Lani's breath catch.

"Then I guess we'll have to work that much harder from now on," Lani said briskly. "Would you like to try the hula today?"

"That's a dumb old dance." Maile's voice was scornful. "Only little kids and tourists do the *hukilau* hula."

"I guess it *is* pretty simple, but it's the only hula I know. I wonder if we could talk Moana into giving us both a few lessons? She told me she used to dance with a hula troupe before she was married. The exercises are important, of course, but there are ways to supplement them, such as dancing and swimming. Do you know how to swim, Maile?"

For a moment she thought Maile wasn't going to answer her. "A little," Maile said. "My father gave me some lessons."

"Well, I'm not a good enough swimmer to give you any lessons," Lani lied, "but didn't your Uncle Jason say something at dinner last night about David Kealoha being a champion swimmer while he was at the University of Hawaii? Maybe he'd have time to give you a few lessons."

She paused, expecting a quick rejection, but Maile was silent. Encouraged, Lani went on, carefully casual. "When we get finished today, maybe you'd like me to tell you a story."

"I don't like made-up things. They're just the same as lies. Don't you know anything about real people?" Maile gave her a sidelong look. "What about that girl who lived with the Gypsies? What was her name?"

"Yana," Lani improvised, borrowing the name of Kore's grandmother. Although she was careful to hide it, she was pleased that her ploy had worked—so far. "She took the name of the dead sister of the boy who found her."

Maile sat up straighter, almost dislodging the doll in her lap. "A *boy* found her? A Gypsy boy? How old was he? What was his name? What did he look like?"

"Whoa! One question at a time. His name is Kore, and he was fourteen when he found Yana hiding under a bridge. The first time she saw him, he almost scared her to death. He moved so quietly he reminded her of a panther, and— and I'll tell you all about him as soon as we get the exercises out of the way."

To her surprise, since she expected at least a token resistance, Maile laid her doll aside and slid off the bench. This time there were no complaints as she did her exercises, closely supervised by Lani. She even seemed to enjoy the hula, and when Lani suggested again that she take hula and swimming lessons from Moana and her son, her nod, while not enthusiastic, was agreeable.

Afterward, Maile settled herself on the bench, her eyes expectant, as Lani told her about her first meeting with Kore. She listened with such flattering attention that Lani found herself expanding the story, describing the blackness inside the drainage pipe, her feeling of dread as she had waited there, not knowing for what. Feeling a little like Scheherazade, spinning a tale to capture the curiosity of her king, she tried to make it as interesting as she could, and like Scheherazade she was careful to break off before Maile's interest lagged.

"I have to finish some typing for your uncle, but I'll tell you more about Yana and Kore tomorrow," she promised. "In the meantime, I'll talk to the Kealohas about giving you hula and swimming lessons."

"Will you tell me how the Gypsy lady told fortunes?"

"I'll do more than that. I'll tell you what happened the first time Yana tried to sell flowers on a street corner. In return, I'd like your promise that you'll do your exercises from now on."

Maile studied her, her hazel eyes opaque. Although she finally nodded, Lani wasn't naïve enough to think she had won the war. *But at least*, she told herself, *I've won the first battle.*

Maile retrieved her doll and trotted off, and Lani went looking for David Kealoha. She found him in the potting shed, oiling a garden tool against the insidious tropical rust. He grinned good-naturedly when Lani asked if he had time to give Maile a few swimming lessons as part of her physical therapy.

"Sure, I always got time for help out Maile, but lately she no got time for me." He gave Lani a searching look. "It good t'ing you come here, take Maile under yo' wing. She sure is one mix-up little *keiki*. Alla time play alone—mo' bettah she play with other *keikis*, but she no like my boys anymore."

"Doesn't she go away to school in the winter?" Lani asked.

"No, her aunt say she too frail, so she stay here, have da kine tutor come over from Kaneohe. That Maile—she no eat right *kaukau*. My boys, they eat plenty poi, make them strong like papa-san." He thumped his thick chest with his thumb.

Lani stared at him suspiciously; when his eyes grew a twinkle, she knew her suspicions were right. "Uh-huh. You don't have to speak pidgin to entertain me—if that's what you're doing," she said dryly. "Jason Richards told me you

110

were a University of Hawaii graduate, that you have a degree in botany."

David's grin was unabashed. "Okay, so you've found me out. Most coast *haoles* expect a kanaka who works with his hands to talk pidgin, so I try to oblige. You're a pretty sharp *wahine*—and that's a good thing. You'll need your wits to make it here, especially when that St. John woman gets back. She's a numbah-one bitch—you watch out for her, Yula."

"Why would she want to cause trouble for me?" Lani asked.

David hesitated; when he spread his hands wide in a gesture she remembered so well, she knew he had said all he intended to on the subject of Berta St. John. "You be careful," he said again, and returned to his tools.

Lani found Moana in the kitchen, rolling out won ton dough on a huge chopping block table. She wore the white shorts and amah jacket that seemed to be a uniform with her; a sprig of pikake was woven into the coiled braids on the top of her head, releasing the odor of jasmine into the steamy air of the kitchen.

Although Moana heard Lani out, she shook her head when Lani was finished.

"I don't want no *huhu*—no trouble—with Berta St. John," she said flatly. Her hands were deft as she marked the dough in squares with a saw-toothed pastry cutter and began putting tiny spoonsful of cooked meat and vegetables in the center. "Of course, if Mr. Wade told me to do it . . ." She paused expectantly.

"Mr. MacMasters told me to do everything I could to keep Maile interested in getting the proper exercise. I don't see how her aunt could possibly object. Besides"—she smiled at Moana—"I'd like to learn to do the hula myself. I'm sure you're a very good teacher."

Moana smiled back—a little warily, Lani decided. "Well, you've got the build for it. Plenty up here and down there, nice and flat in the middle. First time I see you, I think you walk like dancer." She shook her head, looking fretful.

"When Iolani, Maile's sister, was little *keiki*, she dance like—like bird flying. When she come back, I ask her did she still dance the hula, but she say she forgot how, just like she forgot so many things."

"Were you close to her when she was a child?" Lani asked.

"Oh, sure. She was my own mama's *hanai* child—"

"*Hanai?*"

"That's child you love like own *keikis*, only not really have same blood. Ever since Lani was born, Kawena loved that baby. She came too early and Kawena delivered her"—she jerked her thumb upward—" in her mother's room upstairs. Miss Carol was sick long time after that—or maybe not so sick," she added cryptically. "Kawena took care of Lani, fed her, rocked her, loved her. When Mister John sent Lani away, Kawena almost go crazy. For long time she no eat, no sing or dance, no do anything."

Lani found it hard to breathe normally. "Your mother must have been very happy when Iolani was found again," she said.

Moana gave her a brooding look. "Oh, she very happy— till Iolani come back to Maunaloa. Then we find out she no can remember island, no can remember anyone here, so Kawena lose her *hanai* child second time."

"Your mother has grandchildren. David's sons must be a great comfort to her," Lani said.

"Oh, sure. Kawena love those two rascals, love other grandkids, too. But she still got big empty spot in heart for Lani."

"You called her Lani?" Lani said.

Moana's lips tightened. "It was Lani when she was little girl, but her aunt say we call her Miss Iolani now she grown up." She glanced pointedly at the wall clock above the sink, muttered something about having no more time for talk, and returned to her won tons.

Although Lani was tempted to offer her help, she knew she was the outsider here, that the first overtures of friendship must come from Moana. But she felt a little wistful as she thanked Moana and left the kitchen.

The first hula lesson, in the hau arbor the next afternoon, was an unqualified success. Lani was prepared for trouble, but Maile was cooperative, even cheerful. Although she treated Moana coolly at first, she was obviously intrigued by the song Moana taught her, an old classic about Paahana, a girl who had run away from a wicked stepmother and lived on river shrimps and guava in the then-wilderness of Wahiawa. With surprising grace, despite the weakness in her left leg, she picked up the movements, the slow stamps and turns of the simple hula that accompanied the song. Lani, pretending complete ignorance, joined in the dance lesson, and Maile was so busy laughing at her that she forgot her usual lofty treatment of Moana.

When Moana finally returned to her duties, Maile finished off the rest of the exercises and then curled up on the bench, her eyes expectant. It was obvious she had already prepared her questions, because she spat them out quickly, barely giving Lani time to answer—and sometimes to improvise, when the truth was dangerous.

"Could Pearsa really see into the future?" Maile asked, after Lani had described Pearsa and Kore to her satisfaction.

"When Pearsa read the tarot cards or looked in her crystal ball for her customers, she told them what they wanted to hear. She knew how to read the small signs that give away a person's hidden fears and true feelings."

"So she couldn't really see into the future?" Maile asked, looking disappointed.

Lani hesitated, uncomfortably aware of her own ambiguous feelings about Pearsa's fortune-telling. "Pearsa believed the tarot cards were an instrument through which she could sometimes foresee the future, but only when the power moved within her," she said. "You must remember that the Roms are a very old people—like the Hawaiians—and they still believe in the old superstitions."

"Did any of her predictions ever come true?" Maile asked.

"Some of them seemed to, but of course the tarot cards are so vague that afterward they can be made to fit almost anything that happens."

"What do tarot cards look like? Where do they come from?"

"They're larger than regular playing cards, and they have pictures instead of numbers. Although they've been around a long, long time, no one knows where they originated."

"Can you play games with them?"

Lani shook her head. "The Roms believe the tarot cards should never be used for frivolous things like games. Each fortune-teller keeps her cards in a special box, made of wood to ward off evil spirits—"

There was a sound behind Lani; she turned and met Wade's angry grey eyes. Maile slid off the bench and ran to take Wade's hand.

"Yula's been telling me about her friend who lived with the Gypsies—only they call themselves Roms," she said, her face animated. "Yula knows all about tarot cards and fortune-telling and—"

"I forgot my binoculars, Maile," Wade cut in. "Would you be a good girl and fetch them for me? I think I left them in the library."

Maile's eyes sparkled; without a word she went skipping off, her long braids bouncing down her back.

Wade waited until Maile was out of earshot before he spoke to Lani. He was dressed for sailing, and his faded denim shirt and trousers emphasized his strong, muscular body and brought out the grey in his deep-set eyes. At the moment those eyes were as cold as steel, and Lani wished that she too had some excuse to go skipping off with Maile.

"You had explicit orders not to encourage Maile's obsession with the supernatural, Miss Brock," Wade said, his voice reflecting the chill in his eyes. "She already suffers from nightmares because of the tales she's heard from the Kealoha family. When her aunt found out what was causing Maile's nightmares, she forbade her to visit Kawena Kealoha, a decision I had to go along with, much as I respect the old woman. When I told you to be careful what you said to Maile, it wasn't some whim. I can't understand why you've deliberately disobeyed me."

As Lani met the censure in his eyes, she felt a warning flash of heat to her head. Although she seldom showed anger openly, she had a very healthy temper, and right now she was boiling-over mad.

"And you jump to conclusions much too fast," she said. "Yes, I've been telling Maile about the Roms, in return for her promise that she'll do her exercises every day. But I've tried not to romanticize them. Maile knows that the Roms sometimes lie and cheat and steal, that they're a small ethnic group fighting for survival against larger, more powerful cultures. But I haven't tried to justify what they do. I've been careful to point out that there is nothing magical about Gypsy fortune-telling."

Wade tried to speak, but she wasn't finished yet. "What's more, I think your worry is misplaced, Mr. MacMasters. If Maile is curious about the Roms, it's because there's so little in this cotton-wool world here to feed that busy mind of hers. Even in the short time I've been here, it's obvious to me that she has a very poor self-image. She's been told that she's difficult and spoiled and wicked so often that it's no wonder she eavesdrops and—and does other things she shouldn't. You're concerned because you're afraid Maile will develop a morbid interest in the Gypsies. What you *should* worry about is why Maile is so fascinated by them. Maybe Kawena shouldn't have told her about the Night Marchers and the curse, but Maile could learn other things about her own Hawaiian heritage from Kawena. She's starved for something to stimulate that active curiosity of hers. If you're so worried about her, why don't you spend more time with her? Or, if that's impossible, why not send her away to school where she'd at least have to deal with other kids her own age—"

Wade made an angry chopping gesture with his hand, and she broke off, aware that she had gone too far. But by now her pride was involved, and she gave Wade back stare for stare, then had the doubtful satisfaction of seeing him turn away and stalk off without another word.

Her anger had evaporated by the time he was out of sight,

leaving her feeling deflated and strangely disappointed that he hadn't stayed to argue with her. As she gathered up her scarf and prepared to follow him, she told herself that at least he hadn't fired her, but she had an uncomfortable feeling that she hadn't heard the last about her outburst.

Later that afternoon she was typing a letter when she heard a throbbing, whirring sound overhead. She went to the window just in time to see a small helicopter dropping down behind the tennis courts.

A few minutes later she heard women's voices outside her window, and although she went on typing, she knew her short respite was over, that her aunt and the girl who called herself Iolani Stevenson had returned to Maunaloa Island.

X

KNIGHT OF SWORDS

Lani's first meeting with her aunt took place later that afternoon. She was alone in the office, typing a letter to Mrs. Costello, when Berta St. John, looking cool and immaculate in a beige silk shantung suit, came into the office without knocking. Lani's skin prickled as she met her aunt's eyes. They were the same icy blue she remembered, and there was a thinly veiled hostility in them even though her aunt produced a frosty smile.

"Good day," Berta said crisply. "I'm Berta St. John, Miss Stevenson's aunt."

"I'm Yula Brock. Is there something I can do for you, Miss St. John?" Lani asked, proud of the evenness of her voice.

116

"Yes, indeed. We're having a luau to celebrate my niece's twenty-first birthday next week, and I'll need your help the next few days. I've drawn up a guest list, but I still have to coordinate it with Iolani and Mr. MacMasters. I'll need two copies—no, best make it three. As soon as the list is firm, you can start right in on the invitations. You'll find them on the desk in my room."

She paused to make a small moue. "So trite, really, having a luau. I was planning a formal affair, but Wade insists on the traditional coming-of-age luau. It's annoying, but— Oh, and I'll need a copy of my niece's schedule for the next week. I like to coordinate my own appointments with hers as much as possible because of the wretched transportation problem here." Her eyes surveyed Lani before she added, "In the future, you'd better check with me in the morning when I give Moana her orders for the day."

Although there had been no mention that her duties included taking orders from Berta St. John, Lani told herself that the last thing she wanted to do was to antagonize her aunt. So she made a mental note to clear it with Wade and gave her aunt a polite smile.

Berta dropped an appointment calendar and a handwritten list of names on the desk beside Lani's typewriter. "I'm really quite annoyed with Moana," she said smoothly. "She knows very well that Mr. MacMasters's typists always stay in one of the guest cottages. Sometimes I wonder if the stupidity of these people isn't assumed to save themselves work. It's that atrocious pidgin—even after all this time, Moana has yet to properly cook the meals I plan. She can't understand the most simple instructions. I told her very plainly when I called her from the mainland yesterday that I wanted you assigned to one of the guest cottages."

Before Lani could tell Berta that Moana had been following Wade's orders, her aunt had turned away and was gone. Although Lani finished her letter and began making a copy of Vivian's social calendar for the next week, she found it hard to concentrate. Her aunt had given no sign that she recognized her, but why had she been so incensed because

Lani had been assigned a room near Maile? And should she take the sting out of that anger by quietly moving her belongings to a guest cottage on her own?

In the end, she decided to wait until Wade told her to move, and it was with some inner qualms that she got ready for dinner that evening. Although this was the opportunity she had been waiting for, a chance to see Maile and her aunt together, she couldn't seem to shake off her jitters as she showered and then tried to decide what to wear.

After a couple of false starts, she chose the long skirt she'd worn her first evening on the island and an embroidered blouse that had been a last-minute gift from her landlady before she left San Francisco. The blouse wasn't new—it had been in the wardrobe of the society matron Mrs. Costello had served so many years—but it bore a famous Paris label, and its soft green-on-green embroidery set off Lani's eyes.

As she started down the stairs, uncomfortably aware of the décolleté of her neckline and the embroidery that called attention to it, she tried to convince herself that she wouldn't look out of place at the dinner table, no matter how formal it was. When she rounded the curve in the staircase, she looked down and saw Vivian and her aunt, talking together under the hall's ornate Waterford chandelier.

Lani had known, from her glimpses of Vivian at the charity ball, that the impostor was beautiful; she realized now that a better word would have been exquisite. In the dancing light of the crystal chandelier, Vivian's hair glowed like molten silver. Her face was a perfect oval, and her features were small, as clearly cut—and as cold?—as the carvings on an expensive cameo. She was wearing white, a long supple gown that hugged her slim hips and small, high breasts, and she made Lani, in her thirdhand blouse, feel both dowdy and overdressed at the same time.

Lani was almost to the bottom of the stairs before Berta looked up and spotted her. She examined Lani from head to foot, and a look of annoyance flickered across her face.

"Yes? Did you want to speak to me, Miss—uh, Brooks? We're just about to sit down to dinner. Can't it wait until morning?"

It was well done, a carefully calculated put-down, but instead of destroying Lani's poise, it had the opposite effect. Lani's back stiffened, and her mind moved swiftly as she continued down the stairs. She had to say something . . . or did she? No matter what she said, it was bound to sound gauche. On the other hand, if she said nothing, her aunt was the one at a disadvantage.

Silently, as if she hadn't heard Berta, she joined the two women. Her chin slightly elevated, she met her aunt's frown with a cool smile.

Before Berta could speak, Jason's drawl came from the door. "So there you are, Yula," he said. "I was wondering if you'd lost your way in that maze upstairs. There's a family legend, you know, that a guest almost starved to death once before someone found him wandering around the attics."

His words were pure nonsense, not up to Jason's usual lively wit, but Lani was grateful, knowing they were intended as a diversion. As Jason went on talking, embellishing his tale, anger replaced the chill in Berta's eyes—but now it was directed at Jason.

A few minutes later Wade joined them, looking cool and handsome in a Philippine piñacloth shirt. Although his eyes lingered on Lani, he didn't speak to her, and she knew he hadn't forgotten their encounter in the hau arbor. Since she had too much pride to look away first, she returned his stare and saw a muscle tighten in his jawline before he turned to Vivian with a question about her shopping trip to the Coast.

Jason leaned closer to Lani and murmured in her ear: "Glad to have you aboard. These dinners with Berta St. John are so grim, a feller needs a friend—and a bicarb—to get through one."

Lani smiled at him. "Thank you for the diversion," she said.

"Always glad to be of help," he said lazily. "Not that you needed it. You were doing okay on your own."

A young, plump-faced Hawaiian woman opened the wide dining room doors. Lani eyed her with interest, knowing she must be Lehua, David's wife, who had returned from the Big Island that afternoon. The woman seemed curious about Lani, too, but when Lani smiled at her, she quickly looked away. Jason offered Lani his arm, leaving Wade to escort the other two women to the table. She had no illusions about Jason's attention. She suspected that he enjoyed baiting Berta—or was he using her as an instrument to make Vivian jealous?

She had expected, once Berta had returned, that dinner would be more elaborate, so she wasn't surprised to see the dining room table set for a formal meal. The menu, she discovered, had also changed—but not for the better. Gone were the savory Island foods; in their place was the dull, unimaginative fare she remembered from her Boston years. As she chewed on a piece of overdone beef and contemplated an underdone carrot, she remembered the food of the past two days with nostalgia.

Conversation at the dinner table was general and almost totally impersonal. They could have been any group of well-dressed strangers sharing a meal at a stuffy dinner party, politely discussing the weather, a local political scandal, the spiraling cost of living. Lani ate mechanically, careful to avoid Jason's eyes so she wouldn't be drawn into conversation. To her relief, Berta ignored her completely; and Vivian, after a thorough evaluation of Lani's clothes, lost interest and turned her attention to the two men, dividing her sultry glances and her small, catlike smiles equally between them.

Maile, who had joined them at the last moment, was also uncommonly quiet. Gone was her animation of the afternoon; although she seemed completely absorbed in her meal, Lani noticed that again very little of it actually reached her mouth. Even before dessert was served, she asked Wade's permission to go to her room and slipped away as silently as she had come.

Lani pushed a piece of limp lettuce to the side of her salad plate with her fork, wishing she could escape as easily. Berta's voice, butter-smooth, recalled her to her surroundings.

"I understand you'll be supervising my niece's physical therapy in the future, Miss—is it Brook or Brooks?"

"It's Brock," Lani said.

"Oh, yes . . . I've been trying to place your accent, Miss Brock. It's very slight, but—is it Southern?"

"My parents were Southerners, but I've been living in San Francisco since their deaths."

One of Berta's eyebrows rose slightly. "So you've been on your own in San Francisco. You must have had some very interesting—adventures, Miss Brock."

Vivian laughed, a thin tinkle of sound, triggering off Lani's temper again, but she controlled it and said pleasantly, "Yes, I have, and I've had some of them since I've come to the Islands, Miss St. John."

"Touché," Jason said, not quite under his breath.

Berta's eyes narrowed, but she ignored him and said: "My niece is an overly imaginative child with a morbid interest in the supernatural. I hope you've had the proper training to deal with her." She paused, and her eyes moved to Lehua Kealoha, who was refilling Vivian's wineglass. "I was horrified when I discovered that one of the local women was filling the child's head with wild stories about curses and ghost marchers and those wretched *heiau* stones—"

"Better cool it, Berta," Jason said lazily. "I wouldn't get Kawena stirred up if I were you. Half the Hawaiians on Oahu believe she's a *kahuna anaana*—that's a very special type of wizard, Yula—and she just might put a curse on you."

"Rubbish!" There were two spots of color high on Berta's cheekbones. "Kawena is a senile old woman. Her involvement in that radical Ohana movement is proof of that. The old fool! Imagine camping out with a bunch of young ruffians, trying to take over a Navy bombing range, at her age. Another escapade like that, and the Stevensons will be the talk of the Islands."

"They've never needed any outside help along those lines," Wade said, his voice dry.

Jason gave his cousin a startled look; when he threw back

his head in an irrepressible laugh, Berta's lips crimped into a fluted line.

"You won't think it's so funny when the Ohana movement decides to occupy Maunaloa the way they did Kahoolawe Island," she said furiously. "When those hooligans are camped on that beach out front with their bonfires and their noise and their pop-top cans—"

"—I'll be long gone," Jason said cheerfully. "But I admit it might get a little sticky for the rest of you."

Oddly, it was Wade who looked annoyed. "That's your style, isn't it, Jason? At the least sign of inconvenience, off you go on another assignment. It must be gratifying to have a job that sends you all over the world, snapping pictures of other people's misery, never getting involved."

"Hear, hear!" There was a wicked gleam in Jason's eyes. "You do know how to go for the jugular, cousin. You may be right about my low boredom threshold. I know I'd go out of my bird adding up columns of figures for a living. On the other hand, it could be I move around so much because I've never found the right girl at the right time and place. If I did, I might turn out to be as stuffy as—as the average man. Or maybe I'll get really lucky someday and find a girl who'll go adventuring with me, and then I'll have the best of two worlds."

"She'd better be self-supporting," Wade said, his tone short.

Jason's eyes narrowed. "Or be a rich heiress?" he drawled.

The tension in the room was almost palpable as the two men locked stares. Lani discovered that her mouth was so dry she knew it would be impossible to swallow another bite of food. She rose, murmuring something about wanting to finish some typing for Miss St. John before she went to bed. Although she didn't look directly at anyone, she carried away an impression of Wade's brooding stare as she hurried from the room.

It was such a relief to be out of the tension-charged room that she felt almost giddy when she was standing in the front hall again. Since the idea of returning to her typewriter didn't appeal to her, she decided on a walk instead. Careful to shut the door behind her to keep out night-flying insects, she slipped out into a world of silver-grey moonlight. The wind was soft, tinged with the fragrance of pikake, and the concourse was a broad white ribbon pointing the way to the beach.

She told herself it was good to be alone—and certainly safe enough here on this small, reef-protected island in the middle of the Pacific. A gust of wind caught up the ends of her hair and swirled them around her head. She shivered and hugged her arms, wishing she had brought along a sweater, but she went on, following the concourse to the steps and then to the beach. Under her sandals the sand was yielding, pumice-soft, as she followed the seawall, enjoying the sting of the wind against her flushed cheeks. But when she came in sight of the lagoon, she turned and retraced her steps, not yet ready to face the Folly, especially not by moonlight.

Her mind wandered back to the scene at the dining room table—if such a civilized disagreement could be called a scene. She had witnessed so many real fights, even the spilling of blood, during her years with the carnival; why had she been so disturbed tonight? Was it this place, this island with its past of violence and tragedy; or was it because there had been so many undercurrents hidden beneath all that polite chatter, those careful smiles?

Coral crunched under Lani's sandals, and she realized that while she'd been lost in thought, her feet had brought her to the hau arbor. In the flood of moonlight, the untrimmed hau branch that hung over the entrance to the arbor looked like a groping tentacle, and she was careful to avoid it as she ducked inside.

She found a bench that faced the entrance, curled up with her legs under her, and thought about her own disagreement with Wade. It had been a mistake to lose her temper, even though his criticism had been unfair. To accuse Wade of neglecting his niece had been presumptuous, especially since her job depended on his good will. She already was aware that he hadn't forgotten her outburst. Several times during dinner she had looked up to find him watching her. From the intentness of his stare, she suspected he was still smarting over her words. . . .

There was nothing to warn her, no crunch of shoes on the coral path, no thud of footsteps on the sand. When the light was blotted out, she was so startled that she could only gape at the tall, lean figure outlined by moonlight in the arched entrance of the arbor.

"Jason?" she asked thinly. "Is that you, Jason?"

"Who the hell's Jason?"

It was Kore's voice, so unexpected in this place that it was a moment before her mind would accept it. Then she was off the bench and flying toward him. She flung herself into his arms, and when they tightened around her, she realized how much she'd missed him these last four years.

"Well, that was some kind of welcome," Kore said. "Maybe I should stay away more often."

She laughed, her first uninhibited laugh in several days. "Don't you dare! Now that I've found you, I'm not about to let my big brother disappear again."

Kore stiffened and his arms dropped away from her. "I'm not your brother," he growled. "And I think it's time we had this out—"

"What are you doing here, Kore?" she interrupted hurriedly. "I thought you were in San Francisco. And how did you get on the island?"

"What I'm doing here is checking up on you. And I've been in Honolulu since this morning. As to how I got on the island, I found a local fisherman who knows how to navigate those reefs out there. He's waiting for me at the end of the wharf, and he's one scared kanaka. It seems this island of yours has a very bad reputation, and most of the locals won't come near it after dark."

"But how did you know I'd be in the hau arbor?"

"I spotted you walking along the beach. I didn't dare yell at you, so I followed you here."

"Why didn't you come during the day? I have a right to

see my brother—" She broke off, suddenly uncomfortable. "No, that wouldn't do. I told my employer when he hired me that I was an only child. But you could have talked to me on the radio."

"And how the devil was I supposed to do that? I couldn't get anywhere with the marine operator. She wouldn't even admit there was such a place as Maunaloa Island."

"It's unlisted; someone at Wade's office patches the calls through their phone," Lani explained. "I'll give you the number before you leave."

"I hope there won't be any need for that. I want you off this crazy island before something happens to you. Have there been any more of those so-called accidents?"

"Not so-called—they really were accidents." She plunged into an abbreviated account of the hit-and-run incident, her experience in the alley. From there, she went on to tell Kore what she'd found out since she'd come to Maunaloa Island. It was surprising, she thought when she was finished, how little that had been.

Kore must have thought so too, because he said: "You're wasting your time, Lani. From what you say, your kid sister may be spoiled rotten, but no one is mistreating her. Come back with me tonight. You can send for your things in the morning. We have some unfinished business to settle, you know."

"Unfinished business?"

"Yeah—this!" He moved so swiftly that he caught her unaware. He kissed her, and as she felt the warm pressure of his lips, she relaxed against him, lulled by his gentleness. Then his arms tightened around her, and now there was nothing gentle or brotherly about the kiss. She felt panic, and then a rush of warmth that confused and frightened her. She knew she should pull away, say something light and teasing, but she seemed unable to move, and it was Kore who finally released her.

"Marry me, Lani." His voice, usually so smooth, was husky. "You've had plenty of time to get used to the idea now. You must know the two of us are a natural together."

125

It would have been so easy to say yes, to let his lips, his arms shut out the world. So easy to go away with him, to put Maunaloa and the past behind her for good, to build a new life with Kore as her anchor. . . . She sighed deeply, and as if the sigh had released her from a pleasant dream, the temptation was gone. *Not yet*, she thought. *Not until I've finished the job I came here to do.*

Although she hadn't spoken, Kore seemed to sense her rejection. He turned away, lit a cigarette and drew on it slowly. And because the tiny point of light wavered slightly, she knew that his hands, those wonderfully clever hands that could subdue an unruly show horse as easily as they could repair the complicated machinery of a Ferris wheel, weren't quite steady at the moment.

"Who is he?" His voice was like gravel rubbing together. "Is it that MacMasters guy—or the one you call Jason?"

"There's no one else, Kore. I'm just a piece of office equipment to Wade, and Jason isn't serious about anything, much less a woman. I do care for you, Kore, but . . . there's something I have to tell you. Just before Pearsa died, she made me promise that I'd never marry you. That's why I ran away. I was afraid that if I stayed, I'd break my promise. I—I can't go back on my word, not to Pearsa. Forgive me if I misled you just now, but I was so happy to see you that I—I forgot for a moment."

She stopped, waiting for his answer and hoping for his understanding. When he was silent, she put out her hand to touch his arm. Under her fingers his muscles were rigid, bunched, and when he moved away slightly, she knew that she'd hurt his pride again.

He finished his cigarette and ground it out under his foot. "Okay, kid, you're calling the shots," he said. "I think you're wrong, but we'll try it your way—for now."

Lani let out a silent sigh of relief—or was it relief? She had won, so why did she feel so unsettled, so dissatisfied? "When are you returning to San Francisco?" she asked.

"When you're ready to go back with me. You don't think I'd leave you here alone, do you? I haven't forgotten what that bitchy aunt of yours did to you. If she ever figures out who you are, there's no telling what she'll do."

"I'm not afraid of my aunt," Lani said, not quite truthfully.

"Yeah. Well, maybe you should be."

He lit another cigarette, and she told him, "You smoke too much, Kore."

"I also gamble and take a few drinks when I'm in the mood, and sometimes I sleep with women. I didn't say I'd turned into an angel just because I decided it was a bum's game, working cheap scams and maybe ending up in a jail cell for the rest of my life."

He moved to the entrance and stood there with his back to her, staring out into the moon-drenched night. "What I'd like to know is how they pulled this con off. Those big-time lawyers are shrewd. They'd need more than your aunt's word that the girl was you. Maybe she got to one of the lawyers—or to this MacMasters character."

"There *is* a man involved," Lani said reluctantly. "When I overheard my aunt at the charity ball, she mentioned a man, and I think it's someone she's afraid of. It could be Wade, only—" She hesitated, not sure how to explain that Wade didn't fit the role of conspirator.

"Only what?"

"Well, he must draw a big income from the estate," she said lamely. "Surely he doesn't need to steal."

"Every man has his price, and he'd be in a position to set this thing up. There must have been something more than your aunt's identification of the girl—"

"Oh, I know something about that," she said. Briefly she told him about the hairbrush with Vivian's fingerprints on it, the letter in Vivian's handwriting, supposedly written to her father when she was a child.

Kore whistled softly when she was finished. "That's a pretty solid scam."

Lani smiled at the approval in his voice. "And I thought you were a reformed character," she teased.

"I am, but I can still recognize a good scam when I see one."

"They did seem to think of everything," Lani said ruefully.

"Everything but the possibility that you might turn up alive."

Lani felt cold suddenly, aware of the dampness in the air. She rubbed her upper arms and said, "They had a couple of lucky breaks, of course. Kawena's blindness, for one. And the girl they used fits my general description and has a background that could stand an investigation. I'm sure Vivian—"

"Vivian?" he repeated sharply.

"That's the impostor's name. I'm sure there's some legitimate doubt about who she really is. Those things they could hardly fake. Whenever she makes a slip, she can blame it on her amnesia. Without that, it would be almost impossible to fool the Kealohas."

"Do you think they suspect anything? Would they stick out their necks to help you if you decided to step forward and blow this thing wide open?"

"Who would believe them? They have their own axes to grind. After all, they have good reason for wanting Aunt Berta discredited. And anyway, I don't intend to claim the estate, Kore. I meant it when I said I'd never take anything from my father."

"You've never forgiven your old man for dumping you with your aunt, even now that he's dead?"

"It isn't a matter of forgiving him for that. I have my own reasons for feeling the way I do. Vivian and my aunt can have my half of his money as long as they don't try to take Maile's too. I have to be sure she'll be safe."

"Safe? You think the kid's in some kind of danger?"

"That's one of the things I intend to find out before I leave here. She's had a couple of odd accidents—"

"What kind of accidents?"

"For one thing, she ate some akia berries—they're very toxic and could have killed her. I asked Moana Kealoha about the incident, and she told me that Maile insists the only berries she ate that day were in the fruit salad she had for lunch. Moana—and everyone else—is convinced Maile picked the berries from a specimen plant in the greenhouse. But suppose Maile is telling the truth? That would mean someone tried to kill her."

"And the other accident?"

"She fell and broke her leg when the railing on the balcony outside her room gave way."

"Kids do have accidents, and they eat things they aren't supposed to and then lie about it later."

"Maybe, but she's scared to death, Kore. She locks her bedroom door at night, and she won't sleep in a dark room."

"Neither would you when you first came to live with us," he reminded her.

"That's because Aunt Berta used to leave me locked up in her closet for hours, sometimes overnight. What reason does Maile have to be afraid of the dark?"

"Look, if you're all that worried about the kid, why don't you go to your old man's lawyers, tell them who you are and kick your aunt off the island?"

"Why would they believe me? Any investigation into my background would only show that—"

"—that you're a dirty, thieving Gypsy. And my word wouldn't help much, would it? They'd figure it for just another Gypsy hustle."

"Pearsa did too good a job, establishing me as your sister," Lani said. "But it will never come to that. As soon as I'm sure Maile is in no danger, I'll leave."

"And I can't change your mind about leaving tonight?"

"No. I have to be sure, you see."

"Okay, but I'd feel a hell of a lot better if you weren't alone here. If I could think of a way—" He snapped his fingers suddenly. "This Vivian—what kind of chick is she, anyway? Does she like men?"

"I wouldn't be surprised," Lani answered dryly. "She certainly doesn't have any interest in women."

"A barracuda, huh? Well, maybe I can get something going with her and con her into inviting me to the island. You need someone here you can depend on, just in case things get sticky."

"You want me to introduce you to Vivian? But that's—"

"Just tell me some of the places she'll be the next couple of days, and I'll take care of the rest."

"That might not be so easy, Kore. Vivian is—well, I suspect she's sort of a snob."

"She's a chick, isn't she?" There was an unconscious arrogance in Kore's voice, a supreme confidence in his power over women—and with good cause, Lani thought, remembering his devastating effect on them. But Vivian wasn't one of his carnival girls. It might not be so easy to charm her into an invitation—or even into conversation.

But she kept her reservations to herself and told Kore several places where Vivian would be during the next couple of days: a fashion show at the Royal Hawaiian Hotel, a dinner dance at the posh Honolulu Yacht Club, a tennis exhibition at the University of Hawaii.

When she was finished, Kore bent to kiss her—a brief impersonal kiss this time—and was gone as silently as he had come.

For a long time after he left, Lani sat in the darkness of the hau arbor. For better or worse, Kore had come back into her life. She was glad to have an ally, but had she any right to let him get involved in her affairs? Had he really accepted her decision not to marry him, or was he just biding his time? Knowing so well how tenacious Kore could be, she found it hard to believe he would give up so easily . . . or had finding out that Pearsa had been opposed to their marriage made the difference?

If Pearsa had died without regaining consciousness, she surely would have married Kore; shared his life, his bed; had his children. At one time all she had wanted from life was Kore, but she had been a different girl then, terrified of being alone, willing to conform to the demands of those she loved because she had so desperately needed their support. It was this girl whom Kore had proposed to; would he ever be comfortable with a girl who had learned to direct her own life, deal with her own problems? Kore had seemed uneasy with her tonight. Had he begun to realize that she was no longer the girl he remembered, the one who had been so grateful for any crumb of attention from him?

Somewhere close at hand a motorboat throbbed into life, and she thought what a lonely sound it was, maybe because it meant she was alone again on this island, surrounded by strangers. Even the ones who weren't strangers, she reflected painfully, were no comfort to her, since they thought of her as an outsider, too.

She rose and returned to the house, slipping through a side door because she was in no mood to talk with anyone. A few minutes later, as she was putting away her clothes in the armoire, the sight of her suitcase reminded her that, once again, she had forgotten to tell Kore that his mother's *sumadjii* was safe—and his for the asking.

She fell asleep with the light still on, the book she had been reading lying open on her chest, and she dreamed that she was back in Boston, hiding in the fusty dark of the drainage pipe; that Kore, miraculously reverted to a dark-eyed boy of fourteen, was offering her sanctuary—but only if she came immediately. In her dream she reached out longingly for his hand, only to see his face dissolve into blackness, and she was filled with grief, knowing she had waited too long. Then the darkness before her began to glow. She screamed in terror as the patch of light formed into a skull, the grinning skull from the tarot card of death. . . .

She awoke, her skin bathed in cold sweat, and it was a long time before she finally fell asleep again.

XI

Breakfast at Maunaloa House remained informal even after Berta St. John's return. At eight Moana and her daughter-in-law Lehua set out coffee, fruit, cereal, and an assortment of hot dishes on warming trays on the lanai serving table. The family and guests wandered in as they pleased, served themselves and ate at small rattan tables on the lanai.

Lani, hoping to avoid her aunt and Vivian, came down early and dropped half an English muffin into the toaster that was provided. She was sorry now that she hadn't rapped on Maile's door. It would have been a good time to talk to Maile alone without the strain of those enforced therapy exercises between them. She made a mental note to arrange things differently in the future as she buttered her muffin, poured herself a cup of coffee, helped herself to a piece of papaya, and carried her food to a sunny table nearby.

She chose a chair that faced away from the house, and then forgot to eat as she took in the familiar scene. The garden ran riot with island flowers—heliconia, bird-of-paradise, torch and shell ginger. Behind the trees that bordered the garden the cliffs rose, rosy-grey in the morning light. A mist still lingered in the crevices of the bluffs, adding a purple tinge to their usual greyness. A path protected by a waist-high railing zigzagged up the side of the cliff, starting at the rear of the tennis courts. It led through the island's deep central valley and ended at the old deserted village where the ancestors of the Kealoha family had once reigned supreme.

Although it had been years since Lani had been there, she was sure she could find her way along the path in the dark. Engraved on her mind was every turn in the path: the tiny artesian-fed brook it crossed and recrossed; the banana tree thickets; the groves of paper mulberry, pandanus, ironwood and kukui trees; the lush, thick undergrowth of ferns and honeycreepers.

There was something mysterious, something dark and secret, about the valley, which the Hawaiians had called *Po*, believing it to be the habitat of the Night Marchers. She had felt it even as a child, and she wondered if she'd get a chance before she left the island to renew her acquaintance with the valley.

"If that's your usual breakfast," Jason said at her elbow, "it's no wonder you're so slender."

"Sometimes I skip breakfast altogether," she confessed, smiling at him. "It's a terrible habit I fell into while I was working for a free clinic in San Francisco. We worked such long hours that a few more minutes' sleep was worth missing breakfast over."

"Well, you won't be overworked here," he told her. "Wade only needs a part-time typist. Usually, he brings over someone from his office. What he should do is train one of Kawena's teen-aged nieces to help him out when he needs it. It would keep them out of mischief on weekends and during vacations and give them spending money, too."

"Why doesn't he, I wonder?" Lani said. "Is he—" She paused, not sure she wanted to finish the question.

"Is he prejudiced against the Kealohas? No way. He's *hapa-haole* himself, and damned proud of it."

"Wade is part Hawaiian? But he doesn't—" She stopped, trying to grasp this new concept of Wade.

"He doesn't look Hawaiian? Actually, he's only—oh, about an eighth, I think it is. His father was a foreman at Halelaulea, the Stevensons' ranch on the Big Island. John Stevenson took a shine to Wade, sent him to Punahou and then to Stanford Business School, and trained him to take over the management of the ranch. He did so well at it that eventually John moved him to his Honolulu offices."

"Wade must have been very loyal to John Stevenson," Lani said.

"I would say so. Of course, Wade is an enigma to me, and always has been."

"But you're cousins. Surely you've known him all his life?"

"Not really. I lived on the mainland, in Pasadena. I spent part of several summers at Halelaulea, and our families had an occasional reunion, of course." He sat down opposite her and added sugar to his coffee. "Wade's family were the poor relatives. My mother, who is a bit of a snob, always thought her sister had married beneath her. My father was a successful lawyer, you see, and Wade's dad was a cowboy who worked with his hands. Now I'm the working stiff, and Wade controls a multimillion-dollar business."

"That isn't the same as owning it."

"If he marries our Cinderella girl, you can bet it will be the same," he said.

Lani weighed the dryness in his voice. She had assumed that Wade's attentions to Vivian were the normal male response to a seductive woman; was Jason hinting that it was something more cold-blooded? For a moment she almost felt pity for the impostor. No matter whom she married, unless he was a wealthy man, she could never really be sure it wasn't the Stevenson money that was the real attraction.

Jason dropped a plate of scrambled eggs and ham on the table and began eating in a quick, businesslike way. In the sun, his hair was more red than rusty, and his eyelashes were tipped with gold.

"How about posing for me in the hau arbor this morning before the sun gets too high?" he asked, around a mouthful of toast. "I'm going to the Big Island in the morning to do a photo-essay on a balloon meet, but I have today free. Maybe Moana would put us together a picnic lunch and—"

"Forget it," Wade said from the doorway. "Miss Brock has enough work to keep her busy in the office all morning."

"Then I'll have to settle for this afternoon, won't I?" Jason said. "The light's not quite what I want, but I can rig up something."

Lani was sure Wade would refuse, but he gave in with a shrug. "If Miss Brock wants to use her free time, I have no objections."

"Come off it, Wade," Jason said softly. "You don't call any of your other employees by their last names. Why don't you face up to this hang-up of yours? Calling her Miss Brock isn't going to make Yula look any less like that wife of yours."

Lani was immobilized by an agonizing embarrassment as she watched the pupils of Wade's eyes contract. From their first meeting, she had sensed that he had a volatile temper. She braced herself for an explosion, sure that Jason had gone too far.

"Don't get any ideas about punching me out, big cousin." There was an edge in Jason's voice. "You may have a good thirty pounds on me, but if I have to, I can give a pretty good account of myself." He looked down into Lani's frozen face, and his eyes softened. "Sorry, Yula. This hasn't really got anything to do with you. Call it a residual hostility from our youth. We got rammed down each other's throats so much as kids, I guess it left a few scars."

He crammed the last bite of egg into his mouth, finished his coffee in one gulp and got up. With a jaunty salute for Lani, he loped off.

Lani kept her eyes fixed on her plate. When Wade remained silent, she risked a look at him. To her surprise he was smiling.

"He's right, you know," Wade said. "I had to scramble for good grades, while Jason held a 4-cum average and never seemed to open a book. My father never got past the fourth grade, so he had a thing for education. Every time Jason won another honor, I knew Dad was wondering why the hell I couldn't do it, too."

"Jason said both of you felt that way. Why does he resent you?"

"I was into sports pretty heavy. Jason's old man had been

a jock while he was at Stanford, so he expected Jason to be the same, only Jason was more interested in photography and writing. I guess he threw my record into Jason's face. We got thoroughly sick of each other as kids and fought like a couple of wild dogs when we were together. Unfortunately, we still like to needle each other."

"If you'd rather I didn't pose for him—"

"Do what you prefer. I suspect Jason would talk you into it anyway. He has a way of—of steamrolling things his way." He gave her a long look. "Maybe I should warn you about my cousin. A girl who took him seriously just might get hurt."

Lani fought back a laugh. Each man had warned her against the charms of the other—did they both think she was some silly schoolgirl, vulnerable to the first man who smiled at her?

There was a flash of blue at the lanai doors and Vivian, looking confident of her welcome, advanced on them. She was dressed in pale blue lounging pajamas, and her skin, only faintly touched by a tan, looked like fine porcelain in the morning sun. She acknowledged Lani's presence with a nod before she turned a radiant smile on Wade. Lani, feeling like an intruder, finished her coffee and excused herself.

Wade's office was located in one corner of the main house, a large room that overlooked the gardens and had once been a ladies' sitting room. Lani finished the last of the luau invitations in short order and looked around for something else to do. A file cabinet she hadn't explored yet caught her eye. When she opened it and read the labels on the folders, she saw that it held household bills. Unable to resist, she found the folder labeled *Iolani Stevenson*. It was packed full of bills, all of them recent, and she winced slightly as she thumbed through them. Why would anyone, much less someone who lived in Hawaii, need three mink coats? Or a dinner gown that cost five thousand dollars? And each bill had been countersigned by Wade; did this mean he was so smitten with Vivian that he was unable to refuse her any extravagance? Or was this a bribe to keep one of his accomplices from getting bored with life on Maunaloa Island?

She heard Wade coming and quickly closed the file, but her thoughts returned to it often during the remainder of the morning.

Maile didn't appear for lunch, so Lani was a little surprised when she turned up, dressed sensibly in a leotard and tights, for her therapy. As they did the exercises, Maile chatted away cheerfully, telling Lani about a book she had been reading. Afterward, as they waited for Moana, Maile plied her with so many questions that Lani knew it was her storytelling skill rather than any desire to be friends that had motivated Maile's cooperation.

She drew upon her memory of a Rom wedding she had once attended and began to describe the lively dances, the plaintive songs, the wedding ceremony, so ancient that no man knew for sure from which culture it had originally been borrowed. Maile was particularly fascinated by her description of the wedding feast, that lavish display of food that no self-respecting father of the bride would ever try to skimp on. If she wondered how Lani, with her secondhand knowledge of the Roms, knew so many details of their customs, she said nothing, but after Moana appeared to give them a hula lesson, Lani felt uneasy, aware of how much she had told Maile about her life with Pearsa and Kore.

Moana took Maile with her when she left, promising her a treat from her kitchen, but Lani sat on, waiting for Jason. He appeared in a few minutes laden with photographic material, and he was all business as he told Lani to change into something more photogenic than her T-shirt and jeans.

"And do something about your hair—it looks like hell up in that tacky washerwoman's knot," he called after her.

Lani, more amused than annoyed, went to change into a summer dress. When she came downstairs, he was waiting for her in the hall. His scrutiny was so thorough that she was glad she had taken the time to brush out her hair and add a touch of makeup. They chatted easily as they walked through the trees toward the lagoon, following the white coral path, and it wasn't until he remarked that the Folly should be getting the afternoon sun by now that she realized where he was taking her.

Her feet faltered and she stopped. "I—I feel a little sick," she said.

Jason studied her. "It came on awfully sudden. You wouldn't be camera shy, would you?"

"No—yes, maybe I am."

"Well, not to worry. Uncle Jason has the cure for that." He seized her arm firmly. "It's a bit like stage fright—or falling in love. Once you get the hang of it, you can relax and enjoy yourself. Just wait until you see yourself in gorgeous color in a magazine spread."

His hand under her elbow, his banter, his assumption that her problem was camera shyness, made it possible for her to move forward again, down the path, past the bathhouse, over the tiny iron bridge that crossed Lono's Spring. When they came in view of the Folly, she took a deep breath and lifted her eyes.

The Folly sat on a natural stone platform to the left of the lagoon. Behind it a cindery cliff, half of which lay in rubble now, formed a starkly severe background for the structure. Built in Canton by Chinese artisans, it had been brought to the island by a clipper ship, and despite the cracks in its teakwood walls and the moss that covered the stone foo dogs that guarded its entrance, the Folly still retained much of its original beauty. It wasn't until they went inside that Lani realized the building hadn't been used for a long time.

Although the hand-carved frieze border on the ceiling and the teakwood doors, inlaid with mother-of-pearl, were still intact, the onyx tables and embroidered screens and scrolled chairs that had delighted her so as a child were gone, and the only furnishings that remained were several derelict wicker chairs. A trickle of memory, an ugly image that she thought she'd suppressed years ago, suddenly surfaced from some dark recess of her mind. Suddenly she couldn't bear to see any more. So she shut her eyes and listened to the liquid sounds of the spring outside, and she wondered if, after all this time, any ghosts still lingered in this place where her mother had died so violently.

"It's a shame to let this old place fall into ruin," Jason said. "Maile is the only one who ever comes here these days. After Carol was shot here, John couldn't stand the sight of the place."

Lani opened her eyes and focused them on Jason. "How did it happen? Was it an accident?" she asked.

"The family always claimed it was, but there was some mystery about the details—which is all pretty irrelevant now, except maybe to Iolani."

"Because it happened to her mother?"

"Because she was the one who found her mother's body. She was—oh, eight or nine, I'd guess. It was such a shock that she lost her voice for quite a while. The doctors convinced John that she would have a faster recovery if she left the island, so he sent her off to Boston to live with Berta."

"That's the only reason he sent her away?"

"So I understand."

"Didn't someone tell me that she—that Iolani lived with her aunt for four years? In all that time, she never spoke?"

Jason regarded her with thoughtful eyes. "Now that you point it out, it does seem rather strange. Well, it's all in the past now, isn't it?"

He went to raise a bamboo window shade, letting in the sun and releasing a shower of dust into the air of the room. In the slanted rays of the sun, dust motes swirled as he pulled up a high-backed wicker chair, setting it in a pool of light.

"For these first shots, I want the light to fall directly across your face, with the rest of you in shadow. Did you know that your eyes are the same color as the lagoon? I'll feature that later when I photograph you sitting on the sea-wall. . . ." He went on talking as he placed her hands in her lap and arranged her hair so that it tumbled artlessly around her face. It was impossible to feel self-conscious when his touch was so impersonal, but Lani was relieved when he finally stepped back to study her.

"Yes, that's exactly what I want," he said. "A smile

now—no, not that way. A real smile. Pretend I've just told you one of my corny jokes."

She gave him one of her best smiles, and he let out a low whistle. "Maybe it's best you don't do that more often. That kind of smile could get you anything you want from a man."

Lani stiffened. "I'm afraid that wouldn't appeal to me."

"No, somehow I didn't think it would," he said.

He returned to his camera, and while he worked, he kept up a running conversation that she suspected was part of his technique for keeping his models relaxed.

"Okay, hold it . . . that's fine, just what I want. A couple more of you smiling, and we're in business. Now, a pensive look . . . that's right, only lower your eyelashes a shade for this one and— That should do it. Okay, you can relax while I get it together here. I want to try a filter this time to see if I can bring out those green eyes."

Lani relaxed and turned her face away from the glare of the sun. The wicker chair was cool under her cheek and she yawned, feeling somnolent and at ease. Although she wasn't vain enough to believe Jason's compliments, there was something undeniably flattering about having the complete attention of an attractive man.

"Damn!" Jason's exclamation made her jump. "Sorry—I just discovered my filter case isn't in my equipment bag. I must have left it in the guest cottage. You wait here—take a nap or something—and I'll be back in a shake."

He was gone before she could answer him. Lani heard his footsteps crunching on the path, and then there was only the sound of the brook to break the silence.

She sat very still, trying not to notice the shadows in the corners. Even though she was sitting in a patch of sunlight, she felt chilled, as if a cold wind had started up in the room. She reminded herself that just a few minutes ago she had been congratulating herself for feeling so relaxed, but it didn't seem to help. The past was all around her again, and the sound of the spring, chuckling and murmuring like a gathering of people at a party, was no longer reassuring.

The feeling that she was being watched came on her so

slowly that at first she didn't recognize the reason for her uneasiness. Then she knew—every instinct told her—that she wasn't alone. She stared around wildly; although the room was empty, her certainty increased. Someone was here with her, if not in the Folly, then just outside, holding his—or her—breath, listening, just as she was listening. . . .

Then the whispering started up, a sibilant crooning sound that raised the small hairs on her arms and chilled her body just as surely as if she'd been doused with ice water.

"Crazy Lani . . . full of hate . . . killed her ma . . . when she was eight. . . ."

She wanted to scream at the voice to stop, wanted to get up from the chair and run from the room, but she couldn't move, couldn't even take a normal breath of air into her frozen lungs. She tried to bring reason to her panic, to find an explanation for the whispering voice. One thing she was sure of: it was no ghost from the past come to haunt her. The chant was the same hateful one the children in Boston had taunted her with—and that meant that someone very much alive was standing out there trying to terrorize her.

"Aunt Berta?" she whispered.

There was a mocking laugh, and the chanting started up again.

"Crazy Lani . . . full of hate . . . killed her ma . . . killed her ma . . . killed her ma . . ."

"Stop it!" she said loudly. She put her hands over her ears. "Go away—I won't listen to you. You're wasting your time, you hear?"

She stopped to listen, but there was only silence now. Had she convinced her tormentor that it was no use trying to frighten her? Or had she imagined the whole thing? Had it been a hallucination, brought on by the trauma of coming back to the place where her mother had met her death?

She sat on, huddled in the wicker chair, listening to the wind at the corners of the roof, to the murmur of Lono's Spring, and it was there Jason found her a few minutes later. He stopped in the door to stare at her, his forehead puckered into a frown.

"Is something wrong, Yula? You look like you've just seen a ghost."

His voice sounded so strange without its usual undercurrent of amusement that she stared at him without speaking; when he saw she didn't mean to answer, he ran his hand through his hair, setting it on end.

"Okay, it's none of my business, but if you ever feel the need to talk with someone, I'm willing to listen."

She stared into his eyes, those oddly colored eyes that gave away so little of the man inside, and she wanted desperately to confide in him, to enlist his aid. Then his mobile mouth curved into a smile, and Pearsa's words—*"The face of the second man is pleasing, but it is greed that drives him, that perverts him"*—echoed in her ears, and she knew she couldn't take the chance. Because it was all so coincidental. First the chanting—to frighten her into relaxing her guard?—and then the offer of help from a man she had just met a few days ago.

"I haven't the foggiest idea what you're talking about," she said.

"No good, huh? You just can't see me in the role of Father Confessor? Well, I can't blame you. But if you ever feel you need a friend, the offer is open-ended, Yula."

He waited a moment; when she didn't answer him, he shrugged and returned to his camera.

During the next half hour, he seemed to have put the incident out of his mind. He was an exacting taskmaster, taking infinite pains to get the effect he wanted, and by the time he finally began packing up his equipment, Lani was glad to call it a day.

As they walked down the path toward the lagoon, she turned and looked back, half expecting to see covert eyes watching her from the blank windows of the old structure, and she had a sudden feeling of unfinished business, a suspicion that the Folly wasn't yet done with her.

XII

She had almost finished dressing for dinner, this time in the neatly mended and freshly laundered dress she'd worn to the charity ball, when there was a rapping on the door.

Although her muscles tightened, she hesitated only a moment before she went to answer it. She had already decided that she would act as normally as possible. If the episode in the Folly hadn't been a hallucination, then it meant that someone here knew who she was and was trying to scare her away. She was determined he—or she?—wouldn't succeed. She would behave as if it had never happened, and if her nerves were a little on edge, no one was going to know, not if she could help it.

But she was relieved that it was Maile who was standing there when she opened the door. Dressed in a yellow satin Chinese jacket and black pants, she looked like a tiny Oriental doll. Her smile was so shy that Lani wondered how many doors she had knocked on lately where she hadn't been welcome.

"Are you going downstairs now?" Maile asked.

It was her first real overture, but Lani didn't make the mistake of overreacting. She nodded and went to slip her feet into sandals.

"You look nice in that dress," Maile said. "Vivian says Hawaiian prints are tacky, but I like them."

"And I like that Chinese jacket you're wearing," Lani said.

"The yellow brings out your hazel eyes."

"Do you really think so?" Maile sounded doubtful. "Uncle Jason bought it for me in Taiwan because he knows yellow is my favorite color, but Aunt Berta says it makes my skin look sallow. She told Uncle Jason she was sure there was a Chink somewhere in my background."

"And what did your uncle say?" Lani's voice was tight.

"He said he'd often wondered what was hidden in the woodpiles of some of those old Boston Beacon Hill families."

Lani laughed, then said, "Well, I doubt that you're part Chinese, but if you were, it wouldn't be anything to be ashamed of. The Chinese are a very old, very wise people—and very sensible about most things, just like the Hawaiians."

Maile wandered over to the mirror and looked into it soberly. "Do you think my skin is sallow?" she asked.

"It's like ivory—with a pink overlay. Your aunt must be color-blind if she doesn't see that you look lovely in yellow."

"She likes ugly colors like tan and brown and grey." A dimple showed in Maile's cheek briefly. "She and Iolani had a fight once because Iolani bought this really bright red dress. Aunt Berta said it made her look like a cheap tart. Do you think Iolani looks cheap?"

"I think she looks very expensive," Lani said, thinking of the bills she'd found.

Maile giggled. "They fight about that too, sometimes. You'd think it was Aunt Berta's money, the way she fusses over Iolani's bills."

"And does Wade fuss about her bills, too?" Lani couldn't resist asking.

"Oh, he thinks everything Iolani does is wonderful." Maile's eyes showed scorn. "I could tell him some things about her he wouldn't think were so great—if I wanted to."

"If it's something important, don't you think you should discuss it with him?" Lani asked.

"Why should I? He wouldn't believe me. Everybody thinks I'm a liar."

"What about your aunt? You must be pretty close to her."

She expected evasion or even hostility, but Maile said listlessly, "We get along okay, I guess."

Lani knew there would be no more confidences, at least not tonight.

"I'm ready to go down now," she said, holding out her hand. When Maile took her hand, Lani felt as though she had just won some kind of victory.

Dinner was much as it had been the night before—dull food, poorly cooked but impeccably served. Vivian, looking lovely in pink chiffon, concentrated most of her attention on the two men, although she did greet Lani cordially enough. Berta seemed preoccupied. Once, when her eyes met Lani's, her lips crimped together as if she'd suddenly found a fly in her soup. Lani wondered if her aunt had finally recognized her. After what had happened in the Folly, it was certain that someone here knew who she was, and Aunt Berta seemed the logical choice. Although Lani knew her aunt was capable of violence, somehow it was hard to see her doing something that could have put her in a ridiculous position if she'd been caught at it by one of the Kealohas. Or had she been acting under the orders of the man she had warned Vivian not to cross? And was that man Jason, who had left Lani alone in the Folly and then offered, so conveniently, to be her friend?

As the meal dragged on, Lani wondered how soon she could slip away to have a quiet visit with Moana in the kitchen. During the past couple of days they had become, if not friendly, at least less reserved with each other. It was difficult, Lani reflected, to remain aloof when you were showing someone how to do the hula.

Lani had noticed to her secret amusement that Moana invariably used the broadest pidgin when she spoke to Berta, pretending she didn't understand her Boston accent and making it necessary for Berta to repeat her orders. Even then Moana managed to get most of them garbled. This morning, for instance, Berta had ordered a leg of lamb for dinner, but it was a pork loin roast, more than a little burned around the edges, that had arrived at the table, much to her aunt's annoyance. Since the condiments and vegetables didn't match the meat, it was a very peculiar meal.

Although Lani knew that Moana had won this round of the battle, she wasn't sure that Berta knew it, too. After all, Berta St. John was at a disadvantage, because she believed that all Hawaiians were ignorant, stupid and lazy. To admit that Moana had been putting something over on her, probably from the first day they had met, would have been to admit that Moana was smarter than she was—and this was something her aunt could never do.

But there are other things Aunt Berta can do, Lani thought suddenly. If the island came under her control when Maile came of age, she would be in a position to evict the Kealohas. Would the island then fall into the hands of the real estate developers? Would the old house be torn down to make way for more of the high-rise monstrosities that already blighted the Honolulu skyline? Would tourists roam the beaches and the rain forests, leaving their trash behind, invading the burial caves in the cliffs and destroying the petroglyphs, those strangely beautiful cave paintings that were all that remained of a vanished people? And would this invasion upset the fragile balance of nature that made Maunaloa Island one of the last refuges for species of birds and plants that were almost extinct elsewhere in the Islands?

She discovered that she'd lost what little appetite she'd had. She pushed away her untouched dessert, glad the meal was almost over. But a few minutes later when Berta rose, said her good-nights and left, signaling the end of the meal, Lani's plan for escape was thwarted when Jason stopped her.

"If you're planning to go back to work tonight, forget it. We're having brandy and coffee on the lanai, and I insist that you join us," he said.

"I'm a little tired. I thought I'd go to my room and read for a while," Lani said.

Vivian made a face. "How boring! I prefer being with—

with other people." Her green-eyed glance touched Wade, then Jason.

Like the vamp in an old-time movie, Lani thought. "I guess I never had any trouble amusing myself," she said, a little too tartly.

Jason laughed. "The kitten has claws."

Vivian gave him a narrow-eyed look which he didn't seem to notice. Not wanting to make an issue of it, Lani let Jason lead her to the lanai, and when he put a brandy in her hand, she sipped it politely and listened while he talked about the trip to the Big Island he was planning for the next day. Despite herself, her eyes strayed toward Vivian and Wade, who seemed completely absorbed in each other. Even when Wade was relaxed, there was a controlled vitality about him that was in direct contrast to Jason's studied indolence. When Wade smiled at something Vivian said, she felt a pang that it was Vivian who could make him laugh instead of she.

As if sensing her inattention, Jason had fallen silent. He bent toward her and said softly, "I warned you not to do that."

"Do what?"

"Not to fall for Wade. You could never handle his hang-ups, you know. His suspicions and cynicism about women would tear you apart."

She felt a prick of anger. "And did you warn Iolani about him, too?"

"Oh, she can take care of herself. There's nothing vulnerable about Iolani."

"Do you think she's in love with Wade?"

Jason turned a thoughtful look on Vivian. She was leaning backward on the couch, the mellow light from an overhead light highlighting her smooth cheekbones, her shimmering hair and feline smile.

"I've been wondering about that myself," Jason said. "Is it possible she could prefer that stuffed shirt to me?" He sounded so chagrined that Lani gave him a sympathetic smile—and then saw that he was laughing at her.

"So you do have a soft heart. I thought so. I can spot a romantic every time."

Lani decided she wasn't going to play his game—whatever it was. She took another sip of the brandy, then rested her head against the back of the chair, trying to look unconcerned.

Jason reached forward and touched the neatly coiled hair at the nape of her neck. "Why do you keep your hair restrained like that?" he asked. "You should let that marvelous mane of yours fall free."

"No wonder your line bombed out with Iolani," she said sweetly. "First I have a dirty face—that *is* what you meant by earthy, isn't it?—and now I look like a horse. Maybe you should ask Wade to teach you *his* line."

"And you have a sense of humor," he said, sounding surprised.

"Doesn't everybody?"

"No, indeed. Berta has absolutely none at all—and neither does Iolani."

"And yet you're in love with her, aren't you?"

"In love? I lust for the gal—but then most men would. She's a very beautiful woman." His voice was serious, but she decided she didn't trust him when he was serious, because maybe that was when he lied the most.

"But I don't want to talk about Iolani," he went on. "At the moment, you're the one who interests me. What goes on inside that lovely head of yours? I'm pretty good at figuring out people, but I have to admit you have an elusive quality that I can't pin down. At first I thought it was shyness, but it isn't that. Reserve, yes; but you're not really shy, just very careful. Now why are you so careful about what you say? What was it—a bad experience with a man? Or does it go further back than that? What's the explanation for that politeness of yours? Were you raised in a foster home or a boardingschool, one of those sterile institutions where they drill the three magic little words, *please* and *thank you*, into you and never allow you to show a good honest human emotion? Or are you one of the walking wounded, Yula

Brock? Were you a battered child, or—"

He broke off and a look of dismay crossed his face. He put out a lean, hard hand and grasped her arm tightly.

"Hell—that was inexcusable. I'm so busy being the big-shot photographer that I sometimes forget how dangerous it is to pry into other people's private pain. Will you accept an apology from a very stupid man?"

She struggled with the constriction in her throat, the prickling under her eyelids. When she was sure she wasn't going to cry, she set her brandy down and rose. "No apology necessary—and if you'll excuse me, I think I'll take a walk before I go to bed."

"Could you use some company?"

"No, thank you. It isn't often I get a chance to walk alone at night."

She gave him a polite smile and left, moving only a shade too fast. By the time she had reached the veranda in front of the house, she had had time to realize that she'd handled the whole incident badly. What she should have done was to brazen it out, made a joke of it. Instead, she had revealed her vulnerability to Jason's probing, quicksilver mind.

She took the path that wound through her grandfather's prized specimen trees, wanting to put as much distance as she could between her and the lanai. The path, a broad white strip of crushed coral, was easy to follow even though a fog was rising, shrouding the moon. With her thoughts in a jumble, she followed the path automatically, driven by the demons of memory. Jason's words had opened up a flood-gate. Was she never to get over these sudden assaults from her own mind? She had been proud this afternoon because she'd faced down one particular demon in the Folly, so why was she trembling now, just because of a few casual words from a stranger?

Through the trees up ahead, she saw the grey outline of the bathhouse, and she felt a sudden primitive urge to plunge into the cool, cleansing waters of the lagoon. Swiftly, before she could change her mind, she hurried down the path toward the bathhouse.

When she went inside and turned on the lights she saw that the bathhouse had changed very little in the past thirteen years. The walls, paneled in grey cypress, looked freshly waxed, and one wall still held specimen cases of sea urchins, starfish, and slices of rare coral, while the opposite wall, covered with cork, was cluttered with photographs of notables who had swum in the lagoon at one time or another—a visiting head of state, a Vice-President, several movie stars, an austere-looking four-star Air Force general.

She found a bathing suit among the collection kept there for guests—two twists of cloth that covered her less than adequately. It took a little longer to find and activate the switch that controlled the lagoon lights her father had installed. When she went outside, her breath caught with pleasure. The discreetly positioned lights intensified the green of the coconut palms, and the fiddle-shaped ferns turned the lagoon into a place for *menehunes*, secret and mysterious and tempting.

She sat on the edge of the seawall for a while, enjoying the luxury of being completely alone, before she slipped into the water. It was colder than she had expected, but she splashed vigorously, restoring her body heat, before she turned over on her back and floated, staring up at the pearly, green-tinged fog, letting her tensions drift away. . . .

It was several minutes later that the lights went out. It happened so quickly, so unexpectedly that she gasped, floundered for a moment, and almost went under.

At first she thought the darkness was total, but when her eyes adjusted, she saw that there was a slight glow overhead, although not enough to see by. The water lapped at her body, and she had the fancy suddenly that she was floating in a vast sea without any shores. Almost immediately her common sense asserted itself. After all, she had learned to swim in the lagoon. She knew very well that there were no dangerous riptides, no sea animals to pull her down. To reach safety, all she had to do was swim forward in any direction until she touched the seawall.

She treaded water, straining her eyes, trying to get

oriented. Wasn't that a patch of grey to her right? If so, it must be the bathhouse, and she had her perspective again. She began swimming toward the slight break in the darkness, moving slowly so she wouldn't crash into the wall.

Then, like a recurring nightmare, a whispering sound came out of nowhere, its sibilance amplified by the peculiar acoustics of the lagoon.

"Crazy Lani . . . full of hate . . . killed her ma . . . when she was eight. . . ."

The whispering rose and fell. The skin on Lani's body prickled as she tried to pinpoint its direction. Did it come from up ahead, from the seawall—or was it closer, from the water that surrounded her? Was someone swimming toward her, coming to seize her legs and pull her down into the airless depths of the lagoon?

"Crazy Lani . . . full of hate . . . killed her ma . . . when she was eight. . . ."

When she discovered that she was warm again, that the chill had left her body, she thought confusedly of warm ocean currents—and then realized that the warmth came from within, that it was anger that had heated her blood.

She stopped swimming and treaded water. "Who are you?" she asked. "What do you want?"

A laugh, low and mocking, came out of the darkness. "I want you, daughter. Your life for my life. An eye for an eye, a life for a life. I want you to stay here with me forever. . . ."

There was a crawling, tingling sensation all over Lani's body as her skin, more atavistic than her reason, reacted to the meaning of the words. But it lasted only a moment. Because the whisperer had made a mistake, and she knew that this was no apparition returned from the dead. Whoever was out there in the dark was alive, very much alive; and while she was still afraid, it was the kind of fear that came from knowing she had an enemy. She began swimming, but this time it wasn't blind panic that drove her.

She sensed the seawall looming up ahead of her, or maybe there was a slight change in the quality of the darkness. She stopped swimming and culled her arms soundlessly through the water to keep afloat. When she heard nothing, she reached out and touched the rough side of the coral wall. It was the chill of displaced air on her wet face that warned her; she recoiled instinctively, kicking outward, using her feet to push her body violently away from the wall. A split second later, something smacked the water where she'd been; she screamed and rolled over, the water closing over her head.

She came up sputtering and coughing, her heart pounding so hard she was sure it would fail her. A heavy object flew through the air and struck her arm a glancing blow. Briefly, fire filled her arm, and the pain galvanized her anger again. Did he—she?—have eyes that could see in the dark? How had her enemy known she would try to climb out at this exact spot? Surely not by sound, since the acoustics in the lagoon distorted all sound. . . .

She swam backward, a little awkwardly because her arm still stung. Her mind, as if stimulated by the danger, moved swiftly, making and discarding plans. Her best chance for escape, she decided, was to climb up on the sea gate, follow it to the beach. Once she reached the beach she was confident she could evade her enemy, especially if it was her aunt, as she suspected. It was possible Aunt Berta had told her co-conspirators about that old doggerel from her past, but who else except her aunt would derive such pleasure from toying with her before trying to kill her?

A few minutes later she stopped swimming to listen again, but the only sound was the rustling of the palm fronds, the sound of water lapping against the seawall. Then, so faint she almost missed it, she heard the pat-pat of footsteps, and she knew her attacker was circling the lagoon, heading for the sea gate.

She felt a stultifying despair. Could her enemy be psychic, have some special powers? She moved her arms slowly, just enough to keep afloat, and the slight shimmer the movement made gave her the answer. From the vantage point of the seawall the moonlight, although too faint to see by, lent a luminescence to the water; her passage through it disturbed that luminescence and told her tormentor exactly where she was.

The knowledge that there was a logical explanation for her enemy's seeming ability to see in the dark steadied her. When the chanting started up again, she discovered it had lost its power to frighten her. In fact, it only made her feel contemptuous. She knew now that her enemy wasn't infallible, and since this was true, she had a good chance of saving herself.

"This is all pretty silly," she said in a normal voice, letting the acoustics carry her voice across the water. "You're wasting your time, you know, trying to scare me. Why don't you stop playing games and go away?"

The silence was total; even the coconut tree fronds seemed to stop rustling to listen.

"I'm not afraid of you, but I also don't intend to let you bash me in the head," she went on. "So I'll just stay out here treading water until someone comes along and chases you away. I can stay afloat for hours, but if you stay away from the house too long, someone might wonder where you are. So why don't you run along and leave me alone?"

The laughter came again, low and mocking, but she caught a note of uncertainty in it now, and she went on with more confidence.

"You made a mistake, pretending to be my mother's ghost. She would never say what you just said to me. So not only are you human, you also aren't very smart, are you?"

She stopped again, but there was no answer, only a listening, hating silence.

"I don't want to scream and cause a fuss," she said, raising her voice slightly. "You can understand that, can't you? But I'll do it if I have to, and someone not in on this scheme of yours just might catch you here. So why don't you run along and save both of us a lot of trouble? Go away—" In spite of herself, her voice wavered, so she repeated the words. "Go away!"

She listened, scarcely breathing. Would it work? Would whoever was out there believe her when she said she wasn't afraid, that she could stay out in the lagoon until morning if necessary? She heard footsteps, and this time there was no attempt at stealth. A moment later, when she heard the crunch of shoes on the coral path, tears of relief began to mingle with the salt water on her face.

But her tears soon dried, and she reminded herself that she still wasn't out of danger. It was possible that her enemy's retreat had been a trick, that he or she was waiting for her in the specimen grove. Her best bet was to try to reach the bathhouse. If she could lock herself in, she could wait there until morning.

Cautiously she began paddling toward the bathhouse again. Although she stopped often to listen, all she heard now were the usual night sounds. When her hand scraped against the coral seawall, she paused, trying to penetrate the darkness around her, regretting the trees that crowded close to the water.

As soundlessly as she could manage, she lifted herself onto the seawall and crouched there, listening to her own rapid heartbeat.

Maybe she heard a sound, or maybe it was pure instinct, but when the attack came, the reflexes of her body saved her again. She flung herself backward into the lagoon, creating a wave that washed over her head, swamping her. She did a backward roll and swam underwater until she was forced to come up for air. Her lungs straining, she struggled for breath. When she had cleared her nose and throat, she flung back her head and screamed.

The first scream was spontaneous, born of terror and anger, but she didn't stop then. At the moment she didn't care if she made a fool of herself. This had narrowed down to a duel between her enemy and her, a matter of life and death, and she didn't intend to die young in this lonely place.

So she kept on screaming, even after she heard footsteps pounding along the path. The lights came on, flooding the lagoon and pushing back the darkness. When she saw that Jason wasn't alone, that Wade and her aunt were coming up behind him, she finally stopped screaming and swam toward them.

When she reached the seawall, Wade grabbed her hands, hauled her out of the water and deposited her, none too gently, on the seawall, but it was Jason who took off his shirt and put it around her shoulders.

"Okay, what happened here?" Wade demanded.

"I—I went for a swim," she said, her teeth chattering. "I was in the middle of the lagoon when the lights went off. I lost my—my bearings in the dark. I must have been swimming around in circles, because I couldn't find the seawall. I guess I panicked then, and once I started screaming, I couldn't seem to stop."

"Well, you're safe now." Wade gave Jason a hard look. "You didn't turn off the lights as a joke, did you, Jason?"

"Come off it, Wade." Jason's voice was irritated. "I'm not given to practical jokes. There's nothing remotely funny about scaring someone half to death. I suspect the light lever wasn't all the way down and it snapped back to OFF."

"I can think of another explanation," Berta said silkily. "You wouldn't be trying to stir up a little excitement, would you, Miss Brock?"

A sharp reply rose to Lani's lips, but the expression on Wade's face stopped her. The greenish cast of the light shadowed his deep-set eyes, but there was no mistaking the suspicion there.

She turned her attention to her aunt. "You can believe what you like, Miss St. John," she said evenly.

She shrugged off the shirt Jason had put around her shoulders, handed it to him, and stalked away toward the house. She didn't bother to look back to see if anyone was following her.

XIII

THE FOOL

It was Maile who awakened Lani the next morning. She had locked herself in the night before, and the incessant rapping and rattling of the doorknob jangled her nerves as she got up, pulled on a robe, and opened the door to Maile's flushed face.

"Hurry up and get dressed, Yula." Maile's eyes were snapping with excitement. "Uncle Wade is taking us across the island to the old village, and we have to leave right away. We're taking along food and we're going to build a fire and—and Iolani is mad because Uncle Wade was supposed to take her to a tennis exhibition and now he isn't and"—she took a gasping breath—"he said for you to wear comfortable shoes and old clothes—"

"Wait, wait!" Lani said, half-laughing. "Are you sure you haven't made a mistake? Why does your uncle want me to come along?"

"Because you're supposed to see that I don't get too tired. When I went down for breakfast, he said to tell Yula he was declaring a holiday, to wear something old—and you're supposed to bring along a swimsuit, too."

She danced out of the room, leaving Lani dazed and a little suspicious. Was this another of Maile's games? At dinner last night Vivian and Wade had discussed the tennis exhibition, then talked about their plan to go out to dinner later. Why would Wade suddenly change his plans? And why would he invite—no, order—her to go along, too?

She took a quick shower and, using her bathing suit as

underwear, pulled on jeans and a denim shirt, which she knotted at the waist. Although she didn't bother with makeup, she tied a strip of gay scarf around her head.

Still expecting to find that it was some kind of joke, she went downstairs and found Wade and Maile waiting for her in the hall. Three knapsacks were lying at their feet. Wade took in Lani's jeans and sneakers and gave an approving nod.

"Look, Yula, that one belongs to me! Uncle Wade says I can keep it after our trip." Maile picked up one of the knapsacks and began squirming into it. "They're packed with food and stuff, and we're going to cook on the beach, so hurry up and eat your breakfast, 'cause we're all ready to go."

Wade helped Maile with the straps of her knapsack, and she flew out the door, saying she was going to show it to Jason.

"This is all pretty sudden," Lani said. "Is there any special reason for this excursion?"

"Yes, Wade, do explain why the hell you're breaking a date with me to go off with Maile and Miss Brock?"

Vivian was standing on the stairs, dressed in town clothes, and it was obvious she was in a blazing temper. Lani stared up at the taut muscles in her throat; it occurred to her that not only was Vivian an impostor, she also was older than twenty-one years.

"I went into all this at breakfast, Iolani." There was a coolness in Wade's voice that Lani had never heard him use to Vivian before. He picked up the heaviest of the knapsacks, shrugged into it and pulled the straps taut over his chest.

"Oh, yes . . . you think it's time that Maile got acquainted with her Hawaiian heritage, wasn't that it? That's all very admirable, but why today? Why must you mess up my plans, and why is it necessary to take Miss Brock with you?"

"I don't want Maile to overdo, and Yula is the best judge of the child's physical strength. Why don't we discuss this later tonight?"

"I'm afraid that's impossible, since I won't be returning to the island tonight. I'm sure Jason would be delighted to take your place as my escort."

Wade's jaw tightened. "As you wish," he said curtly. He stalked from the hall, leaving Lani alone with Vivian. She avoided Vivian's eyes as she fumbled with the unfamiliar straps of the knapsack, trying to get it settled comfortably on her back.

"Here—you're going to have blisters if you wear it low like that." To Lani's surprise, Vivian gave the knapsack an expert heave, then fastened the strap deftly.

"Thank you. I'm sorry if this interferes with your plans, Miss Stevenson."

"Oh, I know this wasn't your idea." She studied Lani, and while her eyes weren't friendly, there was no personal animosity in them, either. "A word of warning, Miss Brock. Don't get any heavy ideas about Wade—or Jason. They're both out of your league, you know, and you could get hurt."

Before Lani could think of an answer, Maile danced back into the hall. Ignoring Vivian, she seized Lani by the hand and pulled her toward the door. Her excitement was so infectious that Lani didn't have the heart to remind her that she hadn't had her morning coffee yet. As they hurried toward Wade, waiting for them on the path, she was determined not to let Vivian—and her curious warning—spoil her day.

Lani held back as they circled the house, letting Maile walk beside her uncle. Remembering Vivian's remark to Wade about Maile's Hawaiian heritage, she suspected that her own pointed words to Wade in the hau arbor had drawn blood. If so, today's outing was probably an attempt by Wade to establish more closeness with Maile, and Lani wanted to give him every chance to succeed.

There was another reason why she hung back, a personal one. Today would be another excursion into the past for her; she didn't want to have to guard her expression every minute of the day.

They climbed the cliff path at a slow, easy pace, and it took them half an hour to reach the top. Below, the leeward side of the island was spread out before them—the great, sprawling house with its brown tile roofs, its orderly gardens, and the huge monkeypod trees that dwarfed everything else except the house itself. Beyond a strip of white beach the blue-green waters of the cove shimmered in the morning sun. To the right, the scarlet roof of Abigail's Folly brooded over the lagoon, while at the left, behind the finger of land that held the hau arbor, the cluster of cottages where the Kealohas lived looked like tiny dollhouses, each with its fruit trees, its neat, postage-stamp garden. The cemetery which lay beyond the cottages was hidden by the curve of the island, but Lani was very much aware that it was there, and as she turned away to follow Wade and Maile, she remembered that she'd made herself a promise to visit her parents' graves before she left the island.

With the leeward cliff at their back, they plunged into another world, a world of giant trees, of ferns and honeycreepers and, in places where the sun shone through in small muted pools, clusters of the red-fringed ti plants that grew wild on the island. The stone path passed through the center of the saddle-shaped valley that separated the island's two ranges of hills. Although not a true rain forest, the valley was lush and green and primitive. It pointed directly into the prevailing winds, and the trees—mango, ironwood, paper mulberry, koa, kukui, the versatile hala, an occasional sandalwood—all bent their majestic heads slightly to the southeast, as if paying tribute to the power of the trade winds.

Lani, bringing up the rear, listened silently as Wade pointed out a grove of kukui trees, their pale green standing out against the darker green of the other trees. He helped Maile gather up several handfuls of the nuts and told her that when the rough cover was filed away, the oily nut inside would be as black and shiny as a bit of coal.

It was late morning when they finally stood on the rim of the windward cliffs. They stared down at a magnificent cloud-dappled valley, choked with green, that ended in a wash of white froth where the land met the ocean. Although it was almost noon, the air was crisp and cool, and the wind carried a strong, rich odor, a mixture of earth and sea, to their nostrils. The sky was alive with birds, wheeling and soaring and swooping.

"So many birds," Lani murmured. "I didn't—" She stopped, appalled that she had been about to say she didn't remember so many birds on Maunaloa Island.

"You didn't realize there was such a variety of birds in Hawaii?" Wade said. "Most are *haole* species—from other places, imported into the Islands." He stopped to point out a tern and two varieties of frigate birds. "They thrive here on Maunaloa. There are no natural enemies—no rats or mongooses or predatory animals, not even man, just as there are no snails to destroy the honeycreepers."

"Wouldn't all that change if the family sold the island to a hotel chain?" she said.

"Where did you hear that?" Wade asked sharply.

Lani hesitated. "I didn't *hear* it anywhere. But with land so limited in the Islands, it seems logical that real estate developers would be after Maunaloa," she said.

"Well, I prefer that you keep that kind of speculation to yourself. What we don't need right now is more rumors about the Stevensons or the island—"

Maile came up with a wildflower for him to identify and he turned away. From the top of the cliff, he pointed out the ruins of the deserted village, the ancient taro patches, the fishponds that predated by a millennium the coming of the white men. The embankments that defined the taro patches were in ruins now, but the taro still grew rank and wild there. Here and there, light lavender patches among the green taro, water lilies bloomed. A mist, not yet dispersed by the soft-edged wind, hugged the sides of the bluff as they descended a steep, narrow path to the valley floor.

At the bottom, they stopped under a huge mango tree to rest, and Wade showed Maile how to cut a wedge of skin from the fruit with her thumbnail, so she could eat the sweet pulpy meat underneath. Lani, sitting a little apart, ate a mango, then leaned back, the wind fresh and cool against

160

her face, and thought about her conversation with Wade. There had been a proprietary tone in his voice when he talked about Maunaloa—did he already think of himself as Vivian's husband, as owner of the island? Was this why he was cultivating Maile? Was he thinking ahead to the day when she would come of age and be in control of her half of the island?

She watched their two heads, so close together as they bent over the lacy petals of a coral hibiscus, and it was inevitable that she would think of another excursion to this side of the island.

She had been eight years old, and the man who had taken her to see the old village had been her father. It had been a wonderful day, and because she had relived it so often in her memory, she had never forgotten any detail of it. The outing, like this one, had been a spur-of-the-moment thing. Although her father tried to get her mother to come along, she was furious because he had disrupted some plans of her own, so in the end they went alone. Lani knew her father was angry, but after a while he seemed to throw off his mood as they explored the village where the Kealohas had once lived.

Later, he made a seine from coconut fronds and dredged up small striped fish from an abandoned fishpond. They gathered breadfruit and green bananas, dug up yams growing wild near the site of the ruined village, and cut broad, fleshy taro tops to cook their food in. He dug a small *imu*, an underground oven, in the sand, and she wove him a wreath of fern to keep the sweat out of his eyes as he built a fire to heat the stones for the *imu*.

With the green wreath around his dark hair, he had looked like a young Olympic hero, but his feet had been made of clay, and now the memory of that day was tarnished by his rejection of her so soon afterward. So why was it that even now, knowing how he had failed her, she still would have given ten years of her own life to have him here, alive and well and smiling at her in the sun?

It took them another half hour to cross the valley. When

161

they reached the beach, the sand beneath their feet was ovaline, the remnants of some ancient lava flow, and Maile was enchanted by sand that was tinted green instead of white.

The wind tossed their hair and swallowed up their voices until they found a sheltered place in the lee of a protruding spar of rock. They gathered driftwood and Wade built a fire. When it had burned down to coals, they broiled strips of *pipikaula*, meat soaked in shoyu and dried, which Moana had already threaded onto bamboo slivers. There was cheese, French bread, fruit, coconut cake wrapped in foil. Lani smiled when she saw how much food Moana had provided for them, but it disappeared with such rapidity that she knew Moana's judgment had been right.

As Maile stuffed her pink little mouth with food, she listened avidly to Wade's tales about the ancient Hawaiians who had braved the treacherous waters surrounding the island in their frail boats, using the products of the sea and the land to provide them with all of their needs. It pleased Lani that while he didn't try to gloss over the bad parts of their culture, the cruelties of the rigid caste system and the brutality of their religion, he made Maile see how the stark reality of living always on the brink of starvation, at the mercy of the vicissitudes of weather and tidal waves and drought, had formed their belief in a multitude of jealous, brutal gods.

After they had eaten, they looked for shells in the tepid waters of the tidal pools and explored the ruins of the old village. Wade showed them the foundation of an ancient *heiau*, his description so vivid that they could almost see how it had looked before its destruction. When Maile's eyes began to droop, Wade rolled her in a towel and carried her to a shady crevice of the cliff. When he stripped to his bathing suit, Lani, who had thought he was on the stocky side, saw that there wasn't a superfluous ounce of flesh on his taut, well-knit body. Feeling self-conscious suddenly, she undressed quickly and joined him in the surf.

Exhilarated by the boiling, tumbling water, they bodysurfed until they were exhausted and then sat in the sun, content to let the wind dry their suits. From his knapsack Wade produced a comb and handed it to her. She fought the wind, trying to comb the tangles from her hair. He watched her lazily for a while, then took the comb away from her. "Here—you're just making a mess of it. I'll do it."

With surprising gentleness he smoothed out the tangles, then tossed the ends of her hair with the comb so the wind could dry it. She sat motionless, her eyes half-closed, filled with a deep languor.

It was later, when her hair was almost dry, that a small disquiet started up inside her. She was aware suddenly of Wade's nearness, of the ripple of muscles under his brown skin as he drew the comb through her hair. Most of all she was aware of her own constricted breathing and the rapid beat of her heart. Although her nerves shrieked *Danger! Danger!* it seemed unimportant at the moment that this man might very well be her enemy. Even when he dropped the comb on the sand and reached forward to put the tip of his finger on the pulse that throbbed in her throat, she seemed unable to move.

He turned her head gently between his hands and kissed her, and she knew the pressure of his lips was much too intense, too probing, that it was madness to let it continue, but the fire that had sprung into being inside her was not to be denied. Their near-naked bodies were touching now, and as his hand slid down her back, she pressed closer to him.

"You're wicked! You're both wicked, and—and I hate both of you!"

Maile's shrill voice broke them apart. Lani scrambled to her feet, clutching at the strip of material that covered her breasts. Her heart dropped when she saw her sister's face. There was nothing childlike about the jealousy in Maile's eyes, and Lani knew she had just made a serious mistake.

"Maile—" she began, and then stopped, realizing that an apology would only make things worse and lend importance to what was, under the circumstances, a very natural kiss.

163

Wade must have realized it too, because he began picking up his clothes from the sand. "I was wondering if I should awaken you, Maile," he said casually. "As soon as we police the area, we'd better start back. I promised to show you the sinkhole, but it's a few hundred yards off the main path, and we want to be back down the cliff before dark."

Lani, following his cue, dressed quickly and then helped pick up the campsite. Later, when Maile had cooled off, she would explain that—explain what? That proximity to an attractive man, the whole long carefree day, had conspired to make her drop her guard? That for a little while she had put her suspicions away and made a fool of herself with a man who, even if he wasn't her enemy, still thought of her as an appendage of his office?

The trip back to Maunaloa House was a drudgery, something to be gotten over with as quickly as possible. They stopped often to rest, but Maile refused to sit with them. Gone were her eager questions, her darting curiosity. Although she seemed more dispirited than angry now, she ignored Lani completely and spoke to Wade only when he asked her a direct question.

Wade seemed not to notice her silence. As before, he led the way, and during their rest stops he talked quietly to Lani about impersonal things. Lani found it hard to respond to him. She was still too much aware of him, of his smoke-grey eyes, the iodine odor of sea water that clung to his hard, muscular body, the warmth of his hand when he helped her over a fallen log.

Once, when they were sitting side by side, their backs against the trunk of an ironwood tree, she looked up to find Maile's hostile eyes watching. When they started on, Maile changed her tactics. Now she clung to Wade's hand, and when they crossed the small silver stream that flowed down the middle of Po Valley, she insisted that he carry her. She clung to his neck, her eyes triumphant, while Lani found her own way across the stream.

Lani, feeling increasingly depressed, wished Wade would postpone the side trip to the sinkhole. The day that had started out so promising had ended with an even wider gulf than ever between Maile and her. How could she have forgotten, even for a moment, the tightrope she was walking? One moment's carelessness, and the days she'd spent cultivating Maile had all been wasted. And there was something else, too. With Maile's penchant for gossiping, how long would it be before Vivian and Aunt Berta knew that Wade had kissed her on the beach today?

Ahead of her, Wade stopped so suddenly that she almost ran into him. He caught her by the arm to keep her from falling, and for a moment his hand seemed to burn into her flesh. She stared at the pulse that leaped to life at his temple, and she knew that whatever he thought of her as a person, he was not indifferent to her physically.

Maile, her eyes jealous, crowded in between them, and Wade dropped Lani's arm to take Maile's hand as they left the main path for a more narrow one. It was very dark here, with the branches of the trees forming a green roof overhead, so thick it shut out the sun. The air seemed oppressively heavy, and there was the constant drip-drip of water somewhere close at hand. The only other sound was the distant cawing of a mynah bird and a rustling among the ferns that formed an undergrowth so dense that it sometimes obscured the path.

A few minutes later, as they were passing a thicket of mountain banana trees, they heard a rumbling sound, like distant thunder. Although she had been expecting it, Lani jumped nervously. Maile gave her a scornful look, but her eyes betrayed her own uneasiness.

"It's the tide," Wade told them. "There's a channel that connects underground sea caves in the edge of the cliffs to the sinkhole—it's probably an old lava vent. When a large wave rolls in, the air in the tunnel is compressed, and it creates a rumbling sound. Right now the tide is out, but when it's high, it sometimes sounds like a giant's whistle." Wade smiled at Maile. "That's the explanation for those nose flutes you've heard, Maile—the sinkhole is located in the hills directly behind the Folly, you know."

A *giant's whistle* . . . those were the same words her father had used, Lani thought, the day he'd shown her the sinkhole and told her the family secret. She had felt very adult when he'd made her promise that she would never tell anyone—except one of her own children someday—about the burial cave that was hidden under a ledge in the walls of the sinkhole.

It had been Captain Aaron's son who had found the burial cave. Although he had no way of knowing who was buried there, he knew it must have been a great chief, since the taboo against entering any lava vent, especially one that was believed to have been sacred to Lono, was so strict. Other burial caves on the island had already been plundered for their feather capes, their artifacts, even their bones, and Captain Aaron's son had been determined it wouldn't happen to this one. So he'd told no one about his discovery, not even his father. Later he had passed the secret along to one of his own sons, and it had come down to her father—and to her. She had been so proud that day, so sure of her father's love. And yet, just a few days later, he had turned his back on her and sent her away from Maunaloa.

"There it is. You can see the barrier through that break in the trees," Wade said, pointing to a plank fence, grey with age, that formed a barrier around the sinkhole. A cold draft, rank with the odor of rotting seaweed, blew against Lani's face, and she fought back an impulse to call out a warning as Wade and Maile drew closer to the sinkhole.

Holding Wade's hand, Maile peered through the planks at the yawning blackness of the collapsed lava vent. The opening was several yards in diameter, and its edges were undefined, blurred by the lush vegetation that grew around its rim.

Sensing Lani's reluctance to approach the fence, Wade held out his free hand toward her. "It's safe, Yula, as long as you're careful. The lava formation is very interesting, well worth seeing. I promise to hold onto you so you can take a closer look."

Maile's eyes darted from Wade's outstretched hand to

Lani, and an ugly flush stained her face. "I know a secret," she blurted. "Nobody else in the whole world knows it, and I promised I'd never, never tell except to one of my own children someday." Her eyes flickered toward Wade. "When I got so sick from those berries, I thought maybe I should tell someone about it, but now I'm glad I didn't. People pretend to be your friend and then you find out they aren't, so I'm not going to tell anyone my secret, not even when I get old."

She knows about the burial cave, Lani thought. *He told her because he thought I was dead.*

"Maile—" she said, and then paused. Because what could she say without giving herself away? "I think I'll skip looking into the sinkhole," she went on. "Heights make me nervous."

Maile looked scornful. "You sure scare easy. Well, *I'm* not afraid—"

Afterward, Lani couldn't reconstruct exactly what happened. Did Maile pull away from Wade's hand, or did he release her? But somehow Maile was free, had slipped under the bottom plank of the fence and was stepping boldly up to the edge of the sinkhole. Lani screamed just as Wade reached forward to grab Maile, but she seemed to slip through his hands. One moment she was there, her eyes bright with mischief as she looked over her shoulder at them, and the next she was gone.

Lani darted forward, past Wade's frozen body. She rolled under the fence and, careless of her own safety, flung herself full length on the damp ground inside the enclosure. She thrust her head and shoulders over the rim of the sinkhole. Below, Maile's terrified eyes stared up at her, and she saw that Maile had landed on a ledge about five feet below the rim. It was the same ledge that hid the entrance of the burial cave, but Lani didn't think of this until later.

She met the entreaty, the terror in Maile's eyes. "Don't move, Maile," she said, her voice surprisingly calm. "You're perfectly safe as long as you don't move. We'll get you out—only don't move."

She reached down, clasped Maile's upstretched hands. A

crushing weight pressed into the small of her back, and she felt a rolling wave of panic before she realized that Wade had climbed over the fence and was holding her down with his body while he reached past her to grasp Maile's wrists. Together they pulled her frail body upward, over the rim of the sinkhole, and then Maile was in Wade's arms, her body shaking, clutching at him with frantic hands.

"It's all your fault, Yula," Maile wailed. "If you hadn't yelled and scared me, I wouldn't have fallen—"

She began to sob, and Lani wanted desperately to start off down the path, to be alone with her own tears, but something stronger than hurt kept her there. Earlier, she had wondered why Wade was so insistent about her coming along on the outing; now she asked herself if it was because he needed a witness. If the ledge hadn't broken Maile's fall, she surely would have pitched to her death at the bottom of the sinkhole, and Lani would have been there to testify that it had been an accident. But had it really been? Wade's body had blocked her view during that moment when he'd reached out to grab Maile. Had his hands missed her, as it seemed, or had he touched Maile, given her frail body that extra nudge that had made her lose her balance?

Lani discovered that her whole body was shaking with cold, and she turned away, afraid of what Wade might see on her face. When Wade asked her if she was all right, his voice solicitous, she produced a smile for him, but as she followed Wade and Maile down the path, the coldness, the suspicion, stayed with her.

XIV

Pleading a headache, Lani fixed herself a sandwich in the kitchen and took it to her room for dinner that night, and the next morning she went down to breakfast late, knowing it would be best to avoid Maile as much as possible.

Maile, as she expected, failed to turn up for her therapy session in the hau arbor that afternoon, but to Lani's surprise, when she talked to Moana just before dinner, she discovered that Maile had coaxed the Hawaiian woman away from her chores long enough for a hula lesson on the lanai. Hoping for the best, Lani said nothing to Maile about the missed exercise session at dinner that night, instinct telling her to avoid anything that could stir up Maile's hostility.

She didn't see Wade until dinner. He had left a note for her on her desk, laying out some work he wanted finished, and had taken off in the company helicopter before she came down to breakfast. That evening, Jason and Vivian returned with him on the *Kauhelani*, and during dinner Vivian was her usual smiling, bland self. Lani wasn't sure whether she was relieved or chagrined that everything seemed to be back to normal between Wade and Vivian.

They were sitting on the lanai, having their after-dinner brandy, when Vivian said, very casually, that she had invited a guest to the island for a few days, a man she had met at the tennis exhibition.

"He's in the import business in Seattle, and he says he's a

169

whiz on the tennis courts. He promised to improve my backhand in a few easy lessons, so I thought—why not?" She directed one of her smiles at Wade.

Wade's face tightened, and Lani wondered if Vivian knew that it had been a professional tennis player who had broken up his marriage.

Berta, sitting across from Vivian, frowned at her. "Do you think it's wise to have a guest here just now? You know we'll be very busy for the next few days, getting ready for the luau—"

"Oh, I'm sure he'll fit right in," Vivian said lazily. "And after all, this *is* my home, isn't it? I do have the right to invite anyone I want here."

Berta's sallow face stiffened, but it was Wade who asked, "Who is this man, Iolani? What do you know about him?"

"Well, I know he dances like a dream and that he looks rather like a young Omar Sharif. He has these black, black eyes and the most devastatingly long lashes, and he also has a very good opinion of himself. I'm sure he thinks he's God's gift to lonely heiresses." She gave a small secret smile. "I thought it might be amusing to string him along."

"Someday you're going to get into trouble teasing the animals, ole dear," Jason said.

"Oh, but that's what is so exciting. There's something very dangerous about the man." Vivian closed her eyes, her small teeth nibbling at her lower lip. "He has this way of moving, like a panther stalking a rabbit. . . . Yes, I think he'll be quite an addition to the luau guest list."

Lani was careful to keep her face a perfect blank. She wasn't sure if she wanted to laugh or to scratch Vivian's eyes out. Despite Vivian's disparaging remarks about Kore, there was a current of excitement under her drawl, and Lani had a hunch she was more impressed by Kore than she had admitted. And why should she be surprised? As Kore had said with so much unconscious arrogance, Vivian was a woman, wasn't she? And she, of all people, knew how charismatic Kore could be.

The brandy Lani was sipping had a bitter taste suddenly.

She set it down, murmured an excuse to Jason about being tired and left the lanai, glad that he seemed too preoccupied with his own thoughts tonight to try to stop her. Still thinking of Kore, she had almost reached her room before she realized the door was open and light was spilling out into the hall. She stopped in the doorway, staring at Maile.

Dressed in pajamas and clutching her doll, Maile was sitting in the middle of the bed. "I've been waiting for you. I thought you'd never get here," she said, pouting.

"Is something wrong?"

"I want you to tell me a story."

"Oh?" Lani pumped surprise into the word. "I thought we had a bargain. You would do your exercises every day and I would tell you all I know about the Gypsies."

Maile's eyes wavered. "My leg hurt from all that walking yesterday, but I promise to do my exercises tomorrow."

Lani's first instinct was to refuse, to make Maile stick to their bargain, but she felt herself weakening as she took in the droop of Maile's mouth. She nodded, and Maile gave a little bounce on the bed.

"Tell me about the Gypsy lady," she ordered. "Where did she get the gold coins she wore around her neck? Wasn't she afraid someone would steal them?"

Lani pulled a chair up close to the bed. She answered Maile's eager questions about Pearsa's *sumadjii*, then about Kore, describing his grace, his easy mastery of sports. When she realized she was treading on dangerous ground, she changed the subject to carnival life, which continued to fascinate Maile, even though Lani hadn't tried to play down its harsh, sordid side.

When Lani finally ran down, she began getting ready for bed, but Maile lingered, watching as she braided her hair for the night.

"I heard them talking about you before dinner," she said abruptly.

"Them?"

"Aunt Berta and Iolani. They were talking in Aunt Berta's room, but they left the door open."

"People who eavesdrop often hear things about themselves they don't like," Lani said.

"They were talking about you, not me," Maile retorted. "Iolani was fussing at Aunt Berta about those books she keeps locked in her desk. She said if Aunt Berta didn't get rid of them, she would be sorry someday. What did she mean by that, Yula?"

"Sometimes—well, sometimes people write things they shouldn't in diaries. Maybe she meant that."

Maile thought about that for a moment, then shrugged. "Anyway, they started talking about you then." She looked mutinous suddenly. "If Aunt Berta tries to send you away, she'll be sorry—they'll both be sorry."

"Why would you care?" Lani said. "I thought you blamed me because you fell into the sinkhole."

"I just said that because I was scared. Uncle Wade was awful mad at me. He said I hurt your feelings and should apologize. Did I really hurt your feelings, Yula?"

Lani smiled at her. "Yes, for a little bit. But I was pretty sure you didn't mean it."

"Well, I'm sorry—and I don't want you to leave. Aunt Berta told Vivian she was going to make Uncle Wade send you away."

"Whatever for?" Lani kept her voice light. "I haven't talked to your aunt half a dozen times since I came here."

"It's because Uncle Wade wouldn't make you move to one of the guest cottages, I think. And Iolani doesn't like the way Uncle Wade and Uncle Jason pay so much attention to you." She was silent for a moment, staring at Lani. "I guess it isn't your fault. You can't help it if you're pretty. But Iolani is mad because Uncle Wade took you with us yesterday."

Lani decided it was time to change the subject. "I'm still surprised that you care whether or not I stay."

"If you go away, they'll just bring someone else here. At least you tell good stories, and you don't wear too much perfume like Miss Choy or have knuckly hands like Miss Simmons."

"I wonder what Miss Choy and Miss Simmons are saying about *you* right now," Lani said thoughtfully.

"They're probably saying I was the worst patient they ever had," Maile said with satisfaction.

Lani smiled at her. "Well, I've had worse."

"Really? Worse than *me?*"

"There was a little boy who bit me on the hand and another who poured hot soup into my lap."

"Did you punish them?"

"Of course not. They were very frightened. Both of them had been badly treated by their—by people. We became good friends after they began to trust me."

Maile regarded her with thoughtful eyes. "I trust you," she said abruptly.

"Do you mean you want to be friends, Maile?"

"I guess so." Maile's eyes slid sideways. "People are supposed to do nice things for their friends, aren't they?"

"That's usually how it works."

"If you're really my friend, then—then you'll do something nice for me to prove it, won't you?"

"If I can. What is it you want, Maile?"

"I heard Uncle Jason ask you before dinner if you'd go to the Bon Dance at Haliewa with him tomorrow so he could take pictures of you. After dinner, I asked him if I could go along too, but he said you probably needed a rest from me—and besides, people who listen at keyholes don't deserve treats. I told him I didn't listen at any keyhole, that you two were talking right down there in the hall. He laughed then and said it was up to you."

"And you want me to prove that I'm your friend by saying you can come along?"

"Uh-huh. It's just the same as giving me a present."

Her words jogged Lani's memory, and she realized that Maile had given her the opening she'd been waiting for. "Well, I did have a real present for you, Maile. I was going to give you that locket you admired so much the first day I came here—you know, to put your father's picture in?—but when I looked for it, it was gone. The chain must have broken in the garden or maybe in the hau arbor. I'd appreciate it if you'd keep an eye out for it."

Maile's eyelids dropped over her eyes. She fingered the bit of ribbon in her doll's hair. "I'll look for it," she said.

"Good—and about the Bon-odori ceremony tomorrow: you do know it's a Japanese religious ceremony, don't you? I'm a little surprised you'd be interested. Didn't you tell me you didn't like the Japanese, that they were yellow-skinned barbarians?"

"That's what Aunt Berta says." Maile's voice was defensive. "Only—only she was wrong about the Hawaiians being lazy and stupid, so maybe she's wrong about other things, too."

Lani eyed her suspiciously. Were Maile's eyes a shade too ingenuous, her words a little too glib?

"You can go with us tomorrow, provided your Uncle Wade says it's okay," she said, making up her mind. "But this is a business outing for your Uncle Jason. You'll have to promise not to be a pest."

"I promise. Do you think he'll take my picture, too?"

"I'm sure he will. And since we both want to look our best tomorrow, I think we should get some sleep now."

Obediently Maile scooted off the bed. She gave Lani a tiny smile and was gone. Lani stared after her, frowning. She had a strong suspicion that she'd just been very cleverly maneuvered by an eleven-year-old child. How was it that Maile seemed to know exactly which buttons to push to get her own way?

The next morning, Lani got Wade's permission to take Maile on the outing to Haliewa. Maile, looking like a small Hawaiian princess in a yellow muumuu with a crown of maile vines in her dark hair, was on her best behavior. On the ride across the choppy waters of Kaneohe Bay, she hung on Jason's every word, laughing at his jokes, and spoke to Lani as if they were the best of friends.

Earlier, Jason had made arrangements at the Buddhist temple in Haliewa for Lani and Maile to be provided with colorful—and very costly—Japanese kimonos. A tiny Japanese woman, giggling politely, helped them dress. It was a lengthy process, since each fold of the kimono, each tuck of the obi had to be painstakingly arranged according to ancient custom. When their helper was finally satisfied, she provided them each with an elaborately arranged black wig before she allowed them to look at themselves in the mirror. Standing side by side, they stared at their transformed images with fascinated eyes.

"Little sister look ver' Japanese," the woman told them. "Big sister got green eyes, so don't look so much Japanese, but she ver' pretty, too."

Maile giggled; she seized Lani by the hand, barely allowing her time to thank the woman. When they went out into the hall where Jason was waiting, they had the pleasure of seeing his eyes widen with surprise.

"You both look wonderful," he said. "I can see this is going to be one of my better projects."

"Why did you decide to use an outsider?" Lani asked curiously. "Wouldn't a girl from the Japanese community be much more authentic?"

"Not really. You have a certain quality—call it universality—that makes you perfect for a series I have in mind. If I can pry you away from Wade often enough, I'd like to photograph you in costume, attending the festivals of several Island cultures. I have a good reason for using an outsider. The excitement of encountering a new experience for the first time is almost impossible to fake. To a Japanese girl, this celebration today would be old hat. To you—and to Maile—it's fresh and exotic, and that's the quality I want to capture on film."

For the next hour he concentrated on doing just that, remaining so unobtrusive that Lani and Maile almost forgot he was there as they explored the temple yard, fragrant with incense; stared with awe at a giant bronze Buddha and visited the booths that sold ice cream and *saimin* and teriyaki-on-a-stick, or offered games of chance to passersby. When Jason was satisfied, he put aside his cameras and his professional manner and took them to a nearby Japanese restaurant for tempura and sukiyaki and honey-sweetened rice cakes.

As she had on the excursion with Wade, Maile ate ravenously, her eyes darting around the restaurant, appraising the other patrons, the scroll-and-flowers arrangement near the door of the austerely decorated room, the elaborate paper lanterns overhead. In their bright kimonos, they attracted a lot of attention, which delighted Maile but made Lani very uncomfortable.

It was almost dusk by the time they returned to the temple yard. Lights from a multitude of octagon-shaped lanterns glinted on the bronze Buddha and on the copper roof of the pagoda, while incense from the temple, where five black-robed priests were reciting passages from the Sutra, accompanied by the beating of wooden blocks, perfumed the air.

A circle of dancers had already formed around a lantern-decked platform in the middle of the courtyard. They stepped out in a ritualized pattern of advance-and-retreat, advance-and-retreat, while on the platform, drummers and singers began the reedy, singsong chanting that would continue without pause for several hours. Among the dancers were middle-aged businessmen in somber kimonos; plump housewives, looking exotic and mysterious in elaborate kimonos and powder-white faces; followed by children of all ages who imitated their elders, step by step.

To Lani's amusement and Maile's delight, Jason joined the dancers and made a circle with them, executing the steps as if he had been born in Japan. He gestured for them to join him as he passed the first time. Maile was too shy and hung back, but Lani, caught up by the color, the hypnotic beat of the drums, the incense-heavy air, slipped into line next to him and followed his lead as he went through the stylized postures and gestures, keeping time to the wailing of the flutes and the offbeat of the drums.

When they were tired they dropped out, panting and very pleased with themselves. "You missed your calling, Yula," Jason told her. "You caught on to that like a professional dancer."

"What about you?" she countered. "Where did you learn to do a Japanese Bon dance?"

"I spent a little time in Japan, doing—"

"—an article for *National Geographic*."

He grinned down at her. "Nope. As a matter of fact, it was for a book on Pacific Island dances. You should see me do a Filipino stick dance."

Maile pulled at his arm, and they went to get soft drinks at a stand. Afterward, they watched as the priests lighted hundreds of candles, enclosing each in an eight-sided paper lantern and setting the lanterns afloat in the shallows. Soon the current swept the flickering flotilla of lanterns out to sea, bearing with them, Jason told Maile, the contented souls of the dead, who now knew that they had not been forgotten.

When Maile began to yawn, they returned to the temple and changed into their own clothes. Maile fell asleep on Jason's shoulder as he was carrying her to the car and didn't awaken when he tucked her into the back seat and covered her with his jacket.

On the hour-long trip back to Kahaluu, Jason was unusually silent, and Lani was content to watch the road ahead, busy with her own thoughts. It had been a good day, one she would remember for a long time. More importantly, Maile would remember it, too; after today, it would be hard to convince her that the Japanese were yellow-skinned barbarians.

"How are you and Wade hitting it off?" Jason asked, breaking his silence.

"He's a very considerate employer," Lani said evasively.

"That trip to the other side of the island was rather a surprise. Maile tells me she had a narrow escape at the sinkhole. What exactly did happen?"

Lani hesitated, wishing she knew what Maile had told him. Reluctantly she described the incident, but she was careful to keep any of her secret doubts out of her voice.

"Maile seems to have a talent for this sort of thing," Jason commented when she was finished. "This is the third close call she's had in the past few months. She was a very sick girl after she ate some akia berries she'd picked in the greenhouse."

"I heard about it—and also that Maile claims the berries

were in the fruit salad she had for lunch," she said, her tone neutral.

"We all ate that fruit salad, and Maile was the only one who got sick. Of course it's natural she'd deny picking those berries. She's been told often enough not to play in the greenhouse."

"*You* were there when it happened?" Lani asked sharply.

"Uh-huh. I flew in the night before on one of my lightning visits, hoping for a couple of days' rest, but Maile's illness took care of that. She gave us a good scare there for a few hours."

"Were you there when she fell off the balcony and broke her leg?"

"As it happens, yes. Why do you ask?"

"I—I was just wondering how it happened."

"I'm not really sure. The railing had pulled out, I understand, and when Maile leaned on it, it gave way." He shook his head. "This latest incident makes you wonder if it isn't true that some people are accident-prone."

"I doubt if that applies to Maile," Lani said stiffly. "After all, I had two accidents within days of each other, and I'm certainly not accident-prone."

"What kind of accidents?"

"I was almost hit by a car before I came to Hawaii, and then, two days later, I was mugged in a Honolulu alley—" She broke off, biting her lip. Why had she called it a mugging when she had taken such pains to tell Wade she'd had a fall?

"Haven't you forgotten something? You've had another accident, too. You almost drowned in the lagoon two nights ago."

"Oh, but that wasn't an—" She broke off and gave him a hostile look. Why was it that she always seemed to be lulled into saying too much around Jason? Was this ability of his to make her let down her hair part of his journalistic bag of tricks?

"Wasn't what? An accident? You don't think someone, like maybe Maile, turned off those lights as a joke, do you?"

"I do not. Maile was in bed when I got back to the house. Of course, I have no idea where the rest of you were," she added.

"As it happened, we were all in our rooms when we heard you yelling." He took his eyes off the road long enough to glance at her. "You're pretty defensive about Maile, aren't you? Are you getting fond of the kid?"

"Of course. Aren't you?"

He didn't answer immediately. "Yes, I think I am." There was a hint of surprise in his voice. "Most of the time she acts like a spoiled brat, but she can be a pretty decent kid, like today. Maybe you bring out the best in her, Lani."

"Or maybe you do," she said.

Jason shrugged. "It's easy playing the indulgent uncle when it isn't a full-time job."

"Haven't you ever been tempted to—to settle down in one place?" she asked curiously.

"Are you asking me if I've ever been in love? Of course— several times. If you mean did anyone ever make me think of orange blossoms, the answer is yes again. It did happen, but only once—so far."

"What happened?"

"She married another man, and it sent me into a tailspin for a couple of years."

"I'm sorry. I know I shouldn't have pried into your private—" She broke off, staring at his profile. In the light of an oncoming car, she saw he was smiling.

"Aren't you ever serious?" she said crossly. "What about that truth you say you always tell?"

"Sorry. I couldn't resist. You are such a romantic, despite that cool exterior. And I was speaking the truth. There was a woman once, and she did marry another man—my cousin Wade—and promptly made his life a hell on earth. Now I tend to be a little cynical about quick physical attractions. However, I'm willing to make an exception in your case." He paused to cut around a slow-moving car, his eyes on the road. "You do know that I'm very much attracted to you, don't you? When you went off with Wade on that outing, with only Maile for a chaperone, I have to admit I was jealous as hell."

"Oh, I suspect you had a good time with Iolani," she said.

"Not really. She couldn't understand why I didn't chuck my appointment on the Big Island to escort her to that tennis exhibition. When we did meet for dinner, she had her mysterious importer in tow and devoted most of her attention to him."

"What is he like?" Lani couldn't help asking.

"Very attractive, very charming, and also very cagey. And I don't want to talk about him. It's possible that I'm falling in love with you. How does that grab you, Yula?"

"It makes me feel uncomfortable," Lani said truthfully. "I'm not very good at playing games with men."

"I've noticed that. Now I wonder why you freeze like a scared rabbit when a man pays you a compliment. I hate to use an old cliché, but—are you afraid of your own sexuality, Miss Brock?"

Lani felt a stab of disappointment. "That *is* an old cliché," she said coolly. "Why don't we talk about something else?"

Jason looked amused; he immediately launched into an entertaining account of a disastrous interview he'd once had with a reigning movie queen. She found herself laughing—and wondering what had happened to her sense of humor earlier, since it was obvious he had been teasing her.

When they reached Kahaluu, the cabin cruiser hadn't yet arrived at the landing. Jason looked at his watch, and told her they were a bit early. He glanced back at Maile, still asleep in the back seat, and opened his door. "Come on, let's stretch our legs. We can walk up and down the wharf and still keep an eye on the car. I feel restless, sitting still. It might even be dangerous, the two of us in cozy proximity in the front seat with Maile asleep in the back."

"Oh, I don't think *you'd* be in any danger," she said dryly.

But she joined him as he strolled up and down the wharf, and when he locked arms with her, she didn't pull away. His arm was surprisingly hard, and she reflected that in his line of work, a well-conditioned body might well be a prerequisite.

When they were tired, they sat on the edge of the wharf, their legs dangling over the water. Although there were still a few yellow streaks in the western sky, the sun had been down for a long time now, and the lights of Kaneohe Marine Base were sparkling like tiny fireflies on the long arm of the peninsula that jutted out at the end of the bay.

"'For me, its balmy airs are always blowing,'" Jason said softly, "'it's summer seas flashing in the sun, the pulsing of its surf beat in my ears; in my nostrils lives the breath of flowers that perished twenty years ago. . . .'"

Lani took a deep breath. "That was lovely."

"Unfortunately, Mark Twain said it first. I think of those lines every time I return to the Islands."

"You wonder why anyone born here would want to live elsewhere, don't you?"

"Even Paradise has its growing pains these days. And there are other places just as beautiful in this world, places that I personally wouldn't want to miss. When I've seen them all, I'll probably come back here to spend the remainder of my days." He turned to look at her. "You're still in transit, too, aren't you, Yula? I sensed it the first time I saw you. Life on that island out there is unreal, as unsubstantial as a dream. It's like a *kipuka*, one of those beds of growth left behind after a lava flow where life goes on undisturbed by the outside world."

"Why are you telling *me* this?"

"Because you might be tempted to stay there too long. You're much too young to get strung out on lotus blossoms."

"There's no danger of that. It's only a temporary job. As for trying my wings, aren't you being a little unrealistic? Most people don't have your options, you know. You have an exciting job that takes you to glamorous places, but as a visitor who can afford the best hotels, the finest restaurants. You don't see those places as the ordinary people do who live there. Do you really think an eight-to-five grocery clerk's job is so different in Paris from one in Columbus, Ohio? It still means grubby rooms and economy food and bill collectors."

"So you'd settle for a steady paycheck?"

"Why do you keep misunderstanding what I'm saying?" she asked, suddenly exasperated with him. "I'm not talking about money; I'm talking about options, about reality. You shouldn't be so contemptuous of people who have to settle for what they can get."

To her horror her voice wavered. She started to get up, but he pulled her back down and swung her around to face him. His hands were gentle as he smoothed her hair back from her face. She didn't try to get away; there was something inherently humiliating about struggling with him like a scared virgin. So when he kissed her, she didn't resist. She sat there quietly, only to discover that she'd waited too long to pull away. His hands moved over her hair, down to her shoulders; and his arms, lean and hard, tightened around her. With a swiftness that startled and dismayed her, her body responded to his closeness, and she found herself kissing him back.

The weakness lasted only a moment before a thread of caution stirred. Suddenly she was remembering the day in the Folly when Jason had left her alone—and then, after she'd had a good scare, had returned with his unprovoked offer of friendship. Was this more of the same? An attempt to get past her defenses, get her to confide in him? Or was it something more sinister? After all, they were all alone out here on this isolated wharf.

She stiffened in Jason's arms, and he released her immediately, his smile crooked. "Well, that answers one of my questions. You certainly aren't frigid, Yula."

She found it impossible to meet his eyes, so she stared down at his hand, still holding her arm lightly. It was a strong, well-shaped hand, and in the last yellowish light of sunset the hairs on his wrist looked like tiny golden wires. She remembered his gentleness as he'd stroked her hair, and suddenly she was wishing she hadn't been so quick to pull away.

The thought shamed her. What was wrong with her lately? Three men had kissed her in the past few days, and she had responded strongly to all three. Was she becoming some kind of sex freak?

Her self-disgust changed to anger, and the anger fastened on Jason. She removed his hand from her arm, jumped to her feet and stalked away. Although she didn't look back, she was sure that if she had, she would have seen that clown's smile of his on his face.

Until David arrived in the *Kauhelani*, she sat in the car, watching as Jason strolled up and down the wharf. What infuriated her most was the suspicion that his ease was natural, that he had already dismissed the incident from his mind.

During the trip back to Maunaloa, she stayed in the cabin, Maile's head cradled in her lap. After they docked, Jason carried Maile to the house, and somehow it added fuel to her anger that he showed no sign of fatigue, even though Maile was a dead weight in his arm. After he deposited Maile on her bed, he gave Lani an amicable smile and strolled out the door.

Lani stared after him. "Damn," she said loudly.

She undressed Maile and got her into pajamas, then awakened her to go to the bathroom. Maile was cross and whining, and Lani was relieved when she was finally tucked into bed. She left the bedside lamp on and started to turn away. Maile's sleepy voice stopped her.

"Don't go, Yula," she said drowsily. "Promise me you'll stay."

Lani picked up Maile's hand and held it tightly. "I'll stay here until you fall asleep," she promised.

"No, I didn't mean that. I don't want you to go away from Maunaloa. Everybody I like always goes away. She always finds a way to get rid of them."

"She?"

"Aunt Berta. She doesn't want me to have any friends. She tells them lies about me, and then they don't like me anymore. She sent Miss Moore away, too. I didn't want her to go. While she was here I didn't hear the voice so often."

Lani found it suddenly hard to breathe. "The voice?"

"The night voice."

"Do you hear it often?"

"Sometimes—but not since you came here."

"What does it say to you, Maile?"

"It says I'm a wicked girl and I should be punished for what I did."

"What you *did*?"

"I killed my mother and father, or at least it was my fault they drowned. They wouldn't let me go fishing with them because I hadn't cleaned up my room, and I told them I hoped a big wave would come along and sink the boat. I put a curse on them, only—only I didn't mean it." Under her eyelids two tears welled up and ran down the sides of her face. "My *aumakua* heard me say I wished the boat would sink and it killed them. So it's my fault."

"But that's just superstition," Lani said gently. "There are no such things as personal spirits, and even if there were, an *aumakua* would watch over *you*, not go around hurting other people."

"But my *aumakua* is very strong, and that's why it killed them. Now the voice says I have to kill myself. Then everything will be all right."

The hairs on the back of Lani's neck stirred. "It was a nightmare. You've been having nightmares, Maile. There isn't really any voice—"

"Yes, there is. Miss Moore heard it, too. It was raining, and she came to my room to see if the windows were open, and that's when she heard the voice. She was awful mad, and she said she was going to Aunt Berta's room to talk to her. They had a terrible fight, and Aunt Berta told Miss Moore she was a troublemaker, that she was trying to—to cement her position here by making up stories, and then she fired Miss Moore. I didn't even get to say good-bye to her, because Aunt Berta locked me in my room."

"Why didn't you tell your Uncle Wade about the voice—and that Miss Moore heard it too?"

"I did, but he said she was a bad influence on me. He said

there were some things a child my age didn't understand about people with sick minds. He told me not to think about the voice, that it was just Miss Moore playing a trick on me." Her eyes showed her hurt, and Lani bent to kiss her gently.

"I'll stay here as long as I can, Maile. And I believe that you really did hear a voice. I think someone in this house is playing a practical joke on you, pretending to be— something supernatural. If you hear the voice again, yell for me and I'll be here in a few seconds."

Maile stared up at her, and a smile started up in the corners of her mouth. "I love you, Yula," she said. She closed her eyes, and even before Lani had time to pull up a chair and sit down, she was fast asleep again.

XV

Lani sat by Maile's bed, watching her sister's sleep-flushed face. There was a slight tremor in her fingers, born of rage—and of frustration because there was so little she could do about the rage. Although the worst of her suspicions had been confirmed, she still found it hard to believe that anyone, even her aunt, could be so cruel as to try to drive a child to suicide. And yet—why was she surprised? She knew what her aunt was capable of. Was she working alone, or were her two co-conspirators also involved? Had they helped her slip akia berries into Maile's fruit salad and loosen the railing so she would tumble from the balcony? And why use such a risky, uncertain method as this latest one? Maybe it was because the first two attempts on Maile's life had failed and they were afraid three accidents in a row would arouse suspicion. And what about the incident at the sinkhole? Had it really been an accident—or the third attempt on Maile's life?

Suddenly the realization of her own helplessness almost overwhelmed her. She could do so little except watch over Maile and try to convince her that the voice was someone's idea of a bad joke and not to be taken seriously. But what could she really do about protecting her from other dangers, from some new scheme? It was foolish, maybe even dangerous, to go to Wade or Jason with her suspicions. Even if she tried to prove that Vivian was a fraud, who would believe her—an outsider with a background that couldn't stand even the most casual investigation? Although she had never participated in any of her foster parents' more dubious schemes, who would believe that—or that she wasn't their real daughter? It was a matter of record that she had been involved in at least one bunko attempt. That she hadn't been guilty would be impossible to prove at this late date.

And if she went to the police and was herself discredited, then she would have to leave Maunaloa, and who would watch over Maile? No, her wisest course was to remain quiet—and watchful. Kore would be here tomorrow. Maybe he could think of a way to help Maile. At the very least, she wouldn't be alone with her fears and her suspicions.

The next morning the tempo of activity picked up as caterers and crews of workmen descended on the island, bearing food supplies, lumber, cartons of folding chairs and rolls of heavy tapa paper. David supervised one crew, transforming the gardens into a fairyland with potted orchids, rare palms and other exotic plants from the greenhouses. Moana, her kitchen invaded by strangers, went around with a long face, complaining about the noise, about dirt tracked onto the kitchen floor, and the *haole* food piling up in the freezers.

Maile, on the other hand, was in seventh heaven as she tagged along behind David, watching as the workmen dug the *imu* for the luau pig, built a temporary bandstand for the musicians, and put together planks for the long tables that would be covered with tapa paper just before the guests arrived.

She turned up on the lanai for lunch, full of gossip and ravenously hungry. Since her two excursions, she had developed a proprietary attitude toward her uncles, and to Vivian's obvious annoyance she competed very effectively for Wade's and Jason's attention.

At first Berta seemed preoccupied with her own thoughts, but she finally took notice of Maile's unusual vivaciousness. "I understand Maile has been taking swimming and hula lessons from the Kealohas," she said to Lani. "Surely you remember that I've forbidden her to associate with those—with that family. The next thing we know, she'll be having those dreadful nightmares again."

Although Lani couldn't control the flash of heat to her face, she kept her voice even as she said: "I doubt that, Miss St. John. I plan to check up on her often during the night from now on. I doubt if she'll be having any more of those—nightmares."

Something dark and secret moved below the surface of Berta's china-blue eyes, and a nerve twitched ominously beside her mouth. Unexpectedly, it was Jason she turned her next attack upon.

"In the future, Jason, I'd appreciate it if you'd consult me before you take Maile off the island. I *am* responsible for her, and it's obvious to me that she had far too much excitement yesterday."

"No, I didn't!" Maile burst out. "We had a wonderful time—and anyway, I slept all the way home."

"There—that proves my point." Berta didn't try to hide her satisfaction. "You can see she's overstimulated, Wade. Maile is a very delicate child, and—"

"Oh, come off it, Berta. She's a tough little bird," Jason said. "What she needs is to get off this island once in a while and play with other kids her own age."

"You're very quick with your advice today. Isn't it a little late for you to take an interest in Maile? Is it possible you're trying to impress Miss Brock?"

Maile, who had been following the conversation with interest, looked a little frightened as Jason's face took on a wolfish look.

"Please—we're upsetting Maile," Lani said quickly. "I think we should talk about something else."

"And I agree," Wade said. "This isn't the time or place for this kind of discussion. We'll talk about it later, Berta."

Berta started to say something; then she met Wade's hard stare and evidently thought better of it. Although she was silent for the remainder of the meal, Lani was aware of her baleful scrutiny, and she was glad when it was time for Maile and her to go change into their exercise clothes.

They had finished their hula practice—without the supervision of Moana, who was busy defending her kitchen today—and had collapsed on the sand in front of the hau arbor to rest when Jason appeared, loaded down with cameras, equipment bags and a tripod.

He looked them over, decided their leotard-and-tights outfits were piquant, and, to Maile's delight, included her in the photography session. He took a dozen or more shots of the two of them together, then worked with Maile alone.

Lani curled up on a stone bench, watching as Maile pirouetted in the sun, following Jason's exacting directions as flawlessly as if she had been doing it all her life. From her rapt expression, it was obvious how much she enjoyed being the center of Jason's attention. Lani tried to decide whether his apparent affection for his niece was genuine, but she finally gave it up and told herself that Jason was like a mirror, reflecting only what he saw. Maybe when Kore got here, he could figure Jason—and Wade—out. She certainly couldn't.

"There—hold that expression, Yula," Jason said. He was squatting in a clump of ice plants at her feet, squinting at her through the viewfinder of his camera. "Whatever you're thinking about, keep on thinking it. You look as if you have a thousand secrets hidden behind those green eyes."

Obediently Lani tried to hold the expression on her face, but she thought how lucky it was that while she couldn't read Jason's thoughts, neither could he read hers.

Later, as they walked toward the house, Maile skipping on ahead, Jason said abruptly, "Berta was way off base today, you know. I don't know what's been eating her lately, but she had no right attacking you."

"I have the feeling that she doesn't like me. I wonder why?" Lani said.

Jason shrugged. "Who knows? She's a strange lady, that one. Maybe she doesn't care for the way Wade looks at you. She likes her position here; if he got seriously interested in a woman, it might change things for her."

"I don't believe a word of that—and neither do you," Lani said crossly. "It's obvious Wade is completely indifferent to me."

"I don't think anyone could be completely indifferent to you, Yula," Jason said softly. "The question is—are you indifferent to Wade? Tell me, were you thinking of him when you got that faraway look in your eyes a while ago?"

"I was thinking of my brother," she said, her tone short.

"Your brother? And here I was hoping you were remembering that kiss on the wharf last night."

"Wrong again," she snapped, glad they had reached the house—and the end of the conversation.

She and Maile spent the rest of the afternoon in the potting shed, working on the kukui nuts they had gathered on their trip across the island. David took a few minutes away from his work to show them how to file off the rough crust of the nuts and promised that when they had enough for a necklace, he would drill holes in the velvety black nuts.

"Maunaloa Island is a treasure house for seed collectors," he told Maile as he showed her a mason jar full of nuts. "Next time I take the boys to look for seeds, why don't you come along, Maile?"

The corners of Maile's mouth drooped. "They won't want me to come along," she said. "They don't like me."

"Sure they do, little sistah. But you make them plenty

mad, you know, when you call them names. You talk nice to them and then they play with you. You think you can do that?"

Maile, after only the smallest hesitation, nodded.

As they were returning to the house, they heard the company helicopter settling down behind the tennis courts. Lani's heart beat a little faster, knowing Kore was on the helicopter, that she would soon be seeing him. She coaxed Maile into taking a nap and then went off to her own room to look over her wardrobe.

She finally decided on the embroidered blouse Mrs. Costello had given her, remembering that Kore had always liked her best in vivid colors, but it was with mixed feelings that she began to dress. It was going to be a difficult evening, pretending that Kore was a stranger—and how would Kore make out tonight? Although he had enough self-possession for ten men, he wasn't dealing with ordinary people now. Wade and Jason, despite their dissimilar personalities, were both sophisticated and shrewd men, and Aunt Berta had already aired her disapproval of the stranger Vivian had invited to the island.

So it was with misgivings that she heard the bell ring in the hall. Since Maile had elected to eat in the kitchen tonight, declaring herself too tired to change her clothes, Lani went downstairs alone.

Kore was the first person she saw as she started down the stairs. He was standing with the others, smiling down at Vivian. To Lani's relief, the cut of his dinner jacket was as impeccable as Wade's, and he looked perfectly at ease, as if he were the host and the others his guests. Unless Vivian was putting on an act, she was very much intrigued by him, and the other men were eying him warily, as if some instinct told them that he could be a very dangerous opponent—in a business deal, in a fight, for the favors of a woman.

Kore turned as Lani came up. His eyes widened briefly, which could have been his signal that everything was under control—or that he was surprised to see the changes four years had made in her. Maybe his smile was a shade too warm during Vivian's perfunctory introduction, because she gave Lani a sharp look and then deftly extracted Kore under the pretext of showing him the gardens. They didn't reappear until Lelua opened the dining room doors.

The dinner conversation was unusually lively. Vivian, dressed in white chiffon and wearing a spectacular emerald necklace, had eyes for Kore only—to Aunt Berta's obvious disapproval. Kore was representing himself as Shane O'Neill, an importer of Oriental antiques, and he handled the role without effort, at least outwardly. As Lani listened to his account of how he acquired a prized white jade pony, she wondered what facet of his checkered career he was drawing on for his information. Only once did he show anything but perfect control; not so oddly, it was with Jason.

"I've been trying to decide what your national roots are, Mr. O'Neill," Jason said during a lull in the conversation. "Your name is Irish, of course, but somehow I wouldn't have guessed you as Irish. You look more Arabic—or perhaps East Indian."

"Oh, I'm pure Irish—or maybe not so pure," Kore said easily. "There's a lot of Moorish blood in the south of Ireland—that's Black Irish country, you know." His black eyes glittered above his wineglass as he paused to take a sip of Pinot Noir. "Are you a genealogist—or just curious, Mr. Richards?"

"I'm a journalist, and curiosity is my stock in trade. I thought I was pretty good at guessing national origins, but I've been striking out right and left lately. For instance"—he gestured lazily toward Lani—"I couldn't begin to tell you what Yula's background is. She has a chameleon quality that makes her a very exciting model to work with."

Kore's black eyes considered Yula. She sat frozen, wishing furiously that Jason would change the subject. "Miss Brock is very attractive," he said finally.

"Yes, but that isn't what makes her interesting to a photographer." He studied Kore's dark face, frowning. "I'd be interested in seeing how you photograph, O'Neill."

"Sorry. I have a thing about cameras."

There was a slight edge in Kore's voice. Lani was glad when Jason dropped the subject and the conversation became general again. Although Kore looked perfectly relaxed, Lani sensed his tension and wondered what nerve Jason had touched. Was it his old protectiveness toward her surfacing—or simply his Rom aversion to having his picture taken? Whatever it was, he held his own during the rest of the meal, skillfully fielding anything that became too personal; and there was no denying that his charm was very effective. Even Aunt Berta forgot her disapproval long enough to ask him, a bit stiffly, if he was comfortable in the guest cottage.

Lani resisted an impulse to smile at Kore. No matter how often she'd seen Kore's magnetism at work, it still amused her, mainly because she was convinced it was largely unconscious on his part. So she wasn't surprised that Vivian took him off immediately after dinner to see the lagoon by moonlight, pointedly not inviting anyone else along.

Shortly afterward, Lani found an excuse to leave. She felt restive as she went up to her room; not even to herself would she admit the reason she felt so out of sorts.

Although she tried to get interested in a book, she had a hard time concentrating. Again and again her thoughts wandered back to the dinner party. Was it imagination, or had there been an unusual current of discord during dinner, more than the presence of an outsider could account for? Did someone there suspect a connection between Kore and her, or was she becoming paranoid, seeing conspiracies and plots everywhere?

Even a good night's sleep didn't dispel her restlessness. She spent the morning in the office typing an inventory list for Wade, who had gone to his office in Honolulu for the day. Not particularly eager to see Vivian fawning over Kore, she ate breakfast early, skipped lunch altogether and spent the afternoon with Maile in the potting shed, working on kukui nuts.

When Maile went up to her room for her afternoon rest, the thought of a walk tempted her. She started off without any particular destination in mind, but somewhere between the house and the beach she made the decision to visit her parents' graves, something she had put off far too long.

The sun was low enough in the eastern sky that the seawall cast a long shadow over the sand, and she walked in shade as she skirted the promontory where the hau arbor was located. A few yards farther, she passed the cluster of neat cottages where the Kealohas lived. She heard a radio playing rock-and-roll music, and a boy's shrill voice, and she remembered Moana telling her that David's sons had returned the day before from their annual summer visit to their grandparents in Hilo.

She moved into sun again as she rounded a long curve in the beach. The cemetery was hidden from the beach by a grove of plumeria trees, and the jasminelike fragrance of plumeria blossoms filled her nostrils as she left the beach and climbed the narrow path that ended at an ornate iron gate.

The cemetery was a peaceful, timeless place, looking more like New England than Hawaii, with its simple white stone crosses and its iron picket fence. Six generations of Stevensons and Kealohas lay here in ivy-covered graves; although some of the graves bore other names, the stones always included the family name of the occupant. There was no segregation. From the first, the plots had been assigned in order of demise.

The iron gate moved noiselessly on well-oiled hinges as she opened it and went inside. She walked between the well-tended graves, searching the stone markers for her parents' names. She found their graves together near the gate. Next to her father, flanking his other side, was the grave of his second wife, Maile's mother. Until now, Lani hadn't known that her stepmother's name had been Lilia.

She stood there for a long time, staring at her parents' graves, waiting for some revelation, some sign or message from the past, but all she felt was a gentle, soft-edged grief.

After a while she turned away and began walking aimlessly among the markers, stopping now and then to read the name engraved on a cross. She found Captain Aaron and his beloved Abigail, who had died so young. Had it been because of the curse, as the Hawaiians believed? Other early deaths were recorded on other stones, some shrouded so far in the past that Lani had no idea what their relationship to her had been. Near Captain Aaron's grave she found a stone that bore the single name KEALOHA and the dates 1800–1865. Had this been the *kahuna* who had put the curse on the Stevensons? If so, how strange that he, a heathen by Aaron Stevenson's standards, should be buried with a cross to mark his grave, within touching distance of the man toward whom he had been so vindictive.

She was passing a cluster of trees when she heard a low humming, then a snatch of song.

"—*kuu pua, kuu lei, kuu milimili e.* . . ."

She threaded her way through the trees, and it seemed perfectly natural, an extension of her own thoughts, that Kawena should be sitting there on a mound of ivy, her frail body framed by a clump of torch ginger.

Lani's throat tightened as she saw how Kawena had aged. She was wearing a high-necked muumuu; the wicker basket in her lap was filled with plumeria blossoms, and the ground beside her was heaped with leis. As Lani watched, Kawena's fingers, brown and still nimble, pierced a flower with a needle and drew the waxy blossom down the thread. A small brown-skinned boy was squatting at her feet, watching her.

Although Lani's feet had made no sound on the spongy ivy, Kawena stopped and lifted her head. Except for the slight milkiness in her brown eyes, Lani would have thought it was all some mistake, that Kawena could see her standing there.

"*Aloha nui kakow*." Kawena's voice was soft and lilting as a young girl's. "You come visit with Kawena? Maybe you like to help make leis for luau tomorrow?"

Lani was silent, afraid to try to talk around the lump in her throat. She sat down near Kawena, cross-legged on the ivy. The boy looked at her shyly and ducked his head.

"That's Peter, David and Lehua's *keiki*. He's one rascal boy, but ver' big for ten, I t'ink."

"Yes, he is. He looks like his father," Lani said.

The feathery wrinkles around Kawena's eyes deepened. "All Kealoha men good-looking. They marry good, strong women—like me—and we give them strong *keikis*." She picked up the lei in her lap and began stringing blossoms again. "Moana say you come to help Maile get strong again. Maybe you like to stay here on Maunaloa long time?"

"Maunaloa is a very beautiful place," Lani said evasively.

"One time, this island was belong to Hawaiian people. Someday it belong to us again. We ver' proud people, but we got no place just for us. At University, they teach people how to talk Hawaiian, but they call it foreign language. *Auwe! We* not the foreigners here! *Aloha aina*—love of land is part of Hawaiian, part of blood that pump through our hearts. So we make plenty *pilikia*, make trouble for Navy on Kahoolawe, and someday they pay attention."

"Do you think the Stevensons will return Maunaloa Island to the Hawaiian people eventually?"

"Yes, that happen, but maybe not while I still alive. Mr. John say he want Maunaloa to be place where Hawaiian people come, fish in bay and walk in forests like in old times, but then he die too young, that man, before he can sign da kine papers that make it park, make old house into place for old Hawaiian t'ings like Bishop Museum."

"Wouldn't you lose your home if that happened?"

"That not matter. Mr. John say he put David in charge of Maunaloa, and David ver' *hauoli*, ver' happy, make plans for restore old village, rebuild fishponds and taro fields so people can see how old Hawaiians live. Then Mr. John have accident and so that never happen. Not right time, I tell David. First, sacred stones come back to Lono's Spring. Curse will end, and then maybe Maunaloa belong to Hawaiian people again."

"Maybe—maybe Miss Stevenson will turn it over eventually."

Kawena shook her head. "That one no care for Hawaiians, no care for nothing but pretty t'ings to wear. She was *hanai* child to Kawena, but now she forget old friends, not care about island."

There was grief on Kawena's face and the telltale sheen of tears in her blind eyes. Lani felt a surge of compassion, of love for her old nurse, and something happened to her caution, to her resolution to keep a tight rein on her emotions. Before she had time to reconsider, she had already reached out to pick up Kawena's frail hand.

"When I used to come to you, crying because someone had hurt my feelings or because I had a skinned knee," she said softly, "you would put your arms around me and tell me, 'No need for cry, Lani. Cry no good, only make *pilikia*. All *pau* cry—we laugh and have plenty good time now.'"

Kawena bent toward her, her head tilted to one side as if listening to something audible only to her own ears. She reached out and touched Lani, and Lani sat quietly, waiting, as Kawena's fingers explored her face.

Kawena sighed deeply and her hands dropped away. She turned her face toward her grandson, who was watching them with awed eyes. "Run to house, Peter—*wikiwiki* now!—and tell Lehua to put on pot for tea. You say to mama—Kawena got special guest. Say ver' old friend come back to Maunaloa."

She waited, her face composed, until he was gone before she spoke to Lani. "Why you no come back to Maunaloa before this, Lani? Why you stay away so long from yo' *hanai* mama? You t'ink yo' old friends believe you shoot yo' mama? We nevah believe that—nevah!"

A trembling started up inside Lani. She found herself in Kawena's sinewy arms, not sure if she went to Kawena or if Kawena found her first. She let Kawena rock her, pet her, scold her, and when the storm was over, she told her old nurse what had happened the day her mother died, something she had never been able to tell anyone before, not even Kore.

The day it happened, everybody had been too busy for her. Kawena and Moana had been cleaning house, getting it ready for an influx of weekend guests. David and his twin brothers were working in the gardens, and even if it had occurred to Lani to seek out her aunt, she knew Aunt Berta was busy too, writing letters in her room.

As usual when there were no guests, her mother had retired to the Folly with a book and a decanter of wine. Her father had gone off in his sailboat before Lani came down to breakfast, another source of Lani's discontent. Although she had strict orders never to bother her mother when she was resting in the Folly, Lani was so bored that she went there to try to coax her into a game of Monopoly, which she had recently developed a passion for.

On the way, thinking to soften her mother up, she gathered feathery lehua blossoms and made a lei; but her mother, lying on a chaise longue, tossed the lei aside and told Lani to run along and stop bothering her. Hurt and angry, Lani ran off to nurse her grievance in her favorite hiding place, the clump of a'pe plants behind the Folly.

She fell asleep there, curled up under an umbrella of giant a'pe leaves. Later, angry voices awakened her. She recognized her father's voice, and she knew he was very angry because he was shouting, accusing her mother of things Lani only half understood. But she understood her mother all too well when she screamed back and told him that if he tried to get a divorce, she would stand up in court and swear that he wasn't Lani's father, that she had been pregnant by another man before she'd met him.

Lani crouched there, her mother's hateful words echoing in her ears, and something cold and vindictive inside her was glad when she heard a slapping sound and knew her father had struck her mother. A few moments later she heard the shot, and she could only cower there, afraid to move, almost afraid to breathe.

There was the crunch of feet on the path. She looked through an opening in the a'pe leaves and saw her father, his face so distorted by anger that she hardly recognized him, hurrying down the path toward the wharf. A few minutes later his sailboat was heading out into the bay.

It was a long time before she found the courage to move. When she did, she ran to her room and hid in her closet. But she found no peace there, and eventually she was driven to return to the Folly to find out what had happened to her mother. Why hadn't she gone to Kawena for help? Maybe it was because, even that early, she had known that she would have to cover up for her father, protect him.

So she was alone when she returned to the Folly. Her mother was dead, lying on her back, her chest covered with blood, and next to her was the gun that Lani had last seen in her father's desk drawer. At that moment, with her own world collapsing around her, she had only one thought—to hide her father's gun. She crept forward, skirting her mother's body, and picked up the gun—and this was how her aunt found her, standing over her mother with the gun in her hand.

Her aunt screamed at her, called her a monster, an unnatural child; and when Lani tried to defend herself, she found she had lost her voice. She ran from the Folly then and hid in the greenhouse under a potting table, but not for long. Later, she couldn't remember who found her and brought her back to Maunaloa. Her memory of the rest of the day was clouded too. She moved through it like a shadow, a ghost among ghosts, but she never forgot her father's grey face when he finally appeared and was told what had happened, just as she never forgot her hurt when he turned and walked away from her and she realized that he was going to let her take the blame. . . .

When she was finished, Lani sat there, holding Kawena's hand, feeling drained, but strangely at peace. Kawena rocked back and forth, her sightless eyes moist.

"*Auwe!* Such a big burden for a *keiki*," she said. "We nevah t'ink you do this t'ing, kill yo' mama, but we t'ink it was accident. I tell Mr. John, you no can send that *keiki* away with her aunt. That woman is bad, not good for Lani. Give Lani to me, I tell him. I take her, raise her, make her well; but no, he say the doctors t'ink you no get well if you stay here. Now I know why he no listen. It was bad t'ing he did, let you take the blame, but I t'ink he ver' sorry. He talk about you alla time, say he nevah happy since he send you away. Then we hear you are kidnap, maybe dead. Why you nevah come back, Lani? Where you been all these years?"

Lani talked for a long time, telling Kawena about her life since she'd left Boston, and by the time she finally ran down, the sun had disappeared behind the cliffs. There was still no wind, and the air was warm, oppressively moist.

"Wind drop its wings," Kawena said, sighing. "Air ver' heavy—not good sign. Kona wind come soon and bring storm with it, maybe tomorrow, maybe next day." She smiled at Lani. "Now we go to house and have tea, and you tell Kawena more about that Gypsy woman who take you in."

As they walked toward the settlement, Kawena's hand rested lightly on Lani's arm, but it was obvious that she had taken this path so often that she didn't need guidance.

"After Mr. John die and that woman come here, we watch out for Maile best we can," Kawena said suddenly. "Then you come back and we t'ink everyt'ing be okay, that soon you get rid of your aunt and that girl. But then you no speak up, no say anyt'ing."

It was a few seconds before the significance of her words sank in. Lani stopped in the middle of the path to stare at her. "You already knew who I was?"

"Not at first. But you no can fool Moana and David for long."

"But—they never said anything to me."

"They afraid for you. They t'ink you lose memory, that you got da kine amnesia. So if they tell anybody, maybe somet'ing bad happen to you."

Lani discovered that her mouth was dry. "Who were they afraid of, Kawena?"

"Afraid of yo' aunt. She ver' bad, that one, got *he naau kuko*."

Lani found herself nodding, although she knew Kawena couldn't see. "Yes, Aunt Berta does have a covetous heart."

Kawena moved her head restlessly. "Big *pilikia* coming. Can feel it, getting closer and closer. You still have *aumakua* Kawena gave you, Lani?"

"I still have the shark's tooth."

"You wear it—wear it alla time. Ver' strong *mana*—maybe it protect you from evil. I can feel dark cloud all around you—ver' bad business, da kine cloud."

"I'll be careful. I promise to keep my doors locked at night," Lani said, smiling.

"Maybe not kind of evil you can lock outside. Maybe danger come from inside. Mo' bettah you watch yo' heart, not let it fool you."

Lani's pulse jumped. "That's odd. Just before Pearsa had her stroke, she said almost those same words to me."

"This Pearsa—she was yo' *hanai* mama, too? She make room in her heart for you?"

"She was very good to me."

"She was *kahuna*?"

"I thought she was at first, but now I know she was just a very wise woman."

Kawena made an impatient gesture. "Alla same t'ing, that. So you mind what Pearsa tell you; mind Kawena, too. Plenty big trouble heading this way, coming to Maunaloa Island, coming to you."

And it seemed to Lani, as they started up the path again, that the air, which had been so warm and sultry, had suddenly taken on a chill, and that Kawena's words had a prophetic ring.

XVI

It was dusk when Lani finally left Kawena's cottage. She walked along the path that led from the settlement to Maunaloa House, thinking how many generations of Kealohas had traveled over these same worn stones during the decades. Despite Kawena's warning, she felt revitalized, as if an intolerable burden had been lifted from her. Just to say the words aloud, to share the secret of her mother's death with someone she could trust, was reason enough for her change of mood. Another reason, equally strong, was her reunion with Kawena. It occurred to her that the three people—Kawena, Maile, Kore—that she cared for most were here on the island. How could she feel anything but hopeful that things would work out right in the end?

She had intended to take the back stairs to her room, but when she reached the *mauka* wing the small service door was locked, and she remembered that Berta had ordered Moana to lock up the house that morning because there were so many outsiders on the island.

She retraced her steps and went in through the front entrance of the main house, hoping to reach her room unseen. But as she was passing the living room, her aunt came to the door and beckoned to her.

"Would you step in here a moment, Miss Brock?" she said.

Lani, aware of her tousled hair and rumpled dress, followed Berta into the living room. It was a large room, of near-ballroom size, and its furnishings were old, some pieces dating back to Captain Aaron's time. But it wasn't the familiar room or its mellow old furniture that made Lani stare around. To her surprise, since she had heard no voices as she let herself into the house, the room seemed full of people—everyone on the island, in fact, except Kore and the members of Kawena's family she'd just left in the settlement.

Moana and David Kealoha, their brown faces impassive, stood side by side near the door, so close that she could have touched David's muscular arm. Maile, her hazel eyes watchful, sat between her two uncles on one of the room's graceful Empire sofas. Although Wade was grim-faced, it was Jason's smile that told Lani something was wrong. It was tight-lipped, more grimace than real, and there was the same wolfish look in his eyes that she had noticed once before.

Of them all, only Vivian seemed at ease. She lounged in a high-backed chair, looking so complacent that Lani knew that whatever was going on, it had something to do with Vivian.

"We've been waiting for you, Miss Brock." Berta's voice was icy. "Would you mind telling me where you've been for the past two hours?"

Lani met the suppressed fury in her aunt's eyes; she braced herself for a surge of the old fear. When it didn't come, when all she felt was contempt tinged with caution, she knew that what she had told Kore was true, that she was no longer afraid of her aunt. *Why, she's just a greedy old woman*, she thought.

"I went for a walk," she said. "I met Kawena Kealoha and her grandson in the cemetery. They were making garlands to decorate the bandstand for the luau tomorrow, so I stayed to help them. Later, Kawena invited me to her house for tea to meet several of her grandchildren who are visiting." She turned her head and smiled at Moana and David. "It was very pleasant. By the time I left, I felt as if we were old friends."

Moana didn't smile back; the only sign that she under-stood was the slight movement of her eyelids. David wasn't so restrained; a smile split his broad face and he chuckled low in his throat.

Berta gave them a sharp look. "You two can go now," she said. "You'd better delay dinner for an hour."

She waited, not trying to hide her impatience, until they were gone before she turned back to Lani. "I advise you to consider my questions very carefully before you answer them, Miss Brock."

"Is something wrong?" Lani asked.

"Yes, indeed. Someone has taken my niece's emerald necklace, the one she wore to dinner last night."

"Taken? You mean it's been stolen?"

"Iolani remembers taking it off and putting it away in her jewel chest last night after dinner. Now it's missing. What have you to say about that, Miss Brock?"

Until this moment it hadn't occurred to Lani what her aunt's questions, her hostile attitude, implied. When she realized she was being accused of theft, her first reaction was incredulity.

"Are you accusing *me* of taking the necklace?" she de-manded. "Why, that's absurd!"

"I haven't made any accusations, but I think you'd better explain what you were doing in my niece's room this morn-ing."

"But—but that's not true. I spent the whole morning in the office, finishing up a household inventory list for Mr. MacMasters."

Vivian widened her eyes at Lani. "But I saw you coming out of my room," she said sweetly.

"That's a—you've made a mistake, Miss Stevenson. I've never been in your room. I have no reason to go into that part of the house."

She paused, taking in the disbelief on her aunt's face and the suspicion in Wade's grey eyes. Instinctively she looked at Jason, but it was impossible to guess what he was think-ing. *The compleat spectator*, she thought, irrationally an-noyed with him.

"If you think the necklace has been stolen," she said, forcing the words through stiff lips, "then you should call the police. But be careful whom you accuse. There's such a thing as slander."

Jason laughed softly. "Your move, Berta," he murmured.

"If you've had nothing to do with this business," Berta said, ignoring Jason, "then you won't have any objections if we search your room, will you?"

"You'd better search the guest cottages, too," Maile piped up. "I saw that friend of Vivian's going up the staircase this morning, pretending he was looking at the paintings."

"Mr. O'Neill waited in the hall while I changed into tennis clothes—which is when I saw Miss Brock leaving my room. What's more, we spent the whole morning together." Vivian considered Maile thoughtfully. "You're quite the little troublemaker, aren't you? It's about time someone took you in hand and taught you some manners."

Color flooded Maile's face. "That necklace doesn't even belong to you," she spat. "It was *my* mother's, not yours—and you didn't even ask me if you could take it out of the bank vault!"

"This quarreling is getting us nowhere," Wade said sharply. He turned an unsmiling look on Lani. "Do you have any objection to having your room searched, Yula? It might be the quickest way to settle this thing."

Lani hesitated—and saw his eyes darken. Reluctantly she nodded, and then, too late, realized that she might have fallen into a trap. If the theft was Berta and Vivian's way of getting rid of her, then they probably had planted the necklace in her room, and she was a fool to have made it so easy for them. Was Wade in on it? He had boxed her in very neatly, making it almost impossible for her to refuse.

Silently Lani led the way up the stairs, through the main house and down the long hall to the *mauka* wing. The others followed just as silently, but only Maile walked beside Lani. Just before they reached Lani's room, she whispered, "Don't worry, Yula," just as if she were the adult and Lani the child.

After Lani switched on the lights, she went to stand by the windows. There was something inherently degrading about having another person touching her possessions, opening drawers, shaking out her shoes, but she kept her temper under rigid control. Vivian, after a half-hearted attempt to help Berta, gave it up and sat in one of the chairs looking bored. As Berta searched swiftly, Vivian surveyed Lani's possessions, her eyes weighing the value of the trinkets that Berta tumbled onto the bed from Lani's small jewel case.

Feeling increasingly humiliated, Lani stared at the bits of jewelry, and a feeling that something was wrong came to her. She examined them more closely, and the anger inside her simmered higher, as she realized that the shark's tooth that Kawena had given her was missing. She started to speak, then reconsidered. Who would believe that she also had been the victim of a theft? Wouldn't they think it was an attempt to cover up her guilt?

"What do you have in here?" her aunt said, holding up the small metal box that Lani had hidden in her suitcase. "Why is this locked?"

"I keep my private papers in there," Lani said quickly.

"Indeed. Well, something's rattling inside, and it doesn't sound like paper to me. If you have nothing to hide, then I'm sure you won't mind opening it for me, will you?"

"But I do mind."

"Maybe you should open the box, Yula," Wade said. "I promise you that no one will read your private papers."

Lani knew she had no choice. She took a tiny key from its hiding place in the lining of her suitcase, opened the box and turned it upside down on the bed. The envelope that held her papers, bound with a cord, fell onto the bed—and so did Pearsa's breastpiece of gold coins.

Before Lani could move, Berta pounced on the breastpiece, holding it up. "These are real gold coins. What on earth are you doing with this?"

"It belongs to a friend of mine." Lani held out her hand for it. "Please be careful; some of those fittings are very old and fragile."

Berta dropped the breastpiece on the bed, but she wasn't finished yet. "Whom does it really belong to—your last employer?" she asked nastily.

Lani took a deep breath. "It was entrusted to me by a friend just before she died. It belongs to her son. When I find him, I'll turn it over, but until then I'm responsible for it."

Jason ambled over to stare at the coins. He touched a gold eagle with his fingertips. "It's a *sumadjii*, isn't it?" he said. At Lani's start, he added, "I did a photo-essay on a Rom *familia* once for a national magazine. The old matriarch of the tribe wore one of these to her son's wedding."

"Yes, it's a *sumadjii*," Lani said reluctantly.

"Do you have anyone who can verify your story?" Wade asked.

Lani turned and faced him. "I don't have to verify it, any more than you have to verify where you got your wristwatch or your golf clubs. If my word isn't good enough—"

"Why should we believe the word of an ex-con?" Vivian said. Unnoticed by Lani, she had moved to the bed. Lani's heart jumped as she saw the papers in Vivian's hand. "This is a social worker's report. It says you confessed to being involved in a bunko charge. And this one"—she extracted another paper and waved it triumphantly—"is from your parole officer. According to it, you got a suspended sentence because of your youth. It also says you belong to a notorious family of Gypsies."

Lani stalked to the bed. She took the papers from Vivian's hand, folded them neatly, inserted them into the envelope, put it and the *sumadjii* into the box, locked it. She swung around then, hot words trembling on her lips, but before she could speak Maile flew out of her chair and confronted Vivian.

"Yula didn't do anything wrong," she stormed. "It was her mother—she was old and sick, and Yula knew she would die if they shut her up in that jail. So she said she was the one who switched that lady's ten-dollar bills to one-dollar bills."

"How do you know all this, Maile?" Jason asked.

"Yula has been telling me stories about her friend who lived with the Roms, only—only she was talking about herself, and there wasn't any friend, I guess."

"Why are you so ready to believe that Yula was telling you the truth about the bunko charge?"

"Why would she lie?" Maile replied. "Now I know why she looked so sad when she told me about it. I guess it was awful, being in that detention hall, waiting to find out if she would have to go to a real prison. She was scared that if the judge put her away, her mother would confess, and Yula was sure she would die in—"

"You're getting overexcited, Maile!" Berta interrupted, her voice sharp. "Go to your room! I won't have you upset by something that doesn't concern you."

Lani saw rebellion flare in Maile's eyes. To forestall another outburst, she gave her sister's hand a squeeze. "If you really want to help me, you'll do as your aunt says, Maile. You don't want anyone thinking I'm responsible for upsetting you, do you?"

She was sure Maile would give her an argument, but to her surprise her sister turned and walked out of the room without another word.

Berta gave Lani a venomous look. "I don't believe that story about your mother, not for one moment." She was breathing so hard that the words had a strangled sound. "I refuse to have my niece associated with a Gypsy and a jailbird. I want you off this island as quickly as you can pack your—"

"That's enough, Berta." Wade's voice had a steeliness that matched the chill in his eyes. "Yula works for me, and I'm not convinced she had anything to do with that necklace. Now the rest of you clear out of here. I want to talk with Yula alone."

Lani didn't watch them leave. Wade's unexpected support—*if that's what it is*, she thought—had almost been her undoing. She turned her back on them, fighting for control, and when she turned around again, it was to find that only Jason and Wade remained. For whatever reason,

Vivian and Berta had left without argument.

Jason was still leaning against the wall near the door, his arms folded across his chest. "If you want Wade to go too, just say so," he told Lani. "I think you've already had enough of this family for one day."

A look of annoyance crossed Wade's face. "I have no intention of giving Yula a hard time."

"I'll be okay—and thank you, Jason," Lani said, suddenly wanting it over with so she could be alone.

Jason pushed himself away from the wall. He gave her a wink and sauntered out the door, leaving a pulsating silence behind him.

Lani forced herself to look at Wade. "I hope you meant that about believing I know nothing about Miss Stevenson's necklace," she said stiffly.

"I think there've been enough accusations tossed around here tonight. And I want to apologize for Iolani. She had no right to read your papers. As for Berta, she overstepped her authority. I'll see that she apologizes for her rudeness tomorrow. But that isn't what I want to talk to you about. I'm curious why you thought you had to lie to me about being a Rom. If my memory's correct, you denied it even before I offered you a job. Are you ashamed of your heritage? You gave me quite a lecture on ethnic pride a few days ago. I'd hate to think you were a hypocrite, or a pathological liar like—" He broke off.

"Like your wife?" she said.

The words lay between them. She watched the chill come back into his eyes, and when he swung around and left the room, she knew she had found an effective way, after all, to be alone.

For a long time she stood there, staring at the closed door. If she could have recalled her words, she would have; since she couldn't, she went to put her shoes back in the armoire, to replace her trinkets in the jewel case.

The dinner bell rang a few minutes later. Maile's footsteps came down the hall and stopped at her door. Lani waited for a knock, but the steps moved on again.

Since it would have been impossible to face the others so soon, she had already decided to skip dinner. She took her time preparing for bed, stretching her bath out, washing and blow-drying her hair, filing her nails and replacing the clear lacquer. When she finally came out of the bathroom wearing pajamas, the room felt very hot and stuffy. Even after she opened the hall door, there was no wind to stir the curtains or cool the room.

She was sitting by the window, hoping a breeze would start up, when she heard a sound behind her. She looked around to find Jason standing in the doorway, smiling at her over a covered tray.

"Compliments of the chef," he said.

She got up to take the tray from him and put it on the dressing table. "I didn't realize you and Moana were such good friends," she said.

"Oh, we get along—but very warily on Moana's part. She thinks I'm something of a kolea, I'm afraid."

"A kolea?"

"Yeah. That's an Island bird that stays in one place only long enough to fill its belly before it moves on somewhere else."

Lani laughed at his rueful grimace. "Whose idea was the tray?" she asked.

"Moana was putting the finishing touches on it when I went into the kitchen for—to talk with David. I volunteered to make the long trek to your room so I could check up on you."

"Aren't you afraid you may be contaminated if you associate with an ex-con—or a thieving Gypsy?"

She hadn't intended to sound bitter, but some of her resentment must have crept into her voice, because Jason's eyes sharpened. "But I *have* associated with Roms—and also with jewel thieves—and I'm still reasonably uncontaminated. And there's no percentage in hiding in your room, wallowing in self-pity, Yula. That's as unproductive as hell. You should have come down to dinner and looked them all straight in the eye."

Lani flushed, knowing he was right. She *had* been feeling sorry for herself. On the other hand, who was this—this kolea bird to give her advice?

"What was the real reason you volunteered to bring the tray to me?" she asked coolly. "To satisfy your curiosity? You really are something of an elephant child, aren't you?"

"That's my girl," he said approvingly. "Fight back. Why should you care what Berta, what any of us think about you? And you're so right about me. I do have a well-developed curiosity bump. For instance, I'm very curious why you broke with your *familia*. That's rare with Roms, isn't it? No matter how much they fight among themselves, they present a unified front to outsiders, don't they? Somehow I can't believe you're ashamed of your own people, so it must be something else. You want to talk about it, Yula?"

She met his eyes. Although there was no censure there, it was important suddenly that he not think she was ashamed of her own roots.

"I'm not really a Rom," she said, choosing her words carefully, "but I was raised by a Rom woman. When my foster mother died, I found I had no real ties with the rest of the family, so I went off on my own."

"She's the one who gave you the *sumadjii*?"

"I'm keeping it for her son. There was a quarrel and we lost track of each other. Someday I hope to turn it over to him."

"Do you have any other relatives—real ones, I mean?"

"I'm an orphan. I had a very—very mixed up childhood. After my mother died no one wanted me, so Pearsa took me in. She treated me as if I were her own daughter."

"Then you were a lucky girl, weren't you? Some kids drift from foster home to foster home and never find anyone who really gives a damn about them."

"I was very lucky," she agreed.

"Okay, so now let's figure out how to pull ole Berta's sting. Were you really in Iolani's room this morning?"

"As I've already said, I was working in the office all morning."

210

Jason smiled briefly at the edge in her voice. "I wonder why Berta was so riled up about that necklace," he said. "You'd think it belonged to her instead of to Iolani."

"I don't know—maybe it's because she thinks I took it. She's been hostile to me ever since I came here."

Jason wandered around the room, stopping once to examine an ornately framed seascape, another time to finger an acanthus-leaf carving on the tall headboard of the bed.

"Why are you trying to help me?" Lani asked suddenly.

"Maybe because I have a thing for underdogs."

"A dog?" She raised her eyebrows. "I thought I reminded you of a horse."

"When you were facing up to Berta, you reminded me of a tiger. And I think I'd better go and let you eat your dinner before it gets cold. From what I saw of it, it beats the over-cooked chicken we had tonight." He gave her a speculative look. "The Kealohas seem to have taken you under their wings. First Kawena has you to tea, then Moana fixes you special goodies for dinner. Right now David is in the kitchen, glowering like one of those koa carvings of Ku, the Hawaiian war god, muttering what he'd like to do to Berta."

"I guess it's part of Hawaiian character to—to be friendly to strangers," she said.

"Not as much as *malihinis*—outsiders—would like to think. The old image of the happy-go-lucky Hawaiian is a little obsolete these days, and with good cause, since that's how they lost the Islands in the first place. The Kealohas in particular are a very clannish bunch."

It was hard to think of an answer to that, so she was glad when he smiled at her and added, "You look very fetching in those thin pajamas, you know, with your hair still a little damp around the edges. Maybe I'd better leave before my baser impulses take over and I make a serious pass at you after all."

He was gone, leaving the door standing open behind him. Lani discovered she was smiling. Whatever Jason's reason for coming here, she had to admit she felt much better than she had before he came, especially when she took the domed cover off the tray and found that it was loaded with an assortment of Island food. All her old favorites were there—crisp won ton, pork tofu, lomi-lomi salmon, a salad of watercress and taro tops, and fried rice made with bits of crab, the way she liked it.

Her eyes smarted when she saw the small bowl of one-finger poi, laced with cream and sugar. On the occasions when her mother allowed her to eat breakfast at Kawena's house, she had always asked for poi served this way. After all this time Moana had remembered, and it was like a warm hand on her shoulder to know that she had taken this way to say, "Welcome back to Maunaloa, Lani!"

Although she would have sworn she couldn't eat a bite, she realized now that she was ravenously hungry. But as she picked up a fork to spear a piece of salmon, there was a low whistle—a peculiar, two-level sound—outside her window. When the whistle came again, she forgot all about eating. One whistle was Kore's signal that he wanted to see her, and two meant she should come as quickly as possible.

XVII

Lani changed into a skirt and blouse and hurried out of the house. Although she followed the path to the hau arbor, she was careful to walk on the sand beside it so that her feet would make no telltale sound. It was so still tonight that every noise was amplified, and the surf, usually so unobtrusive in the cove, seemed very close as it seethed against the shore somewhere in the soft darkness. There was still no wind, and the night air, which should have been cool and fresh, was sultry, and tainted with the acrid odor of burning cane which had drifted over from Oahu.

When she reached the arched entrance of the arbor, she paused briefly, listening. There was no sound inside, but she caught a whiff of cigarette smoke and knew Kore was already there, waiting for her.

As she ducked under the trailing hau branch, Kore's voice came out of the darkness. "Well, kid, you've had one hell of a day, haven't you?"

His voice was so familiar, so much a part of a good time in her life, that she forgot her resolution to stay cool and convince Kore that she could take care of herself. She flew toward him and almost bowled him over in the dark. When he caught her and steadied her so she wouldn't fall, she burrowed her face into his chest. His arms closed around her; under her cheek, she heard his heart pumping so rapidly that she wondered if he'd been worried about her.

"Okay, tell me about it," he ordered. "Why weren't you at

213

dinner? Something's happened, hasn't it?"

Inside the circle of his arms, it was easy to treat the whole humiliating episode lightly, to pass it off as a joke. But Kore wasn't fooled. As she talked, his body stiffened and his arms tightened until she could hardly breathe.

"The bloody old fool," he said when she was finished. "She must have really spooked you. It's a wonder you didn't give the whole thing away."

"Actually, she didn't scare me at all. It came to me suddenly that she's just a—a dried-up old woman. Of course she can still cause me a lot of trouble. I'd feel a lot better if that necklace turned up."

"Maybe one of the workmen snatched it."

"I suppose that's the answer; only I wonder how anyone got into the house? Aunt Berta had the doors locked, even the ones into the kitchen wing. Moana was grumbling about the inconvenience all day." She hesitated, then added, "Maile saw you looking at the pictures on the staircase wall while you were waiting for Vivian to change into her tennis clothes. The police may question you tomorrow—can you stand an investigation, Kore?"

Kore gave a low laugh. "I didn't take that damned necklace, if that's what's bugging you. I do my robbing legally now, like the *gadje* do. I really do have an import business in Seattle. So, you see, your ex-brother is legit these days."

"I'm glad," she said lightly. Not even to herself would she admit how relieved she felt.

"How about the Kealohas? Any chance they took those emeralds?"

"No, that's impossible," Lani said. "But maybe Vivian cooked up the whole thing to get rid of me. After all, I wasn't anywhere near Vivian's room today, so she deliberately lied."

Kore grunted. "She wouldn't have the brains to set up anything like this."

"Why, I thought you were very impressed with her. You've seemed to enjoy her company these past two days," Lani teased.

Kore brushed aside her words. "Don't change the subject. How is this going to affect your job?"

"Wade apologized for Vivian and Aunt Berta—he *says* he doesn't believe I took the necklace. On the other hand, he didn't like it because he thinks I lied to him about not being a Rom."

"Why did you tell the kid so much about yourself, anyway? That was pretty careless, wasn't it?"

Lani smiled in the dark. Kore may have changed some of his ways, but he still had the Rom instinct for secrecy. "It was an accident at first, something that slipped out. Maile was so fascinated that I promised to tell her more about the Roms and carnival life if she would do her exercises every day." Her words reminded her that she hadn't talked to Kore for several days, and she went on to tell him about the voice that had been tormenting Maile at night, of her determination to protect Maile.

Kore was silent for a long time when she was finished. "What are you going to do? Step forward and try to prove who you are?" he asked finally.

"I may have to. After what happened today, I could be fired any minute, and then there'd only be the Kealohas to watch out for Maile. There's something else, Kore: I don't want to see Maunaloa Island turned into a resort, a playground for rich *malihinis*. Captain Aaron bought it for a few hundred dollars, but the island wasn't really part of the royal estate. It had always been a place apart, sacred to the Hawaiians. Someday I want to see it returned to them."

Kore whistled softly through his teeth. "You always were as impractical as hell—which is why you made such a lousy Rom," he said.

He touched her face, pushed back her hair with a curiously tender gesture. His hands were very warm as he squeezed her cheeks between his palms, using his thumbs to lift her chin. His kiss was gentle, undemanding, and she leaned against him, feeling comforted and more relaxed than she had all day.

She wasn't sure when the contentment disappeared, when the feeling of being snug and safe deserted her, but suddenly she was aware of a deep uneasiness, and even with Kore's arms around her, his warm mouth on hers in the sultry darkness, she felt cold.

There was a rustling sound, furtive and barely audible, in the bushes near the arbor, and she knew that her instincts had been right. Someone was standing out there in the dark, listening. How much had he—or she—overheard?

She pulled away from Kore. "Someone's out there," she whispered. "I heard something moving in the bushes—"

Kore's hand closed over her arm, silencing her. For the space of several heartbeats he stood motionless, and she knew he was weighing the night sounds, trying to separate them. His hand dropped away from her arm, but she wasn't sure he was gone until she heard light, swift footsteps moving away from the arbor. She wanted to call after him, tell him not to leave her alone, but she forced the words back and waited for him silently, her hands pressed over her mouth.

He was back in a few minutes. His voice sounded angry as he told her, "You were right. Someone was out there."

"Who was it?"

"Hell, how do I know? All I saw was a flicker of white. Before I reached the house, I heard a door slam. It could have been anyone."

"Do you think someone followed me here? If so, he probably heard everything we said."

"Dammit, this could blow the whole thing sky high."

"Not if it was one of the Kealohas." She went on swiftly to tell him about her meeting with Kawena.

"So the kanakas recognized you even before you talked to the old lady today," he said when she was finished. "They must be a closemouthed bunch."

"Like the Roms," she said.

He grunted. "Well, it was probably just someone taking a walk. Unless he stood there and deliberately listened, he'd just think you were having a rendezvous with Richards—or MacMasters."

She was silent, still doubtful. He reached out and

touched her arm. "And that reminds me," he said softly, "we still have some unfinished business to take care of, don't we? Where were we when we were interrupted?"

But Lani evaded him now. "We do have some unfinished business—Pearsa's *sumadjii*," she said firmly. "It's in my room. I should have put it in a safe-deposit box a long time ago, but I had this fantasy of finding you someday and dropping it casually into your lap." She gave a shaky laugh. "Maile isn't the only one who loves stories."

Kore's hand tightened on her arm. "Pearsa gave the *sumadjii* to you," he said gruffly.

"To keep for you," she lied. "I—I think she was hoping that you'd marry a Rom girl someday."

Kore was silent so long that she grew uneasy. When he drew her close again, she didn't pull away, but this time when he kissed her it was on the cheek, a good-night kiss between friends.

She knew she should be glad that Kore had finally accepted her decision, but, perversely, she felt bereft, as if something precious and irreplaceable had been taken from her. She agreed listlessly as he told her that since it would be risky to meet in the hau arbor again, she should come to the guest cottage after the luau the next night. Somehow this meeting which she had been so eager for was a letdown, tinged with sadness. She reminded herself that Kore was no longer the big brother who could solve all her problems and cure all her hurts, just as she was no longer the frightened, unsure little girl he had rescued from the creek bank. *Things change; people change—but oh, how I wish they didn't have to*, she thought as she left Kore and walked slowly back to the house alone.

XVIII

During the night the wind returned, but it wasn't the balmy trades that give the Islands their near-perfect climate. This wind was from the east, and it was humid and hot, oppressively heavy, like the air inside a greenhouse.

When Lani awakened, her pillow was unpleasantly damp and her pajamas clung to her moist body. Her head seemed to be filled with bubbles, and she felt headachy as she sat on the edge of the bed, dreading the day ahead.

It was pride, not hunger, that finally took her downstairs for breakfast. At some point during the night it had come to her that if she avoided the others today, it would look as if Aunt Berta's accusations were true—or as if she were ashamed of what they had found in the metal box. It was only after she had made the decision to carry on as usual that she had finally been able to sleep.

The same pride demanded that she look her best, and she took pains with her makeup and hair and chose her one really gay summer dress to wear. When she was finished, she stared at her image in the mirror and concluded that no one would guess at the butterflies in her stomach—unless it was Kore, who knew her so well.

As she turned away from the mirror, she heard Maile's door slam. She listened as Maile's light footsteps moved along the hall, but again, as she had the night before, Maile went on without knocking, leaving Lani feeling a little hurt and wondering if Maile had had second thoughts about her innocence.

She waited a few minutes before she followed Maile downstairs. When she came out on the lanai, she saw that they were all there—her aunt, Kore, Wade, Jason, Maile and Vivian—sitting at two tables that had been pushed together in a patch of shade.

She forced herself to smile, to murmur a general "Good morning," before she moved to the serving table. Whether or not anyone returned her greeting or smile, she couldn't remember later. She was proud of her steady hands as she poured herself a cup of coffee and put a piece of fruit on a plate, but it took all her courage to turn around and walk to the table, to sit down in the empty chair next to Jason.

She kept her eyes on her cup as she put sugar, which she ordinarily didn't use, into her coffee and stirred it carefully.

It was Aunt Berta who broke the silence.

"It seems we owe you an apology, Miss Brock." There was a brittle quality in her voice that tightened Lani's nerves. "Iolani's necklace has turned up, after all. The clasp was loose, and she put it in her pocket for safekeeping before she took a walk with Mr. O'Neill. She only remembered it this morning."

Lani looked at Vivian. The blond girl was wearing outsized sunglasses, so it was impossible to see her eyes, but her face had a puffy look, as if she too had had a hard time going to sleep the night before.

"I do hope you aren't too upset over this, Miss Brock," she said, her voice thin. "After I'd had time to think, I realized that it must have been Lehua I saw coming out of my room yesterday. You *are* both about the same size, and I only caught a glimpse of her back, of course."

Lani's vindication had come too quickly for her to absorb. She stared at Vivian, wondering why she had lied in the first place—and why she was lying now.

"A necklace?" Kore said easily. "Was it that emerald necklace you were wearing at dinner a couple of nights ago?"

"It's a family heirloom," Berta said. "Somehow Miss Brock got the impression we suspected her of taking the necklace. It was just a misunderstanding, of course. Since it's all been cleared up, I suggest we all forget it and—"

"Well, I'm not going to forget it!" Maile burst out. "Iolani had no right wearing the necklace without asking me. Daddy gave it to *my* mother, not hers, so it belongs to me now."

"If you don't behave yourself," Vivian said lazily, "you're going to be spending the evening in your room instead of at the luau."

"You aren't my boss." The whine was back in Maile's voice. "And anyway, who wants to go to your luau? All those stuck-up old people—"

"Okay, knock it off, Maile," Jason said. "Just because some of us behaved like a bunch of three-year-olds last night is no reason for you to copy us."

"Jason is right," Wade said. "Maybe we should set Maile a better example." He gave Vivian a cool look. "I've already apologized for my own part in that business last night. I think you owe Yula an apology, too, for reading her private papers."

Vivian's face tightened. She started to take off her sunglasses, and then, as if the morning light were too bright for her, she quickly replaced them, but not before Lani caught a glimpse of swollen eyelids. Unexpectedly, she felt pity for the girl.

"No apologies are necessary," Lani said briskly. "If I lost something as lovely as that necklace, I would be upset, too. Why don't we put the whole thing out of our minds and forget it."

Across the table Wade was studying her, as if wondering whether she was sincere. Unexpectedly, his eyes softened, and one of his rare smiles lit up his face. Before anyone could speak, there was a chopping sound overhead that made further conversation impossible. Grateful for the interruption, Lani stared up as the company helicopter, its blue bubble of glass catching the morning sun, passed over the lanai. By the time it had settled down behind the trees, Berta was pushing back her chair, leaving the table.

Wade stood up too. "When you've finished your breakfast, come to the office," he told Lani in a low voice. "I want to talk with you."

Lani met his eyes, and a small thrill went through her. Always before, even when he had kissed her on the beach, those grey eyes had held a reservation when he looked at her. Now they were so warm that she looked away quickly, afraid of what her own eyes might reveal.

After he was gone, she ate her fruit and finished her coffee. She chatted with Jason, even laughed at one of his quips, and all the time she was wondering what Wade wanted to talk with her about.

At the end of the table, Kore was devoting himself to Vivian, but Lani sensed the tension under his flattery, his lazy smiles; and when she got up to leave the table, she felt his eyes following her.

The office, at the northwest corner of the main house, was dark when she got there, and she thought at first that Wade had changed his mind. But when she came in through the open door, she saw that he was sitting in his desk chair, his back to the door, staring out the window at a small group of men who were setting up chairs and covering the bandstand with layers of fresh ti leaves.

His chair creaked as she switched on her desk lamp and opened the drawer where she kept her shorthand pads and pencils, and she knew he had turned to watch her.

"Leave that," he said. "I don't have any work for you today, but I do want to talk with you."

He rose and came toward her. When he took her hand and led her to a pair of leather chairs, she came along without protest. The leather cushion crackled as she settled herself, folded her hands in her lap and gave him an inquiring look.

"What do you want to talk about?" she asked.

He ran his hand over his hair, ruffling it. "You're making this hard for me," he said. "That little-girl politeness of yours is a hard nut to crack, you know—or maybe you don't know."

Lani didn't answer him; she discovered that she was enjoying herself.

He expelled a long breath. "First I want to apologize again for that business last night. The only one of us who suspended judgment was Jason—"

"And Maile. She didn't believe for one moment that I'd taken the necklace."

"You're right. The rest of us acted like damned fools. I apologize for that, and I also want to explain why I stormed out of your room last night. Jason accused me once of confusing you with my wife. Well, there *is* a superficial resemblance. Intellectually, I knew it was purely physical, but it got in the way of my seeing you as the decent, obviously honest person you are."

But you were right—I am a liar, Lani thought, and the enjoyment went away. *I've lied to you from the first moment I met you in that alley. . . .*

"Why are you saying all this?" she asked aloud.

"Because I owe you an explanation for last night. I hired you originally because I needed a secretary who could conform to my irregular schedule. I also thought Maile could use someone young and active around her. Later—well, I found myself becoming interested in you as a person, as a woman. Or maybe it happened even earlier, when we first met. Something odd happened in that alley when I picked you out of the air. I hadn't really had a good look at you, and yet I knew you would be important to me."

Lani remembered her own physical response, and a flush spread over her face. Suddenly she didn't want him to go on, not when there were so many unanswered questions, so many suspicions on her part, between them. "Please," she said hurriedly. "I'm really not angry about what happened last night. What I'd like to do is forget it, once and for all."

"You really could do that—forget it, I mean?"

"Of course. I'm very happy with my job here, Mr. Mac-Masters. I like living on Maunaloa. I wouldn't want anyone to feel uncomfortable over what was a very natural mistake."

Wade stood up, towering above her. When he took her hands and pulled her to her feet she felt a moment of panic, an impulse to push him away and run from the room.

"Why don't we make a pact, Yula? I'll see that no one ever mentions that damned necklace again, and you'll stop calling me Mr. MacMasters every time you want to put a little distance between us."

Involuntarily she smiled, and his hands tightened on hers. She knew he was going to kiss her, and she wanted him to, wanted to go on from where they had left off on the beach, but something—a stir of caution—made her free her hands gently and move out of his reach.

"If you don't need me today, maybe I can give Moana a hand," she said, avoiding his eyes.

There was a short silence, but when he spoke, his voice was still warm. "If you like, although it isn't necessary. What are you going to wear tonight? Do you have anything Hawaiian?"

"Just the dress I wore to the charity ball. I mended the torn place. It doesn't show unless I raise my arm."

"You could borrow something from Iolani. She has enough clothing to outfit a dozen girls."

"I couldn't do that," she said—a little too quickly. "It should be interesting, going to a genuine luau," she added.

"Interesting, yes; genuine, no." His voice was dry. "A genuine luau is strictly homemade—entertainment, food, decorations."

"Well, I wouldn't know the difference, so I expect to enjoy this one." She edged toward the door. "Is there anything I can do for you before I leave?"

"No. The helicopter is waiting to take me to Honolulu. I have a couple of business appointments I can't postpone. Take the day off, Yula. Try to get a little rest so you can enjoy yourself tonight."

He turned away and went to his desk to pick up his briefcase, making it easy for her to slip out the door.

She spent the next few hours in the spacious kitchen of Maunaloa House, helping Moana with last-minute preparations which she insisted, to the annoyance of the head caterer, on doing herself. The kitchen, hot and humid from the steam, swarmed with caterer-helpers. After one of them accidentally broke Moana's favorite koawood serving spoon, there was a sharp exchange of words that threatened to end up with all of them walking out.

Lani soothed Moana's ruffled feathers and got her to sit down on the lanai with a glass of iced tea. With so many people coming and going, there was little opportunity for private conversation. Only once, when they were standing on the edge of the lanai, watching the men covering the luau tables with brown tapa paper, did Moana say, her voice low, "Tomorrow we have plenty time for *hooponopono*, huh?"

A *time for talking out problems with a friend*. . . . Lani nodded, not trusting herself to speak, and she was glad when one of the caterers interrupted with a question.

By late afternoon the guests had already begun to arrive. Some came in their own private boats, others were flown over from Honolulu in the company helicopter; and David was kept busy making trips back and forth to Kaneohe on the *Kauhelani*. When Moana finally took off for her cottage to rest, Lani left too and went to her room.

A blast of hot air struck her as she opened the door and went to open the window louvers as wide as they would go, grateful that the sun had finally dropped below the bluffs. She stripped to her panties and bra, pulled down the bedspread and stretched out on the cool sheets. Although she had intended merely to rest her eyes, her lack of sleep the night before caught up with her, and the last thing she heard before she fell asleep was the drumming of the helicopter, arriving with yet another load of guests.

The room was full of shadows when she awakened. Through the open windows she heard the distant thump of a drum, the tinkle of ukuleles, the twang of guitars. She lay there, listening drowsily for a few minutes, before she got up and went to take a shower.

The sting of cold water on her body chased away the last residue of drowsiness, and she hummed as she dried herself and pulled on a robe. It would be good to watch some entertainment, to be part of a crowd having fun, she told herself, pushing away her doubts. After all, today was *her* twenty-first birthday, not Vivian's. . . .

She was sitting at the dressing table, trying to decide what to do with her hair, when there was a rapping at the door. She opened it to find Moana standing there, a basket over one arm and something green and silky draped over the other.

With a flourish Moana produced a holoku, long and fitted, with a tiny train. It was the same shade of green as Lani's eyes, and inside the neckline she saw the label of an exclusive Honolulu dress shop.

Moana grinned broadly at Lani's gasp of delight. "Mr. Wade says you should wear it tonight—and Kawena sent you something to wear with the holoku."

She handed Lani the basket. Inside, nestling on a bed of ferns, was an orchid lei, but not the usual purple vanda. These were tiny spider orchids, and they were green, a few shades lighter than the holoku.

"But these are some of David's prize hybrids," Lani protested. "It seems such a waste, cutting them for a lei."

"Not a waste. Today you turn twenty-one—that is very special birthday." She patted Lani's arm. "You wear lei tonight, give you plenty good luck."

Looking very pleased with herself, she went off down the hall, her thongs slapping cheerfully against the floor.

Lani laid the holoku on the bed and returned to her dressing table. On impulse she swept her hair away from her face and tied it in a Grecian knot before she made up her face, using a touch more makeup than usual. When she slid into the holoku and zippered it up the back, it fit as if it had been custom-made for her. Either Wade had a good eye for women's sizes, or he had made a very lucky guess.

She put a dab of perfume behind each ear and then went to look at herself in the mirror. The color of the holoku brought out the tawniness of her skin, her green eyes, and the gold highlights in her hair, and she looked older, certainly more sophisticated—and maybe even a little exotic.

Carefully she lifted the lei from the basket and slipped it over her head. As the tiny green orchids snuggled against the silky material of the holoku, she decided that no jewels, no matter how expensive, could possibly set off the dress as beautifully as the lei.

She heard voices in the living room as she came down the stairs. To avoid being drawn into conversation with any of the guests, all of whom were strangers to her, she went out the front doors and took the path that circled the house.

In the shadow of a bird-of-paradise planting, she stood unnoticed, bemused by what she saw. With the Japanese lanterns and a scattering of luau torches for light, the garden had been transformed into a fairy grotto in which the milling guests seemed intruders. On the garland-decked bandstand, a small Hawaiian group was playing Island music, almost totally ignored by the guests. Long plank tables covered with tapa paper circled a large cleared area in front of the bandstand. The centerpieces for the tables were sprays of orchids lying on beds of fern. At each table were assortments of fruit and plates of hors d'oeuvres, the *haole* food that had earned Moana's contempt. Berta had also broken tradition by providing chairs for her guests, and as Lani looked around she saw why. Most of the guests were past middle age, and almost totally *haole*, although she did see one dignified elderly Japanese couple. Although the guests wore muumuus, holokus, aloha shirts, with a sprinkling of lava-lavas and sarongs, there was something self-conscious about the way they wore their Island garb, as if they were dressed for a costume ball. She was watching one white-haired woman whose lacquered coiffure and orthopedic shoes were at odds with her Tahitian *pareu* when a hand touched her shoulder.

"So this is one of the luaus you used to talk about so much," Kore's derisive voice said in her ear.

She turned to smile at him. He was looking very handsome in white flannel trousers and a white silk shirt, open at the neck, with a red carnation lei around his shoulders. She wondered if Vivian had given him the lei—and the kiss that traditionally went with it.

"It's all pretty plastic, I'm afraid," she said. "The ones I told you about were given at the beach by the Kealohas and were quite different from this."

"Yeah, this reminds me of those Rom movies where a Marlene Dietrich type goes around snapping her fingers and doing a Mexican hat dance." He smiled briefly at her laugh and added, "Not that I have any particular love for the Roms. I cut myself off completely from the *familia* after Mom died."

"They never really accepted me, even after Pearsa made up with her *familia*," Lani said ruefully. "But it was different with you. It must have been hard for you to break with them."

"Not all that hard. I always felt like an outsider with both sides of my family. Dad's hillbilly relatives treated me like I was some kind of freak, and most of Mom's *familia* hated my guts. Sure, her old man made a fuss over me—until a couple of pure-blooded grandsons came along. So it's me against the world these days—with one small crack in my armor you managed to get through."

"I'm glad," she said, more warmly than she intended.

Kore moved until he was almost touching her. "It isn't too late, Lani. You can still change your mind. Say you'll marry me and we'll cut out of here tonight."

She felt a weakness in her legs, a quickening of her pulses. What would it be like if she said yes, took up her life where it had broken off four years ago? It would be two against the world—she and Kore, with no secrets between them, each knowing the other's faults and strengths. They could make a new life for themselves, forget the past, build their own snug, safe wall against loneliness. . . .

Behind her, someone called out a greeting to a friend, and the dream dissolved. She sighed and smiled at Kore. "You've already done enough for me, Kore. You don't have to go on feeling responsible for me. And—and anyway, there's my promise to Pearsa."

She stopped, staring at Kore. His face was so tense that

she knew she had trampled on his pride again without intending to. Why couldn't he understand what she was saying? How could she break her promise, when she owed so much to Pearsa? And how could she turn her back on Maile, leave her here alone with only the Kealohas to protect her?

It was with relief that she saw Maile threading her way through the crowd toward them. She was wearing a long yellow muumuu, and she looked flushed, very pretty, as she rushed up, bursting with importance.

"I've been looking all over for you, Yula," she said reproachfully. She gave Kore a speculative glance, then turned her attention back to Lani. "You look beautiful. Wait until Iolani sees you in that holoku. She'll be green with jealousy. I saw it first, even before you did. Uncle Wade showed it to me when he got back from Honolulu this afternoon. He had me take a dress out of your wardrobe so the size would be right." She touched the lei with a fingertip. "Did he give you the lei too, Yula?"

"It was a present from the Kealohas," Lani replied, aware of Kore's darkening face.

"Uncle Wade sent me to find you. You're supposed to sit with us, and you'd better hurry, because the *imu*'s already been opened, and David is going to blow the *pu* any minute now."

She darted off again, looking like a skimming canary in her voluminous yellow muumuu.

"So that's how it is," Kore said heavily. "You've got something going with MacMasters."

"It isn't that way at all," she said. "Wade knew the only Hawaiian outfit I had was torn when I was mugged the night I met him. The holoku is his way of apologizing to me about—about the way he acted over the necklace."

Kore gave her a dark, unreadable look. He turned on his heel and stalked away, leaving her wishing she could give him a good hard shake. He hadn't changed at all, she told herself. He was still acting like the macho big brother who thought he had the right to choose her friends for her, tell her how to live her life.

She waited, watching from the shadows, as he settled himself beside Vivian at the table where the family and a few favored guests were sitting. David Kealoha, looking very impressive in a lava-lava, his burly chest bare except for a lei of ilima blossoms, blew the *pu*, the traditional triton shell trumpet, summoning the guests to the tables and signaling the serving of the *kalua* pig. Girls in bright *pareus* served the guests from calabashes piled high with an assortment of shrimp and crab; chicken with rice; yams and breadfruit and green bananas, roasted brown in the *imu*; platters of fish— butterfish with garlic, ahi tuna, baked mahimahi—and great chunks of the succulent *kalua* pig, steaming hot from the *imu*.

In the flurry of activity, she had hoped to find a place at another table, away from her aunt, but Wade spotted her as she was approaching. He sprang to his feet and escorted her to his table, and she had no choice but to join the family.

Across the table, her aunt stared at her, her forehead creased in a frown, and Vivian's eyes raked her, taking in the holoku, the green orchid lei. Jason, sitting next to Lani, leaned close and murmured that if he'd known she was going to turn up looking like a Hawaiian princess, he would have brought along his camera. After one hard glance, Kore ignored her and bent his dark head toward Vivian.

Despite her misgivings, the luau started off pleasantly enough. The musicians played languid Island songs, and the food, for all Moana's grumblings, was excellent. Even the weather seemed to be cooperating. Although the clouds continued to pile up overhead, the wind was warm as it tossed the plumeria garlands on the bandstand, fluttered the flames of the torches and rustled the leaves of the monkeypod trees.

Lani ate some of the food in front of her, smiled until she was sure her face would crack; and all the time apprehension was building up inside her. From the speculation in the eyes of the other guests, she knew they had noted Wade's attentions to her and were wondering just what her status was at Maunaloa House.

Once she turned her head and met Jason's eyes. He was

wearing an outrageously gaudy aloha shirt and an orange lei that clashed with his russet hair, and the maile wreath he wore on his head had slipped down on one side, giving him a raffish look. Lani smiled at him, resisting the impulse to straighten it. He winked back, but before she could speak, he turned to the woman on his other side with one of his quips.

Feeling a little miffed, Lani gave her full attention to Wade. Like Jason, he was wearing an aloha shirt, open at the neck, but Wade's shirt was raw silk, etched with a small brown tiki on the breast pocket, and he wore a lei of leatherlike St. Thomas nuts. For the first time, Lani fancied she could see a hint of his Hawaiian blood in the powerful line of his throat, his strong features, the slight flaring of his nostrils.

She listened, her interest stirred, as he described a first-year luau he had attended when he was a child on the Big Island. The thought of him as a small brown-skinned boy running wild in the sun made him seem less intimidating, and she found it easy to ask him questions about ranch life.

There was a roll from the drummer on the bandstand as a troupe of professional entertainers from Honolulu started their program. Three Island girls wearing halters, plumeria leis and artificial grass skirts danced the hula. A Samoan boy, his brown face glistening with sweat, did a fire dance that caused Maile to shriek with excitement. He was followed by a throaty-voiced singer who sang several popular Island songs about love and betrayals and partings. The guests, mellowed by their Mai-Tais and the abundance of food, had loosened up, and the applause was generous as he ended up with one of the ballads made popular by Alfred Apaka.

The music took on a faster tempo as an amply endowed Tahitian girl did a frenzied version of the *tiare tarus*, the spirited Tahitian dance, her hips rotating rapidly under her ti-leaf skirt.

"If this were a real luau," Jason said in Lani's ear, "some of the younger male guests would jump up there and join in, and if one of them was favored by the lady, he would carry her off on his shoulder into the darkness."

"I suppose you learned how to dance the *tiare tarus*, too?"

"I'm a whiz at it," he said smugly. The brown specks in his eyes seemed to whirl as he leaned closer. "And you do pick up things quickly, don't you? Where did you learn the names of Tahitian dances?"

A ripple of whispers among the guests spared Lani the necessity of thinking up an answer. She caught the frown on her aunt's face, and even before she turned her head she felt a premonition of disaster.

Kawena, her right hand resting lightly on David's broad arm, was standing in front of the bandstand. She wore a formal holoku of maroon silk; its long train was caught up on one side and looped over her left wrist. A pikake wreath crowned her white hair, and an open-ended maile-vine lei hung almost to her waist. She looked as regal and self-possessed as one of her own *alii* ancestors as she waited for the whispers to subside.

When there was complete silence, she inclined her head in a tiny bow.

"I will do a special hula for the twenty-first birthday of my *hanai* child, Iolani Stevenson," she said. Although her voice was low, it carried to every corner of the garden. She turned her blind eyes toward the table where Lani sat. "*Me ke aloha o Kawena*," she added softly.

With the love of Kawena . . . Lani took several deep breaths, fighting tears.

While Kawena waited, David spoke to the musicians in a low voice. There was respect in the glances they gave Kawena as they picked up their ukuleles, their steel guitars, their gourd drums.

The music began and Kawena's arms rose, slowly, gracefully. Her hips swayed; her feet moved in the gentle, delicate movements of the true hula. Every gesture, every arching of her supple fingers seemed to carry its own message. What matter if her face was lined, her hair white? She was a child chasing a butterfly across a meadow, a young girl dancing for her first lover, a mother celebrating the birth of her son.

The music changed and her brown hands wove a simpler pattern now. She began to sing in a tremulous falsetto that awakened echoes from Lani's childhood. She sang of the flowers of the earth, the hawk in the sky; and Lani's body slowly chilled and a prickling started up at the back of her neck.

Involuntarily she turned to look at her aunt. Berta's skin was mottled; her hands were clenched so tightly together that they looked like small, ugly claws. She was staring directly at Lani, and when Lani saw the naked hatred in her eyes, she knew that Kawena's song, the one she had been singing the day she ran away, had broken through some barrier in Berta's mind. If her aunt hadn't recognized her earlier, she did now; and her hatred was still as virulent as it had ever been.

Mercifully the conversation flowed around Lani, leaving her isolated in a small pool of silence. After a tremendous wave of applause, which Kawena had acknowledged with a sedate bow, she had left on David's arm without turning her face again toward the table where Lani sat, frozen with apprehension.

To Lani's relief, no one seemed to notice her silence, or maybe they were all fooled, as Wade obviously was, by her fixed smile, the calm expression on her face. Only Kore might have guessed her inner turmoil, and he was still ignoring her, directing all his attention to Vivian, who had been abnormally quiet all evening. Across the table Berta was silent, too. Although Lani hadn't looked at her since that one involuntary glance, every nerve in her body was aware of the ominous quality of her aunt's silence.

It was the weather that finally released Lani from her ordeal. The wind, as if waiting for a lull in the entertainment, was suddenly upon them, brusque and insistent, ruffling the coifed hair of the women, undulating the strings of Japanese lanterns, and bringing the smell of distant rain to their nostrils.

There was a. rush of activity as the guests, eager to be home before the storm broke, retrieved their wraps from the house and took leave of their hosts. When Lani was sure no one was watching her, she eased into the shadows and hurried toward the guest cottages. Although Kore had continued to ignore her, she had decided to meet him anyway, as planned. She had to talk to him, tell Kore about her certainty that her aunt knew who she was.

The cottage was dark when she got there, but when she went inside, she decided against a light. As she groped around in the dark, her hand touched the cool smoothness of rattan, and she settled herself in a chair to wait. The wind, moaning at the corners of the cabin, had a lonely sound. Even inside the snug cottage, there was the acrid, parched odor that precedes rain, and she felt a sudden impatience to be back in her own room before the storm broke.

Behind the tennis courts, there was a rush of sound as the helicopter lifted off its pad, returning guests to Oahu. The cottage was too far from the wharf for her to hear any of the activity there, but Lani was sure the guests' boats were gone by now, that the *Kauhelani* was already on its way across the bay with a load of guests. They would have a choppy ride, but in their condition, she thought, they probably wouldn't notice. Tomorrow they would keep their phones busy, telling their friends what it was really like on Maunaloa Island, and none of them would come within a hundred miles of the truth.

She leaned her head against the back of the chair. Although she tried to relax, images from the luau, from the past few days, sped through her mind, and her brain felt charged with energy. The feeling of impending danger deepened. Although she tried to blame it on the dropping barometer, she really knew better.

Suddenly too restless to sit there waiting, she rose and went to the door. She opened it a crack, using her foot as a brace against the pressure of the wind. The sound of voices made her stiffen. Surely Kore wouldn't bring anyone to his cabin tonight when he knew she would be waiting for him—or had he forgotten their appointment?

As she started to close the door, a light flared in the window of the cabin across the tiny courtyard—Jason's cabin. Two people were silhouetted against the light, and there was no mistaking Jason's tall, rangy figure—or Vivian's, willowy as a reed. Lani watched as the two figures moved closer together. Then Vivian's arms were locked around Jason's neck, her fingers clawing at his back, and Lani closed the door and turned away, feeling a little sick.

She leaned against the closed door and tried to understand what she had just seen. How long had this been going on? Had Jason's rueful complaints about losing out to Wade been some kind of coverup? Vivian, at least in Lani's presence, had treated Jason as if he were a casual admirer and nothing more; had that been part of the game they were playing? But why would they go to so much trouble to hide their—what was it, anyway? A flirtation, or a full-blown affair? There had been something desperate about the way Vivian had flung herself into Jason's arms. Did it have anything to do with the change she'd noticed in Vivian today, as if some inner dissolution were taking place?

And why was *she* standing here, fighting tears? Was it because she had come to think of Jason as a friend, someone she could trust, the most unlikely person to be Vivian's accomplice? If so, she had been a fool. After all, he had once told her that he—how had he put it?—lusted after Vivian's body.

She returned to the chair, and as the air inside the cabin

began to chill, she felt increasingly restive. The wind was gusting, blowing leaves and bits of twigs against the windowpanes, adding to her nervousness. Where was Kore? Was he staying away to punish her? If so, any meeting between them tonight, no matter how urgent the reason, was going to be difficult. With Vivian and Jason so close by, it might even be dangerous.

It was the last thought that made up her mind for her. She let herself out the back door, circled the cottage and walked swiftly along the path, the wind tearing at her hair and slapping her skirt against her legs. A drop of rain, the prelude to what was coming, struck her cheek as she was crossing the garden. Not wanting to get wet, she began to run. The lei of green orchids she was still wearing bounced around her neck, and she took it off, doubled it and slid it over her arm.

Although a few lights were still on in the house, the lanai and garden were deserted. The luau tables had been disassembled, reduced to a stack of lumber again, the chairs removed and all the debris cleared away. Only the bandstand, looking forlorn without its gay garlands and ti-leaf covering, still remained to show that a party had taken place there.

She went into the *mauka* wing through the service door and hurried up the stairs. Although the hall at the top of the stairs was dark, she didn't bother pressing the light switch.

Light trickled through the crack at the bottom of Maile's door at the end of the hall, and she heard the soft sound of a radio. Not in the mood for casual talk, she turned into her own room, closing the door before she reached for the light switch. The burst of light blinded her briefly, and it was a few seconds before she realized she had a visitor.

She stopped short as her aunt rose from a chair by the window. Her eyes were glittering, and there were streaks of red on her cheeks, as if she had been clawing at her flesh with her fingernails.

"You always were a nasty little troublemaker," she said.

Although Lani's first impulse was to turn and run, she

held her ground, her eyes defiant. "You haven't changed either, Aunt Berta," she said.

Her aunt's fingers clenched, and she took a step toward Lani.

"Don't come near me," Lani warned. "I'm not a child any longer. I know how to defend myself now."

Strangely, instead of angering Berta further, Lani's words seemed to give her some satisfaction.

"I knew that wild blood of yours would find its own level," she said. "What else did you learn from those Gypsies? How to lie and whore and steal?"

"They treated me with kindness and love, which is more than you ever did. What's more, it would be abhorrent to them to kill a child or to try to drive her to suicide by pretending to be her dead mother."

For a moment, naked hatred looked out at her from her aunt's eyes. "What did you come back here for? Surely you don't think anyone will believe you, a nasty Gypsy tramp with a police record? Or do you think the Kealohas will help you? You don't think they'd stick out their necks for you, do you?"

"I don't need the Kealohas," Lani answered, her voice hard. "I can prove who I am without them. And I can also pass a lie detector test. Can you, Aunt Berta? I know things about my own childhood that Vivian couldn't possibly know."

"Such as the fact that your father killed your mother, and then sent you away so you couldn't tattle on him?"

Her words seemed to bounce off the walls of the room, puncturing Lani's spurious confidence and leaving her speechless.

"You didn't think I knew, did you?" Berta's voice was gloating, vindictive. "Well, I did, and your father paid dearly for my silence before he died. Oh, I never pushed him too far. Just a hint here and there about the necessity of protecting you from scandal, and he was only too glad to see that I lived in comfort."

"It's a lie—it's all a lie," Lani spoke loudly, as if she could drown out the truth by raising her voice.

"Oh, it's true enough. That's why you acted like a dummy for such a long time, isn't it? Afraid you would let something slip and give away that precious father of yours."

"All the time you were telling your friends that I had killed my mother, you knew it was a lie," Lani said. "Was it just for the money that you kept quiet? Or did you hate me even more than you did him?"

"You were John Stevenson's daughter, as like as peas in a pod." Berta's face was suffused with an ugly dark red, and her eyes looked so wild that for the first time Lani wondered if her aunt was insane. "He destroyed my sister long before he put that bullet in her. Well, I made him pay, and I made you pay, too, for trying to cover up for him."

"But if you loved your sister, how could you hate me, her daughter, so much?" Lani whispered.

"She never wanted you—never! He tricked her, got her pregnant so he could perpetuate that filthy half-breed line of his. Well, she never had another baby by him, never gave him the son he wanted so much—and neither did that Island girl he married after he'd killed Carol. The Stevenson name is finished; nothing can change that part. If Maile had been on that motorboat the day it went down, the whole bloodline would be gone—except for you."

"You hate Maile, too—that's the real reason you've been tormenting her."

Aunt Berta shrugged off her words. "Carol didn't want to bring any half-breeds into the world. When she realized she was pregnant, she wanted to get an abortion, but he promised her that if she'd have the baby, she could write her own ticket financially and have complete freedom to—"

"To have other men," Lani finished. "Yes, I know about that."

"Oh, he had his women, too, but he was discreet about it. He never came near her after you were born—did you know that? So she knew he must be crawling into someone else's bed. Why do you think she brought those men here and flaunted them in his face? And that's why he killed her. His masculine pride couldn't take it—"

"That isn't why he wanted a divorce," Lani said. "I heard

them quarreling that day. He didn't want me to grow up with the knowledge that my mother was a—a tramp." She stared at her aunt, frowning. "Why are you so sure you know what happened in the Folly that day? You were in your room—or were you?"

Berta's eyes got very still; her face seemed to swell, or maybe, Lani thought, it was her distended eyes that gave that impression. Until now, she hadn't really been physically afraid of her aunt, but she was suddenly aware of their isolation from the main part of the house, of the rain lashing against the windowpanes, the wail of the wind against the eaves.

She forced words past her stiff lips. "So we've reached an impasse, haven't we, Aunt Berta? I may have a hard time proving who I am, but on the other hand, who would believe you at this late date if you claimed my father was a murderer? How would you explain why you kept quiet so long or why you accepted a generous allowance from the man who killed your sister? Of course your accusations alone would cause a lot of talk, which I wouldn't want Maile to hear, so I'll make a bargain with you. I'm willing to share my inheritance with you, provided you leave Maunaloa Island." She paused to take a deep breath. "Otherwise, I'll go to the police tomorrow and take my chances that they'll believe me."

Berta moved, so swiftly that Lani only had time for one gasp before her aunt's body was between her and the door. She stood there, frozen with shock, staring at the small black gun in Berta's hand.

"You aren't going anywhere tomorrow—or any other day," Berta said. "If you disappear tonight, who can say what happened to you? There were over a hundred outsiders on the island tonight, including a crew of locals who stayed late to clean up. Any one of them could have attacked you, then killed you to keep you quiet and tossed your body into the surf. Maybe the police will decide you had too much to drink and wandered into the surf. Or maybe I'll clear out your closet, and then they'll think you went away on the *Kauhelani* with the other guests, left without giving notice, like the Gypsy tramp you are."

Her voice was matter-of-fact, but Lani, staring at her aunt, knew she was looking into the eyes of an obsessed woman. She felt a deep despair. Berta had all the advantages on her side, even the weather. With the wind howling around the house, obscuring all lesser sounds, would anyone hear a gunshot? All her aunt had to do was force her to go with her to the beach, where Lani's blood would be washed away by the tide—and where Berta could easily bury her body deep in the sand. There would be a brief search, speculations, rumors; but it would all come to nothing in the end, and in a little while Maunaloa Island would be just as it had been before a girl who called herself Yula Brock had come there. . . .

Lani's mind went blank for a moment. She shivered so violently that the lei on her arm slapped against her body. *The green orchid lei* . . . was it possible that the lei, given to her with such aloha by the Kealohas, could be the instrument of her salvation?

She shifted her position slightly and let her arm drop to her side. The lei slid down to her wrist, then to the palm of her hand. The tiny orchids felt cool, very fragile, as her fingers closed around them, reminding her of the vanda she'd found on the street the day she'd run away from her aunt.

She let her body sway, blinked her eyes several times. Berta watched her closely as she brought her hand up toward her face, as if to rub her eyes. But when her hand was midway to her eyes, she flung her arm outward as hard as she could, releasing the lei at the same time. The lei, pliant as a whip, lashed out and slapped her aunt across the eyes. Instinctively Berta's hands flew upward, and the gun struck her forehead, making a slapping sound. She lost her balance and tumbled over backward—but to Lani's horror she managed to hold onto the gun.

Lani fled from the room as if all the horrors from all the nightmares of her life were pursuing her. She sped down the dark hall, down the stairs, out into the full fury of the storm. It was only when she had almost reached Kore's cabin that she realized she had left Maile behind, at the mercy of a madwoman who hated her.

She stopped, oblivious to the rain pelting her head and bare arms. Only the realization that she couldn't fight Berta's gun alone kept her from turning back.

Although the windows of Kore's cabin were still dark, it didn't occur to her that he wouldn't be there. Expecting him to be in bed, she opened the door without knocking and went inside. Only when she had called his name several times and there was no answer did she turn on the light. When she saw the empty bed and realized he hadn't returned, she dropped into a chair, shivering with cold, her nerves seething with mingled anger and worry. Was this Kore's way of punishing her for hurting that damnable pride of his, or had something happened to him? Surely he hadn't returned to Oahu for the night and left her here alone.

When a gust of wind tossed a torn-off tree branch against the windowpane, she jumped, gave a small scream. She realized then that she was on the verge of hysteria, and also that she didn't dare wait any longer. She went to Kore's closet and felt around until she found one of his jackets. When she put it on, its warmth, the faint odor of aftershave lotion, of tobacco, spelled comfort and safety to her, and almost immediately she felt stronger.

It was a temptation to wait a little longer, to remain in the snug cabin, out of the cold rain; but the feeling of urgency was back, warning her that she could wait too long. She had assumed that Berta would return to her room, ready to deny any accusations that Lani might make, but what if Berta's hatred got the upper hand? Would it occur to her that while Lani was beyond her reach, Maile was not—and that Maile too was the daughter of the man she still hated so much?

Lani went to a small rattan desk, found notepaper and a pen, and scribbled out a note, telling Kore to come to her room as quickly as possible. She didn't bother to sign it, knowing he would recognize her handwriting. To make sure he didn't overlook the note, she propped it up on a pillow in the middle of his bed and left the lights on when she stepped out into the storm again.

The rain, driven almost horizontal by the wind, struck her in the face, almost blinding her. She gasped and flung her arm up to shield her eyes, but she didn't turn back. The jacket was soon drenched; it flapped around her, but it gave her a certain amount of protection from the rain as she stumbled down the path.

She was passing under the windows of Maile's room when she glanced up and saw that the windows were dark. Before she had time to think what this might mean, she heard a sharp, barking sound. The sound was muffled by the rain, by the wind, but she knew instantly that someone had fired a gun close by.

She stood there, paralyzed by shock. It could have been a minute—or maybe longer—before she found she could move again. She ran then—around the corner, down the long side of the wing, through the door and up the stairs, not caring that her wet sandals were making loud thumping noises on the hollow stairs. She was pounding down the hall, headed for Maile's room, when she saw light streaming through the open door of her own room and heard a whimpering sound, like a small puppy left out in the rain.

She turned into her room and then stopped sharp in the doorway. Maile was there, standing in the middle of the room. She was wearing pajamas and her hair was braided for bed; there was a dazed, vacant look in her eyes, and the whimpering sounds were coming from her throat. One hand, her left, was clamped over her mouth as if she were afraid she would be sick. And in her other hand she held Berta's small black gun.

Lani forced her eyes downward. Berta lay at Maile's feet, stretched out on her back, her eyes staring at the ceiling. Lani's sick eyes took in the blood that covered her aunt's throat, that was already spreading out across the rug, and she knew that Berta would never give another fancy party for her friends, would never lie or cheat or hurt anyone again.

Lani looked into Maile's stunned eyes and held out her

hand. "Give me the gun, Maile," she said, fighting to control her voice. "You don't need it now."

Maile's eyes widened and her face turned the color of wax. She gave a little scream and thrust the gun away from her. It fell to the floor between them with a thud. Before Lani could bend to pick it up, Maile had pushed past her and was running down the hall.

A few seconds later, just before Lani started screaming, she heard Maile's footsteps pounding down the stairs.

XX

It was Kore who reached her first. When he appeared in the doorway, his black eyes blazing, she stopped screaming and rushed into his arms. His arms tightened around her, but his body was so stiff that she looked up at him and saw that he was staring at the gun on the floor. Slowly his eyes moved to Berta's body, then back to Lani's face.

"Did you—" He broke off in mid-sentence.

"I didn't kill her, but—oh God, I think Maile did. I found her with the gun in her hand, and now she's out there in the storm and—and she's such a *little* girl, Kore." The tears began slipping down her face.

"It won't help any if you lose your cool," Kore said. He produced a handkerchief, handed it to her, then watched silently as she dried her face. "Okay, we've got some decisions to make—and fast," he said, his voice urgent and quick. "The way you were yelling, someone's bound to be along any minute now. They're going to toss a lot of questions at you, and you'd better have some answers ready. If you want them to believe you had nothing to do with your aunt's death, you'd be smart to keep on playing the outsider—at least for now."

Although Lani knew he was right, she felt a rush of impatience for his Rom instinct for secrecy. "I don't care about any of that. The important thing is Maile. We have to find her before she gets hurt, or—" But she couldn't say the words. The tears flooded back, and this time Kore held her face against his damp windbreaker and stroked her hair with gentle hands.

"What the hell's going on here?"

Lani broke away from Kore to stare into Wade's scornful face. His eyes were the color of storm clouds as he took in her wet jacket, obviously a man's, her disheveled hair.

"You're a fast worker, O'Neill," he said.

"And you have a very suspicious mind, MacMasters," Kore said, his voice dangerously soft. "Miss Brock was taking a walk near the guest cottages when it started to rain. I made her take my jacket and was seeing her back to her room when we heard a gunshot. At the time we thought it was a branch breaking off one of the trees. I left her at the door downstairs and was heading back to my cottage when I heard her scream."

He moved aside and pointed to Berta's body. "You'd better start a search for your niece. Yula found her standing over Miss St. John, holding a gun. When she saw Yula, she dropped the gun on the floor and ran out."

Lani knew that Kore, protective as always, had just given her an alibi, but she felt no gratitude. He had also made it impossible for her to tell the truth, at least for the present, and she was suddenly sick of lies, of evasions and distortions of the truth.

Wade's face was stiff and expressionless as he stared at Berta's body, then at the gun. He took a step forward, then stopped. When he looked up at Lani, his eyes bit into hers, as if to force the truth from her.

"Are you saying that Maile killed her aunt?" he asked.

"I don't know what happened," Lani said. "When I found Maile, she seemed dazed, as if she were in a trance. I must have frightened her when I spoke, because she screamed, dropped the gun, and ran out the door. Maybe—maybe she saw the gun on the floor and picked it up—"

Wade interrupted her. "We can talk about this later. Our first priority is to find Maile. You'd better get some dry clothes together, Yula—you can dress somewhere else. I'll have to lock up this room until the police get here."

The police. . . . Involuntarily, Lani looked around at Kore. She wasn't the only one the police would question. How much probing could Kore's new identity take? Was he going to have to face the suspicions of the police because of his concern for her?

"I'll notify them as soon as I can get to the radio shack," Wade went on, "but I doubt if they can bring a helicopter in here until the storm slackens. I'm afraid we'll have to find Maile without any help from outsiders." He gave Kore a hard look. "While I try to get a phone patch to the Kaneohe police, you'd better get Jason and David Kealoha. You'll find flashlights and extra batteries in the service room off the kitchen. And be careful; the path to the Kealoha compound is slippery as hell when it's wet."

To Lani, there was something reassuring about the way Wade took charge, but she was sure that Kore, who hated taking orders from anyone, didn't share her opinion. To her surprise he nodded, gave her a reassuring smile and the covert hand gesture that meant she should be careful, and left without argument.

Wade turned back to Lani. "You'd better get out of those wet clothes as soon as possible, Yula."

Lani shook her head. "I'd just get wet again. I'm going to help with the search."

"You'd only get in the way, and I want you here when we bring Maile back to the house," he said, his voice tight. "If you want to do something constructive, you can search the house. It's possible Maile came back in through another door when she saw how bad the storm was. Maybe you'd better get Iolani to help you—" He paused and a shadow crossed his face. "Iolani's going to take her aunt's death pretty hard, I'm afraid."

Lani had her reservations about that, but she kept them to herself. While Wade, looking grim, covered Berta's body with a sheet, Lani selected jeans, a sweater, and a scarf to put around her wet hair. She felt numb, as if her brain had been overloaded with too many emotions, too much fear. Even the white mound on the floor seemed unreal as she stepped around it and went out the door.

Wade locked the door behind her and pocketed the key. Although he asked her if she would be okay, his tone was perfunctory, and anger stirred under her apathy.

"No," she snapped. "I won't be okay until I know that Maile is safe."

Wade rubbed the small line between his eyes. "You're right. The most important thing is to find Maile."

He went off down the hall, leaving her standing there alone.

She changed her clothes in Maile's room and left her wet garments lying in a heap on the floor. Even if the rain hadn't ruined the holoku, she would never wear it again. It would always remind her of this night—a night that still hadn't ended.

She was passing along the hall at the top of the stairs, heading toward Vivian's suite of rooms in the *makai* wing, when she heard Jason's voice below in the hall. When Kore's voice answered, she paused, but before she could call down, the two men had already disappeared through the front door.

Bracing herself, she went to tap on Vivian's door. Almost immediately Vivian answered her knock. She was wearing a negligée, filmy and expensive-looking, but there were lines of strain on her face even before Lani told her, as gently as she could, that Berta had been shot.

Vivian turned away; she went to the table next to her bed, got a cigarette from an open pack, lit it with shaking fingers.

"Any chance she's still alive?" she asked then.

"No—and Maile is missing. Wade wants us to search the house for her while he and the other men search the grounds and beach."

Vivian stared at her, but her eyes were vacant, as if her thoughts were far away. "This blows it," she said. "This bloody well blows it."

Lani didn't ask her what she meant. "I think we should start with the *mauka* wing," she said. "Maile may be hiding in one of the downstairs bedrooms."

Vivian crushed out her cigarette in an overflowing tray. She stripped off her negligée, pulled on slacks and a jersey tunic, belted a linked chain around her narrow waist and slid her feet into open sandals.

"Let's go," she said.

It took them almost half an hour to search the house. There was little conversation between them as Lani led the way from room to room. Vivian trailed behind Lani, making no attempt to help with the search. She watched, smoking one cigarette after another, as Lani opened doors, looked into wardrobes and closets, searched under beds and behind screens. When Lani opened the door to her aunt's room, the odor of lilac perfume made her wince, and after a quick search she was glad to close the door behind her again.

When it was obvious that Maile was not in the house, they went to the living room to wait. The spacious room with its antique furnishings and priceless rugs looked cold and unlived-in, like the rooms of a museum, Lani thought. She listened to the rain lashing at the windows and breathed a prayer that Maile had found a refuge somewhere, out of the full fury of the storm.

Across the room, Vivian was curled up in a high-backed wing chair, her hands cupped around a mug of coffee. Lani wondered what she was thinking behind that sphinxlike face. Was she regretting that she had become involved in Berta's scheme? Or was she just beginning to realize the ramifications of Berta's death? True, she had lost her confidante; but now she would have no one to hold her extravagances in check, to force her to associate with people who obviously bored her, or to share her half of the Stevenson estate with—unless it was the man who had been the third conspirator.

The minutes, the seconds, seemed to crawl past now. Finally unable to endure the waiting any longer, Lani told Vivian that she was going to search the house again. Vivian didn't offer to go along, and Lani escaped from the room with a feeling of relief, leaving Vivian sitting there alone with her coffee, with yet another cigarette and her own brooding thoughts.

Although Lani went through the motions of searching the house, she already knew it was hopeless. Half an hour later, she ended up in Maile's room, standing in the middle of the floor. As she stared at the rumpled bedcovers, at Maile's favorite doll lying on its back beside the bed, she tried to reconstruct what must have happened.

Something—a nightmare or the storm or maybe the sound of quarreling voices in the next room—had awakened Maile. She had left her bed in such a hurry that she hadn't even stopped to pick up the doll she'd knocked off onto the floor. Why had she turned off her lamp? Was it so she could open the hall door without the light giving her away? Had it been her insatiable curiosity, her penchant for eavesdropping, that had sent her down the hall to Lani's room? If so, what had happened in those few minutes before Lani had returned to find Berta dead and Maile standing over her with a gun in her hand?

Lani rubbed her smarting eyes. She felt sick with fear—and guilt. She had left Maile alone and unprotected while she ran away, concerned only with saving her own life. And now her sister would grow up with the stigma of having killed her aunt, and for the rest of her life, no matter where she went, whispers and rumors would follow her.

It was bad enough to be branded a murderer when you were innocent, Lani thought bleakly, but to have to live with the knowledge that you had killed another human being, no matter what the provocation, would be even worse. But why was she so sure Maile had killed her aunt? Because of the gun? She herself had picked up the gun that had shot her mother, and *she* hadn't been guilty. She had run away afterward, too—had the same thing happened to Maile? Did she know who had killed her aunt, and had she run away because it was someone she couldn't bear to betray?

Lani moaned aloud, remembering her own hasty words that had shown Maile, all too clearly, that she thought she had killed her aunt.

Suddenly the rumpled covers on Maile's bed, the small concave place on her pillow, seemed to reproach Lani, and she turned away and wandered over to the wall-wide closet that years ago had held her own clothes. She opened the louvered doors and studied the orderly rows of clothing, of shoes. It had surprised her that Maile, whose emotions were often so chaotic, should be orderly in her personal habits. Every dress, every blouse and jacket had its own padded hanger and was facing the same direction; every pair of shoes had its place in the racks on the floor, while her games and toys and other treasures were lined up on shelves at one end of the closet.

Lani stared at an empty space on one of the shelves, and a small excitement stirred. Ever since the trip to the other side of the island, the knapsack that Wade had given Maile had held a place of honor in the center of the most accessible shelf. Now the knapsack was gone. Had Maile come back to the house during the past hour, walked past the room where her aunt lay dead, to get her knapsack? If so, what else had she taken from her room?

Lani searched quickly, and now the empty space among a row of sneakers, a half-opened chest drawer, had significance. When she found the pajamas Maile had been wearing in the bathroom clothes hamper, she knew that Maile had tricked them. Since the pajamas were dry, she couldn't have left the house. She must have hidden somewhere until it was safe to return to her room for her clothes. But why had she taken the knapsack? To carry a blanket, maybe a supply of food? Surely she didn't think she could hide out indefinitely. She must know that every inch of the island would be combed as soon as it was light.

No, not every inch, Lani thought suddenly, her whole body chilling. Because Maile believed she was the only person alive who knew the existence of the burial cave in the sinkhole.

An insidious image crept into Lani's mind—the watersoaked rim of the sinkhole, the slippery ledge, the dark pit below, where, according to legend, a *kaku*, one of the guardian spirits who watch over sacred places, lurked in wait for intruders. For a moment the black mouth of superstition yawned before her, but she struggled with it and finally put it away from her. If Maile had gone to the sinkhole to hide in the burial cave, her life was in danger, yes, but the danger had nothing to do with the dead, or with evil spirits who might guard their bones.

She returned to the living room and found Vivian still sitting in the chair, looking sleepy and bored.

"Find anything?" she asked languidly.

Lani shook her head. "Has anyone returned to the house yet?" she asked.

"I haven't seen a soul. Maybe they all drowned in the rain. If you ask me, that kid is holed up somewhere, waiting out the storm, while we're all knocking ourselves out looking for her." She hesitated briefly. "What got into her, anyway? Did it have anything to do with—what happened to Berta?"

"I don't know the whole story," Lani said evasively, "but I do have an idea where she could be. As soon as the men return, tell them—" She broke off. How could she leave a message for Kore with Vivian, of all people? And yet— someone should know where she was going, someone she could trust. Did she dare wait around until Kore or David returned?

The thought of further delay was abhorrent to her, and she made up her mind quickly. "I have a hunch that Maile is hiding near the Folly," she said. "If the men come back before I do, tell them I went there to look for Maile."

"That's probably the first place they looked."

"Maile told me once she had a secret hiding place among the a'pe plants behind the Folly," Lani improvised. "Wade and David might not know about it."

"I think you're wasting your time," Vivian said, shrugging, "but if you want to play the little heroine, go ahead." She leaned back in the chair and closed her eyes, effectively ending the conversation.

Lani found a plastic raincoat and a brimmed rain hat on a hook behind a kitchen closet door and donned them thankfully. It took her a few precious minutes longer to locate a flashlight that worked, as the men had taken the supply kept in the service room, but she finally found one in a desk drawer in Wade's office.

She bypassed the living room and went out through the kitchen. Despite the protection of the raincoat and hat, she was drenched within a few feet of the house. Although she regretted the delay, she headed for Kore's cottage first to leave another note. Briefly she thought of leaving a message with Kawena, too, as double insurance, but she decided against it. It would take fifteen minutes or more to go to the Kealoha compound, and she had a feeling that she had already wasted too much time.

She battled her way through the rain to Kore's cabin and found it blazing with lights. When she went inside, dripping puddles of rain on the lauhala rug, she saw that the note she'd left on Kore's pillow was gone. She scribbled another note, her hands shaking with cold and with her impatience to be gone.

"I've gone to find Maile in the place I told you about once where the old Hawaiian chief is buried. Come quickly—and come alone."

She left the note on his pillow as before, but she took the precaution of tilting the shade of a lamp so its light would fall on the piece of notepaper. Before she left the cabin, she turned off all the other lights to alert Kore that someone had been there.

250

Although she wasn't satisfied that Kore would return to the cottage before morning, she was sure he would understand her cryptic note if he did. As a boy he'd been intrigued by her stories of the burial cave, and she'd never regretted telling him the family secret, knowing it would be safe with him.

The question now was, she thought as she opened the rear door of the cottage to stare out at the wind-driven rain, would Kore find the note in time to be of any help to her and Maile?

XXI

The trip up the side of the bluff seemed interminable. Although the wind had died, at least temporarily, and the rain was now coming straight down, the constant drumming on the crown of Lani's rain hat set her teeth on edge.

After the first few minutes, she tucked the flashlight into the belt of her raincoat, its beam directed downward, and used both hands to propel herself up the path, holding onto the metal railing.

Although the railing was sturdy, without gaps, the path was steep, and she knew it would be dangerous to lose her footing on the slippery stones, so she moved carefully, gripping the railing so tightly that her wet fingers were soon numb with cold.

When she reached the summit, she switched off the flashlight to save its batteries and leaned against the guardrail to catch her breath. Shielding her eyes against the rain with her hand, she looked back the way she'd come and only then realized that she could see the path, a whitish strip that zigzagged up the side of the cliff. Without her noticing, the sky to the east had cleared; it had already taken on the pearl-grey of first dawn.

In a little while it would be morning, she thought. What further tragedies and horrors would the new day bring? She closed her eyes and offered up a prayer—and a promise. If Maile was found, alive and unharmed, she would tell the police the whole truth, hold nothing back, no matter what the consequences to herself. What's more, she would fight for the estate her father had left her, and if she won, she would do everything in her power to see that her father's dream of turning the island over to the Hawaiian people would be honored. . . .

The decision seemed to give her strength, and she was smiling as she opened her eyes. Below, through a thin veil of rain, she saw the lights of Maunaloa House and remembered that during her second search she had left them on as she moved from room to room. There was another light, too—a pale rectangle at the edge of the grove of trees behind the house. Was it the lamp she had left burning in Kore's cottage? She strained her eyes and was sure she saw a shadow passing in front of the light.

The temptation to wait there in the hope that Kore had found her note and would soon join her was strong, but the urgency that had driven her out into the rain to search for Maile was even stronger. After a brief struggle with herself, she turned away from the railing and plunged into the rain forest behind her.

Although there was a certain amount of shelter from the rain under the overhanging branches of the trees, she had another enemy now—the heavy growth of shrubs and ferns that encroached on the path. Wet fronds lashed at her face and hands, and spiny twigs tore at her clothes as she pushed past, while underfoot, the mud that surrounded the path stones, covering them completely in spots, made every step a hazard.

Ahead of her, the rain made tiny streaks of white in the beam of the flashlight as she moved down the path toward the sinkhole. Although there were no footprints in the mud that covered some of the stones, she wouldn't allow herself to hope that Maile had gone to some safer place to hide. She knew that any footprints Maile might have made would have been washed away by the rain, just as hers were being obliterated behind her now.

A few minutes later she reached the junction where the path divided. Briefly, she paused to call Maile's name. The lush, rain-washed green of the forest, its rich, earthy odors assaulted her senses as she listened for an answer that didn't come. From somewhere up ahead, she heard the sound of rushing water and was glad that she wouldn't have to ford the brook that flowed through the center of Po Valley.

Thankful that the rain had almost stopped, she took the path to the left. The trees were closer together here. Their branches formed a dark ceiling overhead that dripped water down on her head, and she was glad for the light of the electric torch as she moved down the path.

Once she made a detour around a fallen tree limb and stepped into mud up to her ankles. There was a sucking, viscous sound as she pulled her feet out, one at a time, leaving her shoes and socks behind in the mud. Begrudging even the few minutes it would take to fish them out, she went on without them.

It was harder going now, with the wet stones like glass under her bare feet. Although she wanted to run, she made herself move slowly, testing each stone before she put her weight on it. A few minutes later her flashlight picked out the grey boards of the fence that guarded the sinkhole. Even before she ran toward it, she was shouting Maile's name.

For a moment her eyes played a trick on her, and she thought she saw a small, dark figure huddled just inside the fence; then she drew closer, and she realized it was the shadow of one of the fence posts. Holding her breath so she could hear better, she leaned over the fence and called

Maile's name, but the only answer was the liquid sound of running water, the plop-plop of rain dripping off the saturated trees.

The yawning mouth of the sinkhole seemed to mock her, as if it knew a thousand secrets it would never reveal. Although the rain had almost stopped, water still poured over the lip of the hole and splashed against the bottom far below. Moving like an old woman on her numb legs, Lani climbed over the fence, stretched out full-length beside the sinkhole, and thrust her head over the edge.

But, except for a strip of sodden cloth, the small ledge was empty. For a long time she played the flashlight beam over the bit of yellow cloth. Maile had been wearing a yellow scarf the day they'd explored the old village. Had she lost it when they'd pulled her off the ledge, or had she dropped it here tonight?

Lani realized she was shaking, and not just from the cold. Her voice held the thin edge of hysteria as she called Maile's name again and again. Maile's name came back a dozenfold as the pit, acting as a giant echo chamber, splintered her voice and amplified the sound. She waited for a long time, but there was no answer.

Everything sensible and cautious in her nature told Lani to wait, that there was nothing she could do without help; but something stronger than reason, something intuitive and not to be denied, told her differently.

It took all her courage to ease her legs over the rim of the sinkhole, to lower herself into the black pit. By the time she was standing on the ledge, her heart was pounding wildly and her throat was so dry that she scooped up a handful of rainwater from a shallow depression in the rock and drank it greedily.

Not allowing herself any time for second thoughts, she knelt and felt along the edge of the ledge for the small wedge-shaped groove that her father had told her about.

"I replaced the sennit rope I found there with a rope ladder," he'd told her. "It's anchored to metal pitons and stored in a natural pocket under the lip of the ledge. Getting it uncoiled and then lowering yourself to the first rung of the ladder is pretty tricky business. When you're older, I'll take you to the burial cave to satisfy your curiosity. Until then, stay away from the sinkhole."

Lani shook her head as if to rid it of the past. Her fingers found the wedge-shaped indentation that marked the position of the rope ladder. She reached under the ledge—only to find that the ladder had already been lowered.

She took a deep breath, then another, and reminded herself that six generations of her ancestors had safely navigated this same ledge and the descent into the pit, but her mouth was dry again as she rolled to her stomach, her upper body flattened against the rock ledge, and swung her legs over the edge. She groped with her toes until they touched wet rope. When both feet were firmly planted on the ladder, she twisted her body sideways and reached down to grasp the top rung. An image of Maile making the same maneuver flashed through her mind, and the feeling of urgency flooded back, stronger than before.

Holding onto the ledge with one hand, she lowered her body the remaining few inches, every nerve aware of the black hole yawning behind her, of the cold draft and rank odor that rose from the bowels of the pit.

The ladder swayed disconcertingly with her full weight on it, but she took some comfort from knowing that the rain had finally stopped altogether. She began her descent, counting as she went, rung by rung. When she reached the tenth rung she stopped and, hooking one arm around the rope, took the flashlight from her raincoat pocket and switched it on.

Her heart sank as she played the beam over the rough sides of the pit. Her father had described a boulder resting on a ledge, but all she saw was grey rock covered here and there by a layer of cindery lava. Was her memory faulty? Maybe he had said the twentieth rung. She moved the beam and stared fixedly at a rough protrusion in the wall, and now she realized that what she had taken for a bulge in the side of the sinkhole was really a separate boulder, resting on a narrow ledge.

Moving carefully, she tucked the flashlight into her belt,

leaving it on so that the beam was directed downward, and stretched out her right arm, feeling for the metal ring her father had installed there as a safety measure. It took her a while to locate it; it was only when her groping fingers touched the chill of metal that she realized he had camouflaged it with grey paint.

Holding on to the piton, she swung herself across the narrow gap and onto the ledge. To her relief the small ridge of stone she was standing on was wider than it appeared from the ladder. Her arms outstretched, she hugged the boulder and inched her way along the ledge. When she had circled the boulder, she lifted the flashlight from her belt and stared with dismay at the opening of the cave, which seemed little more than a sliver between the boulder and the side of the pit.

The beam of the flashlight slid through the opening and reflected off rock just a few inches away inside. Surely this shallow niche couldn't be the cave her father had described.

Putting aside her doubts, she bent and slid sideways through the dark opening, only to find that there was plenty of room, even for a large man, to get through.

The rock wall opposite the opening was an illusion, too, since the tunnel slanted off sharply to the right. Trying not to notice the ebony darkness that lay just beyond the comforting circle of light, she stepped forward, eager to find Maile, to explain to her sister that she hadn't really thought she had killed her aunt.

As she moved deeper into the cave, there was a rancid odor that made her nostrils flare, and she was suddenly reminded of the drainpipe she'd hidden in so long ago. It came to her that what she smelled was death—decades-old, maybe centuries-old death. The hairs on the back of her neck stirred, and she felt an almost overwhelming compulsion to look behind her. Only the thought that Maile was up ahead kept her moving forward.

The passageway soon narrowed, and she had to crouch slightly to keep from scraping her head on the jagged ceiling. Ahead of her, the flashlight reflected off an archway of saplings set into the solid rock. Stripped of their bark, they looked like bleached bones as they loomed up out of the darkness.

Although her father's descriptions of the cave had prepared her for what came next, she gave a small involuntary scream as the light picked out three mounds of bones, each topped by a gleaming skull.

"The *alii* chief—or, more likely, king—who was buried in the cave," her father had told her, "must have been quite a warrior. His bones obviously had so much *mana* that the brothers or friends entrusted with preserving them were forced to go to great lengths, even to using a place of taboo—the sinkhole—to save them from grave robbers. They sacrificed three men, possibly slaves or men under a strong taboo, and left their bodies under the archway so their spirits would guard the burial chamber from intruders."

Lani edged her way through the mounds of bones that had once been living, breathing men, her eyes shrinking away as she saw the blue tattoo on a bit of skin that still clung to a shinbone.

The tunnel widened again, then opened into a chamber carved out of the granite that formed the spine of the island. She ran the beam of light over the piles of articles that covered the floor and the tops of stone benches on two sides of the chamber. Some of the articles she recognized— wooden fishhooks, tattoo needles for etching human skin, cooking utensils, body ornaments made of ivory, bone and pearl shell—but most of the objects were unfamiliar to her.

Opposite the entrance, in a niche that had been hollowed out of the rock, a coffin, an effigy of an outrigger canoe, rested. Although it seemed unlikely that Maile would hide herself in a coffin, Lani drew closer and directed the flashlight beam inside. Except for the bones of the dead chief, wrapped in a moldy tapa-cloth covering, the coffin was empty. Even the red-and-yellow feather helmet and cloak that had proclaimed his chiefhood in life had been reduced to a few moldy remnants by time and the damp.

She turned away and stood in the middle of the chamber, sick with disappointment. She had been so sure she'd find Maile here, especially after she'd found the scarf and the lowered rope ladder. Was it possible that the force of water cascading down the sides of the sinkhole had washed the ladder out of its hiding place under the ledge?

She stared at a pile of fishhooks carved from human bone, and suddenly the walls of the cave seemed to be moving toward her, and she knew she had to get out of this musty, airless place with its grisly relics and its bones and its reminder of ancient murder.

She ran from the burial chamber, back down the tunnel, past the remains of the retainers who had been slaughtered so cruelly to protect the bones of their dead chief. She was almost to the entrance when she heard a moaning sound. For a moment, until her reason told her it was the wind, she felt a superstitious dread, and she wasn't surprised that the Hawaiians believed the sinkhole to be the habitat of the Night Marchers.

When she was standing on the ledge again, she slid the flashlight under her belt and inched her way around the boulder. Her fingers felt stiff and nerveless, very cold, as she knelt on the ledge and turned the flashlight beam downward. Although the light didn't quite reach the bottom, she was sure she saw something white below. Was it more of the granite, another boulder, that had been torn away from the side of the pit when the top caved in millenniums ago?

She called Maile's name, then called it again, but when she stopped, the only sound was the faint echo of her own voice. This time, when she made the harrowing transfer from the ledge to the ladder, she had no time for personal fear. All her energy was concentrated on one thing—reaching the bottom of the pit as quickly as possible—and she begrudged the time she'd already wasted.

Thankful that her father had had the foresight to choose a ladder long enough to reach the bottom, she started down. She began automatically counting the rungs and had reached the twentieth when a voice came out of the darkness below her.

258

"Yula—help me, Yula," it said.

Lani clung to the ladder, weak with relief, but only for a moment. With the flashlight beam bouncing crazily off the walls of the pit, she scrambled down the remaining rungs of the swaying ladder. The bobbing light reflected off water, and then she saw Maile, lying on a mound of rocks just below the ladder, the water lapping at her feet.

In her impatience she skipped the last two rungs and jumped to the top of the mound. In a moment she was kneeling beside Maile, her arms around the shivering girl.

"I fell," Maile said. "First the knapsack slipped off my back, and when I tried to grab it I dropped my flashlight, and then I fell. I guess I landed on top of the knapsack, because I hit something squishy."

"Are you hurt? Can you walk?"

"I think something's wrong with my leg. It hurt awful when I tried to move. I kept yelling and yelling, but nobody heard me, and then I went to sleep and I dreamed I heard you calling my name."

"That wasn't a dream, and everything's going to be all right now," Lani said soothingly.

"I know. I'm not afraid now that you're here."

Lani's eyes prickled as she asked quickly, "Do you hurt anyplace besides your leg?"

"No, and my leg doesn't hurt now. I guess it went to sleep, too."

Lani laid the flashlight on a pile of leaves and bent over Maile. Her breath caught sharply as she saw the odd twist in Maile's leg. Maile didn't cry out as she touched the leg gently to find out if the flesh had been punctured, and she felt a new fear. Had there been some nerve damage? She probed her memory of the broken bones she'd seen treated at the clinic. Wasn't there a natural numbness sometimes just after an injury, or was that wishful thinking?

Quickly she finished examining Maile. Except for the broken leg, a rope burn in the palm of her hand and a few bruises, she seemed to have survived the fall in remarkably good condition.

"Your leg is broken," Lani explained gently. "Luckily it's

not the same leg you broke before, and it doesn't seem to be a compound fracture this time. Help will be along any time now—I left word that I was coming here to look for you. All we have to do is wait."

"But, Yula, what about the water?"

"It's stopped raining—see? There's hardly any runoff now."

"Not the rain," Maile said with a touch of her old asperity. "I meant the tide. It's almost morning, isn't it? Won't the tide come in soon?"

The muscles in Lani's throat tightened, and it was all she could do not to groan aloud. The tide—how could she have forgotten the tide? Already there was a drumming sound, still faint but getting louder, as sea water began to fill the underground passages. Soon the whistling that sounded like nose flutes would start, and then the water would begin to rise. . . .

"By the time the water is high enough to be a—a bother, we'll already be gone," she told Maile, wishing she felt as confident as she sounded. "Even if help doesn't come soon, we have the ladder. I'll tie you to my back and climb up above the water. It would be too risky to try to reach the ledge in front of the cave, but—"

"We aren't supposed to talk about the cave," Maile said sharply. "It's a secret. I had to promise I'd never, never tell anyone except one of my own children someday. If Vivian finds out, she'll tell all her silly old friends, and they'll come down and tear up everything and—" She broke off abruptly.

Lani stared at her, at the wary look in her eyes. "You know Vivian isn't your sister, don't you?" she said.

"She's a big fake," Maile burst out. "They're in it together, Aunt Berta and Vivian. I heard them talking—Aunt Berta was telling Vivian not to worry, that Iolani was dead and could never cause them any trouble."

"Why didn't you go to your uncles with this?"

"Because—because they wouldn't have believed me. Nobody believed I didn't pick those akia berries. Everybody thinks I'm a liar—Aunt Berta saw to that. Always telling

Uncle Wade stories about me. Once, when I was mad at Vivian, I told Uncle Wade I thought she wasn't my sister, but he got mad and said I musn't ever say that again, not to anyone."

"What about your Uncle Jason? Maybe he would have listened to you."

"I was afraid he'd laugh and tease me about having such a big imagination," she said. "Nobody ever believes what I say—that's why I ran away tonight. I knew they'd think I killed Aunt Berta, and I didn't! I didn't, Yula!"

"I believe you," Lani said softly. "I believe what you told me about Vivian and your aunt, too."

Maile stared up at her. In the yellowish light of the electric torch her face had a pinched, sallow look. "Do *you* know who killed Aunt Berta?" she asked, her voice hushed.

"No. Do you, Maile?"

"I—I'm not sure. I heard people talking loud, yelling at each other in your room, and then I heard a big bang. Someone ran down the hall, but the lights were out, and— and I'm not sure who it was. I was afraid you were hurt, so I ran into your room, and that's when I saw Aunt Berta—"

She stopped, and a shudder shook her frail body. Lani found a blanket in the knapsack and wrapped it around her. Maile smiled up at her, and she felt a wave of love, of pity for the small girl who, all alone, had been fighting against such a formidable enemy.

"You haven't asked me why I believe that Vivian isn't your sister," she said impulsively.

"Oh, I already know that. Ever since I found that shark's tooth in your room, I knew you were Iolani."

Lani felt the shock through every inch of her body. "You *knew*—and yet you didn't tell anyone?"

"I was afraid Aunt Berta would do something to you if she found out." Maile's voice was drowsy. She yawned and closed her eyes. Lani sat beside her, watching her. When she was sure Maile was asleep, she rose quietly and went to the knapsack. She removed the straps and began trying to devise a harness to hold Maile on her back—just in case

Kore didn't get there soon, she thought grimly.

Preoccupied as she was with her task, the scraping sound overhead didn't really register at first, but when a pebble fell into the water, sending ripples radiating outward, she stiffened, raised her eyes—just in time to see the ladder moving upward.

Disbelief held her immobile for a split second, and then she lunged for the ladder. But the ladder was already beyond her reach, and she watched helplessly as it moved inexorably higher, up the wall of the pit.

A sudden feeling of being exposed and vulnerable sent her scrambling to switch off the flashlight. She looked up again, and now that her eyes weren't blinded by the light, she saw the head and shoulders of a man silhouetted against the grey-rose flush of early morning.

XXII

With some small part of her mind Lani was aware of Maile's sonorous breathing behind her, of the whistlelike sound, still faint and faraway, that filtered up from the underground passages beneath the sinkhole. But these things had no immediate meaning, any more than did her icy feet and the wet clothes that were draining away her body heat. All that mattered at the moment was the identity of the man who had removed the ladder.

"Who are you?" Her voice was loud; it set up an echo along the stone-cold walls of the pit.

At first, when there was only silence, she was sure that he

would go away without answering, that she would die in this dark, evil-smelling place without ever knowing the name of her murderer.

Then he laughed. "*Sarishart*, Lani," he said.

She felt a shock as painful as a physical blow, and she gave an involuntary gasp. Because she knew that laugh, that voice; and the Rom word of greeting he had used came straight out of her childhood.

"Kore . . ." Although she had whispered his name, the peculiar acoustics of the sinkhole carried her voice upward, and he heard her.

"You should have married me while you had the chance, Lani," he said, and it seemed unnatural, obscene, that there should be genuine regret in his voice. "If you had married me four years ago, this wouldn't be necessary. I would have had the island, the money, without bringing Vivian and that old harpy Berta into it. If you had married me that night, we would have had it all—"

"Not all." Even to her own ears, her voice had a hollow sound. "Half of the estate belongs to Maile. What would you have done when you found out about her?"

"Oh, I probably would have let her live. By the time she was twenty-one, she would have sold her share of the island to me and let me manage her half of the estate."

Until this moment, the familiar arrogance in his voice would have made her smile; now it chilled her, made her aware suddenly of the water lapping near her feet.

"My mistake was that I handled you with kid gloves," he went on. "I should have gotten you pregnant, and then Pearsa would have gone along with our marriage."

Lani remembered the pity, the pain in Pearsa's eyes those last few minutes before she'd slipped into a coma. "She knew it was the money you really wanted. That's why she made me promise I wouldn't marry you," she said.

"Not just the money. It was the island—I've wanted it ever since the first time you told me about it. Pearsa could always read me like a book—that's why I waited until she was gone before I asked you to marry me."

Lani felt a stirring of old grief, but it seemed unreal, from another life now. "Who is Vivian?" she asked.

"A piece of fluff I met in Las Vegas. She called herself an actress, but she was just a high-class call girl. When I realized that her background and physical description made her a perfect substitute for you, I recruited her. By then I was sure you were dead—after all, it had been four years. I had every carny and Rom I knew looking for you, but not a sign of you. I figured that even if you did turn up I could handle you—one way or another."

"How did you talk Aunt Berta into helping you?"

"She was a very greedy lady—and she had a yen for the society thing, too. She took Vivian in hand, smoothed off the rough edges, showed her how to behave like a lady. And it was going down until—"

"Until you got one of my letters."

"That was some kind of shock, all right, finding out you were still alive."

"So you came to San Francisco, pretended to be a detective, found out what you could about me from my landlady—and then you tried to run me down in a stolen car. When that didn't work, you tried again. You found out from Mrs. Costello what hotel I was staying at in Honolulu and—did you follow me from my hotel that night? Is that how you happened to be in the alley?"

"I was right behind you when you went out that door. It would have ended right there if those men hadn't come along."

Lani rubbed her aching eyes. "I should have guessed it was you. When I was a kid, I was sure you could see in the dark."

He laughed softly. "I was beginning to think there was something to that shark's tooth of yours when you lucked out the third time, in the lagoon."

"That was you in the Folly, too—you remembered the chant from the day in Boston. How did you happen to be there? How could you know that Jason would take me to the Folly?"

264

"I didn't. I never left the island after I talked to you in the hau arbor that first time. I was hiding out in the Folly. When Richards left you alone, I couldn't resist giving you a good scare, but you were tougher than I thought. And this is all irrelevant. Because the fifth time will be the last—"

"The fifth time?"

"I almost strangled you last night in the hau arbor when you told me you were going to the police. Then the kid—it was Maile, by the way—came snooping around. I was afraid she had recognized my voice, so I changed my plans."

"I felt the evil," she said dully. "Pearsa warned me about a devil who hides behind a pleasing face, but how could I suspect it was you?"

"I asked you to marry me, even after you came back to the island. I even tried to talk you into dropping the whole thing and going away. If you hadn't been so stubborn, I might have let you live." His voice softened suddenly. "You threw me for a loop when you told me you had been keeping the *sumadjii* for me. Hell, I thought you'd sold those coins years ago."

Under Lani's fear a faint hope stirred. "Pearsa did love you best," she said. "That's why she left the *sumadjii* to you."

"And you're a liar, little sister." Kore's laugh set up an echo in the pit. "But I still prefer you to that tart Vivian. As soon as I saw you, I realized I still wanted you. If you had gone along with me, you wouldn't be in this fix."

"If I had, what would you have done with Vivian?"

"Paid her off. All she wanted was enough money so she could make a try at the movies."

"You never told her who I was, did you?"

"No way. She would have blown it for sure if she'd found out you were still alive. Berta, too—she was running scared tonight, afraid she'd have to face an extortion rap. I told her you were bluffing, but she wouldn't listen—"

"Is that why you killed her?" Lani asked.

"Yeah. It was an accident, but I would have had to get rid of her eventually, anyway." The casualness in his voice sent a shudder through her. "After she had that fight with you in your room, she was convinced you had some way of proving who you were. When I told her what I'd do to her if she tried to save her own neck by turning on me, she waved that damned gun at me. I tried to take it away from her and it went off."

"Did you go to my room to kill me?" she asked bitterly.

"I went there to give you one more chance. I was going to make a play for you tonight when you came to the cottage after the luau. Those guest cottages are too damned close together, so I told Vivian to get Jason up to her room and keep him busy for a few hours, but the jerk wasn't interested, even after she went to his cottage and made a play for him."

"I saw her in Jason's cabin," she said. "I thought—"

"It was a good plan," Kore interrupted. "I even picked a fight with you so I could stage a big reconciliation scene. I figured that once I got you in bed with me, I'd have no trouble talking you into marrying me. Then Berta grabbed me before I could get to the cottage. She had recognized you at the luau and she was talking crazy, threatening to blow the whole thing. When I thought I had her calmed down, I went to the cottage, but you were gone. I went to your room and found Berta there. She was raving and ranting again over her fight with you. Then she pulled the gun on me, and the next thing I knew, she was dead. The kid saw me running down the hall, but it was dark and she thought I was Jason—we're about the same size, I guess."

Lani held her breath, then let it out slowly. "How do you know this?" she said.

"Because she was yelling her uncle's name. You can bet I didn't turn and look back at her."

Lani felt a moment of *déjà vu*. It had happened again. Maile had run away to protect Jason, just as she had once protected her father. Only one thing was different: Jason was innocent, and her father had been guilty.

"You can see why I can't let Maile talk to anyone, can't you?" Kore said. "Someone just might remember that I'm the same build as Jason. As for Vivian, I don't know how much pressure she can take. She just might decide to toss me to the wolves to save her own neck. So I'm afraid you and the kid will have to go, Lani."

There was a subtle change in his voice, and Lani knew that time was running out for her. She tried to think of a way to keep him there, to make him change his mind.

"You were very clever tonight," she said. "You gave me an alibi, but you also gave yourself one, too, and made it impossible for me to tell anyone who I am. So you've won, after all, and there's no need for—to leave us here. Maile would never tell what she saw—for thirteen years I knew that my father killed my mother, and I never told anyone, not even you, until he was dead. You can have the money, the island. You know I've never wanted them, and now that Aunt Berta is dead, I'm not worried about Maile—"

"I had nothing to do with tormenting the kid—or those attempts on her life," Korc said abruptly. "As soon as you told me what Berta was up to, I put a stop to it. Planting that damned necklace in your room was her idea, too, although she tried to blame it on Vivian. I think she went off her rocker tonight. She was raving like a loonie after her run-in with you, waving that gun around and threatening to shoot you on sight. That's one reason why—" He broke off.

Lani discovered it was hard to breathe; she forced air into her lungs before she said, "You know you don't want to leave me here to drown, Kore. Those other times—you say that some fluke always saved me, but it was really because you couldn't go through with it. Isn't that the real reason you kept trying to get me to marry you, even though you already had Vivian? Let us go, Kore, and I promise I'll do anything you say, even marry you if you still want me. You know I'll keep my promise. In all the time you've known me, have I ever broken a promise to you or told you a lie?"

She held her breath, waiting. Kore hesitated. After he was gone, she would remember that, for just a moment, Kore hesitated. "I can't do that," he said finally. "This way, it will look like an accident, and I might not get another chance. Without the ladder, which I'll take with me, every-body will assume you fell in, trying to rescue Maile from the ledge. It's just too perfect—you can see that I have to do it this way, can't you?" He hesitated again, and then, so softly she wasn't sure if she heard it or only imagined it, he added, "I'm sorry, Lani."

She heard the click of metal on stone, and a rubbing sound that could have been a knife cutting through rope. Then, as she stared up with agonized eyes, she saw that the circle of light was unbroken, that the silhouette of Kore's head was gone.

She wanted to scream, to beg him to come back, but she knew it would only frighten Maile. Even if he heard her he wouldn't come back. She dropped down beside Maile. The whistling was louder now, and she listened to it with dread, knowing that when it stopped, the tide would pour in.

The draft was stronger too, and she covered her bare feet with the edge of Maile's blanket. Above, the patch of sky had changed from grey to pale blue, but little of the daylight filtered down into the depths of the pit. She found the flashlight and switched it on, needing the comfort of its light, only to discover that the island of debris and rock they were on was smaller, that the water had already begun to rise.

She got up to inspect the sides of the pit. There were irregularities, places where the lava rock still clung to its granite base, but even if she could climb up above the water, she knew she could never manage it with Maile on her back.

Behind her, Maile stirred. "Yula?" she said fretfully.

Lani went to her and cradled her head in her lap, using her body to block off the sight of the rising water. How could she possibly tell Maile that the ladder was gone, and yet how long could she keep her from finding out the truth?

"Yula, I have to tell you something," Maile said. "I—I did some mean things to you—"

"It isn't important."

"But it is. I *have* to tell you, don't you see? I took your locket that first day, the one you thought you lost, and I took the other one, too—the shark's tooth on a chain. They're both in the knapsack with the emerald necklace."

"*You* took Vivian's necklace, Maile?" Lani said sharply.

"Yes, but I'm not sorry about *that*. The necklace didn't really belong to her, you know. I knew she was up to something when I saw her going into your room yesterday. After she came out, I found the necklace hidden in your pillow case, so I took it—it's in my knapsack." She gave Lani a sober look. "Do you hate me now, Yula?"

"You'd better start calling me Lani," Lani said, smiling at her. "And I don't think you could do anything that would make me hate you, Maile."

Maile stared up at her. "I haven't finished yet. I should have told you about your mother, too."

"My mother? What do you mean, Maile?"

"Everybody thinks you killed your mother, but it was really an accident."

"How do you know that, Maile?"

"Because I read about it in one of Aunt Berta's diaries. She keeps them locked up in her desk, but I know where she keeps the key. I stole—took one of the old ones and read it."

Lani took a deep breath. "You called it an accident. What did you read in Aunt Berta's diary, Maile?"

"About the day your mother was shot. I guess she was mad at Daddy because he wanted a divorce, so she shot at him with a gun to scare him. He went away in his boat, and she began drinking wine, and then she dropped the gun and it went off and shot her."

"But how could Berta possibly know that?"

"Your mother was still alive when Aunt Berta found her. She said a few words—I forget exactly what she said, but the diary's in my knapsack if you want to read it. Then Aunt Berta ran down to the wharf to get Daddy, only he was gone. When she came back to the Folly you were there, and you had the gun in your hand. She started yelling at you, and you lost your voice, and that's when she saw how she could get some money from Daddy. She never told anyone

269

it was an accident, and all those years, Daddy thought you had killed your mother." She was quiet for a moment. "Aunt Berta was a very bad woman. I've tried to feel sorry that she's dead, only—only I can't."

Lani turned off the flashlight so Maile couldn't see her face. All those wasted years; the love and family life she had been robbed of because of her aunt's lies, her greed, her vindictiveness. No, she wasn't sorry Berta was dead, either.

Maile's cold hand touched her arm. "Don't worry, Lani. Uncle Jason and Uncle Wade will be here before the water gets too high. You'll see—it's going to be okay."

There was such confidence in her voice that Lani felt ashamed of her own fear. Surely there was some way they could escape the deadly tide even now creeping up the dark passages beneath the sinkhole toward them. . . .

As she stared up at the circle of sky, she was seized with a sudden, irrational fancy. If only Maile and she could grow wings and fly away from this grim place. The sky was so clear, washed clean by the storm, without a cloud to mar its blueness. Even the kukui tree that drooped its pale green branches over one corner of the sinkhole was still, as if resting from its ordeal. It was going to be a perfect day, and on this windless, cloudless day Maile and she would die in this black pit unless she thought of some way out.

A *windless, cloudless day*. . . .

The words echoed through her mind, and an idea took root, grew. It was such a long chance, but what other choices did she have? It was something to do, a way of fighting back. *Even if it fails*, she thought.

Maile watched silently as she switched on the flashlight and bent over the knapsack. She found matches, neatly wrapped in aluminum foil, tucked inside a small sewing kit. Maile, as methodical as ever, had been prepared for a long stay in the burial cave, it seemed. Her aunt's diary was hidden in an inside pocket. As she stared down at her aunt's cramped writing, she was tempted to save the pages that proved her—and her father's—innocence, but there wasn't enough time. With only a small pang of regret, she ripped out all the pages and put Maile to work twisting them into tapers while she gathered all the leaves and twigs and kukui nuts she could find and piled them up beside the mound of crumpled paper.

On a flat chunk of lava rock, she stacked several of the paper tapers and topped them with the driest leaves she could find, reserving the wetter ones for later. She struck a match, but her hands were clumsy with cold, and its head, still burning, flew off into the water.

She was more successful with the second match. When she held it to the edge of the paper it caught fire, and she squatted beside it, adding leaves and nuts, nursing the flames carefully until a thin blue vapor began to form. The oily kukui nuts caught fire and burned with a smoky gusto, and when the vapor thickened into grey smoke, she breathed a prayer that the natural draft in the pit would carry it upward.

In a few minutes a thick column of black smoke was rising up the center of the pit. She watched it anxiously, wondering how far it would rise before it dissipated. Would it escape the pit, rise above the tops of the trees that surrounded the sinkhole? If so, would someone see it—and would he guess what it meant?

Maile coughed, and she realized that her own eyes were streaming tears from the smoke. She wet Maile's yellow scarf and gave it to her to hold over her face, but she didn't put out the fire. When the leaves and kukui nuts and other bits of vegetation were gone, when she'd added everything that would burn from Maile's knapsack, she turned back to Maile, knowing it was time to tell her about the ladder.

"There's something important I have to tell you about the ladder, Maile—"

"I know something's happened to it. Tell me about the Rom wedding," Maile ordered.

Lani sat down beside her sister and turned off the flashlight so Maile couldn't see the black water creeping toward them. For yet another time, she told her about the Rom dances, the songs, the chains of gold coins the bride wore around her neck, the kidnapping ritual that was as old as time, the passing around of the loaf of bread so the guests could stuff it with money for the young couple.

The water crept over their legs as she was describing the wedding feast—the roast goose with its crackling brown skin, the chilled eggplant squares succulent with spices, the meat-stuffed pastries called *bokoli*, the fragrant black bread. . . .

When the water swirled around Maile's shoulder, she lifted her and held her higher in the water. Although she was as gentle as possible, Maile moaned and then slumped in her arms, and Lani was thankful that she had fainted.

She braced herself against the wall of the sinkhole, Maile's body a dead weight in her arms, and she had a crazy image of Alice in Wonderland, swimming around in the tears she had shed herself as a giant.

And still the water, icy and evil-smelling, rose around them. When it reached her breasts, she held Maile's chin up and let the rest of her body float, hoping the air trapped in Maile's clothes would make her buoyant and prolong her life for a few minutes longer.

This is a nightmare, she thought; *it isn't really happening. . . .*

At first she thought the voices were part of the nightmare, and when she realized they were real, that someone was calling her name over and over, she began to cry, her tears mingling with the water in the pit.

It was Wade who slid down the rope they lowered, who held Maile while David and Jason devised a harness to pull her out of the water. It was only after Lani saw Maile's limp body rising inch by inch that she stopped treading water and let Wade hold her up.

Thank God, she thought. *Thank God, it's all over now.*

But it wasn't over, of course. She realized Wade was talking urgently in her ear, and she tried to make sense from his words.

"—then David spotted the smoke, and he realized what it must mean. There was a landslide sometime during the night, and it took down part of the cliff behind the Folly and—oh God, we thought both of you were buried under all that rubble. I found out something the past couple of hours—I'm in love with you, Yula. I don't give a damn about anything else. We'll put the past behind us and start out fresh, as if we'd just met in that alley in Honolulu."

She tried to tell him that the past couldn't be shoved aside so easily, that sometimes it had to be exorcised, like an evil spirit, but she discovered she had lost her voice. Wade was still talking, but she could no longer make any sense out of his words. She felt her hold on reality loosen, and she knew the long sleepless night, her physical and mental ordeal, had finally taken their toll.

Willingly, thankfully, she slid into unconsciousness.

XXIII

Although Lani knew that the men were taking turns carrying Maile and her through the dripping rain forest and down the cliff path, she wasn't really aware of what was going on until they reached the bottom.

When she came to her senses again she was in Jason's arms, her head cradled on his lean shoulder. Even before she looked around for Maile, she saw there were strain lines in Jason's face that she'd never noticed before.

Maile, her leg in a makeshift cast made of tree branches, smiled at her from David's burly arms. For all that had happened to her, she looked surprisingly cheerful. It was obvious she was enjoying the attention when, a few minutes later, David carried her aboard the helicopter that would take her to Queen's Hospital in Honolulu. Despite her bedraggled appearance, she had the aplomb of a young princess as she waved to them grandly through the helicopter window.

Lani stared after the helicopter as it lifted off its pad. With Lehua and David Kealoha in attendance, she knew Maile was in good hands; so why did she feel so depressed? Was it because she also knew that Maile no longer needed her?

She realized suddenly that Jason was still holding her, and she insisted that he let her down immediately. Although Wade tried to argue that she was still too weak to walk, Jason only grinned and let her slip to the ground.

"She's a big girl now," he told his cousin. "If Yula wants to walk, let her walk."

So Lani returned to Maunaloa House as she'd left it—on her own two feet. Moana, clucking and fussing like a plump brown hen, met them in the hall and tried to carry Lani off to her room for a bath and a nap. But there was still some unfinished business Lani had to attend to, and she resisted all efforts to get her off to her room, although she did allow Moana to strip off her soggy raincoat and wrap her in a tartan plaid afghan.

Through the open doors of the living room, she saw Vivian. She was still sitting in the same high-backed chair, but it was obvious she wasn't the same girl Lani had left there. Her face looked like wax that had just begun to melt under high heat, and her eyes had a blank look, as if she were sleepwalking.

She looked up as Lani, followed by Wade and Jason, came into the room. For a long moment the two women stared at each other, ignoring the two men as if they didn't exist.

"Where is Kore?" Lani asked.

Nothing moved on Vivian's face, not even surprise. "He's dead. I went to the Folly to meet him, like he told me, but the Folly is gone. He's buried under all that rock . . . all that rock—"

She began to cry. The tears slipped down her cheeks, over her crumpled mouth, and splashed on the front of her tunic. As if her arms were too heavy to lift, she didn't try to wipe them away.

Lani felt a wrenching grief, as if part of her own body had just been torn away, but even in the middle of her pain, she felt compassion for Vivian. Until this moment she hadn't known that Vivian was in love with Kore.

"Are you saying that someone was killed in that landslide behind the Folly?" Wade asked sharply. "Who is Kore?"

"You knew him as Sean O'Neill, but his real name was Kore," Lani said.

Vivian's eyes moved over Lani. "Were you one of his women?" she asked.

"Not in the way you mean, but I've known Kore most of my life. He was a Rom—my foster brother."

Strangely, Vivian didn't seem surprised. "He never talked about himself, you know; but once, on the street, this Gypsy woman came up to us and called him Kore." She stared at Lani fixedly. "He killed Berta—did you know that? When she threatened him with a gun, he tried to take it away from her and it went off—it was an accident." She didn't seem to notice Wade's start, Jason's low whistle. "He put the whole thing together, made it work. We were living together in Las Vegas when he got the idea—or maybe he'd had it a long time before that. I accused him once of taking up with me because what happened to me as a kid—you know, losing my family and my memory—made it easy for me to pass as the Stevenson girl, but he just laughed. He was good to me. He never put me down because I had to turn a few tricks to get along between modeling and acting jobs. He did love me—he couldn't fake that, could he?"

"I'm sure he loved you," Lani lied, out of pity.

Vivian gave a long sigh. "He made it sound so easy, such a sure thing. Berta was willing to go along for a share of the money, and any mistakes I made could be put down to my loss of memory. I did have amnesia, you see. Sometimes, I even got to thinking I really was Iolani."

"You did a good job of fooling everybody," Lani said. She didn't look at Wade and Jason.

"Well, I'm a pretty good actress, only I never got a break. Kore told me what to say to the psychiatrist, how to let bits and pieces of my memory come back. You should have seen how excited that old shrink got the day I told him I was sure my name was Iolani, that I remembered living on an island called Maunaloa."

She looked at Wade, and for a brief moment a spark of amusement replaced the apathy in her eyes. "You swallowed my whole act, didn't you? You were so sorry for me because of all I'd been through that you didn't even fuss over the bills I ran up."

Although Wade's face tightened, he didn't answer, and she moved her head restlessly. "Everything went wrong tonight," she said. She gave Jason an accusing look. "Kore wanted you out of the way for some reason. He told me to get you up to my room, to keep you busy for a couple of hours, but you weren't interested, not even when I made a big play for you."

Jason lit a cigarette and handed it to Vivian. "That's because I'm a realist. It was just too hard to believe that you'd suddenly succumbed to my charms with two male specimens like Wade and O'Neill around. I figured you were using me to make one of them jealous—and I don't like being used."

"Did your lover give you orders to be nice to me, too?" Wade's voice was tight.

Vivian shrugged. "He said I should keep you happy, but I have to admit I didn't mind. You're quite a man—and you didn't get cheated, did you? Besides, you lost interest after Yula came to the island. That's why I went along with Berta when she told me to hide the emerald necklace in Yula's room. I figured it was a good way to get rid of the competition; only it backfired, and Kore was furious with me. He knocked me around, forced me to change my story, and I ended up looking like a fool."

She drew on her cigarette greedily, her eyes narrowed against the smoke. "It all began to fall apart after Kore changed the plan. We were going to wait until I came into the money before we staged a big romance and got married, but Kore decided to move the whole schedule up. After he came to the island, Berta got edgy, and Kore—he wasn't the same, either. And now he's dead, and none of it matters anymore. It's all over—"

She began to cry again. Lani turned away, unable to look at Vivian's ravaged face. An image of Kore as he'd been the first time she'd met him—his intense black eyes, his self-possession, his elaborate indifference—flashed before her. When had that boy changed into a stranger who could leave Maile and her to die in a black hole in the ground? Or had he really changed? Maybe the signs had been there all along. The first thing he'd done after he'd met her on that creek bank had been to con her out of every cent she had. And why had he really taken her home with him? She had thought he was joking when he'd told her once that he'd been planning to marry her since he was fourteen. Now, remembering Kore's maturity, his self-reliance, it wasn't hard to believe that, even at fourteen, he had been looking ahead, planning how to get his hands on the island, on her father's money. . . .

Wade's hand on her arm brought her back to the present. "Why didn't you tell me that O'Neill was your foster brother? Did you know what these two were up to?"

Lani locked stares with him. "And if I did?" she asked quietly.

For a long moment he was silent. "Then I'll have to learn to live with it," he said. "You've proved yourself tonight by saving Maile's life. Maybe I'm a fool, but I meant it when I told you I wanted to forget the past."

Lani told herself that these were the words she wanted to hear, so why did she feel so dissatisfied, so apathetic? Was she still in shock from the news about Kore, from her own brush with death?

"What are you going to do about Vivian?" she asked.

"The storm damage on Oahu delayed the police, but

they'll be here soon. When they've finished questioning Iolani—Vivian—about Berta's death, I'm going to see that extortion charges are filed against her."

"But she was Kore's tool—"

"She's a whore, a liar and an extortionist," he said, his voice cold.

"Don't you think she's suffered enough, losing Kore? And whom did she really hurt?"

"Yula's right," Jason said. "Why not forget about the extortion charge? Let it out that Vivian finally got all her memory back and now she's sure she isn't Iolani Stevenson after all. It will cause a little talk, but not an open scandal—and you can keep Yula out of it."

Wade's lips tightened, but he turned to Vivian, who sat listening, her face expressionless, as they discussed her future. "As soon as the police are satisfied, you can pack the things you brought with you and clear off the island."

"No," Lani said. "Let her take her clothes and jewelry. She'll need a stake until she gets established again. Maybe this time she can make it as an actress."

Wade hesitated, then nodded. "Okay, we'll do it your way, but I think you're both wasting your pity. Just in case she changes her mind, I want a signed confession from her, too." He took Lani by the shoulders and turned her toward the door. "And now you're going up to bed—and no arguments this time. Moana is fixing you some food. I'll send her up with you to make sure you're all right."

Lani looked down at her bare feet, at the streaks of dirt on her hands. "I must look awful," she said ruefully.

Jason laughed. "You're a mess. Where did you pick up that tacky hat, Yula?"

Lani gasped and put her hand to her head. Through all the things that had happened to her, somehow she had managed to retain the droopy rain hat. She smiled and then realized she felt surprisingly normal. *I'm alive*, she thought, *and so is Maile. I'll have to keep remembering what a miracle it is just to be alive. . . .*

The next hours were vague, unreal. Later, she remembered Moana's scolding voice, her gentle hands, the blessed warmth of scented bath water, the softness of her bed. She slept, then awoke. When Moana put food in front of her, she ate every bite, even though it had no taste. She slept again, and the next time she awoke, a tall, thin man was talking to her, but before she could decide whether he was a doctor or a policeman, she was asleep again.

It was late afternoon when she awoke the third time. She sat up in bed and stared out at the sunlit garden below her window, and suddenly she was hungry for company, for someone to talk to. She brushed the tangles from her hair, pulled on her jeans and denim shirt and went downstairs. When she heard voices on the lanai, she went outside and found Wade and Jason sitting at a table, drinking coffee.

Although both men greeted her warmly, she sensed the strain between them and wondered if they had been quarreling again. Jason was very quiet as Wade brought her up to date on what had happened while she slept. Although it wasn't all over yet and the police wanted a statement from her, Wade was reasonably sure they had accepted Vivian's explanation of Berta's death. If so, the whole thing was over—at least where the police were concerned, he added.

Lani listened in silence, the sun warm against her arms and face. She felt strangely removed from the events of the past day, and she was relieved when Wade began telling her about Maile, who was keeping the staff at Queen's Hospital hopping.

Lani had fallen asleep when the police took away Berta's body, but she was a witness to Vivian's departure from Maunaloa Island. There was no drama in her going. Vivian didn't even turn her head to look at them as she passed the lanai, although she must have heard their voices. She was wearing one of her spectacular town suits; her silver hair was immaculate, her face an ivory mask as she swept past on her way to the helicopter, with David and the helicopter pilot following in her wake, both loaded down with luggage.

No one spoke as they waited for the helicopter to leave. When Lani heard the whirring of its rotors, she breathed a long silent sigh. It was time to tell Wade and Jason the truth, to put the last piece into place. The problem was where to begin, what words to use.

Busy with her own thoughts, she was only half-listening as Wade talked about the storm damage to the island—the total destruction of the Folly, several uprooted coconut palms, severe glass breakage in the greenhouses, a missing sailboat—

Lani's breath caught as Wade's words sank in. She gave him her full attention as he told them that the sailboat had broken from its moorings and disappeared at some point during the night or early morning.

A *missing sailboat* . . . and Kore had learned how to handle small boats during his stint as a sailor. Was it possible that Kore had escaped after all? Had he seen the smoke rising from the sinkhole and realized that it was all over? It was even possible that he had already known about the landslide when he'd ordered Vivian to meet him there. Had he hoped that she would assume he was dead and give him time to leave the Islands?

Lani felt a stirring of sadness for Vivian and for herself. They had both cared about Kore, but to Kore they had never been anything more than *gadje*, to be exploited, then discarded when he no longer had any need for them.

Sitting there on the sun-drenched lanai, Lani searched her own heart. She discovered sorrow there, but no bitterness. Although Kore had betrayed her, used her, the habit of caring what happened to him was still too strong for her to wish him ill. It would take time before she could see him with complete objectivity.

And maybe I never will, she thought.

David Kealoha called to Wade from the garden, and he excused himself, saying he would be right back. Lani stared after him, remembering those minutes with him in the sinkhole. They seemed like a dream now, something that had happened to another girl.

Jason drained his coffee cup. "Well, at least the landslide should put an end to the curse," he said. "The legend says the curse will end when the *heiau* stones are returned to their original site, and there's no doubting they have returned—along with half the mountain."

Lani nodded slowly. Did Kore lie beneath those stones? Would she ever know for sure? Somehow, she doubted that the police would go to the trouble and expense of excavating the Folly.

She gave a start when Jason reached across the table and picked up her hand. "I wouldn't worry too much about that foster brother of yours," he said. "If he's like most Roms, he has a dozen identification cards on him at all times. He could disappear into any city in the world without a ripple and never be found."

"What makes you think he's still alive?" she said.

"Because he's a survivor. And no, I'm not going to tell this to the police, or even to Wade. I'm just saying what you already suspect."

"How could you possibly know what I suspect?"

"I was watching you while Wade was telling us about his missing sailboat."

Lani sighed deeply. "You're right. Is it so wrong to hope that he's still alive, that he's never caught?"

"Wrong? There'd be something wrong with you if you didn't give a damn what happened to him. When you care about someone, you don't turn it off like a faucet just because he doesn't live up to your expectations."

She stared at him, at his wide, humorous mouth, at his amber eyes that looked almost bronze in the sun now. How strange that Jason, who made such a fetish of not getting entangled in personal relationships, could understand her ambiguous feelings toward Kore. It was also strange how much alike they were. Was that why it was so easy to be herself with Jason, knowing that he wasn't making judgments or expecting too much of her?

The pressure on her hand increased as Jason leaned toward her slightly. He wasn't smiling now, and there was a tightness around his mouth.

"It looks like I'm odd man out," he said. "Wade tells me

you two are getting married. I won't pretend to be a good sport about it. I still think I'm the right man for you, but I have to respect your right to make your own decisions."

He paused, his eyes very intent. "You'll be safe with Wade. He's a stable man, an anchor for you. But if you ever need a friend, I'm available. I'll always be available."

He gave her hand another squeeze and released it. "It's going to be a little rough on me, watching you two together. I might even end up taking a poke at Wade—and getting my face bashed in. So I think I'll stay in Honolulu until I'm sure Maile is really on the mend; after that—well, there's always another assignment."

Lani felt a curious ache, although she knew he was right. Wade would give her life the stability she had always wanted. Life with Jason would be chaotic, hectic, constantly demanding—and it wasn't as if she had to lose him altogether. She would still have Jason's friendship; his offer to be her friend had not been given lightly.

So Pearsa's predictions had come true, after all. She knew now that it was Kore whom Pearsa had been warning her about, the enemy who hid his greed behind a pleasing face and a protective manner. And Wade was the man she would share her life with, while Jason—why, Jason was her friend. How many people were lucky enough to have a friend like Jason?

So why, when everything was working out so well, when she'd been given more than she'd ever dreamed of, did she still feel as if she wanted to cry? Was it because she knew that while Wade would be a wonderful husband, he would also expect her to be a perfect wife? He would take charge, relieve her of the terrible burden of making decisions, give her life direction—but it would be *his* direction, *his* way of life, *his* decisions.

Twice Wade had told her he wanted to forget the past, but he must have reservations, because he hadn't given her a chance to tell him what her past had been. Because of his experiences with his first wife, would he ever really trust another woman, no matter how much he loved her? Would she spend her life proving herself to Wade, watching what she said, how long she talked with other men at parties, always on trial?

She thought of the years she'd spent with Pearsa, trying to be the daughter Pearsa had lost. There had been a special pain in wearing a dead girl's clothing, answering to a dead girl's name. And even before that, when she had lived with her aunt, she had been forced to conform to Berta's impossibly rigid standards, knowing that no matter what she did, she could never please; that she would always fall short of someone else's expectations.

But I don't want to be on trial for the rest of my life, she thought. *I want to be myself, make my own decisions, be treated as an adult.* The physical attraction she felt for Wade was very strong, but wouldn't any man as attractive as Wade have stirred her at this time of her life? She was young and healthy, with a normal woman's instincts and drives. She had felt the same pull toward Jason, but because she was so inexperienced, she had rejected it. How many girls, she thought bleakly, had been betrayed by something that was only the natural yearnings of their bodies?

She looked up, into Jason's warm and dear—so very dear—eyes.

"When Wade gets back," she said, smiling at him, "I have a long, long story to tell both of you, but first"—she rose and went around the table toward him—"you and I have some personal business to settle."